A PLUME BOOK

RED RUBY HEART IN A COLD BLUE SEA

MORGAN CALLAN ROGERS is a native Mainer who grew up in the shipbuilding city of Bath and splits her time between coastal Maine and western South Dakota. This is her first novel.

"Rendered first-person in confiding, colloquial prose . . . [like] the bittersweet coming-of-age movies (see: *Stand by Me, The Last Picture Show*) that don't get made much anymore." —*Entertainment Weekly*

"Deeply moving . . . Callan Rogers writes with a superb sense of place and period, delving deftly into true-to-life responses to unexplained loss . . . A realistic and resonant coming-of-age novel." —*Kirkus Reviews*

"Callan Rogers's astonishing debut brilliantly illuminates deep loss, impossible longing, and our yearning to hold on to love no matter what, all told in the voice of one remarkable young heroine. So rapturously moving, I could barely bring myself to close the final page."

—Caroline Leavitt, author of *Pictures of You*

"Rich in landscape and character, with regional dialect and phrases that will tip many mouths into grins." —*Booklist*

"Refreshing . . . A piercingly knowing portrait of the complicated thoughts and actions of a maturing teenage girl . . . with a one-of-a-kind setting and dialect straight from the shore." —David Svenson, *Portland Monthly*

"Incredibly detailed, rich, and real . . . You will find yourself drawn into this book quickly and fiercely." —Katy England, *The Maine Edge*

"The young, prickly, and thoroughly endearing narrator of *Red Ruby Heart in a Cold Blue Sea* got to me in a big way. Not since *Ellen Foster* have I rooted so hard for a fictional girl, whose losses, while deep and abiding, show us what she's made of. I loved spending time with Florine, and I'm still thinking about her. She will break your heart and make you glad she did."

—Monica Wood, author of *Any Bitter Thing*

"At once very personal and very broad in theme and atmosphere, *Red Ruby Heart* is a lovely novel, long on heart. Morgan Callan Rogers has a confident, almost playful prose style, and she bears down on this story from the first paragraph, never faltering in her mission to convey her characters and their painful paths with honesty, compassion, and humor."

—Susanna Daniel, author of *Stiltsville*

"Finely nuanced . . . *Red Ruby Heart* follows Florine's coming-of-age all the way through high school. As with the journey all adolescents are forced to endure, the goal is to somehow survive. . . . We can all take a lesson from Florine. And be grateful for the care and talent Morgan Callan Rogers devoted to bringing her so richly to life." —*Portland Press Herald*

"I read it straight through and flipped over it. Florine's voice is pitch-perfect throughout, and the story is both poignant and heartwarming. I love the three-dimensionality of the characters—no pure bad guys or good guys. I love all the Maine stuff; the distinctions between the summer people and the year-rounders of course rang bells. Loved Grand, loved the father, was so happy and relieved that in the middle of all that loss, Bud and Florine found each other. Oh, and I just loved the food: bread, apple pie, mac and cheese, beef stroganoff, Stella's 'gourmet' cooking—both mouthwatering in the descriptions and adding another layer to the you-are-what-you-eat characters."

—Mameve Medwed, author of *Of Men and Their Mothers*

"*Red Ruby Heart in a Cold Blue Sea* spun me deep inside its feisty, honest heroine, Florine. A classic story of paradise lost, this is a beautiful and wise coming-of-age story set on the Maine coast, where grief—harsh as the granite shoreline—is suffered, solaced, and survived. I love this book, with its fresh-baked bread, stars and waves, wind-worn houses, mysteries and truths. A wonderful first novel."   —Beth Powning, author of *The Sea Captain's Wife*

"Filled with a kind of fresh honesty, as well as dry wit—seen most of all in the character of Florine . . . It is almost impossible not to care about her."
—*BookPage*

"A heartwarming 'coming-of-age story' set in what is arguably the continent's most beautiful location."   —*Hudson Valley News*

"Readers who enjoy coming-of-age tales and small-town stories will appreciate this well-crafted debut novel that tugs at the heart without falling into sentimentality."   —*Library Journal*

"Like Ava in Karen Russell's *Swamplandia*, Florine increasingly finds herself creating her own rules for survival, whether they appear rational or not. Recommend this to teens who like coming-of-age novels with strong characters and a vibrant sense of place."   —*School Library Journal*

"It's the Maine voices that carry this book and make it an authentic page-turner: fishermen and the women who love them, as well as a younger generation of girls and boys on the coast who skip town as soon as they get their diplomas. Rogers captures this era of Elvis records and small-town Maine fishing life so vividly that you may wish you'd grown up here."
—*Down East*

"Bittersweet and captivating . . . a profound tale."
—*New York Journal of Books*

Red Ruby Heart

in a

Cold Blue Sea

‿

Morgan Callan Rogers

P

A PLUME BOOK

PLUME
Published by the Penguin Group
Penguin Group (USA) Inc., 375 Hudson Street, New York, New York 10014, USA

USA | Canada | UK | Ireland | Australia | New Zealand | India | South Africa | China
Penguin Books Ltd, Registered Offices: 80 Strand, London WC2R 0RL, England
For more information about the Penguin Group visit penguin.com

First published in the United States of America by Viking,
a member of Penguin Group (USA) Inc., 2012
First Plume Printing 2013

 REGISTERED TRADEMARK—MARCA REGISTRADA

The Library of Congress has catalogued the Viking edition as follows:
Rogers, Morgan Callan.
   Red ruby heart in a cold blue sea / Morgan Callan Rogers.
      p. cm.
   ISBN 978-0-670-02340-0 (hc.)
   ISBN 978-0-452-29863-7 (pbk.)
   I. Title.
   PS3618.O4656R43 2012
   813'.6—dc23   2011033332

Printed in the United States of America
10 9 8 7 6 5 4 3 2

PUBLISHER'S NOTE
This is a work of fiction. Names, characters, places, and incidents either are the product of the
author's imagination or are used fictitiously, and any resemblance to actual persons, living or dead,
businesses, companies, events, or locales is entirely coincidental.

To my brother, John Michael Rogers,
and to my friend Denise Gaul Stilson.

Somewhere else, but always here.

Red Ruby Heart

in a

Cold Blue Sea

After we almost burned down a summer cottage, my friends and I were not allowed to see each other for the rest of July and August. It was 1963, and I was twelve.

After the fire, my parents decided that they should take me in hand lest I end up in jail. Grand, my grandmother who lived across the road from us, usually took care of me while they worked. Daddy made his living as a lobsterman and had to haul traps every day. My mother, Carlie, was a waitress at the Lobster Shack. She cut back on her shifts to keep me out of trouble.

Being under Carlie's playful eye wasn't the worst thing that had ever happened to me. I had her pretty much to myself for the last two weeks of July, and we did something different every day. We got ice cream cones at Ray's General Store up the road and sat on our front steps eating them and watching the water wink at us from the harbor at the end of The Point. We hiked from our backyard through the woods to the nearby State Park and ate snacks at the picnic tables there. We hung out at the Lobster Shack, we window-shopped in Long Reach, the town closest to The Point, danced and sang to Elvis records, played cards, sunned ourselves, and goofed off.

On the day I was to remember best, we packed a picnic, piled into Carlie's 1947 Ford coupe, Petunia, and set off up Route 100. We passed through Long Reach, went over a bridge spanning a wide river, and drove toward Mulgully Beach, which made up the nail on a thick finger of land.

We were to meet Patty, Carlie's friend. Patty waitressed with Carlie. Her hair was buttercup yellow, her eyes were light blue, and her dimples were so big she could have hidden marbles inside of them. She didn't take any crap, either. Rude customers had glasses of water accidentally spilled over their laps, or they'd have to wait a minute too long for her to serve them. Once, a table of ten didn't tip her and had the nerve to show up again. "I'm getting them good," Patty told Carlie and me. In between smiling and serving, she went out into the parking lot and let the air out of one of their car tires. As they stood outside wondering what to do, Patty went out and demanded, and got, her tip. I liked her style, although Grand might have said, "Two wrongs don't make a right."

Carlie always got her tips. Whereas Patty flirted and giggled and made it known that she was full of hell and proud of it, Carlie didn't have to flaunt it. Carlie lit up a room like a bright light and people were drawn to her. I thought the sun and moon circled around her. So did Daddy.

I always called her Carlie, never mother, mom, mommy, mum, or ma. She was eighteen years old when she drove Petunia up from Massachusetts. Daddy told me that she swept him off his feet in front of Ray's store. "I was done hauling for the day," he said, "and I thought I'd walk up to Ray's for a six-pack of 'Gansett. The sun caught on the bumper of a car parked outside the store and I was pretty much blinded by the shine. Then someone blocked it. It was this girl, and she smiled at me. Pretty eyes, red hair. Skinny, but that didn't matter."

Carlie told Daddy that she was working up the road at the Lobster Shack for the summer. "I had supper with Ma that night," Daddy said, "and even though she made me her finnan haddie, Carlie's being down the road was the only thing I could think of."

They got married in August 1950 and I was born on May 18, 1951. They named me Florine, after Daddy's mother, Florence, and Carlie's mother, Maxine.

That day, on our way to Mulgully Beach, Carlie tapped her pink fingernails against Petunia's steering wheel. Her hair curled like red ribbon over her shoulders. *Ah lewie lewa, Oh whoa, I saida we gotta go,* thumped on the radio. My best friend, Dottie Butts, and I spent one afternoon listening to "Louie Louie" every time it came on, because we'd heard it was dirty. But it was hard to figure out the words. Dottie said the singer sounded as if his tongue had been cut to ribbons and he was trying to sing through the blood. We came up with the words, *"Every night, at ten, I lay her again. I chuck that girl then I went away."* I asked Carlie about what she thought the words might be, but she shrugged. "Dunno," she said. "It's all about the beat, I guess."

When we reached the beach, Carlie paid a fee at a booth and we parked in a dirt lot. The sun bounced off the paint on the cars and made me squint.

"Don't do that," Carlie said. "You'll get a line between your eyes and look old before you're twenty. We'll get you sunglasses at the snack bar." She looked into the rearview mirror as she layered on bright pink lipstick, then we got out the picnic basket along with an old blanket and our towels and we headed for the bathhouse. When Carlie pulled off her panties, her thatch shone like copper. Fire crotch. I'd heard those words spoken about my mother one day as I waited for her to get off work. Two men were sitting close to me and one said to the other, "Redhead. I'll bet she's got a fire crotch." Now, when I saw Carlie naked, that's what I thought. She pulled her suit up over her hips, worked it over the penny-sized nipples on her small breasts, then wrestled the straps up over her back. I rolled my suit up over my skinny, hairless body, wishing something would bump out or curve in so I could say I was becoming a woman. Carlie had told me, not too long before when I'd been whining about my girl's body, "Pretty soon you'll be so dreamy the boys will walk into walls." Because she had said it, I held some hope of it in my heart.

"Let's go," Carlie said, and we gathered our belongings and headed for the snack bar. Carlie bought me sunglasses with pink cat rims and we hopped and squeaked barefoot up over the hot boards covering the tarry, hot boardwalk.

"Run!" Carlie said. We pounded over the boards to the top in a rush and took in a strip of sun-beaten sand and curly, bottle-green breakers below us. More people than I would see in a year sprawled on blankets or jumped and screamed in the waves.

About halfway down the beach, a woman in a black bathing suit stood and waved at us from a yellow blanket. When we got close enough, Patty hollered, "Hey Florine," and Carlie and I threw our picnic basket and beach bag down onto the blanket.

"Hot," Carlie said. "I'm going to cool off right away." She grabbed one of my hands and Patty grabbed the other one and they ran me down toward the waves. Before I could scream, a wall of water flung me down, tumbled me like laundry, scraped me along the sand bottom and spat me back onto the beach, where Carlie grabbed me.

"Scared?" she asked. Of course I was, and back we went, time and again, until we were scratched and beat up. We dipped into the backwash between breakers and cleaned the sand from our suits as best we could. We staggered back toward our blanket, me trailing behind the two most beautiful women that I knew. Even though they both were small in height, they walked tall and carried themselves high and proud. They tossed their heads at the same time, and their wet hair flung sprays of salty water into the air. When I tossed my head, I tripped over my big feet and almost fell over.

Back on our blanket, we ate peanut butter and grape jelly sandwiches, chugged root beers, and looked out at the ocean.

"You behaving?" Patty asked me. "Haven't started any fires lately, have you?"

"We didn't mean to do it," I said. "It didn't burn down all the way."

"I'm joshing you," Patty said. "Rich bastards deserve a little smoke in their eyes from time to time."

"Well, let's talk about something else," Carlie said. She took a deep breath and let it out. "Ain't this grand," she said. She pulled her bathing suit strap away from her shoulder. "Do I have a burn?"

"You just got here," Patty said.

"I burn easy," Carlie said. She poured baby oil onto her legs and rubbed it in.

"What about me?" Patty asked. Carlie snorted. Patty was golden in all the places we could see her.

"Am I tan?" I asked. Carlie took off her sunglasses and looked at my shoulders. "No," she said. "You have my skin. Your father, now, there's someone who tans easy."

"How is the old man?" Patty asked. I wanted to say he isn't old (even though he was twelve years older than Carlie) but Patty saw my look and gave me the gift of her dimples. "It's just an expression, Florine," she said. "Your daddy's a stud."

"What's a stud?" I asked.

"He's fine," Carlie said. "Hauling."

"Same old same old," Patty said. "Oh, by the way, someone's missing you."

"Who?" Carlie asked.

Patty grinned like a cat. "You know," she said. I couldn't see Carlie's face, but she must have given Patty a look, because Patty glanced at me and her smile got smaller. She grabbed a yellow-knotted string purse from beside her on the blanket and fished out a dollar. "How about you get an ice cream, my treat," she said to me. "Okay?" she asked Carlie.

"I want to stay," I said. I wanted to hear about who was missing Carlie. But Carlie said to me, "You get an ice cream and you come right back," and I went. Mostly she was easygoing, but when she asked me to do something, I did it.

I traveled fast over the hot sand and skimmed up and down over the boardwalk to the snack bar. I stood in line for what seemed hours but was most likely minutes. I got a chocolate jimmy cone and headed back, paying attention not to get it all over me.

I was halfway back down the beach when I noticed the man with Carlie and Patty. He was a darker gold than Patty, and he had black hair. He was stretched on his back on the blanket, hiked up on his elbows, talking to Carlie, who sat facing him, her knees up near her chin, her hands wrapped around her legs.

I crunched the nubbin end of my sugar cone as I walked up to them. The man turned toward me, shutting one eye to keep down the glare of the sun. When he smiled at me, one tooth snaggled out of the left side of his mouth. "Hi," he said. "You Florine?" His hair was slicked back, shiny. His eyes were blue. He looked at Carlie. "Looks like the old man, I guess," he said. "She's got some of your coloring, but she's going to be bigger in every way." Patty giggled. My ears felt hot. I swallowed the rest of my cone and decided I didn't like him. "Can we go for a walk?" I asked Carlie.

She looked at me over the top of her sunglasses. Her face was turning pink. "Sure," she said. She got up and brushed herself off. The man looked at her legs. He shifted his hips on the blanket and moved himself up onto his elbows a bit more.

"Who's that?" I asked as we walked out of earshot.

"Mike," she said. "He comes into the Shack. He's a customer."

"Is he the someone who misses you?" I asked.

"What do you mean?" Carlie asked.

"Patty said someone missed you."

Carlie shrugged. "I don't know," she said. "It doesn't matter. I don't miss him." She stopped and stretched, looked out over the ocean. Then she said, "Come here. Stand in front of me." I did, and she bent down and pointed toward the line between the sea and the sky. "See the horizon?" she asked.

"Yes."

"If you could walk through that line and come out on the other side, you would be somewhere completely different. Wouldn't that be a gas?"

"Yeah, I guess," I said. A seagull landed nearby, cocked its white head, and studied us with a yellow eye. Carlie waved it off.

We walked toward a pile of rocks and sat on a black one with a flat surface that fit both our butts just fine. We looked out at Carlie's horizon for a few seconds, then she said in a dreamy voice, "When I was a kid, before I'd go to sleep, I'd put myself to flying. I'd go to all these places and touch down, look around, see if I recognized anybody. Then I grew up, drove up here, and there was your father, walking towards me with the sun hitting the back of his head like a halo. Blue eyes, big smile, big shoulders, big man, and I said to myself, 'Well, here he is, Carlie. This is where you stop.' He's a good man, Florine. One of the best men I've ever met."

She looked at me and said, "What do you think about before you drift off?"

"I don't know," I said.

"'Course you don't," she said. "You're your father's girl. And that's not a bad thing." She patted my arm and I winced. "Oh shit," she said. "Honey, you're sunburned. We'll go back to the blanket and pack up. Then let's go home, okay?" It was fine with me.

Patty and snaggletooth Mike were jumping around in the waves. As we came closer, they waved at us and ran for the blanket.

Patty shook drops of cold water on me. "Want to go in some more?" she asked.

Carlie said, "We're going home, Patty. Florine has a sunburn."

Mike lifted the bathing suit strap near Carlie's shoulder and ran his finger along the line between white and red skin. He said, "You got one too."

"Stop it," Carlie snapped.

Mike backed away. "You got to tell me the rules, Carlie. Just gotta know the rules." Head down, he walked toward the pile of rocks we'd just left.

"I'll talk to you later," Carlie said to Patty, and we left her stretched on her back on the blanket, one leg bent, looking toward the rocks where Mike had gone.

We were both quiet on the way home and we didn't play the radio.

About halfway to Long Reach, I saw a boy about my age swing out over
a pond on a thick rope that hung from the branch of a large tree. When
he was over the water, he let go of the rope. His baggy orange bathing
suit flapped against his chopping legs as if he wanted to take it all back.
Maybe he never hit the water. We passed him before I could see him fall.

2

What happened with the fire was this. We made a mess, and we got caught.

The night the whole muddle started, Daddy and Carlie were having a familiar argument. As I waited in my bedroom for Dottie, Glen, and Bud to show up, I listened to them talk. Our house was small. Their bedroom was off the kitchen, and my bedroom was kitty-corner to theirs, so I heard most everything pretty easy.

The problem was, Daddy hated going anywhere, but Carlie loved to travel. She and Patty went on a yearly trip up the coast, but she wanted Daddy to take us somewhere as a family.

Daddy said, "Why do you want us to go somewhere else? Most folks want to come to somewhere like this."

"Because we do the same damn things every day. Get up, eat, work, eat, sleep, and get up. Let's do something we've never done. Go somewhere we've never been."

"I don't do the same damn thing every day," Daddy said.

"You're right. You wear a different shirt on Tuesdays and Thursdays. Look, honey, we don't have to do anything expensive, and I've saved some tips."

"I got to paint the house. I got to paint Ma's house. I got to get in the wood. This is a bad time. We can do it next summer, I promise. We'll make it work, somehow."

"Oh, Leeman, it's always going to be a bad time. You'll always be busy. Let's just do it, honey."

The sharp knock on my bedroom wall made me jump. I waited a few seconds to see if my parents had heard it. But they talked over it, so I slid up the window screen and dropped four feet to the ground. Glen, the tallest of us so far, reached up and pulled down the screen to keep out the mosquitoes.

"Let's go," Bud said. We took off up a worn path close to my house that led to the woods. At the edge of the woods we scrambled over The Cheeks, one big white boulder that was cracked down the middle. Bud switched on a flashlight, and we followed him. I was in back of him, Dottie was behind me, and Glen brought up the rear.

The four of us were twelve, though Bud would turn thirteen in November. Brought up cheek-by-jowl in houses that hunkered down on granite ledge, our families had fished from The Point for generations. We knew each other well, but during the summer of 1963, tempers flared, people stomped off, and eyes darted like minnows trying to avoid becoming lunch. Small bumps took up space on Dottie's wide chest, while Glen's bathing trunks sported a lump in the front. A smattering of brown hairs made themselves to home over Bud's upper lip. Nothing appeared to be changing on me, but I felt as strange as the rest.

The motley crew we made that night sneaked behind the wobbly beam of a flashlight through the State Park's woods along its walking paths. On summer days, the Park swarmed with families eating lunches at picnic tables, playing in the little playground, and hiking the paths. I had never been here at night and it was creepy. The ghosts of those who had been there that day brushed against the hairs on my arms and I crossed them over my chest to keep out dark thoughts.

Glen's sneakers creaked like old hinges, and one of my anklebones snapped. When something blacker than the night flashed across the path right in front of Bud, he stopped dead. Dottie bumped into me so hard I pushed him down. He thrashed around underneath me as I struggled to get up. Glen finally grabbed me and set me on the path while Bud righted himself and brushed dirt off his shirt and shorts. "Get back a little ways, for chrissake," he said to me.

"Don't stop so fast," I said.

"Don't stand so close."

"Thought I was fighting a friggin' skeleton," I said. "You got to eat more."

Dottie moved me between her and Glen. "Now you both got cushion," she said.

We went on, and a short time later, Bud's flashlight picked out a path almost hidden by brush placed there by the park rangers to separate it from the park. This Path led to the big private summer cottages. We'd traveled this path during winter days, when the Park was quiet and the cottages were boarded up, but that summer night was a first for us.

We'd planned a simple firecracker raid. Get in near some cottages, light off the firecrackers, run like hell. The firecracker raid was Glen's idea. His father, Ray Clemmons, owned the general store on the road to town. His customers ranged from The Point folks and the surrounding areas to tourists and summer people. Sometimes, Ray wound up with goods that might not be considered legal. But the local sheriff was Parker Clemmons, Ray's brother and Glen's uncle, and every summer, boxes of fireworks and firecrackers found their way into Ray's backroom. Most of the stuff disappeared after July 4th, except for a few boxes of this and that that Ray always held over for some makeshift celebration.

That year, a box of firecrackers had found its way into Glen's grubby hands.

"We should pay a night visit to the cottages," he said. "Set 'em off. Shake 'em up."

"You foolish?" Bud said. "Why rile 'em up? They're them and we're us. Should keep it that way." He had a point, yet here he was, leading the way through the woods.

The trail to the cottages wound around trees so thick the sky couldn't

bleed through the branches. The skin on my head crawled as I imagined a vicious fisher cat leaping from a branch above me and digging its
teeth and claws into my scalp. But the sound of adults laughing shattered my fear like glass. Lights from the cottages pierced the trees and
Bud shut off his flashlight.

I never understood why people called these places cottages. They
were monster mansions with perfect green lawns that spilled just so
down to private docks and private coves with private brown-sugar
beaches. Sometimes, we caught sight of one of the people who owned
these houses in Ray's store. When they talked, they bent their *R*'s like
willow saplings. The women favored lime-green skirts and carried
wicker bags with whales on them. The men wore old, faded clothes that
always looked ironed. Soft moccasins covered their tanned, blue-blooded
feet. They bought shitloads of lobsters and groceries all summer, and
that made the men on The Point happy. But as Bud had pointed out,
they were them and we were us and we lived in different worlds.

Right now we hung on the hairy edge of breaking rules set by our
fathers and their fathers as we crouched at the edge of a driveway across
from a shingled, shambled cottage with a tower that skimmed the night
sky. We knew from our winter visits that a screened-in porch set on
the front of the house. From this porch, women's voices rose and fell like
gulls nagging at a fishing boat, while the men's voices grumbled
like distant thunder. Ice clinked against glasses. Cigarette smoke hung
like fog in the light.

Glen's black eyes glowed in the back porch light. "Good. They're all
here. The porch sides got gaps big enough so we can crawl underneath.
We set the crackers, light 'em, get back here, and watch the shit hit the
fan when they go off."

"Too many people," Bud said. "We'll get caught for sure."

"They're so loud they won't hear us," I said. "And they sound pretty
drunk."

"That's good," Glen said. "Florine, you and I will go right. Bud and
Dottie go left. We'll meet up under the porch."

The hinges on the back screen door shrieked.

"Someone's coming," Dottie said. We ducked and peeked through the tall grass.

A tall, thin, bald man came down the stairs and headed our way.

Bud and I were crouched in front of Dottie and Glen. When they backed up so Bud and I could follow them, a branch snapped under Dottie's feet.

The man stopped. "Whoze air?" he called in a scratchy slur. It was too late for Bud and me to move without being heard, so we balled ourselves up beneath the brush as close to the ground as we could get. The man's feet crunched to the edge of the gravel and stopped. "Whoo?" he called and then he giggled like a girl. "Whoo? Whoo?"

A few seconds passed, then the man warbled, *"You'd never know it, but I'm a kind of poet."* The scritch of a zipper sounded. Then a hot spray of piss hit the top of my head and drenched my back. I wanted to move in the worst way, but fear of getting caught loomed larger than what was happening so I took it. The spray swung in Bud's direction and he grabbed my hand and squeezed. After what seemed forever, the old man finished and zipped up his fly.

"Hadley?" a woman called from somewhere near the front porch.

"Hold on to your saggy tits, you old bat," the man muttered. His feet crunched over the gravel, and then the back door swung open and snapped back on its hinges.

Bud stood up and peeled off his shirt and his shorts, down to his white skivvies. "Jesus," he said. "Oh Jesus." He wrung out his shirt and shorts, and then not knowing what else to do, put them back on. I skinned off my shirt, wiped my head best I could with the dry parts in front, then pulled it back over my head.

A sapling shook against the weight of Glen's and Dottie's laughter.

"Shut up," Bud said. "Let's go home."

The screen door screeched again and we all ducked.

The voice of someone close to our own age whispered, "I know you're in there."

"Great," Bud said, and he stood up. Then the rest of us followed.

"I saw you from the tower," a boy said to us. "What are you doing? Spying on us?"

"Casing the joint," Glen said.

"Jesus, Glen," Bud said. "No, we're not."

I studied the boy. His lips curved in a little smile. His eyes were dark and his hair was light. His hands twitched as he held them close to his sides. "No really," he said. "What's going on?"

"Might as well tell him," I said. "We got no choice."

"Unless we beat the crap out of you and leave you to die in the driveway," Glen said to the boy. "And don't think we couldn't do it."

The boy shrugged. "You probably could, but not before I get a few yells out."

Glen snorted. "Think they'll hear you over the noise?"

"I know who you are," the boy said to Glen. "You work in the general store off Route 100." He looked at Bud. "You work on a lobster boat." He looked at Dottie. "I've seen you around." He nodded to me. "I'm Andy Barrington."

"I'm Florine Gilham," I said.

"Pleased to meet you," he said.

"Now we got that out of the way," Bud grumbled, "let's go."

"You mean we're not going to . . . ," Glen said.

"Not going to what?" Andy asked. "What were you going to do?"

"We were going to set off some firecrackers under the front porch," Glen said.

"No shit!" Andy said, his dark eyes shining. "Let's do it."

"I'm game," I said.

"Me, too," Dottie said. "We come this far."

We all looked at Bud. He shook his head, then, with no warning he sped across the driveway and slid around the right side of the house. Andy and I followed right after him and the three of us slipped beneath the porch. "If I say yes to Glen again, shoot me," Bud growled as he pulled some loose firecrackers from his pockets, heaped them up, stuck a couple of birthday candles into the pile, and muttered, "Happy god-damn birthday."

Glen and Dottie squeezed through the gap on the other side of the porch. "You were supposed to do it my way," Glen hissed.

"Your way went out the window when he found us," Bud said, jerking his head toward Andy, who knelt in the dirt beside me. "Let's get this done."

Glen piled his crackers. Then he and Bud put more near the center of the porch until four good-sized firecracker hills were set to go. Above us, floorboards creaked and voices grew louder. Andy said, "I have matches. Need matches?"

"We got matches," Glen said. "Florine, Dottie, Bud, get into position." We each took up a post in front of a pile of firecrackers, then Glen said, "One, two, three," and we all lit our candles. Dottie finished first. She bolted from beneath the porch, Bud and me close behind. We sped to the edge of the woods and waited for Glen. And waited.

"Where the hell is he?" Dottie said.

The first pile went off. The noise was even louder than I'd expected. They snapped and snarled. Confused people poured from the porch. Another pile went off. A tongue of fire flickered its way from underneath the porch, and Glen bolted toward us, holding his hand and running as fast as he could go.

A man on the lawn cried out, "There he is," and started our way. I fell over Dottie, who scrambled up, pushed me down behind her, and left me sitting in the path. Bud hauled me into the bushes. Glen tore by us, the man hell-bent after him.

"The garden hose, get the hose," someone on the lawn cried. A group of men grabbed a hose from the side of the cottage and soaked the fire climbing up the latticework. Smoke turned the air blue. Then a third group of crackers went off and people scattered back out of the porch light.

The man who had chased Glen came from the woods and walked back toward the house. Another man met him. "Lose him?" he said. "Did you know who it was?"

"It was the boy from the general store. There was more than one of them, I think. Fishermen's kids. I'm calling the sheriff." He spat onto the grass. His hair was yellow, like Andy's. They walked back toward the house. When the fourth pile of crackers went off, Bud and I ran like hell. We followed Bud's flashlight to the edge of the woods near The Cheeks, where we found Dottie on the ground holding her right ankle. Glen rocked against a tree, holding his hand beneath his arm and hissing pain through his teeth.

"Jesus," he said. "I'm burned bad."

"Let me see," I said. Bud shone the flashlight as Glen held out his hand. Blisters were already bubbling up along his knuckles. "We got to get you some help," I said.

"Help me make up something to tell them first," Glen said.

I said, "They know you set the fire."

"Did not," Glen said. "That kid, Andy, lit a firecracker with a candle, and when everything got to hissing, he threw the candle and ran like hell, the bastard."

"We got to get home," Bud said. "We got to beat Parker."

But we were too late. When we scrabbled over The Cheeks, and down the path that led to my yard, our folks, along with Parker, were already there.

Parker went off with Glen and Ray. Bud and Dottie got hauled off by their own parents. I was left with Daddy and Carlie.

"What the hell were you thinking?" Daddy asked.

"How'd you get so wet?" Carlie asked, touching my shirt, and then she smelled her hand. "Did you roll in pee?" she asked. "Lee, smell her."

"I can smell her," Daddy said. "You're in big trouble, Florine."

After Carlie had scrubbed the pee out of my hair and thrown away the clothes I'd been wearing, we all sat down at the kitchen table.

"It wasn't our fault," I said. And then I asked, "Will I go to jail?"

"Might be best," Daddy said.

"Don't scare her," Carlie said. "She'll go to jail over my dead body."

The next morning, Sam and Ida Warner with Bud; Bert and Madeline Butts with Dottie; Ray Clemmons and Glen (his mother, Germaine, lived in Long Reach and was seldom seen by any of us); and we Gilhams formed a caravan and drove up to apologize. Our fathers set the rules. We were not to look at each other. We were to face front and speak only when spoken to except for the apology each of us was to give to Mr. Edward Barrington, the owner of the cottage.

We took the road that joined The Point to Route 100, turned right, went three fourths of a mile, turned left onto a dirt road, bumped along, then parked in the driveway where we'd hidden the night before. We got out and Ray knocked on the back door.

A woman the color of Grand's cherry headboard swung open the screen door. Her nametag read LOUISA. She said, "Can I help you?" through her milk chocolate lips.

"We brought our kids to apologize to Mr. Barrington," Daddy said.

Louisa walked down the steps and looked us over as if we were yesterday's fish. "So, you're the ones?" she said and she frowned. "Come with me," she said. We all trooped around to the side of the house and stopped in front of the lattice. It was black where the fire had licked up it. A porch screen was scorched, as was some of the wood over it.

Louisa pointed to a tangled mound of shriveled branches. "Look what you children did to Mrs. Barrington's rose bush. It grew the biggest, yellowest roses. She cared for that thing like it was a baby. Dead now, just gone. How you gonna be sorry for that?"

"Just tell Mr. Barrington we're here," Ray said.

"Oh, I'll tell him," Louisa muttered. She climbed up the porch steps and went inside.

"Jesus," Ray said to Glen. "This is going to cost us some bucks."

Glen muttered something.

"Shut up," Ray said and cuffed him one up the side of the head.

Mr. Barrington came to us by way of the screened porch, with Andy following him. In the daylight, Mr. Barrington was tall, with the same blond hair and dark eyes as his son, and although he was a handsome man, his face looked as if it could go from sun to squall in a split pea second. Andy looked down at the ground. His fingers curled and uncurled as he stood beside his father.

"Good morning," Mr. Barrington said in a deep, soft voice. He stepped back and looked at us. Daddy pushed me forward, as I was first in line.

"You got something to say to Mr. Barrington?" he said.

I looked at a spot on Mr. Barrington's chest and said, "I'm sorry."

"Why are you sorry?" he said. I looked up at him and blinked. I hadn't expected a question. His dark eyes snapped.

I shrugged. "I guess I'm sorry we came here."

"You guess?" he said.

"I'm really sorry we came here," I said.

Carlie squeezed my shoulders and said, clear, "She's a good kid for the most part."

Mr. Barrington smirked and moved on. Carlie squeezed my shoulders, harder.

Dottie said she was sorry in a loud voice and she added a " Sir."

Bud mumbled and his father, Sam, made him repeat it.

Mr. Barrington said to Glen, "How's your hand?"

"Okay," Glen muttered. "I'm sorry."

"He don't mean no harm," Ray said. "He's a little thick in the head, sometimes."

Mr. Barrington nodded. "It seems to be going around," he said, and indicated his son cowering in back of him. "I appreciate you coming up. We've been good neighbors. I'll let you know what the insurance company says and we can settle up."

"Sounds fair," Daddy said.

Andy glanced at me and I narrowed my eyes at him. He looked off toward the woods and scratched his head. I hoped he had a tick drilling into his scalp.

"Lucky he didn't press charges," Daddy said as the truck bumped down the road.

Carlie snuggled me beneath her arm. "My little criminal," she whispered. I pulled away and almost said, "I'm not little," but decided against it. Quiet seemed the best resort. When Mr. Barrington sent us a bill, Daddy paid his part.

"There goes any trip money we might have had," he said to Carlie.

"That's just another sad excuse," she said.

3

Carlie went back to the Lobster Shack on Thursday, the first of August. "Got a double today," she said to me. "Go to Grand's house before lunch." She left me sitting in the living room, eating peanut butter toast and watching *The Match Game*.

When Dottie's head popped up in the living room window I hauled up the screen, pulled her inside, and she tumbled onto the floor with a big grin.

She told me that her mother, Madeline, had gone up to town with Evie, her little sister. "I can't stay long," she said. "She finds me gone, I'm dead. She's on the warpath, for sure. Christ, she makes me clean the house mornings, then I have to stay in my room afternoons. I might lose what mind I do have, and I don't have much to begin with."

"How you doing?" she asked. She punched my shoulder and I winced. "How'd you get burned?" she asked.

"Went to the beach a couple days ago with Carlie," I said.

"She's some harsh with the punishment," Dottie said. "What you got to eat?" she asked. We both had our heads in the refrigerator when the screen door whined open so fast I jumped and yelled, "Jesus!"

"Unless Jesus is in that refrigerator, he'll want an apology," Grand said to us.

"I'm sorry," I said.

"You should be. Jesus died for your sins." She looked at Dottie. "I imagine I never saw you, Dorothea?" she said.

"Oh, for sure," Dottie said. She hightailed it out of the house.

"You got to come over now," Grand said to me. "I'm halfway through making bread for the bean supper tomorrow. I got to have some help." She hustled out of the house, her square behind shifting from side to side as I trotted after her.

I called her Grand because she was. She stood five foot nine inches tall and was what people refer to as a big-boned woman. She'd lugged me on her boxy hips until she was sure I could walk around without killing myself.

Her house was the oldest one on The Point. It stood alone on a ledge across the driveway from our house. The front yard was a fifty-foot-wide lip of grass hanging over the ledge, which dropped down to the shore about twenty feet below. A side yard held both a flower and vegetable garden. Wide windows on a year-round porch looked out over the water and let us track which boats went out and when they came back in. A big kitchen with windows on the sunny side of the house faced our house across the road. Two bedrooms and a bathroom made up the second floor. A front hall led to a cozy living room on one side and the kitchen on the other.

At the end of the front hall stood a mahogany china cabinet filled with Grand's collection of red ruby glassware, including a water pitcher, glasses, cups and saucers, candy dishes, and pickle and onion dishes. Four times a year, Grand and I would take each piece of glass out and wash it carefully, dry it, and put it back into the lemon-waxed and polished cabinet. My favorite piece was a small red ruby heart that sat in the middle of the three-shelved cabinet. I loved to hold it up to the sun so I could play the rich color against the walls. My grandfather, Franklin, had given this piece to Grand as a wedding gift. He had keeled over dead from a heart attack at a potluck supper when Daddy was ten, so Grand held that heart dear.

Summer days, we sat on the porch in our rocking chairs and I slugged down a soda and read one of my father's Hardy Boys mysteries from books so old that insects had bored their way through some of the words and the spaces from start to finish. If I held the books upside down and shook them, dried-up bug parts fell out.

No time to rock and read today, though. Grand had to make bread, and she had evidently decided that it was time to teach me how to do it. She gave me a flowered apron to tie around my waist, then pointed me toward the front of her old wooden kitchen table, which was so big it could seat ten people. The strong smell of yeast from the big, mustard-yellow bread bowl on that table knocked me back a step or two.

"What do I do?" I asked, trying not to breathe.

"That's already risen once," she said. "Punch it down. Then sprinkle some flour on the table, slap it down and knead it. Then punch it down some more, pick it up, shape it into a loaf, stick it in one of them pans and put it on the windowsill."

The thought of touching the blob of greasy dough twisted my stomach, but I did what she asked and pushed my fist into its pasty white bulk. It hissed yeast like a secret fart.

"Jumped up Christmas," Grand said. "It's dough, Florine. Don't be so spleeny. Put some muscle into it. Watch me."

She plowed her big fist into the dough, pushed and pulled it, smacked it down, kneaded it, shaped it, then plunked it into a pan. She put a dishtowel over it and set it on the sunny windowsill near four others.

"Sun will power it up," she said. "Now hurry. We want 'em all to rise up together."

I gave the next bowl my all, beating hell out of it best I could. By the time I'd set my second pan on the windowsill, she had a third toad of dough on deck.

We sweated buckets.

"Can you tell me why I agreed to do this, Florine?" Grand said.

I knew why. Yesterday, Stella Drowns had cornered us in Ray's. Stella lived above the store in a little apartment. She ran the deli, picked crabmeat, and did other jobs Ray didn't have time to do. I hated her because she was mean to Carlie. Before Carlie, Daddy had dated Stella off and on for years. Word had it that Stella couldn't get him to ask her to marry him soon enough, so she left The Point to see if he'd chase her. He didn't, Carlie showed up, and they were married by the time Stella decided to come back.

Stella was thin and pale, with a pillow of black hair that shone like a wet mussel shell. She wore red lipstick and mascara and painted the nails on her long fingers. Her light gray eyes were rimmed with black. She was pretty, except for a long scar that ran down her right cheek and petered out under her chin. Stella was the only one out of six high school students to have lived through a bad car crash up on Pine Pitch Hill. The story went that glass had filleted her cheek and set it to flapping against her nose and eye. They'd had to stitch it back on.

Once, when I'd gone into Ray's store alone, she caught me staring at the scar. She ran a finger down the length of it and said, "You looking at this, Florine?" She leaned over the counter and her voice went low. "Imagine all those kids dying around me on a summer night and there I was, right as rain, but for the blood running into my eyes. Stare as much as you want to, dearie, to remind you of what not to do."

She could be scary, but she also knew how to charm. A couple of days ago, when Grand and I had happened in to buy milk, Stella had buttered up Grand about her bread-making talents. Now Grand was helping to bake bread for around the one hundred people who would be coming to the Saturday night supper. I called Stella names I was sure Grand didn't know I knew as we beat up the dough to get it ready.

"My arms hurt," I bitched.

"Least you got arms," Grand said.

A boat horn sounded.

"Jehovah," she said, "they're coming in." Grand greeted the lobster boats every afternoon. She never missed a day. It would have been bad luck, she always said.

We got to the porch windows just as two good-sized boats drifted past Grand's house. The red boat, Bert Butts's *Maddie Dee*, chugged along in front of Daddy's *Carlie Flo*. Her dark green hull carved an easy path through the channel. Bert gave a blart on the *Maddie Dee*'s horn, and Daddy waved to us.

"I'm going to meet Daddy," I told Grand.

"Bring him back up and we'll have supper," she said.

I shed the apron and ran down to the wharf to meet him.

4

S am Warner tossed me a line from the boat and I looped it over a piling. "Hope you're behaving yourself," he said. I noticed that Bud was with them. I started to give him a smile, but Sam spat over the gunwale and gave Bud the eye. Bud moved to the stern and looked back to where they'd just come from.

Daddy squinted his blue-sky eyes at me and asked, "What do you have all over your face and your arms?"

"Flour," I said. "Grand and I are baking bread."

A truck rattled down the road to the wharf; Stinnie Flaherty, come to buy lobsters fresh off the boat so he could turn around and up the price to restaurants and fish markets. Tall and bony, except for his potbelly, Stinnie usually had a cigarette dangling from the right corner of his mouth. He was out of his truck the minute it stopped. He passed me with a grunt and started haggling with Daddy and Sam. While they went back and forth, Bud gave me a sly smile and slipped onto the wharf. "How's it going?" I asked.

"Okay," he said. "You?"

"Okay."

A cream-colored car crept down the steep dirt hill, popping pebbles under its tires as it came. It looked too new for the likes of us. It pulled up beside Stinnie's truck. The driver's door opened and Mr. Barrington climbed out. Andy stared at us through the windshield, then he opened the passenger door and followed his father. Mr. Barrington brushed past us, walked up to Daddy, and said, "Would you sell us lobsters for tonight? We have unexpected guests."

"Could," Daddy said. "Had a good day."

Andy gave Bud and me a nervous smile, but I didn't smile back and Bud shot him a look that made him walk to the other side of the wharf.

"If we pushed him in no one would miss him," Bud mumbled into my ear. His breath tickled and I giggled.

"Bud, get over here," Sam said and Bud went.

"You should be buying them lobsters from me," Stinnie grumbled at Mr. Barrington.

"Why?" Mr. Barrington said. "All they did was cross from the boat to the wharf and you've jacked the price."

"Cost of labor," Stinnie said, waggling his cigarette.

Daddy said, "I got some cripples I was going to have for supper."

"How many?" Mr. Barrington said.

"Six or so," Daddy said.

"Louisa can make stew. It'll taste the same," Mr. Barrington said. He reached into his pocket and pulled out a wad of money held together by a silver clip. He took off the clip and said, "How much?" to Daddy.

"Fifteen dollars ought to do it."

"Jesus," Stinnie said, "what the hell? I can sell you two-clawed for three bucks a pound."

"Never mind," Mr. Barrington said. "Louisa makes a fine stew." When he peeled off two bills for Daddy, the whole wad fell apart. Some of the money fell onto the wharf, and some of it fell in the water beside the *Carlie Flo.*

Bud wasted no time shucking off his shirt and sneakers. He dove into the water and gathered up the bills. We stood and watched him.

Andy wandered over to me. "I could have done that," he said.

"Doubt it," I said.

"Look, I'm sorry," he said. "I got caught, too, just so you know. They're threatening to send me back to Connecticut for the rest of the summer."

"Good riddance," I said, and he shut up.

Bud climbed up the ladder attached to the edge of the wharf and handed the money to Mr. Barrington, who handed him back a ten-dollar bill.

Sam took it from Bud and held it out to Mr. Barrington. "Doesn't need it," he said.

"Let him take it," Mr. Barrington said.

"He's fine," Sam said.

"He worked for it," Mr. Barrington said.

Sam said, "Well, he did, I guess. But five is good enough."

Mr. Barrington handed Bud a five.

Bud grinned at me until Sam poked him and said, "Say thank you," and Bud did.

Mr. Barrington smiled at me. "How are you doing, Florine?" he said and winked.

"Fine," I said.

"That's good," Mr. Barrington said. He said to Daddy, "She's a little pistol."

"She's like her mother," Daddy said.

"Could be," Mr. Barrington said, and he and Andy went back to the car. It bore them up the hill and out of sight with their cripples.

Stinnie followed Mr. Barrington up the hill in his rickety old truck. Sam and Daddy walked up the hill ahead of Bud and me.

From this angle, the four houses on The Point set like crooked teeth stuck into tough grass and granite gums. The Warners' house was closest to the water and above it sat the Buttses' house. Our house huddled under a line of tall pines and across the road from us was Grand's house. Summer visitors didn't see this view much. They liked standing at the top of the hill and taking pictures of the harbor. "So picturesque," they said. "You must love living here." We didn't see many tourists in January, though, when the wind staggered off the water like a nasty drunk and slapped us all silly.

"What are you going to do with the money?" I asked Bud as we walked along.

"Put it away. Going to buy a car," he said.

"You can't drive yet."

"I will sometime."

Sam and Daddy talked about Mr. Barrington.

"Got himself a wad," Sam said.

"He don't have nothing we don't have," Daddy said.

"Hell he don't," Sam said, and they laughed.

Bud and Sam turned off, and we continued on to Grand's house. Sometimes we joined Carlie for dinner at the Shack, but Daddy liked to clean up and settle down at home, and Grand liked to cook for us, so we ate with her.

The smell of warm bread and frying fish in Grand's kitchen drew us in the finest way. She sent me out for cucumbers from the garden and I sliced them up into a red ruby bowl and covered them with cider vinegar and salt and pepper.

I told the story of the money and Daddy said that the day had been good on the water. Grand told Daddy that I might be a decent baker if I put my heart into it, and soon after supper, we went home. Later that night, Daddy and I sat in the living room, him watching a Red Sox game and me reading a Trixie Belden book until my eyelids drooped and I went to bed. I was dreaming that I had fallen into a bowl of slimy bread dough and couldn't get out, when I heard Daddy say, "What the hell did you do?"

"I fell into this bowl," I told him, before I figured that he was talking outside of my dream. I opened my eyes. The Mickey Mouse clock beside my bed said one o'clock.

"I liked your hair," Daddy said. "Why'd you change it?"

"For the fun of it," Carlie said. "Don't you understand fun? Let me answer that. Nope." The refrigerator door opened. "Nothing to eat?"

she said. "Doesn't the woman of the house ever shop?" She sounded as if she was talking through heavy syrup.

"You drunk as you appear to be?" Daddy said.

"Probably, but mostly hungry. Suppose Grand would mind if I raided her fridge?"

"I can't get over your hair. I liked it red, just fine," Daddy said.

"It's there, for heaven's sake," Carlie snapped. "It's just covered up."

I opened my bedroom door and looked into the kitchen. Carlie stood in front of the refrigerator door with a jar of mayonnaise in her hand. She stuck a finger full of it into her mouth and smiled at me. "Hey sweetie!" she called, and her voice turned up at the corners. "What you doing up?"

Carlie's hair was as blond as Marilyn Monroe's. The curl was gone and it was straight as meadow grass, except for a little flip at the ends. She'd gone heavy on the green eye shadow and spread bright red lipstick on her bow mouth.

She put the mayonnaise jar back in the refrigerator. "So, what do you think, Florine? Some of us did our hair. You should see Patty. Her hair is redder than mine."

"It's different," I said. Her shoulders slumped, so I added, "But I like it." She came over and hugged me. She smelled like beer and cigarettes.

"Maybe you can get your father to like it," she said.

"It ain't that I don't like it," Daddy said. "It's that you didn't let me know beforehand." Carlie broke our hug at the sad sound of his voice. He walked into their bedroom and shut the door.

"Oh, Leeman," Carlie said, but so soft he couldn't have heard her. Her eyes filled with tears and she stepped over to the kitchen counter to find something to blow her nose on. She reached into the junk drawer and came up with a napkin from the Shack.

"Go to bed, Florine. I have to talk to your father," she said.

She walked into their bedroom. I went back to bed and listened to a low murmur from her, an occasional grunt from him. Then the sounds stopped and I went to sleep.

In the morning, after Daddy had gone out on the water, I came out of my bedroom to find Carlie slumped at the kitchen table, nursing a mug of coffee. Her new blond hair was bed-messed and hung down over her shoulders, limp and pale. I touched it, and it was soft. I stroked it from top to tip and back again.

"It's nice," I said. "Takes some getting used to, but it's pretty."

"Your father is upset with me," she said in a hoarse crow's voice.

"Can I have some coffee?"

"Lots of milk," she said. I rolled my eyes. Surely I was old enough to drink regular coffee, but I settled for fixing a glass of milk with enough coffee to color it, then added three teaspoons of sugar. I sat down and looked at Carlie. Her lashes were clumped with old mascara and most of the eye shadow had rubbed off during the night.

She picked up a piece of her hair and frowned as she studied it. "Looks like shit disguised as straw," she said. "Do you think I should dye it back?"

I shrugged and chugged the coffee milk, held the glass to my mouth and watched the melted sugar flow toward my tongue in a slow sweet stream. The sugar flooded my mouth and breached my taste buds back to my ears.

"Maybe you should ask Grand what she thinks," I said.

"Oh shit," Carlie said. "Grand. I wonder what she'll say."

"Let's get dressed and go over and find out. I bet she likes it," I said. When she saw Carlie's hair, Grand said, "Well, now, that's a change."

"Leeman hates it," Carlie said.

"He'll get over it," Grand said. "Hattie Butts and Cora Brown and I liked to do each other up. Least Leeman noticed. Franklin never did. I don't see the harm in it."

After our visit, Carlie felt better. Still, we cleaned house until it sparkled and made Daddy a good supper. Carlie got a phone call from Patty midway through the day and I caught the words, "I really screwed up this time," before they hung up.

Daddy came home to the smell of supper and the table set. Carlie moved her chair close to his and he kept looking at her, trying, I guess, to learn who she was with this new hair. About halfway through the meal, I realized I might as well be wallpaper. Carlie kept rubbing his leg under the table and Daddy's eyes were getting bright. When Carlie asked me to go to Ray's for some dessert and to take my time, I knew enough to go.

Stella Drowns was the only one in the store. I headed for the cream horns, took two of them to the counter, and handed Stella a dollar.

"You still being punished for the fire?" she asked.

"I didn't set it."

"Not what I asked," she said. She smiled, shifting the scar a few inches up on her cheek. "Think you've learned your lesson?" she asked.

"Can I have my cream horns?" I said.

"Not getting it until you answer me," she said.

"Give me back my money," I said.

She slapped my dollar into my palm.

"You're a witch," I said, and left the store, determined to tell Daddie and Carlie about her. When I got close to our house, I heard Elvis on the record player. I started to go inside, but then I stopped, wondering at the sight of Daddy holding Carlie to him as he led her in a clumsy slow dance across the kitchen floor. When they saw me in the doorway, I said, "I'm staying at Grand's house. I need my PJ's." I started to walk past them, but they opened their arms as if they were a bridge and then they brought down their arms. Carlie giggled on one side of me, and Daddy's soft chuckle moved against my ear. "Let me go," I said, in a muffled voice. When they freed me, I grabbed my pajamas and ran out the door.

Grand cut me a big piece of her chocolate cake and we watched television, then went up to bed. I snuggled down in Daddy's old bedroom to go to sleep. Just before I dropped off, Stella's voice hissed at me, "Think you've learned your lesson?"

5

Madeline, Dottie's mother, was an artist. She sold watercolors at a little gallery up on Route 100. I loved to watch her paint, and on a Wednesday afternoon during the second week in August, Dottie and I sat on her lawn while she did just that. She gazed out over the water, back at her painting, out again, dabbed a few strokes of color down, looked out. I could have watched her for hours.

That Monday morning, a blond Carlie and a redheaded Patty had driven up north for their yearly trip to Crow's Nest Harbor. They were due back Thursday. Carlie packed a suitcase with some summer things, threw a couple of meals together for Daddy and me, and they were off. But not before she'd made Daddy talk to Bert about Dottie and me seeing each other again. They'd agreed, but no overnights, and the boys were still off limits.

Dottie picked a blade of grass out of the lawn and split it down the middle. She put it between her thumbs, gave it a blow, and got a squeaky honk out of it. I tried it and spit all over my hands.

"I don't know why you can't do that," she said.

"I'm not good at sports like you," I said.

"This ain't sports," Dottie said. "It's grass blowing."

I shrugged. Madeline moved her brush and blue slashed across the top of her painting. She moved it again, and another blue slash, lower and darker, appeared.

"Let's do something," Dottie said.

"What?" I said.

"Keep-away," she said. "You take Evie and I'll take Maureen."

Dottie's sister, Evie, was six, and Bud's sister, Maureen, was five. Dottie called them pinkie girls, doll-playing girls. "Keep-away will be too hard for them," I said.

I watched an orange spider the size of a freckle move up Dottie's leg. When it reached her knee, she smeared it. "Them things bite," she said. "I got bit the other day, and I looked down and it was one of them."

"I never got bit by one," I said.

"You probably did. You just didn't know it," Dottie said.

Madeline shifted in her chair. A little breeze lifted the corner of her paper. Dottie picked a little weed shaped like a spoon and peeled the veins up from the stem and down the back of the leaf. Then she threw the stripped weed onto the lawn. "Grand have cookies?" she asked.

"No," I said. "But she'll let us make some."

"I don't want to make 'em, I want to eat 'em," Dottie said. She said to Madeline, "Ma, when can we go swimming? You almost done?"

"No," Madeline said, in a faraway voice. "Not for a while."

"Let's go to Grand's and make cookies," I said. "Tide'll be in after we do that and then we can go swimming."

"Okay," Dottie said. "It'll pass the time."

Grand was watching a soap opera when we banged through the screen door.

"What you doing in?" she called.

"Can we make some cookies?" I asked.

"Just a second," Grand hollered. "Lisa's going to tell Bob she's leaving him for Howard. Been waiting for months for this. Hold your horses and I'll be with you."

"We can do it," I said, but she didn't hear me.

"Wish we had horses," Dottie said, sitting in Grand's rocker on the porch. "We could ride them somewhere."

"What kind of horse would you have?" I asked, sitting down in my own chair.

"Palomino. Like Trigger."

"I'd have a black stallion," I said. "He'd hate everyone but me. I could ride him without a saddle or a bridle."

"You can't even ride with a saddle," Dottie pointed out.

"Neither can you. We don't even have saddles. Or horses. I'm just saying, if I had a horse, this is what I would want."

The television was pretty loud, so Dottie and I got to listen as Lisa told Bob she was leaving him. Lisa sounded more upset than Bob. *"I'm sorry,"* she cried, *"I wouldn't have hurt you for the world. I do love you, Bob, I do, but . . ."* Bob mumbled a couple of words and Lisa started up again.

"That's crap," Dottie muttered.

"You mad?" I asked.

"No. Just bored."

Bob finally hollered at Lisa. *"You think I haven't noticed you've been acting strange, lately? You haven't wanted to sleep with me. You haven't even wanted to kiss me. Oh, I've noticed, Lisa. I'm not blind."*

"Maybe not," Dottie said, "but you're ugly."

We giggled, and then a commercial came on and Grand got up.

"All right," she said behind us in the kitchen. "Get in here you girls. Dorothea, you get them bowls over there and Florine, you get out the flour and sugar."

"We can do this," I said again, but Grand waved me off.

Dottie got out the bowls and sat down as Grand and I gathered all of the ingredients.

"Dorothea, get up and take a couple sticks of butter out of the fridge," Grand said.

"What kind of people name a kid Dorothea?" Dottie said. "I hate my name."

"It's a beautiful name," Grand said. "Your father's grandmother

Dorothea was a wonderful woman. You cut the butter up into little pieces and wash your hands first."

Dottie dragged herself over to the sink and turned on the tap.

"Use soap," Grand said. "That's right. Just like that." She looked at me. "You too."

"I know," I said, and muttered under my breath, "you don't have to tell me."

"Seems like I do," Grand said, somehow managing to hear me.

I bumped hips with Dottie at the sink and the soap popped out of her hand and flopped onto Grand's kitchen floor. We reached for it at the same time and bumped heads.

"Ow!" I hollered.

"Shit!" Dottie yelled.

Grand bent down and picked up the soap. "If I'd wanted a show, I would've turned on *The Three Stooges*," she said. "Lucky you two got hard heads."

Dottie said, "I'm sorry I swore."

"Sorry accepted," Grand said.

I poured white and brown sugar, cracked eggs, tipped vanilla into a spoon and took a deep snort of it. Grand measured flour, baking soda, and salt. The butter chunks thumped as Dottie cut them into a bowl. A breeze chased through the kitchen, touched the back of my neck, and moved on. Grand hummed "What a Friend We Have in Jesus."

"I got the messiest job," Dottie said.

"You done yet?" Grand asked. She took the bowl from Dottie, dumped the butter pats into the sugar and egg, and began mixing it together with a wooden spoon. Then she added chocolate chips and mixed it again. The back fat on her arm wobbled as she gave the ingredients hell, still humming away. The skin on her elbow reminded me of pictures I'd seen of elephants' knees.

Dottie and I smeared Crisco over cookie sheets, and Grand spooned dough onto them. Dottie picked at the dough. Grand said, "Dorothea," and Dottie took her hand away.

Grand bustled into the living room for a go-round with a second soap opera, leaving us to pick up the kitchen. Dottie scraped the sides of the dough bowl with a fingernail. I took it from her and set it in the sink to soak, put spoons and cups into the soapy water in the bowl.

"I got a black and blue?" Dottie asked, tilting her head so her brown bangs fell away.

"No," I said. "Me?"

"No," Dottie said. "I'm going over and get Ma to let us go swimming. Bring them cookies over when they're done."

"You're supposed to help clean up," I said.

"I got to move," she said. "Come over in a little while. Don't forget them cookies."

"Dorothea gone?" Grand asked when she came to check the cookies. I nodded. "She couldn't even help clean up."

"Well, she's a restless soul. Her great grandmother, the other Dorothea, was, too. I never saw someone keep so busy. I'd see her down in the clam flats, digging up dinner, feet and legs in muck up to the knees. Then, later I'd see her beating carpets she'd hauled out of the house and draped over her clotheslines. Made me tired to watch her." The smell of chocolate chip cookies wafted our way and the bell went off.

"Course," Grand said, "I don't see young Dorothea doing that."

"She hates clams," I said.

Grand gave me all three dozen cookies. I took them to Madeline, who put away her painting supplies, let us each have one cookie, then walked Dottie, Evie, Maureen, and me down to the beach by the wharf.

"I wonder when we'll be able to go swimming by ourselves," I said to Dottie as we trailed the others.

"Probably never," Dottie said. "Might as well get used to it." She hitched up the top of her bathing suit. "This friggin' thing don't fit anymore," she said.

"Stop bragging," I said, and she snorted.

The water was almost as warm as the air. Dottie and I held a contest to see who could do a handstand underwater longest. I was winning for the fourth time when I heard Dottie shout, "Hey!" I came up to see Bud and Glen standing amongst the boulders up above the beach. Bud grinned at me so wide his ears disappeared behind his head.

That grin made me feel strange, so I dove underwater to get away from it. Then I stood up, swept my hair out of my face, and Dottie and I waded toward the boys.

"Hold it. They're not supposed to be here," Madeline shouted from her rock. We froze and looked at her. Then she said, "Oh, the hell with it," and let the boys join us.

Dottie and Glen were busy ducking each other when Bud said to me, "Let's swim out to the mooring." The white mooring that belonged to Bert Butts wasn't too far offshore, but a steep drop-off made the water deep. "One, two, three, go," I said. We raced each other out and Bud won. When we reached the buoy, he let me grab the mooring rope while he treaded water.

"Swim to the bottom?" he said, and down we went on the count of three. I took hold of the rope while Bud swam beside me. As the water got deeper, it got colder. My ears felt as if they were pressing against my brains, and I wanted to head back up in the worst way. But Bud grabbed my hand and we spiraled down, until he stopped and pointed.

We'd reached an underwater city of rusty black rocks, where barnacles dotted the surfaces. Seaweed church steeples reached for the light. The far-above sun filtered through them, and Bud and I wove our way through their paths. An olive-colored crab marched backward between two rocks as two small silver fish swam past. A flash of white belly gave a flounder away as it sped off.

When an extra-cold current wrapped itself around my burning lungs, I tugged at Bud's hand and we swam up. I grabbed the mooring as we gulped in fresh air. I blinked my salt-stung eyes and the world blurred, then cleared.

"Want to go again?" Bud asked.

But Madeline shouted to us to get back to the beach right now, if we knew what was good for us, so we raced each other back. I won, but I think Bud let me do it.

I spent the rest of the afternoon with Grand, knitting and reading on the porch until Daddy came in. We ate supper and I went to bed at nine. As I drifted off to sleep, I thought about Carlie. She had promised me that she would buy me something special. I wondered what it might be. She always seemed to know what I would have picked out for myself.

When the phone rang, I jumped. I looked over at Mickey. It was 10:30 P.M. I heard Daddy get up from his living room chair, heard him walk across the kitchen floor to the wall phone and clear his throat of sleep. Heard the crack of a bat and the crowd roar on television. Heard Daddy say, "Hello? No, I haven't heard from her. Why?"

6

Crow's Nest Harbor was up the coast about three hours away. I knew from Carlie's description that it was a tourist town set on a bay that made our little harbor look like a puddle. Carlie and Patty had traveled up there for a few days every summer since I'd been old enough to wave goodbye to them. They always stayed at the Crow's Nest Harbor Motel, just off the main street, near the bay. The postcards Carlie mailed me every year showed me that the motel had a pool and pretty, light rooms. Carlie had promised to take me with them when I turned thirteen, which would be next spring.

Patty was the one who had called Daddy. She told him that she and Carlie had eaten breakfast together at the motel at about ten o'clock, and then Carlie walked into town to a dress shop to pick up something for me that they'd seen on Tuesday. She told Patty that she would be back in the early afternoon.

By five o'clock when Carlie still wasn't back, Patty began to wonder if she'd misheard her, so she walked into town. The dress shop sales clerk told Patty that she had seen Carlie, but it had been at about eleven o'clock. So Patty walked the streets and went into and out of shops and restaurants until about 7:00 P.M. Then she went back to the motel. At ten thirty that night, when Carlie still hadn't called or shown up, Patty decided to call Daddy.

This is what Daddy told everyone, later. He didn't tell me all of that right then, but I picked up the worry in his voice, so I got up and came into the kitchen. "You hear from her, have her give me a call," Daddy said, and hung up. He rubbed the stubble on his chin and glanced at me. "Why you up?" he said.

"Was that Carlie?" I asked.

"No," he said. "That was Patty."

"Where's Carlie?"

"Good question," he said. He caught my frown and said, "Oh, you know your mother. Sometimes she likes to go off. That's probably what happened, and she didn't check with Patty. I'm pretty sure Carlie will call us in the morning."

He told me to go back to bed, that he was about to do the same thing. I did, but not for long. Carlie not being where she was supposed to be was odd. I got up and stood in their bedroom doorway and said to Daddy, "I'm not going to be able to sleep until I know where she is."

Daddy sat up and turned on the little lamp beside him. He ran his hands through his hair and got out of bed. He hadn't taken off his pants, and he hadn't pulled down the covers. We went into the kitchen and we sat down at the table together.

"You want milk or something?"

"Yuck. No."

"I'll have a glass for myself, if you don't mind," he said. He got up and poured some milk into a little pan and turned on the burner. A blue ring of gas lit up with a hiss. "Grand used to make me hot milk, sometimes," he said.

"What if something has happened to Carlie?" I asked.

"Let's not worry," he said.

The milk fizzed as it got hot, and Daddy turned off the stove. He opened the cupboard over the stove, fetched down a bottle of whiskey, and poured a jigger into a mug. He poured the hot milk over it and sipped at it.

That looked good to me, so he poured a little into the jigger glass and I said, "Bottoms up," chugged it, and felt sleepy soon after.

Daddy tucked my blankets around me. I was too old for that, but I didn't say anything to him. It was comforting, somehow.

"You sleep," he said, brushing my forehead with his lips. "See you in the morning."

Come Thursday morning, Carlie didn't call, and Daddy didn't go out on the boat. He talked to Patty and at ten o'clock, about twenty-four hours after Carlie had disappeared, Daddy called Parker Clemmons, who called the Crow's Nest Harbor police department, who called the State Police.

Grand came over to our house. At eleven o'clock, Parker called and said the police needed a picture. Did we have one? Parker would drive it up. Daddy would go with him. No, it was best if I stayed with Grand. When I threw a fit about being left behind, Daddy held firm. "Why don't you help me look through the pictures," he said.

They were jumbled together in an old yellow suitcase with mouse-chewed leather straps under my parents' bed. Carlie had vowed that one day she and I would put them all into photo albums, but we hadn't gotten around to it. I dragged the suitcase into the kitchen and Daddy lifted it onto the kitchen table and undid the buckles. He and Grand and I began to sort through the pile.

Here was me as a fat baby. Here was me at three with Grand's black-and-white cat named Poker, who had folded his game long ago. Daddy as a boy, standing beside Grand, both of them looking spiffy in their Sunday-go-to-meeting clothes. Daddy and Carlie hugging each other and looking into the camera.

Carlie alone.

I shuffled it out from the pile. Even in the black-and-white picture, I could tell it was summer. Carlie stood back to the harbor, her hair flying around her face. She looked into the camera, not smiling wide, as she was apt to do, but giving the photographer just a hint instead, and her eyes were smoky. "I asked her to marry me after I took that picture," Daddy said. "I couldn't believe she said yes."

"'Course she said yes," Grand said. "You are the best thing happened to her."

Daddy said, "Well, she's the best thing . . ." He put his hand on my head. We looked at Carlie looking back at us from the photograph, and then Daddy said, "She hasn't changed much except for the stupid dye job. I guess we can use this one."

Daddy and Parker left to make the trip to Crow's Nest Harbor at about 3:00 P.M. on Thursday. Grand stayed with me Thursday night. We slept in my parents' bed, and I tossed and turned and breathed in the perfume from my mother's pillowcase. Come Friday morning, Carlie still hadn't made an appearance.

Word spread like measles through The Point, and by noon on Friday, Evie, Dottie, and Madeline came to keep Grand and me company. Then Ida, Bud's mother, showed up with Maureen, and Stella Drowns wandered down from Ray's store. I wasn't happy about Grand letting her into our kitchen, but Grand would have said all were welcome, so Dottie, Evie, Maureen, and I went into the living room. Evie and Maureen cut out paper doll dresses from a book Ida had brought along to keep them busy. Dottie and I picked up a jumbo-sized Archie comic and read the parts to each other. But I kept one ear on to what was being said around the kitchen table, where the women sat drinking pots of tea that Grand kept boiling up.

They didn't know Carlie well. She'd made a nest of her life with Daddy and me, but she was too restless for quilting, like Ida did, or painting, like Madeline did, or knitting and baking, like Grand did. Carlie liked to move. That was Carlie.

Stella, sitting across from Grand at the kitchen table, said, "Seems strange, all the same. It's almost like she and Patty planned it." The kitchen went quiet, then Grand said, pressing down on her words, "How do you mean?"

"I'm just saying, the whole thing is weird," Stella said.

Madeline said, "A wife and mother went shopping and disappeared. That's weird."

A cold band settled around my heart as I realized that they thought something was wrong. I left Dottie and stood in the kitchen doorway. Grand saw me and said, "Florine, do you and Dottie want lunch?"

I ignored her. I glared at Stella Drowns. "Nothing's wrong," I said.

"Oh, Florine, I didn't mean it," Stella Drowns said. "Thinking out loud is all."

"Might think better with your mouth sewn shut," I said.

Grand said, sharp, "Florine, apologize. I won't have you talk like that to anyone."

I muttered, "I'm sorry," and I went back into the living room.

Everyone but Madeline and Dottie left soon afterward and the day passed. Grand went over to her house and welcomed in the boats while we waited for news.

The phone finally rang about six o'clock and Madeline answered it. Daddy told her that the police had Carlie's picture. No, she hadn't been seen but in the morning, the police would show her photograph all around Crow's Nest Harbor. Grand came back over soon after the phone call and Madeline went home.

Dottie and I went outside and sat on the front steps of the house. Thin purple clouds clung like spider webs to the twilight long after the sun set. Fireflies blinked and darted across the front lawn. Usually, Dottie and I would get a jug and collect them, but that night we just sat and didn't talk. Grand called us in at about eight thirty. She made us go to bed in my little room and I tried to sleep but Dottie's chunky body, along with my own ragged thoughts, crowded me into a corner. I thought Dottie was asleep, so I jumped when she suddenly said, "She'll be okay. The police will find her." She fell asleep after that and I listened to her breathe for a little while, then I got up. Grand sat on the sofa, knitting and watching Johnny Carson.

I sat down beside her.

"What you doing up?" she asked.

"I want Carlie," I said. "I want my mother." Grand put down her knitting and pulled me close. I put my head down on her lap and sobbed into her dress as she stroked my hair and shushed me. Johnny Carson said goodnight and the network played the national anthem, and there was nothing but hiss, and still she sat and smoothed my hair and hummed hymns to me. I fell asleep staring into the darkness of her lap.

7

Daddy came home from Crow's Nest Harbor two days later. I sat at the picnic table in our front yard and looked down the driveway all day Sunday, waiting for him. Finally, he rumbled home in the pickup. Before he could shut the pickup door, I was on him and he hugged me tight. We went into the house and he gave Grand a hard, tired look.

"Sam brought a six-pack of 'Gansett by for you," Grand said to him. "Told me to give him a call when you got back. You feel like seeing him?"

"'Spose," he said. "Might as well call everyone, tell them what's going on." Daddy and I sat down at our picnic table and soon, everyone on The Point came by.

Carlie's picture was up all over town, he told us, and it was set to go into the local paper on Monday. They'd already checked all the shops in the village. The Crow's Nest Harbor police, the State Police, and the Coast Guard were searching.

When he brought up the Coast Guard, I dug my fingers into his arm. I'd already started my list of Horrible Things That Might Have Happened. Amnesia or kidnapping were at the top, but now I could add another, more permanent thing.

As if he knew my thoughts, Daddy took my hand and held it.

"Florine, no one knows what happened. They're checking every-thing, though, and they'll find out, I'm sure of it. Someone like your mother doesn't just disappear."

"What'd they ask you?" Sam said.

"First thing was, why'd she bleach her hair? Why did Patty dye her hair?" He shook his head. "What the hell was I supposed to say? She got an itch to do it and she did? Well, that's what I said. Far as I know, that's the only reason. They asked me if she was happy. Was she rest-less? Was she acting funny? Did she make phone calls or try to get the mail before I could see it? Did she spend a lot of money all of a sudden? Did she have her own bank account? What did we fight about? All kinds of things." Daddy took a big gulp of beer and wiped his mouth. "I couldn't tell them so many things. She always got the mail. Don't know if she got phone calls. Didn't have a bank account we could find. Paid for her trip with tip money. Sometimes she was happy, sometimes she wasn't, same as the rest of us. Our fights mostly had to do with us not going anywhere and me being stubborn."

"Did they call her family?" Madeline asked.

"Nothing there. I talked to her brother. He's no help. Christ, you think I don't talk much; you should try to worm things out of Robert. Mother's real sick, he said. Father died a year ago. No one's heard from Carlie."

"Be good to send someone down to talk to them, all the same," said Ida. "Might be something they know about her that we don't."

"They're going to," Daddy said.

We sat at the table for a couple of hours. Daddy smoked Chester-fields down to stubs and drank a six-pack of 'Gansett by himself. Grand brought out fried fish and fresh corn for everyone, but Daddy and I just pushed the food around on our plates.

Dottie set up my croquet set and batted a blue ball and a green ball through the wickets. Everyone left as the dying sun dusted the tops of the pine trees orange.

A swarm of mosquitoes began to whine around our heads, so we went inside.

"I know it's only eight thirty, but I'm bushed," Daddy said. "I got to go to bed."

"I should say so," Grand said. "Florine, you want to come with me for overnight?"

"I want to stay here with Daddy," I said. He rubbed his hands over his face and Grand said, "Why don't we let him get some sleep?"

"What if Carlie calls?" I asked.

Daddy said, "I'll let you know right away."

As Grand and I walked to her house, she said, "We got to give him a little time alone, Florine. He needs to catch up to himself."

The steady rhythm of Grand's snoring knocked me out that night, and I slept until nine o'clock the next morning. When I went downstairs, I looked through the picture window in the kitchen down to the harbor. The *Carlie Flo* was not at her mooring.

"Daddy's gone," I cried, and I ran out the door in my pajamas and went across the road and down the driveway as fast as I could go. What if the phone rang? What if Carlie came home with amnesia and left again because she wasn't sure it was her house?

Grand found me in the kitchen, staring at the phone.

"Florine, my number is next to be called," she said. "Your Daddy's got to work. Doing daily things gives a soul some comfort. Parker's got my number and Carlie knows she can call me. Get dressed and we'll work in the garden before it gets too hot."

I weeded and pinched back the row of sticky pink petunias that made up the border of Grand's garden. But their heavy perfume made me woozy, so Grand moved me to the vegetable garden, where I squashed bugs in the tomato plants.

Around eleven o'clock, Patty drove up and parked in front of Grand's house. Her dyed red hair looked rusted out, and dark rings had settled in underneath her eyes. I ran to her and hugged her, not wanting to let her go. "I'm so sorry, honey," she said. Grand sat her down in the kitchen and she told us what she knew, which is what we'd heard, for the most part. They'd asked her a lot of questions, like they'd asked Daddy. Why had they dyed their hair? Why were they traveling to Crow's Nest Harbor? Did Carlie and Daddy get along? Did she know if Carlie planned to meet anyone? Did Carlie make friends easily? Would she go off with a stranger?

"What about Mike?" I asked her.

Patty looked puzzled. "Mike who?" she asked.

"That guy at the beach with the black hair," I said.

Patty shook her head. "No, Florine, he's just a customer. He's married. He flirts, but he doesn't mean anything."

"He really liked her," I said.

"He did," Patty said. "But she didn't like him that way."

"Well, Carlie loves Leeman," Grand said. "Isn't no one else for her."

Patty agreed. "The police had Carlie's suitcase. Did they give it back to him?"

"I don't know," Grand said. "I haven't seen it."

"I'll go look," I said, and before they could say no, I zipped down the driveway. I found the blue suitcase in Daddy's pickup, stashed on the floor below the passenger seat. I wrestled it out and lugged it inside, sprang the snaps, and opened it up.

Her Carlie smell of oranges and peonies triggered tears even as I stared at her gone-through clothes. It made me mad they'd messed them up so. Someone, I thought, should have had the manners to fold them, so I did it. I remembered when I'd last seen her in this shirt, in those shorts, in the bathing suit she'd worn to Mulgully Beach. When I found her favorite green sundress, I held it to my face and cried until I soaked it.

A little while later, Grand showed up and she sat down on the floor beside me, which wasn't easy for her to do, and put her big old hand on my shoulder.

"Patty had to go," she told me. "Said she'd be right up the road if you needed her."

I later found out from Dottie, who'd heard Madeline talking to Tillie Clemmons, who was married to Parker Clemmons and wasn't supposed to tell anyone anything that her sheriff husband told her in secret, that the police thought Carlie and Patty had planned this. That Carlie had run off and Patty was covering for her. That Patty had had to name every man who'd come into the restaurant and how she thought Carlie acted around them. That she'd been questioned about herself and Daddy maybe having an affair. That she hadn't been charged with anything, and she was free to go, but she had to stay in touch with the police. Patty left two days after she came to see me and Grand. She stopped by on her way out. She needed to get away, she said. She told me, "I wish I could think of something that would help. I miss her too. She's my best friend." She gave me an address and told me she'd keep in touch. Then she left for New Jersey, where her family lived. Not long after she left, I wrote to her, but I never heard back.

The day after Patty left, a state trooper came to the house to see me. Daddy had told me ahead of time that he would be coming. Parker came with him. Unlike his brother, Ray, who was short and round as a root beer barrel, Parker was tall, with gray and black hair and one thick eyebrow standing watch over stormy dark green eyes. But though Parker was big, the trooper beside him dwarfed him.

"This is Trooper Scott Sargent," Parker said, and then Parker, Trooper Sargent, Daddy, and me sat at the kitchen table. Trooper Sargent's shaved head shone over hazel eyes the same color as mine. His face was kind, and his long mouth turned up at the corners. He set his Smokey the Bear–shaped hat on the table and folded his big hands as he questioned me. Why did I call my mother Carlie? Was she ever sad, for no reason? Did she whisper when she got phone calls? Had she said anything about going away at any time? Did she get mad when there was nothing to be mad at? Had she ever had any strange men over to the house when Daddy was out? Did I remember seeing any men I didn't know talking to her at any time?

I said, "Mike," even though Patty had told me that he wasn't to be blamed for sure.

Trooper Sargent looked at Daddy and Parker.

"He's that dipshit—sorry Florine—we talked to before," Parker said to the trooper. "He had an alibi. He was at the hospital with his wife the day Carlie disappeared, waiting for their first baby to be born."

Then Trooper Sargent and Parker left. Daddy saw them out. He sat down across from me and said, "Almost time for supper. What do you want?"

"I want Carlie," I said. The look on my face had him over to me in no time.

August ticked down toward September. I spent a lot of time sitting on the big white rock at the end of our driveway, looking up the road, straining my ears for the sound of a car, or for a glimpse of a small woman walking down the hill toward me. Daddy bought more 'Gansett and added vodka to his drinking inventory. Every night, he sat in front of the TV while I fell asleep on the couch next to his chair. At some point late in the evening, he shook me awake and I stumbled off to bed where I might or might not sleep. Every minute I was awake, I prayed to whoever might be listening for my mother to come home.

8

When I was six, we visited Carlie's family in Massachusetts. We went down in Daddy's old green pickup and it was a long ride. Carlie was quiet on the drive.

I'd never met my grandparents Collins. They'd never sent me a birthday or Christmas present, or even a card. I knew Carlie had a brother, which made him my Uncle Robert, and that his kids were my cousins, but Carlie didn't have pictures of them and she didn't talk about them. I didn't miss not knowing them, because my life was filled with everyone around me. Daddy had never met them, either. But he finally got Carlie to agree to visit, in part because of me.

"Florine should know your family," Daddy said to her. "She might need them someday. Grand and I are all she's got on this side."

Carlie wasn't happy about it, but she agreed to go.

In the town where Carlie had grown up, grass sprouted through cracks in the sidewalks on the main street. People stood on corners, watching us go by. Huge buildings took up blocks of space. Carlie said they'd been linen mills, and they'd closed down either before she was born or when she was a little girl.

We drove along gawking for a while, then Daddy said, "Which way do I go?"

Carlie pointed left and Daddy took the turn.

"You okay?" he asked.

She nodded. "Slow down after the next stop sign. It's the third place on the right."

A black dog with a gray muzzle was taking a dump in front of the first house on the right. Where the lawn should have been in front of the second house was just dirt and weeds. An unpainted picket fence had gaps in it like punched-out teeth.

The third house, where Daddy parked the pickup, had a whole picket fence. It needed painting, but the patches of grass on the lawn had been mowed no more than a couple days back. A black-haired Patti Playpal sat in an old lawn chair above a bunch of scattered Lincoln Logs. "Well, here we are," Carlie sighed, and hopped out of the pickup. She reached for me and gave me a quick hug before putting me down.

Daddy came around to the sidewalk and joined us. "Let's get this over with," Carlie said, and she headed up the walk ahead of Daddy and me. When we got to the front door, she paused to knock, then shook her head, and we walked inside.

We found ourselves in a dark hall cluttered up with a laundry basket, more toys on the floor, and a fat yellow cat spread smack in the middle of the black-and-white-striped runner as if he had melted and stuck to it. He swished his tail and Carlie said, "Tiger," and crooked her finger. Tiger glared at her with shiny orange eyes, then looked down and began to lick his left front leg. Bleach and cigarette smoke tickled my nostrils.

Two little kids came running into the hall. One of them was a toddler who wore diapers and nothing else. The older one, a girl, wore a brown pair of corduroy overalls and a blue-striped shirt underneath. She stuck her fingers in her mouth and stared. Both kids had dark red hair and brown eyes. The little girl smiled at me and I smiled back.

"Hi," Carlie said. "I'm your Aunt Carlie. You must be Robin," she said to the girl. The diapers fell off the toddler, and Daddy said, "This must be Ben." The kids didn't talk, Tiger stopped licking his leg, and no one else came to see who was at the door.

"Nice welcome," Carlie muttered, and she took a deep breath, stepped over Tiger, and walked around the corner to the left. I moved against the wall as Tiger swished his thick tail and sized me up with jack-o'-lantern eyes.

To the left of the hall, where Carlie had gone, was a room so gloomy that the only thing I could see was the picture on a TV, which sat against a wall in the center of the room. It was midday and sunny, but heavy dark curtains blocked out the light. As my eyes sorted through the murk, I saw the outline of an easy chair. The light from the TV showed up a man's arm resting on the left arm of the chair. The hand at the end of the arm held a burning cigarette. A standing ashtray full of butts sat next to the chair. The hand flicked the ashes of the cigarette into the tray.

To the right, a woman sat on a sofa that blended into the wall. She'd been folding clothes when we walked in. Her face flickered from white to whiter, depending on what was on the TV screen. Her hair might have been black or dark brown.

"Hi Mom," Carlie said to her. "Surprise!" She raised herself to her toes and clapped like a little girl. Her voice cracked in a high squeak.

"Well for heaven's sake," the woman said. She got up and said, "Well for heaven's sake," again, and she gave Carlie a quick, fierce hug. Then she looked at Daddy, then down at me. "This is my husband, Mom," Carlie said. "This is Leeman, and this is Florine, our daughter."

"Well for heaven's sake," the woman said again, and I wondered if she knew any other words. She glanced quickly at the back of the chair, then at me. "What a pretty girl," she said. "Florine? That's a different name. And Leeman," she said, and Daddy held out his hand. Some "pleased to meet yous" passed back and forth over my head, but I had stopped paying attention.

Something about the hand holding the cigarette drew me to it. I walked till I stood beside the chair, near the ashtray. I looked down at the hand and saw that it was small, like Carlie's hand. I followed the hand up the arm to find a gray-faced man staring at me out of hollow eyes. He took a drag of his cigarette, blew out the smoke, flicked the ash, and looked back at the television. My eyes followed his. Two men were duking it out in a boxing ring. I looked back at his face.

"What are you staring at?" he croaked. He said that while keeping his eyes on the boxing match.

"Nothing," I said.

He coughed up something and spat it into a handkerchief. "Nothing? Kind of dumb answer is that?"

"Daddy," Carlie put her hand on my head and said, "this is my daughter, Florine."

He didn't say anything to her, and he didn't look at either of us.

But then Daddy said in his best manners voice, "How do you do, sir," and he bent down and held out his hand. The man looked at him, put down the handkerchief, and then held up his hand. They shook hands, and he muttered something I didn't catch, then Daddy and he both turned to the boxing match.

The two kids had crowded into the living room with the rest of us, and Carlie's mother said to Carlie, "Let's go into the kitchen and I'll make us some coffee." I trailed after Carlie, and felt a small hand take mine. I looked at Robin. "You're my cousin," she said. We walked into a kitchen with yellow walls and a red table with five chairs around it. Tiger's dishes sat in a corner by the stove. A fly buzzed on top of a hunk of half-eaten cat food.

Carlie sat down at the kitchen table. Ben, still naked, bounced around the floor, grinned and twirled around, looking at me out of the corner of his eye. Robin held on to my hand. "Where's Robert?" Carlie asked.

"Oh, he's working," Carlie's mother said. She wore a checked green housedress and old sneakers that scuffed as she walked. She emptied coffee grounds into a garbage pail that was almost full, then rinsed out the basket and put fresh coffee into it.

"I'm sorry I haven't been down," Carlie said. "It's a ways away."

"It's good to see you," Carlie's mother said, quickly. She looked at me and said again, "Aren't you pretty, dear?" She smiled and I saw Carlie in her. "How old are you?" she asked me.

"Six," I said.

"She has your hair," Carlie's mother said. "That curl."

Carlie said, "She's got my mouth."

Carlie's mother smiled and said, "God help her."

"How old is Robin?" Carlie asked.

"Four and a half."

"Where's Liz?" Carlie asked.

"She and Robert got divorced," Carlie's mother said. Then she said to Robin, "Why don't you show Florine your toys?" As we left the kitchen, I heard Carlie's mother say, "Got to drinking. Robert had enough, and . . ."

I followed Robin up a steep set of stairs that led to another hall crowded with more plastic baskets of laundry. Robin's room was at the end of the hall, past a bathroom and another room on the right with a crib in it.

Her room was stuffed with dolls of all shapes and sizes. "You got a lot," I said.

"Here's their names," Robin said. She held each one up and told me its name. After each name, I said, "Pleased to meet you," and I shook its hand and we giggled.

"We could be sisters," I said to her.

Robin said, "Okay," and we looked at each other, wide eyed.

"You can come stay with me, sometimes," I said, and Robin jumped up and down. Then she said, "Let me brush your hair." She took a tiny blue brush from a shiny plastic doll case on her bed and combed through my pucker brush of curls. Her small hands tickled like moth's wings as she pushed my hair back from my face. Then I combed her long straight hair. When I finished, I said, "Let's go ask Daddy and Carlie if you can come home with me," but we'd no sooner cleared her room when Ben began to cry downstairs and I heard a man's raised voice. Then Carlie shouted and I said to Robin, "We got to see what's going on," and I dodged around the hall clutter, ran down the stairs, and twisted away from one of Tiger's hooked paws to reach the living room.

Carlie's mother held Ben, the man still sat in his chair, and Daddy stood beside Carlie with his hand around her shoulder. Carlie stood stiff and stared at the man in the chair.

The man pointed one finger at Carlie and said, "I don't care whether you come to see us. Far as I'm concerned, you been dead for years." Then he turned the chair around and went back to the boxing match. Carlie's mother carried Ben out of the room.

"You're wrong, you old bastard. I came alive when I left this place," Carlie said, her voice caught between a cry and a growl, to the back of the man's chair. "I'm done. I'm not coming back." And then she went down the hall and out the door.

The sound of coffee gurgling and punching the top of the pot drew Robin and me into the kitchen, where Carlie's mother stood, head down, arms locked at the elbows, holding on to the sides of the stove. Ben stood beside her, gripping her dress.

Daddy walked out into the kitchen and said, "Come on, Florine." He bent down and I let go of Robin's hand as he picked me up and held me in the crook of his left arm.

"It was nice meeting you, Mrs. Collins," he said.

Carlie's mother took a balled-up tissue from a pocket in her dress and wiped at her eyes. "I'm sorry," she said. "I'm sorry."

"You come up and visit us anytime you want," Daddy said. "You'd like it. I'll take you out on the boat. Bring the kids."

"We'll try to make it," Carlie's mother said.

They never came. I thought about Robin, drew her on paper, and colored in her eyes and hair and the clothes she'd worn the day I saw her. Soon after that visit, I asked Carlie if I could write her a letter. I sent a crayon picture of us in her room surrounded by dolls. I never heard back from her.

When Carlie disappeared, her family was no help. After all, as Carlie's father had said to his only daughter, "Far as I'm concerned, you been dead for years."

9

No sudden disappearances could stop school from coming. The Thursday before Labor Day, Madeline and Grand planned to take Dottie and me shopping.

"She better not make me get nothing plaid," Dottie said. "I hate plaid."

"Carlie always let me pick out what I wanted," I said. Dottie didn't answer me.

The day before the shopping trip, Bud, Glen, Dottie, and I went for a last swim. Dottie climbed into an inner tube and pushed offshore. Her wide, tanned feet stuck out as she used her hands to paddle around.

"Let's have an inner tube fight," she called to Bud, Glen, and me as we stood on the beach.

"Only one tube left," Glen said. Three of them had drifted off with the tide, and it made no sense to have Bert lug a new batch down from Freddie's in Long Reach, because swimming ended with Labor Day. Even now, the water had a nip to it.

"Double up," Dottie said. "Bud and me against you and Florine."

"Nah," Bud said. "We're going to swim out to the mooring."

"We are?" I said. Bud nodded and I shrugged.

"I bet I can paddle out there faster than you can swim," Dottie said. Glen grabbed the other inner tube and waded out toward Dottie.

"You got to come back to shore," Bud said. "We start from here."

"Well shit, why didn't you say so?" Glen muttered and waded back. Dottie paddled in and dumped herself out before she hit the shallows. We stood together in a line that Bud drew in the wet gravel with a stick.

"Who gets to say go?" Dottie asked.

"Ma," Bud called to Ida. "Say one, two, three, go."

Ida looked up from the rock where she'd been sitting and chatting with Madeline. "One, two, three, go," she said, but Bud and I were in the water by the "three." Glen and Dottie hollered at us, but we laughed and struck out toward the mooring.

"Let's go down," Bud said when we reached it, and we kicked and dove together. I was looking forward to seeing the crab and swimming through seaweed like before. Instead, I saw my worst nightmare.

What was left of Carlie rose and fell on the bottom of the sea. She was naked, bloated belly turned to sponge, chunks bitten out of her pocked arms and legs, red hair tangled around the seaweed. Her eyes bulged out, and her mouth stuck open in the last scream she'd ever made. The current turned her over and I saw big holes in her back; little barnacles stuck to the lines along her sharp white ribs. I sucked in water and screamed and thrashed, trying to rid myself of the sight as Bud used all his strength to pull me to the surface. When we reached it, I beat the water in a panic, screeching "No," over and over. Bud reached for me but I wouldn't let him touch me.

"She's drowned," I cried. "She's down there."

"Who?" Bud asked. "I didn't see anyone. Who?"

"Carlie," I sobbed. "Carlie is down there. How could you miss her?"

Dottie had reached us in her inner tube by then. "You mean she's dead and she's down there?" Dottie said.

I nodded.

"No, she isn't," Bud said. "I didn't see nothing, Florine, and I was right beside you. Nothing but seaweed and rocks. Not even a crab."

"I saw her," I insisted. "I saw her."

Then Madeline was beside us.

"What happened?"

"Florine says she saw Carlie down there," Dottie said.

"What?" Madeline said. "Where?"

I pointed straight down. "There," I blubbered.

"I didn't see nothing," Bud said. "I was right with her."

Madeline said, "Show me, Bud," and they dove while I clung to the mooring and shook. They surfaced and Madeline said, "Florine, there's nothing. You imagined it."

"I saw her," I insisted. "I did. She's dead. Drowned."

"Take hold of Dottie's inner tube and we'll get back together," Madeline said. "Go get Grand," she ordered Bud, and he was off.

Grand wrapped me in a blanket and set me on her sofa. She made tea laced with milk and sugar and she threw in a good dollop of whiskey. Someone radioed Daddy out on the water, and he burst through the door like a bear after his cub.

"What in God's name happened?" he asked, kneeling beside me.

I looked at him through sleepy, whiskey-laced eyes. "Carlie drowned," I said.

"How?" Daddy said. "Where?"

"She didn't see anything, Leeman," Grand said. "She imagined it."

Daddy moved strands of hair off my forehead. "You know it ain't real, honey," he said, soft. "I see things too, but it's all in my head. Just our brains, I guess, trying to figure it all out." He held me until the image faded and the only thing that mattered was the fishy smell of his bait-stained T-shirt.

That night, Daddy took me to Long Reach to the last summer band concert and the movies. I hunted for Carlie as we drove down the streets of Long Reach to the square where a brass band was playing. I scanned the crowd for her as we listened to the band and ate hot dogs Daddy bought from a cart. We went to the movies and I studied each head above each seat for the one that I would know anywhere. When the lights dimmed we stared at the screen in front of us. But the main attraction in my head—Carlie mauled and jellied on the ocean floor—played over whatever was showing that night. When Daddy said, "I'll be right back," I followed him up the aisle past the pale faces of the audience. We walked out of the movie theater and headed for the truck. We climbed in and sat, both of us staring at the people walking by. He lit a cigarette and took a deep drag. Smoke snaked out of the driver's window. He looked at me and said, "Florine, the only thing we can do is take it day to day. You got school and I got work. We got to get on with both of them. You with me?" I nodded, and he started the pickup.

We almost hit a big doe near the turnoff to The Point. Daddy slammed on the brakes and threw his arm across me to stop me from jerking forward. The headlights flooded the doe's eyes, and then she flipped her flag tail and slipped into the woods.

Labor Day passed and the first day of school came calling. I wore a pretty, plaid, blue dress Madeline had bought for me. Grand brought me lunch.

Even though I would be thirteen in eight months, Grand and Daddy walked me to the bus stop across from Ray's store. Dottie, Bud, and Glen were boarding the bus. I tried not to look at schoolmates who might be looking down at me. I climbed onto the bus behind Dottie and we plunked down in a seat close to the middle. Daddy and I took in each other as the bus pulled away.

10

During the first few days, kids I'd gone to school with since we'd been five mumbled hellos, and then moved away like they were afraid of catching whatever I had.

"They don't know what to say, Florine," Grand said. "They probably don't want to hurt your feelings or make you cry."

What Grand told me made sense, but it didn't make things easier until I started finding things in my desk, like three blue marbles, a pinecone painted white, and a tiny baby doll wrapped in a pink piece of felt and tied with string to a stick cross. Little notes were tucked into the desk, too. "I'm sad about your mom going lost," said one. "I said a prayer for you," said another. "My dog ran away and I still feel bad about it. If my mother went missing, it would be awful," someone else wrote.

While Daddy kept at Parker and Parker kept at the Crow's Nest Harbor police, the State Police, the Coast Guard, and anyone else on the case, September moved into October, then October 13, which was Carlie's thirty-first birthday. I woke up with her name on my lips. I sang "Happy Birthday" while I looked at the ceiling, and it sounded more like a prayer than a celebration. Daddy was quiet that day.

We joined Grand for supper. She made Carlie's favorite dish, baked scallops, mashed potatoes, and spinach, and she baked a chocolate cake.

We stuck thirty-one candles into the cake and sang. The word "Happy" came out like a dying breath.

October passed its flaming torch to November.

Our schoolwork was harder, now that we'd hit seventh grade. But I welcomed it, because it kept my mind from caving in on itself. I took to math that year. Numbers had a rhyme and reason to them. I craved answers, and math gave them to me.

One Friday in early November, our teacher, Mrs. Richmond, asked me to stay for a minute after the rest of the class filed out for the day. She looked up at me with kind brown eyes through her smudged black cat-frame glasses. A flake of red lipstick clung to the curve of her upper lip and chalk dust sprinkled the top of her navy blue suit.

She said, "Florine, I know you're going through something very hard. You are being brave about it, but let me know if you need help. Okay?" I was embarrassed, but glad that she was watching out for me. Then she asked me to help Rose Clark with math.

Rose had come up from kindergarten with us. While we'd grown, she stayed about the size of a fourth grader, with fuzzy yellow hair and pale eyes the color of water on sand. She didn't mesh with the world we knew, but she was sweet. Besides, Dottie would have killed anyone who dared hurt Rose. Two things about my friend Dottie. She was bone kind and she was strong.

Learning got harder for Rose as we went up through the grades. Each teacher found help for her, but she'd barely squeaked by sixth grade. This year, if she didn't make it, word was that she would be riding the retard bus to Long Reach.

I told Mrs. Richmond that I would help Rose. So, during math period, Rose and I left the classroom and went into a small, empty room with two side-by-side desks and one high window. I showed Rose what to do, then sat back and watched her dirty, chewed-down fingernails trace invisible numbers from the bottom of one column to the top of the next, where she tried to figure out where to go from there.

"Just like the right column," I said. "So, one and one and eight make ten, so what goes on the bottom here?" She giggled and guessed, "Nine?" Then she'd say, "Florine. Your name is so pretty. Like a flower."

"Your name is a flower for sure," I said. "But that isn't going to help you on the next math test. You got to pay attention. Try it again." Each forty-minute period would end with me drained and Rose still happy and stupid.

I complained to Dottie. Her being my best friend and me being in the situation I was in would get me some sympathy, I thought. But when I ventured to say that teaching Rose math was a waste of time, Dottie said, "Not everyone gets to have brains in everything. I ain't that bright, either. I'm just smart enough to get Madeline to help me out every night, else I'd be down the hall with you and Rose."

"She picks her nose and she eats it," I added for a gross-out factor.

"Maybe she don't get breakfast at home," Dottie said, and I finally got the message.

The day I started being mean to Rose, I'd had a scene at home with Daddy. He'd sat up until 2:00 A.M., drinking vodka and making phone calls to Parker. When he stumbled off to his room, I heard him crying. I wanted to go to him, but I knew he'd send me back to bed. Even after his cries turned to snores, I didn't sleep until about 4:00. Both Daddy and I overslept. I woke up at about 6:30, and I flew out of bed and threw on the same clothes I'd taken off the night before.

"Daddy," I shouted at him, "Daddy, get up." I heard him grunt and swear as I washed my face and brushed my teeth. I grabbed an apple and ran for the bus stop, only to find I'd missed the bus.

Daddy was upchucking in the bathroom when I got back home. "I missed the bus," I shouted over his puking.

"Shit," I heard him say, and he let loose again. Then the toilet flushed and he walked out of the bathroom, wiping his face with a hand towel Grand had embroidered for him and Carlie. I could see the L and C on the corner closest to me. "Why don't you stay home?" he said.

"You said we needed to get on with it."

"I ain't in the mood to hear you tell me what I said, Florine."

"You shouldn't drink and you shouldn't stay up so late," I said.

"Well, if you're smart enough to tell me what I shouldn't do, don't you think you're smart enough to get yourself up, eat breakfast, make a goddamn sandwich, and catch the bus?"

"You were crying. You kept me awake."

"Well, excuse me for living here."

"You don't have to be mad at me."

"I'm not mad at you."

"Yes you are."

"No, I'm goddamn not."

"Are you giving me a ride or what?"

"Don't talk to me that way. Say to me, 'Please, Daddy, may I have a ride to school?'"

"PLEASE MAY I HAVE A RIDE TO SCHOOL?"

"Jesus," he said. He went back into the bathroom and threw up again as I slammed out of the house and stomped up the driveway.

Grand came out of her house and said, "You're late today. You okay, Florine?"

"No," I shouted. "No, I'm not. I hate Daddy. He's an asshole."

I walked past her and toward the bus stop; head down, into the sour wind. I picked up the pace as Daddy's truck squealed out of the driveway, but he caught up.

"Get in, Florine," he said. "I ain't got time to dick around."

"No," I said. "I can walk to school."

"It's three miles up the road. Get in, goddamn it."

"No."

He put the emergency brake on, and opened the door, and walked after me. I started to run, but he caught up to me, picked me up, and slung me over his shoulder. I beat at his back with my fists and screamed as loud as I could, but he wasn't having any of it. He opened the passenger side door of the truck and threw me onto the seat. He slammed the door, walked around to his side of the truck, got in, and slammed his door. We both steamed as he drove, and he dropped me off in record time. I climbed out and left the door open so that he'd have to walk around and close it.

When I walked into the classroom, Mrs. Richmond looked at me, then at the clock, then her face changed and I could almost hear her thinking to herself, "Oh, poor Florine. Her mother's either run off or dead. I must be patient." It would have been better if she'd sent me to the principal's office, but she said, "We just started math. Why don't you go down the hall with Rose?"

So off I went, poor Rose toddling behind me. We sat down at our desks, and Rose snuggled next to me. She smelled like dried pee. I moved my chair away and said, "Let's get started."

"I like your shirt. It's pretty," Rose said.

"Same shirt I wore yesterday," I snapped. "Let's go."

As usual, she couldn't do her numbers.

"I just showed you how to do that, Rose," I said, a little too loud, a lot too impatient.

Her smile flickered like a breeze-smacked candle flame. "Forgot," she said.

"Well, don't forget again," I said. "I'm going to show you one more time, then I'm going to be quiet until you get it right."

"All right," she said. She bent to her task, her little finger moving down, then up, her mouth pursed into a tiny pucker. She took a long time to come up with an answer, but she did, and then she put down her pencil and folded her hands.

"Let me see," I said. When I saw it was wrong, I rolled my eyes. "Rose, how do you expect me to help you? Do you want me to tell Mrs. Richmond that you can't do this?"

Still a tiny smile, but she shook her head.

"Well, then you have to learn this stuff."

"I will," she said.

She tried again, and she got it wrong.

I broke.

"You can't do this," I said. "You're just too stupid." Rose's lip quivered and tears spilled out of her eyes.

"I know I'm stupid," she said. "You don't have to be mad at me. I know you're sad because your mother died."

"Don't you say that! She did not die!" I yelled, and then I melted onto the floor. "You can't say that," I sobbed. "No one can say that!"

I scared the hell out of Rose, and she set to crying as hard as me, and neither of us could stop. We watched the ugly masks of each other's faces as tears, snot, and drool ran down our cheeks, into our mouths, dripped onto our clothes.

Why no one heard us, I don't know. No one came running to see what was going on. By and by, shame and sense slunk back into my brain, and I managed to choke out, "I'm sorry, Rose. Don't be scared. I'm sorry," because she was still crying so hard that she shook. I wiped my face with my hands, got up off the floor, and went to her. I said soft words to her, much as Carlie or Grand had to me when I was young and afraid or hurt.

I finally got her calmed down and cleaned up, but the math lesson was over for the day. We walked side-by-side back to the classroom holding hands, still sniffling a little bit. When Mrs. Richmond saw us, she took us into the hall.

"What happened?" she asked me.

Rose said, "Florine didn't do nothing. I just don't feel good."

I didn't feel good, either, and I felt worse later that day when Dottie walked up to me on the playground and stood an inch from my face.

"You tell Rose she was stupid?" she asked.

I studied the tops of my shoes. The unfairness of it all crouched solid and square in my mind and I said, "She is stupid. No sense pretending she isn't."

Dottie said, "Fuck you, Florine," and walked away, taking my breath with her.

11

That night, Daddy hit an all-time-high drunk with a bottle of vodka. By the time I'd gotten home from school, half a fifth had gone down his gullet and he staggered as he warmed up a can of beans for me and him. Grand called just before supper and he said to her, "Oh, juss fine ma. Juss leave us alone. We're fine. Juss fine. Beans're burning. Gotta go." He hung up and scraped the beans out of the pan and onto our plates. I stared at the scorched beans on my plate and burst into tears. Daddy didn't say anything to me; he just picked up the bottle of vodka and went into the living room. He sat down heavy in his chair, and it whined with the weight he threw at it. I threw my supper into the garbage and ran over to Grand's house.

"Daddy's drunk," I said. "He gave me burned beans for supper."

Grand pursed her lips. Then she warmed me up some American chop suey and let me eat it in front of the television while she sat and knitted. Her needles flashed faster and faster as we sat there. A rare scowl creased her handsome old face.

"You mad at Daddy?" I asked.

"Hard to be mad when he's so broke up," she said. "Hard to be patient, too, I guess. Jesus tests us in ways we can't even imagine."

"Daddy's ignoring Jesus, I think," I said. "Me and Jesus."

"He's down deep, Florine, down deep," Grand said. "He's trying to make sense of what happened, not that I approve of the way he's doing it, but before he can come back to the light and love of Jesus, he's got to wrestle with the devil."

I'd always pictured the devil as red, with a pitchfork, like the one on the deviled ham can. But maybe, for Daddy at least, the devil was a clear, sharp liquid.

"What about me?" I asked. "We got to get on with it, he said. Well, I'm trying."

"I know," Grand said. "Jesus is easier on young ones, I guess."

I almost spit chop suey onto the coffee table in front of me. I loved Grand, but if she thought what Jesus was putting me through was easy, then Jesus was full of crap.

Someone opened Grand's front door, and Daddy shouted, "Ma, you seen Florine?"

"In here," Grand called. Daddy leaned against the doorframe to the living room. He looked from Grand to me and back again.

"Dammit, Ma," he said to Grand, "stop messing with us. We can manage juss fine."

And he burst into tears, so I did too, and this time I did spit my food back into my plate. Grand put down her knitting and said, "In the kitchen. Both of you."

"Can't do this," Daddy sobbed, sitting down at the table. "I'm goin' crazy out of my head."

"We got to do it, Daddy," I sobbed. "We got to get on with things. You said so."

"Who the hell tol' you that?" Daddy said. "Some asshole? Can't stop thinking of what god-awful trouble Carlie might have gotten mixed up into. Can't think of nothin' else. Can't do nothin' else. Drink, maybe."

"You can do more than that," Grand said. "But you got to put one foot in front of the other."

"Got no choice," Daddy said, wiping his hand over his wet face. "Got no choice."

The teakettle shrieked, but before Grand could pour the tea, Daddy's soggy thoughts veered in another direction and he decided we had to go home, right then, so across the road we went, me half holding him up. I went to bed to cry some more and to talk to Carlie before I went to sleep. Daddy was on the phone at midnight to Parker, yet again.

Sometime after that, Pastor Billy Krum showed up. I woke to hear him knocking at the door. "This is Billy," he shouted to Daddy. "Let me in, for chrissake."

Pastor Billy ran the white church down the road. Sundays, he was a preacher. Every other day, he hauled lobsters off Spruce Point. He and Daddy had gone to school together. Daddy never went to church, but Billy and he played poker together.

"I ain't letting you in," Daddy shouted, but I ran to the door. I stared at Billy on the other side of the door like he was some night angel.

He smiled, his blue eyes kind. "You going to let me in, Florine?"

So I did, and then Billy said, "You'd probably best go back to bed," and so I lay there and listened as he let Daddy puke up remarks that only a devil would spit out without being embarrassed. He wailed away, saying things like, "What did I do to drive her off? Why did she leave me? I should have treated her better. It's my fault. God damn the bitch to hell. What was she thinking? I hope she's dead, because if she isn't, I'm going to kill her." Billy's answers were soft, when he gave them. Mostly, he let Daddy go on and somehow, together, they wrestled the devil back to hell for the night. I fell asleep at about four in the morning.

A couple of hours later, Billy woke me for school. This was the second time in two nights that I hadn't slept much. But I didn't dare to disagree with God's messenger. He handed me a lunch that Grand had bagged up for me and delivered to him.

Before I went out the door, Billy said to me in his voice made of gravel and honey, "Florine, you are one of God's angels, straight from heaven. And God don't give his angels anything they can't handle."

I pondered that as I walked to the bus. If I was an angel, why couldn't I fly somewhere and find my mother? And where the hell was heaven, anyway? Thoughts pinged around my brain like moths looking for a light. I didn't want to face Dottie, Bud, and Glen. I didn't want to face Rose. I didn't want to face anyone. The bus was at the stop when I reached it and I sat in a seat by myself toward the middle. When Rose's stop came and she got on, she spied me and waved. I sank lower in my seat but she plunked herself down beside me anyway. "Hold out your hand," she said, "I found this for you." She put a heart-shaped pink rock into my palm.

12

Later that day, as Rose and I struggled through her math lesson, the school principal's deep voice came over the intercom.

"Please return to your classrooms," he ordered.

"He sounds like God," Rose said, and we giggled as we walked back to the room.

It was dead quiet, with all eyes on Mrs. Richmond. She stood in front of her desk, her face as serious as I'd ever seen it. "Sit down, Florine. Rose," she said, and we did. Then she said to the class, "I have some very bad news. President Kennedy was shot this morning in Dallas, Texas. I'm sorry to tell you he just died." She took a tissue from the pocket of her Friday suit, lifted her glasses off her nose, and wiped at her eyes.

At least they know what happened to him, I thought. Then I felt bad for thinking that. Rose turned around in her seat and said to me, "My Poppy said the Russians would kill him and they did. Will they bomb us now he's dead? Poppy says they hate us."

I said, "I don't know."

"The buses will be by soon to take you home," Mrs. Richmond said. "I imagine you'll be out for some days next week. We'll let your parents know for sure."

"Shouldn't we stay here?" Rose asked me. "Shouldn't we get under our desks?"

"They want us to go home," I said.

Outside, she held my hand and looked up at the sky—for Russian bomber planes I guess—and we joined Dottie, Bud, and Glen near the bus stop. We looked across the road at the house on the other side. A brown dog sitting on the front steps looked back at us. He was hitched up to a thick rope. He yawned.

"I wonder if they let that dog in when it's cold," Bud said. "They should let that dog in. Even hunting dogs should be taken inside."

"I bet they do," Dottie said. "Otherwise, he'd be ugly. He doesn't look ugly."

"Maybe he wants some bologna," Glen said. "I got some in my lunch bag."

Sam Warner pulled into the schoolyard and we walked toward his car. "I got to go uptown, before they close all the friggin' stores," he said to us through the open driver's window. "Get in, Bud."

"Okay," Bud said, and Glen climbed in with him.

"You two want to come?" Sam asked Dottie and me.

Rose took our hands. "Please stay with me," she said.

"We'll take the bus," I said, and Sam drove away.

Rose sat beside me on the bus. "My Poppy says the Russians have bombs that could blow the whole world up. I don't want to be blown up." She leaned against me. Her hair smelled like dust.

"We're going to die," she said.

"No, we're not," I said, but I wasn't so sure. The world appeared to be made of a dangerous quicksand that could suck down mothers or presidents at any time. What was to stop it from grabbing on to our ankles and dragging us down, too?

When the bus stopped at Rose's road, she said, "Will you come with me? I'm scared I'm going to get bombed going down the road."

"I'll walk you off the bus," I said.

"Her, too," she pointed at Dottie, who sat across from us.

"What?" Dottie asked.

"We're walking her off the bus," I said.

Tillie Clemmons, our bus driver, was blowing her nose and wiping her eyes. "Where do you two think you're going?" she asked.

"We're walking her off the bus," Dottie said.

"Okay," Tillie said. "Hurry it up."

Then Parker drew his cruiser up next to the bus and Tillie cracked open her window and talked down to her husband. We walked Rose to the top of a steep hill that, we supposed, led to her house. And Tillie forgot why she'd stopped, I guess, because when Parker drove off, she put the bus into gear and left Dottie and me stranded.

"What the hell," Dottie said. "Now what?"

"Walk me home?" Rose asked.

I looked up at the milky sky and wished for Tillie to turn around. Surely, someone on the bus knew we were missing. Dottie asked Rose, "How far down is your house?"

"Not far," Rose said.

"Can your father give us a ride home?" Dottie said.

Rose nodded.

"Might as well walk you home, then," Dottie said, and we traipsed down the muddy road, scuffing through piles of yellow leaves that filled deep ruts made by tires. The rusted remains of old cars junked up the sides of the road.

"You sad about the president?" I asked Dottie.

"I don't know," Dottie said. "I can't think of what to feel."

"Did you hear a plane?" Rose said, ducking. "There might be a plane up there."

We walked down, down and down, then Dottie said, "Don't take this wrong, Rose, but are we walking to hell or what? Where's your jeezly house?"

"There," Rose said, pointing toward what looked like more trees to us.

"How does your dad get up this road?" Dottie asked. "It's ruts in search of a road, looks like to me."

"He doesn't go up this road since his truck broke down," Rose said.

We stopped. We both looked at Rose, and then we looked at each other. "How are we supposed to get home?" I asked Dottie. "Walk?"

"We can call Leeman," Dottie said. "You got a telephone, Rose?" she asked.

Rose nodded.

"You sure you got a phone?" Dottie asked again.

Rose nodded again.

"Daddy isn't home, most likely," I said. "What about Madeline?"

"She went uptown to get her hair done," Dottie said.

"Maybe the place is closed," I said, "on account of the president."

A low rumble sounded over the crackle of leaves.

"What's that?" I asked, and then I slipped and fell into a rut, getting mud all over my legs and dress. "Shit," I said. "Grand's gonna have a cow."

Dottie laughed. So did Rose.

"Not funny," I said.

"Yes it is," Dottie said. "You should see your ass."

"Well I'd have to be a giraffe, now wouldn't I?" I said.

"Don't get pissed off at me," Dottie said. "I didn't push you down."

"Where's your house?" I snapped at Rose.

"There," Rose said, pointing at nothing.

"I don't see the house," I said. "Do you live in a house?"

"Hey," Dottie said.

"I'm sorry," I said, brushing mud from my underpants and thighs. "It's just that we got to get home soon."

The rumbling grew closer and louder.

"What is that noise?" I asked.

"Sounds like something growling," Dottie said.

"It's Bigger," Rose said.

"What's a Bigger?" I asked.

In about thirty seconds, we knew.

Bigger was a gigantic black dog with short pointed ears. His mouth was flecked with pinkish foam. He was tied to a tree by a thick rusty chain. He looked at Rose and she must have triggered a spark in his dim brain because for about five seconds, he wagged his mangy crooked tail. Then he figured out he'd never seen us.

Dottie and I jumped back as he lunged at us full throttle with his teeth bared. The chain snapped to a straight line and I said, "Dottie, let's just run." But Dottie was pointing to something. "Jesus, look at that," she said.

A doe deer hung by its neck from a pine tree branch close to Bigger. Her tongue stuck out in a sickish pink brown mass. Her belly had been ripped open and her guts and stomach looped along the ground. I hoped she'd died before she'd been strung up.

"Bigger won't bite," Rose said.

"Who the hell are you?" a man's voice boomed, and I grabbed Dottie's arm as we spun toward the sound.

A giant of a man stood about ten feet away from us. His dirty gray and brown beard fell over his chest like chewed-up pot-roast string. His flannel shirt may have been red and black once, if it had ever been new. His faded blue jeans were soaked with old and new stains that looked like old and new blood. He held a dirty shovel in his hands.

"This is my Poppy," Rose said. "This is Dottie and Florine. They walked me home. I was afraid of the Russians."

"What the hell you talking about, Rose?" Poppy said.

Dottie and I began to take steps backwards.

"What you mean about the Russians, Rose?" Poppy asked again. "Bigger, shut the fuck up." He reached over and smacked the dog up the side of the head with the shovel. Bigger yelped and cringed away to the far end of his chain.

"You know what she's talking about?" Poppy asked us and we stopped, lest we have our heads bashed in by the shovel.

"The president died," I said. "President Kennedy got shot."

Poppy laughed like a full winter moon might sound if it took a mind to have a good guffaw. Then he stopped just as sudden, and he said, "You don't say. Someone finally had the sense to splatter his brains all over hell? This is a good day, Rose."

He reached down and rubbed the top of her head, just like Daddy did to me from time to time. I suddenly wanted to be with him more than anything I'd ever wanted in my life.

"Where you live?" Poppy asked. "You live around here?" He stepped toward us.

"Spruce Point," Dottie said, naming another point five miles away from us. "We got to go. See you in school, Rose." And Dottie gave me a shove to get us started.

When Rose said, "Goodbye," we ran, certain we'd feel the hot, hell-hound breath of Bigger before he ripped out our calves, or Poppy's shovel staving in our skulls. We ran when we reached Route 100 and we ran toward The Point, about three miles away.

We were so scared that the sound of a car prompted Dottie to yell, "Hide!" We hit the ditch on the side of the road. The car whizzed by and when the noise died away, we got up. We ran, walked, and jumped into ditches. We ripped our dresses and scratched up our legs, arms, and hands. We reached Ray's at dusk. Daddy's truck was just turning onto the road. He pulled over and he and Bert jumped out.

"Where have you been?" Daddy cried and grabbed my shoulders and shook me. "Don't you ever do that to me again. You hear?" His haunted eyes filled with tears.

We clung to each other.

Everyone on The Point ended up at Grand's to watch the president's funeral; to see the jumpy horse they called Black Jack with the boots turned backward in the stirrups of the saddle, to listen to the drums, and to cry when John John saluted the casket.

And where was Carlie? Was she in the crowd that lined the streets along the funeral parade? Did she miss me like I missed her? Was she as lost as the rest of us?

School started up again on Tuesday. Dottie and I sat together one seat ahead of Glen and Bud. As we got closer to Rose's stop, we didn't slow down. Tillie beeped at the driver of a smaller school bus stopped at the end of Rose's road as we drove past.

"That's the retard bus," Glen said, and everyone went quiet.

Dottie said, "Maybe them teachers will help her. Might be the only thing saves her."

13

Less than a week after President Kennedy was killed, Thanksgiving came and almost went without a peep. Daddy, Grand, and I went to Bert and Madeline's house for turkey that tasted like sawdust and stuffing I couldn't even look at. Grand's mincemeat pie filling turned sour in my mouth and I swallowed it down with milk gone to chalk. Madeline and Grand talked over dates for the upcoming annual Point wreath-making day. This was a day when all The Point women, including little Evie and Maureen, got together at Grand's house with wire and Christmas whatnots and doodads to make wreaths to sell at the craft fairs in Long Reach, or to ship out of state to some of the summer folks wanting a piece of Maine for Christmas. Sam, Bert, Daddy, Glen, and Bud got permission from the park manager every year to go into the State Park and tip fir and spruce trees for the wreaths. It was usually a fun day, but as they talked about it, I slumped further and further down in my chair in the corner of the overcrowded table, already tired and sad thinking about having to go through it without Carlie.

Lucky for me, on wreath-making day, I had a combination fever and cold that was making its way through school. Dottie got it, too, and the two of us sat in her living room, hacking and sniffling and watching Saturday afternoon bowling, one of Dottie's favorites. Maine's woman bowling champion, Barbara Raymond, was knocking down the big pins like they were feathers. Dottie was a Barb Raymond fan.

"I can't wait to go to junior high," Dottie said at one point. "They got bowling teams and I'm going to get onto one." I nodded off on the couch during one of Barb's strikes and slept that day away.

If I could have, I would have slept Christmas away, too, but Grand told me that I had to make the best of it. So, I came up with some ideas for presents, and we worked on them as the days crept closer.

Carlie had been the heart and soul of Christmas. She loved the music, she loved the presents, she loved the season. I was too old, now, to make a list to send to Santa Claus, much less believe in him, but that year, I took a piece of paper out of the little lift-up-top desk in the corner of my room and wrote, *Dear Santa, Please send my mother home. I will never be bad again. I promise. I mean it. Thank you, Florine.* I put it into an envelope, addressed it to the North Pole, and put it back in the desk. Then I waited for the day to arrive, so we could get it over with.

On Christmas morning, my stocking fell off my bed with a clink. I let it lie on the floor and stared at the ceiling knowing that Daddy had filled it and put it there. A newspaper rustled in the kitchen and he cleared his throat. I got dressed, picked up my stocking, joined him and said, "Let's go to Grand's."

Daddy had said that we should have our special times, but he was quick to agree that we should walk across the road, so we gathered up our gifts and walked to Grand's house against a frigid wind and pellets of snippy snow swirling up from the water.

We reached Grand's house and stomped our boots as we went inside. Grand didn't seem surprised to see us so early. I arranged the presents just so under Grand's tree, and then we opened them. For Daddy and me, Madeline had painted and framed a watercolor of the harbor near sunset that showed the *Carlie Flo* at her mooring. Ida had quilted me a blue wall hanging with colorful butterflies stitched onto it. Dottie wrapped up two thick *Archie* comic books in old Sunday funny papers. Grand knitted me a thick warm sweater out of soft light green yarn. And Daddy had somehow found time to buy me a stack of Nancy Drew mysteries. With Grand's help, I had knitted Daddy a sky-blue scarf and a matching watch cap that made his eyes shine. With Madeline's help, I had painted a wavy watercolor picture of Grand's summer garden.

I could have sworn that Carlie sat cross-legged beside me, breathing down my neck as I opened my presents. I swallowed my tears and made as much noise as I could when I opened them. I was relieved when all of our gifts had been unwrapped and it was over. Grand made the three of us hold hands during grace. It was the most comforting part of the day, clinging to Daddy's dry, scarred hand on one side of me, and Grand's soft old hand on the other. Both of them squeezed my hands at different times during the prayer, and I held them tight. Then the three of us ate a quiet dinner.

Later, Daddy and I plowed home with our presents through about three inches of snow, chuffing out air as sharp as hard cider. That night when I went to bed, I reached into my desk, took out the letter I'd written to Santa, and ripped it into little pieces. "Bastard," I said. I slept with no dreams that night, and that might have been my best present since Carlie's disappearance.

I was eating breakfast the next morning as Daddy bundled up and got ready to go out and shovel. He looked out of the kitchen window, then jumped back and said, "Oh Jesus. What does she want?"

"Who? What's the matter?" I asked.

"Hide me," he said. He headed for the door that led to the cold upstairs. We'd never heated those two rooms. They'd always served as an attic for our junk, including items left behind by Hattie Butts, who'd lived there before us, moved to Florida, and died there.

"Tell her I'm not here," he said, and shut the door behind him.

I looked out the kitchen window and saw Stella Drowns wading through the snow. "What the hell *is* she doing here?" I thought. I sat back down to wait for her. She saw me through the window in the kitchen door when she knocked and she waved a red-gloved hand as if we were friends. I just stared at her. When she called through the glass, "Good morning, Florine," hot air from her mouth clouded the glass and hid her face. She wiped it away and smiled at me as I walked, heel to toe, to open the door.

"Morning," she said, cold air clouding her black hair. Her cheeks, except for the scar, were rosy and her gray eyes were light, like the snow-filled sky. "Was Christmas okay?"

I snorted. "What do you think?" I said.

Stella hesitated for a few seconds, and then said, "I made a coffee cake for you both."

"We ate," I said.

"Is your father home?" she asked me.

"Yes," I said. "But he saw you coming and told me to say that he wasn't here."

Stella cocked her head like a confused puppy. "What do you mean?"

I was about to repeat it louder when Daddy came downstairs and joined us at the door. He stuck his hands in his pockets and gave me a foolish look.

"Morning Stella," he said. "Come in out of the cold."

"Oh, thank you," she said. "Florine said you told her to tell me you weren't here."

"Well, that's what you said to say," I said. Daddy gave me a look and Stella laughed.

She and Daddy sat at the kitchen table and had coffee and cake. She asked if I wanted some. It smelled wonderful, but I refused. Instead, I watched television and waited for her to leave.

If I'd been thinking, I would have planted myself at that table. I might have read some words between the words. But I wasn't thinking, so I didn't catch Daddy's slow thaw.

14

New Year's Eve parties at the Buttses' house were tradition. We kids ate sweets till we got sick, while the adults boozed it up, smoked, played cards, and did it all louder as the night went on. Last year, we'd counted down outside the house, looking into the sky at the stars, Carlie holding up Daddy as he swayed. Her fruity wine breath tickled my nose as I cuddled into the curve of her waist. On the way home, Daddy fell down in the snow. He tripped up Carlie, who fell down in front of him. When she tried to get up, he grabbed her ankle and held on. He pulled me down, too, and Carlie and I wet our pants laughing before we managed to struggle up and lug him, between us, into the house.

That had been only last year. This year, Daddy said he thought we'd stay home.

"I thought it might be a good idea to do something a little quieter this year. So, we're having company over," Daddy said. "Stella offered to cook us a nice supper."

He might as well have said, "The devil's coming over to burn holes in your ass with a hot iron poker."

When he saw my look, he said, "Now, Florine, stop with the faces. You can have supper with us, then you can go to Dottie's house."

"I thought you didn't want to see her," I said. "You tried to hide from her."

"That wasn't very nice of me," Daddy said.

"What would Carlie think?"

"This has nothing to do with your mother. It's just supper with Stella. Be nice to talk to a friend, Florine. Be like talking to Dottie for you."

"That's bullshit, Daddy," I said.

"Where in hell did you get that mouth?" he asked. "That's enough of that."

"I don't like her. She didn't like Carlie."

"Well, she feels bad about it," Daddy said. "She's a friend and she's good company."

"So's a dog, and it'd be better looking," I said. His jaw dropped, and then he slapped me across the face.

He'd never hit me before. We looked at each other like we'd suddenly been separated by a high barbed-wire fence. I stormed off and I slammed my bedroom door. I threw my books, one by one, at the wall, swiped all of the things on my bureau onto my floor and ripped the bedding off the bed and tossed it around. Then I flopped onto the mattress facedown, and screamed into my pillow until I was hoarse. I didn't hear Daddy come in until he said, "Grow up, Florine. You can start by picking up this mess."

"I want my mother," I said into my pillow.

Daddy said, his tone softer, "I want her too, but she isn't here. Pick up your room, now. Stella will be by in a couple of hours and we got to get this place tidy."

This battle was lost, and I knew it. I put everything back, then swept the floors while Daddy shoveled the walk and put down sand so our honored jeezly guest wouldn't slip.

She was due at five, and when the sweeper hand kissed the second hand on the twelve, she was at the door like her first day to a new job.

Daddy took a deep breath. "Jesus, what am I doing?" he muttered.

"Tell me and we'll both know," I said.

He opened the door and Stella stepped in holding an orange dish between two brown pot holders. She and Daddy did a dance where she put down the casserole and went to take her coat off, then he tried to help her, and she put it back on so he could help her, and they laughed. Daddy finally hung her coat on the rack near the door.

Stella wore a red dress with a wide belt around her tiny waist. She'd squeezed every ounce of her thin nothing into a curvy something. I was certain it wasn't for my benefit.

"How you doing, Florine?" she asked.

"Fine, thank you," I said.

"Glad you could come," Daddy said.

"Isn't the weather lovely?" I said. Daddy shot me a look.

Stella said, "Well, it's better than nothing, as poor my father used to say."

"Florine, why don't you set the table," Daddy said.

As I did that, Stella put her casserole dish onto a black trivet she'd brought that read, "No matter where I serve my guests, it seems they like my kitchen best." We all sat down and Stella said a short grace, no holding hands thanks be to Jesus, then served us up something with ham, cream sauce, and potatoes. I wish I could say it was awful, but it was one of the best things I'd ever eaten. Flavors popped up like spicy surprises throughout my mouth. I wanted seconds, but I was damned if I'd ask for them. Daddy, on the other hand, kept saying, "This is so good," over and over again. I caught the satisfied glitter in Stella's eyes as she watched him eat. She had him, at least for this meal. I drank my milk down in a couple of good swallows so that I could be excused.

"I'm glad to see a girl drink her milk," Stella said to me. "You're growing, and you need your calcium. Makes strong bones and teeth."

"Thank you for pointing that out," I said. "May I please be excused, Daddy?"

Daddy raised his head from his plate, nodded, and then went back to the food.

I went into my bedroom and rolled up some pajamas and grabbed my toothbrush from the bathroom. While I did this, Stella talked until the air was thick with words. Words about people who came in the store, people she and Daddy had in common, people in church, and on and on. Daddy made sounds once and a while, but it seemed clear that his job was to gobble down everything except Carlie's good tablecloth. Carlie and I had found that tablecloth one day at a yard sale and brought it home. It was fine white cotton with whiter cotton flowers embroidered on top of it. A little rip in a corner was all that was wrong with it. Stella wasn't noticing how pretty the tablecloth was, though. She sat with her elbows on the table eyeing Daddy as if he was the bird to her cat.

"I'm going to Dottie's," I said on my way out.

"Okay," Daddy said.

"Happy New Year," Stella called as I went out the door.

"Happy New Year your ass," I muttered, and slammed the door, just a little.

"She's after him, bad," I said to Dottie. "She laughs at anything he says. It's this jackass hee-haw that she lets out and reels back in again."

"They got a name for that hee-haw noise," Dottie said.

"Bray," I said. "She brays. She prays, too. Says grace."

"That's just god-awful," Bud said. "Thanking the Lord before a meal. Bitch should be shot and skinned."

I smacked his arm.

Dottie and Bud and I were playing gin rummy in Dottie's kitchen. Bud was winning. Or he thought he was winning. I was just about to show him what was what. Carlie and I had played gin rummy for hours on rainy days. She always won, but I had gotten close to beating her a couple of times, which meant I was good, and I was about to prove it.

"Gin," I said to Dottie and Bud. It was a big win—both of them lost points. Dottie had been trailing anyway, and now she was way back. Bud and I were about equal points, now, although I won the next four hands. I could have played all night, but finally, Dottie had enough. "I'm done. Let's go, Florine."

"Night," I said to Bud, and followed Dottie into the hellhole she called her bedroom. A row of dolls her mother had bought her, hoping in vain that she might somehow learn to love them, lined a shelf on one side of her room. I thought about the dolls that Robin had shown me. She had named each one; each one was precious to her. But not to Dottie. The lonely dolls were the only neat thing in Dottie's room because Madeline dusted them from time to time. The rest of the room was a pig pile of clothes and junk that I hoped wouldn't somehow come to life and attack me. The bed was made—Madeline had seen to that, seeing as how I'd be staying—and I pulled on my pajamas and jumped in before Dottie.

As Dottie and I settled side-by-side in her big bed, I listened to the adults partying in the living room and thought about other voices, other years, when Daddy's surprising guffaw and Carlie's girlish giggle had been part of the mix. I wondered if Daddy was missing her as much as I was missing her right now. Then I thought of Stella and her goddamn ham dish and her cinched-in, tiny waist.

"I hate Stella," I said.

"Isn't worth it," Dottie said, and yawned.

"Well, how would you like it if your mother's worst enemy came by and made eyes at Bert and acted all nicey-nice when you knew she was a witch?"

This woke Dottie up a little bit. "Hah!" she said. "That's funny. You really think someone would come by and make up to Bert?" It's true that Bert wasn't much of a looker. His ears stuck out so far he looked like a taxicab coming with the doors open.

My heart drooped. "I miss Carlie so much," I said.

"Wish I could tell you something to make you feel better," Dottie said, and then she fell asleep. I leaned my head against her warm flanneled back as the adults shouted, "Happy New Year!"

"Happy New Year, Carlie," I whispered to the night.

I wasn't anywhere near tired, so I decided to go and sit out of the way in a corner and listen to the adults. I got up, pulled my clothes back on, and went out into the living room. When I showed up, they stopped talking and looked at me as if they might burn in hell for laughing in my presence.

"You okay, honey?" Madeline said.

I nodded. "Dottie's snoring." Everyone laughed.

Bert shook his head. "She was snoring when she was born."

"How would you know? You wasn't there," Madeline said.

"I heard her from the waiting room," Bert said, and everyone laughed again and forgot about me. Madeline went back to talking to Ida while Bert, Ray, and Sam Warner got up and went into the kitchen for a gab and another beer.

Then I noticed Bud, sitting in an overstuffed chair in a corner, taking it all in with his curious dark eyes, a small smile on his lips.

He got up, brushed by me, and said, "Let's blow this popsicle stand." I followed him into Madeline's studio, where the paints and brushes sat quiet and sober. Bud sat down on Madeline's painting chair backwards, his long, thin legs sticking out like pipe cleaners bent just so. I fell into the cushions on an old, soft couch sitting against the wall, opposite Bud.

"Wonder how Glen's making out," I said. His mother had made him dress up and join her in Long Reach for a New Year's Eve variety show at the Opera House.

"Wasn't too pleased to go," Bud said.

"'Spose Germaine had to threaten him to get him into a suit?"

"Probably paid him to do it."

I thought about Germaine, who looked like a quick and angry monkey. I pictured Ray and Germaine making Glen and the picture made me cover my mouth.

"What?" Bud said.

"Nothing." We went quiet. I pictured Daddy and Carlie making me. It made more sense to me as my head clicked through the times I'd seen them dancing, touching, kissing, fighting, laughing, and making up. I disappeared into thinking about that, I guess, because Bud suddenly said, "You doing okay?"

"I'm okay," I said, too quick. *Love me tender* . . . her feet on his shoes. *Love me sweet* . . . his hand on her hip. Me sandwiched between them.

"Must be hard," Bud said.

His eyes were soft and serious, and they opened me up, somehow. "It's all I can do not to scream, sometimes," I said. "I don't want to talk to Daddy about it because he's so messed up. I don't want to keep crying to Grand, she's heard me enough. Dottie doesn't know what to say. Most of the time, I don't know what to say. It fills my head, all the time. And I miss her. I miss her so much, Bud."

By the second "miss her" he was by my side with his arm wrapped around me. I rested my head on his shoulder until I was cried out. We sat like that until we heard footsteps and he claimed his arm again. Madeline wandered into her studio.

"Well hi," she said, her voice pitched high and low and everywhere in between. "I thought you'd left, Bud, and you'd gone to bed, Florine."

"I'm on my way home," Bud said. "We was just talking."

I don't know how Madeline could have thought that, seeing as how I couldn't see because my eyes were swollen to the size of ping-pong balls, but she didn't say anything, just swooped in and wrapped Bud in a big hug.

"Happy New Year," she said, and gave him a big smack on his cheek. "You get some good rest now, Buddy." And he left, then I got up and she shawled me up in a soft hug and led me back to Dottie's bedroom. I counted her snores instead of sheep.

15

Dottie and I woke up about nine on New Year's Day. We shoved beer bottles to one side of the kitchen table so we could feed Evie and us some breakfast. Evie's black curls bounced in the dim winter light as she ate her cereal. Her pink cheeks nestled into her little heart-shaped face and red lips. She was going to be a beauty, something neither Dottie nor I would ever be. Me, skinny as a fishing pole, and Dottie with her build like a brick shithouse. What would become of us? I wondered suddenly.

"Want to watch cartoons?" Dottie asked.

"No," I said. "It's red ruby glass day."

Every New Year's Day, Grand and I cleaned the red ruby glass while she told me the story of her mother, Emma, who had been orphaned in Boston when she was a child and danced on the streets for pennies. Somehow, she got shipped up to relatives in Spruce Point. She married Harold Morse, who was twenty-five years older. He moved them to The Point and Emma gave birth to four children, three of whom died young. Grand was just a kid when her father died of meanness at age sixty.

Harold had died penniless, and Emma thought about selling the house and moving to town and working as a housekeeper until one day, when Grand was playing hide and seek under her parents' bed, she looked up and saw green paper hanging out of a small rip in the bottom of the mattress. She pulled out fistfuls of it and took it to her mother because she thought it was pretty.

It turned out that Harold had filled the ticking with twenties, tens, and not a few fifty-dollar bills that Emma straightaway took to a bank in Long Reach. He'd been a fisherman, and only the devil knew how he'd come by such a stash, Grand said, but it didn't matter. It was enough to make Emma and Grand comfortable until Grand married Franklin Gilham some twelve years later. Emma had lived with them until she passed.

Grand shared her father's Yankee thrift and had a little nest egg socked away to make sure she made it all the way through her old age. She didn't want for anything more than she had. She surrounded herself with her favorite things and she had her garden. I was walking toward Grand's house and thinking how I couldn't wait for summer to come so I could stick my nose into the center of one of her peonies and suck the perfume straight down to my heart when I glanced to my right and saw Stella Drowns walking up our snowy driveway with her casserole dish.

When she saw me, her pale face went pink as the peony I'd been imagining, and she said, "Happy New Year, Florine. Did you have fun at Dottie's house?"

I went to the heart of it. "Did you have fun at Daddy's house?" The January wind picked up the pace and snow began to fall.

Stella hugged the casserole dish to the bulk of her green wool coat with one hand while she freed up a hand to turn up her collar against the cold. "I had a wonderful time," she said, looking me right in the eye.

"Did you spend the night?"

She took a deep breath, and let out a frosted exhale. "Yes, I did," she said.

"Daddy is a married man," I yelled.

"He's a lonely man, Florine. Just because he wanted company for a night doesn't mean he doesn't love your mother," Stella said. "Do you want him to be lonely?"

"Lonely would be better than you," I said.

Stella's scar flushed purple. "I want to be friends," she said.

"Why? You never did before."

Stella lifted a bit of snow onto her boot toe and then tossed it off. "Happy New Year, Florine," she said. "I'll see you later." She walked off up the hill, backside swishing like a cat that's had her cream and sausage, too.

"You can't cook, either," I shouted, although we both knew that was a lie. I turned and stormed into Grand's house, slamming the door behind me.

Grand was walking from the cabinet to the kitchen with a ruby glass water pitcher. "God's sake, no need to bust in here like that, Florine," she said.

"Stella Drowns spent the night with Daddy," I shouted.

"You calm yourself. Sit while I put this pitcher down so I don't break it."

I sat on the sofa, stiff backed, jiggling my knees up and down. How could she? How could he? How could they? Daddy had deserted Carlie and me for a skinny, scar-faced bitch. I wanted to kill them both.

"Let me take your coat," Grand said. I shucked out of it and she hung it on a hook in the hall. Then she sat down next to me.

"Now, what's all this?" she asked.

"I was coming from Dottie's and I saw Stella walking up our driveway. She said she stayed overnight with Daddy. She did it with him, Grand, I'm sure of it."

"Did what? Oh. Well, for heaven's sake."

"They can't do that, Grand," I said. "Daddy's married to Carlie."

"All right, all right," Grand said. "Just set here and be for a minute."

My fists hit the tops of my thighs as if they meant to flatten them and I yelled, "I don't want her near Daddy. How could he do that to Carlie and me?"

Grand gathered my hands in her own and said, "I don't know, honey. He's lonely and mixed up, I imagine."

"You talk to Daddy. Tell him he can't do this. Tell him Jesus wouldn't like it."

"Florine, I don't use Jesus to threaten anyone."

I took my hands from hers and stood up. I paced back and forth, then needing a purpose, I remembered the reason I'd come, and I went toward the china cabinet. I took the heart from the center of the cabinet and walked toward the kitchen with it.

"Not right now, Florine," Grand said. "You need to calm down. You might break something and then we'd both feel bad."

"Your goddamn glass is more important than me?" I hollered. Then, I ran down the hall, out of the door and down our driveway to the path that led to The Cheeks. I scrambled over the rocks and waded through calf-high snow to the State Park. Once there, coatless and cold and hidden in the park's deserted aloneness, I barged toward the ledges by the ocean, trying to ignore the bully wind that pinched my face and the snow that nipped at my feet. I slipped on the icy path, belly flopped, and dropped the little heart in the snow. "Shit," I said, as I groped, found, and clutched it to me. I reached the ledges. Icy spray planted frozen kisses on my face.

I screamed out all my rage, sadness, and hurt over winter's hellish marriage of sleeted water and bastard wind. "MOTHER," I shrieked, "come home. NOW." But the ocean and the rocks kept up their own icy battle and ignored me. In my desperation, I shouted, "Here! Now give her back to me!" and I threw the red ruby heart into the cold blue sea.

And then Carlie was with me. Sudden heat hugged me from my head to my toes, as my mother wrapped her arms around me. I smelled her perfume and pressed my nose into her hair and it was just us, in a little glowing circle of warmth. *Love me sweet, never let me go . . .* , we sang, and I would have been happy to end things there.

But here was Glen, throwing his heavy flannel hunting jacket over me.

"Let's go, Florine," he said. I looked up and smiled at him, and at Bud and Dottie.

"See? I found her," I said as Carlie's arms tightened around me.

"Florine, your lips are blue," Dottie said. "Where's your coat?"

"Can you get up?" Bud asked.

"I don't want to get up," I said.

"Jesus, Glen, pick her up," Dottie said. "She's hypodermic."

Glen slung me over his right shoulder as if I was a rag doll, and hurried back down the trail, my head and arms dangling down his back. Carlie slipped away from me as Dottie kept shouting, "Don't go to sleep. Stay awake. Don't go to . . ."

When I woke up in my bed around dusk, my eyelids felt like someone had placed bricks on them. It was a struggle to open them, so I gave up and kept them shut. Grand was talking to Daddy in our kitchen.

"Well, Florine isn't ready for you to find someone else. She's tougher than tripe, but still she's a girl as lost her mother."

"The last thing I want to do is hurt my girl. If I'd known how bad she would've felt, 'course I wouldn't have done it," Daddy said. "But, Ma, it's like living in hell. Taking some comfort for a night made me forget. Is that so wrong?"

"What do you think?" Grand asked. Then it went quiet, while Daddy thought, I guess. Grand said, "Carlie might come back. Or even if she doesn't, Florine needs to wrap her mind around that fact."

Daddy said, in a voice so low it scraped the floor, "Ma, Carlie ain't coming back. I can't do no more there. I hate calling Parker and the rest of them. They hate it that they ain't got nothing to report. Jesus, we're circling our circles. I loved that woman more than I can say, and if she was to walk through that door, I would welcome her back with a parade. But Ma, she's not coming back. And Ma, I can't do this." He cried for a while, and I heard Grand's "There, there," and could imagine her patting his back.

Sometime later, I felt his damp hand heavy on my forehead. I forced my lids up and stared into his worried blue eyes. Then I turned over and faced my bedroom wall.

"Leave me alone," I said.

16

Soon after Carlie and Daddy got married, Daddy built a small shed beside the house to shelter Carlie's car, Petunia, during bad weather. His trucks sat out in the snow and rain and rusted, but not Petunia. I never got the full story of how Carlie had come by her—something about waitress tips and winks—but Petunia was her traveling companion. When she'd left for Crow's Nest Harbor in Patty's car, she'd left Petunia parked in the driveway, it being summer. After the disappearance, the police went through her like gulls on fish bait. But they found nothing that might be considered suspicious, unless gum wrappers, a tube of pink lipstick, and a melted Hershey bar (mine) in the glove compartment could be toted up as evidence. It got too sad to see Petunia sitting there and so about two months after Carlie's disappearance, Daddy moved her into her shed, drained her fluids, and shut the door on her.

Sometimes, I went out and sat in the driver's seat and let the tears fall as I looked through the windshield, or I climbed into the backseat and curled up on Petunia's soft musty seats. Sometimes I napped there.

During the winter of 1964, though, I didn't sit in her at all. After my trip out to the ledges, going outside unless I had to didn't set well with my fingers and toes. I was content to guard the house against a possible Stella Drowns invasion.

But Petunia wasn't lonely that winter.

One Saturday in late January, when Daddy was uptown and I was in the kitchen, I spied Bud Warner walking up the hill through the Buttses' yard. He veered to the left and walked toward the shed. He looked around, and then slipped inside the shed door.

I threw a coat on and barged out, opened the door, and glared at a sheepish Bud, who was sitting in the driver's seat, gloved hands on the steering wheel. I walked up to the window and he rolled it down.

"What are you doing?" I said.

Bud shrugged. "Feeling stupid."

"You look stupid," I said. "What are you doing in my mother's car?"

"You'll laugh."

"Better I laugh than knock you sideways to Sunday."

Bud smiled. "Probably could, too, mad as you are. Move, so I can get out."

I stepped back and he got out and shut the door. We walked around to the front of the car and he leaned on the grill. He patted Petunia's hood. "She's a nice car," he said.

"She's Carlie's car," I said.

"Think Carlie would mind that I sat in her and pretended I was driving her?"

"Why?"

"Well, I know it sounds foolish," Bud said. "But I like to pretend I'm taking her out on the road, people looking at us, thinking what a beauty she is."

He looked at me with steady dark eyes and a little smile, trusting me to understand something about him. I liked that, but I didn't know what to do about it.

"Well, you can sit in her, I guess," I said. "Long as you don't smoke."

"I don't smoke, you know that."

"I didn't know you came up and sat in my mother's car. For all I know, you could be lighting up a pack a day."

"Nah," Bud said. He moved away from Petunia and we walked to my front door. "Guess I'll go home now," he said. "You sure you're okay with me sitting in the car?"

"I'm okay with it," I said.

"Thanks," Bud said. "I'll see you," and he walked down our driveway, arms and legs too long and loose. He turned around and waved. I waved back and then he disappeared behind the Buttses' house.

As the longest winter of my life dragged its ass across the calendar, I welcomed every minute of returning light, and I welcomed Bud's visits to the car.

Sometimes he left behind little presents. On Valentine's Day, he set a white candy heart that read SOME GIRL on the passenger seat, and on Saint Patrick's Day, I found a green ribbon tied to Petunia's steering wheel. I knitted a black watch cap for him and found it gone, replaced with a Charms cherry lollipop.

One day in late March, I spied him slipping into the shed and I decided to join him in the passenger seat. We looked through the windshield, down over the hill to the harbor, where ice cakes glided to a salty death in the spring ocean.

"Be warm soon," Bud said.

"For sure," I said.

"Someday," Bud said, "I'm going to drive away from here for good."

"Why?"

"I don't want to be here for all of my life. I don't want to fish."

"Where will you go?"

"Someplace where I don't know everybody. Maybe Long Reach. Maybe beyond that. Don't you feel cramped in, sometimes?"

"Mostly I feel like I got a hole inside," I said.

Gulls landed on the chunks of ice in the harbor, riding them past us and out of sight. "Carlie felt cramped here," I said. "She wanted to go places all the time."

"I know how she felt," Bud said. "Sometimes, I get so crazy that I get up at night, go outside and walk until I'm tired. I just have to move. My legs can't be still."

I thought about his lonely, restless, skinny self walking down the dark roads, feet crunching on the gravel or scuffing over tar.

"You think I'm crazy?" he asked. I turned to look at him.

We saw each other different at the same time. We'd always looked at each other as through water, a wavy, liquid, safe distance. But in that car, in that moment, that water evaporated and became air, clear, dry, and true.

"I don't think you're crazy," I said.

Bud's eyes got wide. Then he turned toward the windshield and shook his head. "I don't want to get stuck here," he said, more to himself than me. He opened the car door and hopped out, startling me into a series of blinks. He said, "Don't tell no one I go walking in the night, okay?" He shut the car door and off he ran. I let myself out of Petunia, shut the door to the shed, and went into the empty house. I tugged at the string holding my heart aloft and gently lowered it back into place.

17

One day in early April, the school bus dropped Dottie and me off, and we walked to Ray's so we could buy a snack and split it. Dottie always bought the goods, because I didn't want to go in and see Stella. That day, after coming out of the store and while trying to work the cellophane off some Hostess cupcakes, Dottie said, "Your dad's in there."

"Is he? What's he . . . God damn it," I said. I ignored the cupcake Dottie held out and I marched inside. Daddy was leaning up against Stella's counter, but he straightened when he saw me and looked guilty as hell. I turned and stormed out of the store. Daddy followed me.

"You seeing her again?" I asked. "Just let me know."

"No, I'm not seeing her," Daddy said.

"Good," I said.

"What do you want for supper?" he asked.

"Too busy talking to pick up something at the store?" I asked.

"Jesus," Daddy said. "Why would I need a wife? I've got you to nag me."

Maybe he wasn't lying, then, but late one night not long after that, I heard the sound of footsteps on the driveway. I bolted up out of bed and looked out of my window. Two figures walked up the driveway, away from the house. I figured out that the tall one was Daddy, but who was the smaller one? Then I knew.

I got out of bed and went into the kitchen. The faint trace of Stella's cologne and something I would later come to know as the smell of sex hung in the darkened kitchen.

"Screw you, Stella," I said, then realized someone already had. A little later, Daddy sneaked back down the driveway, came into the house and went to bed.

In the morning I said to him, "Thought you weren't seeing her."

Daddy put the coffeepot on the burner and said, "I wasn't."

"But you are now?"

"I want to," he said. "But I want you to be all right with it."

"Can't have both," I said.

"What the hell does that mean?"

"It's me or her."

Daddy sat down across the table from me.

"Florine," he said, "how can I explain this so you'll understand it?"

"Explain what?"

"I like this woman," Daddy said. "I've known her a long time. If your mother hadn't come along, I might have married her, and she could just as well have been your mother." I gave him such a look of disgust that he added, quickly, " 'Course, that didn't happen."

"Good thing," I said.

"But all that put to one side, I need some company."

"What's wrong with the company you got? You got Grand, me, Sam, Bert, Ray, Pastor Billy, and more. What's wrong with us?"

"You're all good company," he said. "I mean someone I can really talk to. A good friend I can spend time with. And she can cook like no one I've ever known." Daddy smiled. "And I know you liked that meal she cooked, too, even though you pretended you didn't like it. I ain't totally ignorant. I know you, some."

"What you mean is you need someone you can fuck," I said. "Isn't that it?"

I could tell that he wanted to hit me, or yell at me so loud it would blow me off the chair. But instead, he let out a long, slow breath, then he said, his blue eyes sharp, "I suppose it's too much to ask that you don't use that word. But I don't want to ever, ever hear you use it like that again. I hope that when you're ready to be with someone—you treat that time with the goodness it deserves."

He got up and walked to the front door. He put on his coat and turned back to me. "I got to get out of here for a few minutes, I guess. I never thought I'd hear my girl talk that way and I'm ashamed of you. And I'll tell you right now, Florine, the real reason why I want to see Stella. I'm dying inside with missing your mother. I could suck on some bitch of a bottle, but I'd rather talk to someone. Be with someone who can help me get through this. You think about that and I hope you can dig down and haul up some kindness from somewhere inside you." And he left the house.

I tried. I did. When I got home from school a couple of nights later, Daddy was in his woodworking workshop, off the living room. The smell of pine tickled my nostrils as I looked in on him.

"You mind picking up the house?" he asked, not looking up.

"Why?"

"Stella's bringing dinner," he said. "And I expect you to be nice to her."

My good intentions scattered like marbles the minute she came through our door. I hated the way she stretched like a snake shedding its skin when Daddy took her coat, the way she wore full war paint on her face.

"Hello, Florine," she said to me.

"I got homework," I said. I went into my room, sat at my desk, took out a couple of pieces of lined notebook paper and wrote *I hate Stella Drowns* until Daddy knocked on the door and called me to supper.

"Not hungry," I said.

"Get out here," he said. "Please."

Stella heaped noodles, brown sauce, and dark chunks of beef onto my plate.

"That looks good," Daddy said.

"Beef Stroganoff," Stella said.

"Beef strong enough?" Daddy said. Stella giggled. "Silly," she said.

Daddy started to take a bite, but Stella put her hand on his arm. "Aren't you forgetting something?" she asked.

Daddy looked confused.

"She means grace," I said. "Remember, she said it before."

Stella bent her head and said some words.

Daddy added an Amen and then forked food into his mouth. He sat back in his chair and gave Stella a broad smile. "My God," he said, "I don't know when I've ever tasted anything so good. But," he added, and winked at Stella, "it needs a little salt."

"Oh dear," Stella said. "Not enough?"

"Plenty," he said. "I just like a lot of it."

"Salt's not good for you," she said.

Daddy laughed. "Oh, I know, but I got to have some fun, don't I?"

She lifted an eyebrow and said, "I'm not fun enough?"

"I just like more salt than normal," he stammered.

"Well." Stella sniffed. "I'll put more in, I guess."

Daddy put the saltshaker down. "It's fine the way it is, isn't it, Florine?" he said.

"A turd is dinner to a dog, but that doesn't mean I have to eat it," I said.

Stella's eyes turned to glassy shards. "Well," she said, "you're honest."

"She's not fit to sit here," Daddy said, his face red. "Go to your room."

"Should have let me stay there in the first place," I said.

I slid off my chair, went into my room, slammed the door, and put Elvis on my record player. I played "Jailhouse Rock" loud. I imagined

Carlie coming back home right now, in the middle of their dinner. She'd look at Stella, smile and say, "Hey there, Stella!" sit down, serve herself up, thank Stella for coming, and we'd all go on from there.

After a long time, I took Elvis off the turntable, climbed into bed, and slept. I woke later to the sound of Stella crying and Daddy talking. I crept from my bed and cracked the door so I could see them. They were by the front door and Stella had her coat on.

"This is too soon," she said. "Carlie is still in your eyes. I can't live with that."

"It'll take me awhile," Daddy said. "You got to be patient with me."

"Florine doesn't want me here. I don't want to force her."

Daddy walked toward her and she backed off. "Stella," he said.

Stella said, "I waited for years for you, Leeman. It was hard for me to watch Carlie have your baby. I wanted that for us."

"I'm sorry," Daddy said.

"Good night," she said, and left.

"The witch is dead," I told Dottie at school the next day.

"Ding dong," Dottie said.

But that night as I lay in bed, I heard Daddy answer the door in the dark. I opened my bedroom door just enough to see Daddy and Stella locked together in a kiss, making noises deep in their throats. They moved toward Daddy's bedroom and in less than a minute, the bed squeaked faster than a hamster running on a rusty wheel.

That did it. I dragged Carlie's suitcase from under the bed. I'd already packed some clothes and other things I'd need. I put Carlie's favorite Elvis album on top and shut the lid. I opened my window and dropped the suitcase, then myself, to the ground. Daddy hadn't been the only sneaky one. While he'd been making nice with Stella, I'd been taking little dribs and drabs of money from his wallet and his pockets. I had enough money so I could walk to Long Reach, get a one-way ticket on a bus to Crow's Nest Harbor, and start looking for my mother.

It was about eleven o'clock, and the April night was dark and chilly. I hustled up the driveway. I glanced down toward the water and I saw that the lights were out at the Warner and Butts houses. I pictured them sleeping with no cares, and jealousy broke over me like a rogue wave. They had each other and now, Daddy had Stella. I was alone.

The sheer weight of that fact made me sit down on the large white rock at the end of our driveway. Then, like a single, fat raindrop that warns of something bigger coming, a little noise came from somewhere deep inside and worked its way out of my throat. Self-pity played with grief and I knew that no one would give a flying fig if I wandered up the road and went away to become an orphan.

But then, a light snapped on in Grand's bedroom. She parted her curtains and peered out, closed them up. Then the front door light went on and she came outside and walked to where I sat on the rock. When she reached me, she said, "Well, Florine, what in the world?"

Without waiting for an answer, she picked up my suitcase and we walked to her house, where she sat me down at the kitchen table.

"Nobody loves me," I wailed.

"Oh for heaven's sake, that's not true," Grand said. "Now, I was sound asleep and I heard you crying and I woke right up. Guess that's love, don't you think?"

"I guess."

"I should think so," she said. "Come on with me." I climbed into bed with her and cuddled back to her warm soft side.

I woke up late the next morning to find Daddy sitting on the side of the bed.

"I want to stay here," I said.

He didn't argue. "Maybe we need a break," he said. "You can stay with Grand for a while, but I expect you home for supper."

We tried. But it made me crazy to know that Stella would probably come by after I left for the night. I began to skip suppers, saying I had too much homework and I needed to eat at Grand's, so I could get on with it. Soon, I hardly went to Daddy's house at all.

My thirteenth birthday on May 18, 1964, was held at Grand's house. The gift I most wanted in the world was not to be mine, and I knew that, but how I wished she were with us that day. I knew that if she was anywhere, she would know it was my birthday, and she would have called, or come home, if it were at all possible. The beginning of my understanding that she wouldn't be coming home hit me hard on that otherwise bright, sunny, warm day.

Grand made a confetti angel food cake and she, Daddy, me, and Dottie ate it with chocolate ice cream. Since Dottie's birthday was on May 19, we usually shared some part of our days, and always our cakes and ice creams.

Dottie brought me two of her lonely dolls, with Madeline's permission. These dolls were my favorites and I had named them Caroline and Patricia, for Carlie's and Patty's real first names, long ago. Dolls on my thirteenth birthday may have seemed odd, but Dottie knew what I needed, and I held them in my arms as Daddy took a tiny box wrapped in gold paper with white ribbon curls out of his pocket. He handed it to me and said, quiet, "This is from your mother and me."

I looked at him, confused.

"Go on and open it," he said.

A green velvet box nestled inside. I lifted the lid, said, "Oh," and shut it again.

Grand took the box, opened it, and pulled out a gold ring set with a tiny green stone.

"Your birthstone," she said. "A real emerald. Hold out your hand."

It slid around on my right ring finger, and Daddy said, "Too big. Damn it."

"We'll get it fitted," Grand said. "Until then, I have just the thing."

She hurried upstairs. I stared at the ring, rubbed my fingers over the prongs.

Daddy said, "We wanted you to have this for your thirteenth birthday. Carlie picked it out way back in June. I hope you like it, honey."

Grand came downstairs holding a golden chain. She took the ring from me, slid it onto the chain, and fastened it around my neck as tears ran down my cheeks. In all the time I had it, it never left my neck, or later, my finger.

18

I loved living with Grand. For one, she wasn't likely to go hunting for a man, nor was a man likely to call for her. Probably she wouldn't just disappear and I wasn't waiting for the phone to ring. Here, sorrow was allowed to perch and settle inside of me, instead of digging its claws into my heart and flapping its wings, trying to rip it out. When my longing for Carlie got too strong, Grand was there to comfort me in her plain, strong way. We knew each other's routines and I knew what was expected of me.

Church, for instance.

I'd been to service with Grand before. It was the only thing she'd asked of Carlie and Daddy, that I go with her a few times each year. So ever since I'd been able to sit for any length of time, Carlie had rousted me up on certain Sunday mornings and trotted me over to Grand's house in my church clothes. Daddy and Carlie didn't go to church. Daddy said the water was his church. Carlie thought God was part of everything, everywhere. "And in you," she'd say, and touch her finger to my heart.

The Baptist church was up on Route 100. Sam Warner drove us there, every Sunday. I doubt he would have gone, except that Ida loved Jesus, too. Despite quiet Ida's friendship with silence, she got her point across, and if she wanted Sam in church, Sam went. He might sell his soul to the devil with as much drink as he wanted any night of the week, but he had to get it back, intact, by Sunday morning for his come-to-Jesus meeting.

Grand sat in the backseat between Bud and me. Maureen, who so far in her life appeared to be as quiet as her mother, sat up front between her parents, the top of her smooth brown head barely visible. Grand hummed "The Old Rugged Cross" in a wavery voice, and Ida hummed along with Grand. Bud looked out the window, thinking about escape, I figured.

After Sam parked the car, we went inside the little white church, and Grand marched me down to the front row. We sat with three or four older ladies who made room for us by scooting down along a seat worn smooth by warm, shifting bottoms. There, Grand left me for Jesus, lifting her eyes to the ceiling and saying "Amen" in a sure voice.

In this place, Pastor Billy carried himself like a he-gull in his prime. His sermons were both strong and gentle, filled with stories of love and forgiveness. He never preached hell and damnation. Because he was a fisherman, too, he understood what his congregation faced as they rode the waves; how things could get out of hand in a mad minute. They needed comfort, not threats.

Every Sunday, he asked me how I was doing. His big hands, like my father's, were tough and callused. He always set one of those hands on the top of my head and left it there for a few seconds, as if he was wishing good things into my heart.

One Sunday afternoon in late June, after Sam had dropped Grand and me back home, I got it into my head to take a walk to the spot where I'd thrown the red ruby heart into the sea. Pastor Billy had been preaching about Jonah being cast into the raging waters, and how the sea had become calm, and it reminded me of that time.

"I'm going out for a little while," I told Grand.

"Not too long," she said. "I'm making Sunday dinner and I'll need your help."

The air in the woods was sweet and warm like baby's breath, and it seemed that Carlie walked beside me. I hadn't been wrong, I thought to myself. She was here, just as she had been on that bitter New Year's Day. My heart rose as I neared the rocks. But I stopped when I saw someone sitting on a stone bench that hadn't been there last winter.

The sitter, a man, turned his yellow head and our eyes locked. It was Mr. Barrington. Had it only been a year ago that he'd walked down the line of us, and each of us had said we were sorry for almost burning down his house? I felt the ghosts of Carlie's hands squeeze my shoulders and I reached up to touch them.

Mr. Barrington squinted at me. "Is it you?" he whispered.

"It's Florine Gilham," I said, trying to figure out how to back up and bolt the other way without looking like that's what I was trying to do.

"Of course," he said, and he stood up and held out his hand. I didn't see why we needed to shake hands in the woods. Still, Grand would have wanted me to be polite and Mr. Barrington wasn't a stranger, so I took his hand. He gave it a firm squeeze.

Then he said, "It's nice to see you, Florine. I've been coming down here for years." He looked out over the water. "Since way before you were born. I finally paid the park to put a bench here." He pointed at a small brass plaque that read, *On life's vast ocean diversely we sail, Reason the card, but passion is the gale.* Alexander Pope. I wondered if Alexander Pope was a relative, but I didn't dare to ask.

"Sit," he said, and pointed to the bench. I sat. I looked down at Mr. Barrington's new Top-Sider moccasins. Then I looked at my feet. One of the shoelaces on my right sneaker had broken and I'd tied it back together. A big knot snarled up the laces.

"You're about the same age as Andy, aren't you?" Mr. Barrington asked. "He was born in December 1950."

"May," I said. "1951."

Mr. Barrington said, "They say that spring babies are easier to get along with than winter babies. Maybe it's the weather."

I knew that some might argue that easy-to-get-along-with spring baby part about me, but I let it go.

"Your father's probably been out on the water for a few months already," Mr. Barrington said. "We just arrived. Seems we get here later every year."

"Yes, he's working," I said.

Then Mr. Barrington turned and held me with those dark eyes. "I wanted to say how sorry I am about your mother," he said. "She was a lovely woman."

"Thank you," I said.

That being said, he switched back to his son. "Andy is taking an Outward Bound course this summer," he said. "Hurricane Island, up the coast. New program. Hear of it?"

"No," I said.

"'Course not," Mr. Barrington said. "No reason you should. You live Outward Bound on The Point." He smiled. I noticed the stubble on his face, and how the rough blackness of that made his lips look smooth. He had a beautiful mouth, something I'd never particularly paid attention to before in a man or a boy. It disturbed me that I was noticing it on him. I stood up. "I have to go, Mr. Barrington," I said.

He stood, too. "Of course," he said. "I'm sorry I kept you. I need to get back as well. Barbara and I are celebrating our fourteenth wedding anniversary this weekend. The guests will be arriving even as I take this quiet time for contemplation. Do me a favor," he said, and he winked at me. "You bring that gang back. We could probably use some fireworks this weekend to get things going."

"Bye," I said.

"Yes," he said. He held out his hand again and I took it. He didn't let it go, this time, though. He lifted my hand to those smooth lips and I felt their coolness, even as the stubble pricked the back of my hand. I pulled away as a park ranger walked down the trail with a group of nature walkers.

Mr. Barrington and I brushed by them and I walked in front of him as fast as I could without seeming rude. We reached a fork in the trail and he said, "Goodbye, Florine."

"Goodbye," I said, and I started to hurry away.

"Florine," he called, and I stopped and turned around.

"You're lovely," he said. "Just like your mother."

19

O ne July day when Dottie and I were sitting in her room doing nothing, Dottie said, "You want to see something?" Before I could say yes or no, she pulled down her shorts and hauled down her blue cotton panties. She pointed to the chubby V between her legs. "Look," she said. "Isn't that gross?"

"What?"

"Look closer."

"I'm close enough."

"Jesus, Florine," Dottie said. "Look. Can't you see them things?"

When I squinted, I saw four or five little blond hairs rooted like unfurled ferns in her smooth pink skin.

"Wish I had some," I said. I was hairless.

"I don't," Dottie said. "I'm going to shave them off."

"And I don't want to be flat forever," I said. "I want boobs. You got boobs." Dottie did have real boobs now. They wobbled on her chest like half-baked custard.

"I'd give you some if I could," Dottie said. We looked at her doll shelf. "Look at them stupid dolls watching me like they expect something," she said. "You want the rest of 'em for when you have kids?"

"Caroline and Patricia are enough. Give Evie the dolls," I said.

Dottie snorted. "She's got enough friggin' dolls."

"You might change your mind. Your kids might like the dolls, even if you don't."

"I don't want kids," Dottie said.

That alarmed me. I'd always pictured us growing up and living in these houses with our husbands and children. I decided to let the whole thing drop. "Want to go get a tan?" I said, just to change the subject.

"For a little while," Dottie said.

We changed into our bathing suits, walked down to the shore, and spread our blankets on the pebbly sand. Now that we were both thirteen, the adults let us go down to the water by ourselves. The boys weren't around. They were too busy. Glen worked with Ray at the store, and Bud went out on the boat with Sam and Daddy. Bud had stayed pretty clear of me since the day we'd locked eyes while sitting in Petunia. A few days back, though, I had run into him as I was walking down the hill from Ray's store and he was walking up.

"Hey," he said.

"Hey," I said.

"Been fishing?" I asked.

"Yeah," he said. "Been to the store?"

"Yeah."

"Bye," he said and passed me.

But I caught him looking at me when I turned around to watch him walk away. He ducked his head, made a half-assed wave with his hand, and kept on moving.

Now, as Dottie tanned and I burned, words strange to me popped out of my mouth. I raised myself on my elbows and said to her, "I got to tell you something. I like Bud for a boyfriend."

Dottie shaded her eyes from the glare of the sun and squinted up at me.

"That won't work," she said. "That'd mean I have to like Glen."

"It doesn't mean that."

"It would follow."

"I like Bud, anyway," I said. "You don't have to like Glen."

"Look," Dottie said, "Bud's a good guy. Hell, Glen's a good guy. But they're like our brothers. Be odd if you two was to get together."

"Well, let's see what happens," I said.

What happened is that I did get odd. I wouldn't wave if I saw Bud onboard the *Carlie Flo* or the *Maddie Dee*. When the men came up from the boat, sometimes I went to say hello to Daddy and Sam. I couldn't look Bud in the face and I barely spoke. Bud wouldn't look at me, either.

After about two weeks of this foolishness, I decided I'd had enough.

One day, I said to Dottie, "I don't like Bud anymore. It's weird. You were right."

Later that day, I ran into Bud as he was walking down the hill from Ray's store and I was walking up. My heart jumped and tried to run, but I forced it back into a sitting position and I said, "Hey" to Bud.

"Hey," he said back.

It took a mountain of will on my part, but I didn't look back.

The rest of the summer ticked down to the anniversary of Carlie's disappearance. When the day came, it hit me like a stone to the heart. Daddy took me out on the boat with Sam and Bud for the two weeks before school. Out on the water, I was too busy to worry about whether or not Bud liked me or I liked Bud. I helped with the bait, I steered the boat, I plugged lobsters, and did what they asked me to do. Sometimes, I sat in a chair and stared at the water and the sky. None of us talked much. Their quiet company calmed me, and I liked being near Daddy without Stella around. While we worked, Grand took some of Carlie's old clothes and she and Ida made a beautiful quilt for me. I wrapped it around me at night and slept better than I had in a long time.

20

Nothing much happened for the rest of the summer. I grew a few pubic hairs and that cheered me up a little bit. Stella and Daddy stayed locked together in his house, I still lived with Grand, and then it was time to head for junior high for the eighth grade. This meant we had to travel by bus to Long Reach. The comfort of small numbers vanished when we entered a school that contained three grades with about two hundred students per grade. Corridors and hallways had to be navigated by twists and turns to find our classrooms. They called us fish, at first, and they said we smelled, because we were from The Point. Dottie laughed at them, Glen didn't notice, Bud thought they were ass-holes, and I tried to become invisible. It didn't work.

I was tall for thirteen, and skinny, with hair that curled any way it wanted to go, no matter what I did. I was shy as a shit poke, but Carlie's absence was what made me stand out. When we first went to junior high, the Long Reach kids whispered about it just loud enough so that I heard it, clear. *"Ran off with some guy. Dad's a drunk. I heard she got around. Murdered, maybe?"* Although it didn't make any sense, it made me mad that Carlie wasn't there to stick up for me. Talking to Daddy about it was out of the question. I went, as always, to Grand.

"Best to ignore it, Florine," she said. "Don't give 'em the satisfaction of letting it bother you. Soon they'll forget all about it and find something else to talk about." Why Grand thought that I could ignore it was beyond me. Grand hadn't had to go to junior high school. I kept my head down and my ears closed as best I could.

Grand was slowing down some, and forgetting things. One day, when I got home from school, she was sitting on the sofa watching a show on television. Her apron was on and flour spotted her face. She was knitting away on something.

A bowl of flour sat on the bread block in the kitchen. "That flour going to make itself into dough?" I called to her.

"What did you say?"

I walked into the living room. She peered up at me over glasses that glinted with the changing scenes on the television.

"You want me to finish the bread?" I asked.

She puckered her brow. "For heaven's sake, I'm losing my mind," she said to herself more than me. She set her knitting down and shuffled past me into the kitchen.

"I can do it, Grand," I offered, but she wouldn't let me do it alone. I noticed her swollen knuckles, and how the skin around her jaws formed jowls that wobbled as she worked. She had turned seventy-nine years old in late March. What might other people think if I brought them home to meet her? Most of the girls probably had young, pretty mothers, much as I had had once. How would Grand measure up to them? It shamed me to think that way, so I took it out on the bread dough.

Grand was right about them forgetting about me, sure enough. People did begin talking about something else besides me and my missing mother. They zeroed in on poor Glen.

Ray and Germaine, his parents, didn't live together, we all knew that. She lived in Long Reach with a roommate, Sarah. That's the way it was, and we all tended to business with Glen in our midst. But evidently it was important for everyone in junior high to know that Glen Clemmons's mother was a lesbo, which was short for lesbian. Around the end of September, the rumors started.

"She ain't," Glen said to me on the bus going home to The Point one night soon after word got out. Big fat tears rolled down his full-moon face. I noticed that a few pimples had set up housekeeping near his chin.

"So if she is. So if she ain't. Don't let them get to you," I said, sounding like an echo of Grand. Easy to say, I knew. Harder to do, for sure.

"I'm gonna kill anyone says it," he said. I left that one alone. That was up to him.

Dottie joined Grand and me for supper that night for some tuna noodle casserole, one of Dottie's favorites. After we set the table, we sat up in my room. We could hear Grand in the kitchen humming over the TV news blaring in the living room.

"She's getting a little hard of hearing," I said to Dottie.

"She's getting on," Dottie said. "I wished one of my grandmothers was still alive."

Dottie's grandparents, both sides, had passed before she'd been born. This life was tough on the old people. Grand was the last of her generation to live on The Point.

"You suppose Grand knows what a lesbo is?" I asked Dottie.

"I'm not sure I know what it is," Dottie said. "I been trying to figure out what goes where, or who does what."

"You girls come down," Grand called.

On the way down the stairs, I said to Dottie, "I'm going to ask her. Get her going."

"Maybe not," Dottie said.

During supper, I said, "You know what a lesbo is, Grand?"

"A what?" Grand said. "A lesbo? Can't say I do."

"People at school say that Glen's mother is a lesbo."

"No she's not. She's a Whitman, from Georgetown. I knew her mother. Wonderful woman."

Dottie looked down at her plate as if the food there was the most important meal ever put together. Her eyebrows were wiggling, which meant she wasn't far from laughing.

"No, Grand," I said. "People are saying that Glen's mother likes girls."

Grand helped herself to a tablespoon of casserole. "What's wrong with Germaine liking girls?" She gave me a look loaded with questions. Probably I should have stopped there, but Grand said, again, "What's wrong with that?"

Dottie picked peas out of the tuna casserole and pushed them to one side.

"Nothing," I said. "It's just that I thought girls were supposed to like boys, not girls."

Grand shook her empty tablespoon at me. "I want you to listen to me," she said, "and you Dorothea, too. Life's too short to worry about what other people think. And I got a question for you both. Is whatever Germaine likes hurting you?"

"No," I said. "I was just wondering . . ."

"What about you, Dorothea? She hurting you?"

"I don't care," she said. "Don't matter to me."

"That's good, because I say it's none of your business. I say that it's nobody's business. Jesus don't care who likes what or who does what, long as they believe in him and listen to what he has to say far as loving each other, no matter what, no matter who. That's what I think." Grand finished her supper and got up to clear the table, even though Dottie and I were still eating. "Jesus loves everyone," she muttered as she cleaned up the kitchen. "All of us."

After supper, Dottie said, "She got some wound up."

"She did," I said. "Wish I'd never brought it up."

That night, in the half place between sleep and awake, I saw Jesus walking down a deserted Mulgully Beach. I ran so that I could walk along with him, and we headed for the rock where Carlie and I had gone on to that day together. Carlie sat on that rock, facing away from Jesus and me, her back pale against a black swimsuit I'd never seen her wear. She was looking out over the ocean at her precious horizon.

I stopped, but Jesus kept going. "Carlie?" I said. She didn't turn around. She didn't let on that she heard me. When I turned to tell Jesus to make her listen he faded away, and when I turned back, Carlie was gone, too. I opened my eyes and stared up at the ceiling. The television downstairs was still on, loud.

I went downstairs and sat beside Grand as she knitted.

"Bad dream," I said.

"Everyone has 'em, Florine," Grand said. "Everyone has 'em."

"I love you, Grand," I said.

"That's good," she said. "We're stuck with one another, looks like. That helps."

At the bus stop the next day, I said to Glen, "You should be glad you have a mother. Doesn't matter what she does. You should just be glad you have your mother."

But Glen let them get to him, and he wouldn't go to Long Beach to stay with Germaine. Germaine was made of stout stuff, though, and she wouldn't let him ignore her. One night, as we walked from the bus stop to Ray's store, Germaine was waiting outside. I wondered, sometimes, how she and Ray had produced such a big son. Germaine was tiny, with a pixie-cut to her pale blond hair. Ray wasn't tall. But Parker was big, and maybe Ray had passed that on to Glen.

Seeing Germaine standing in front of the store, her eyes desperate with the need for Glen's understanding, made me jealous. How many days had I wanted to see Carlie waiting for me when I got off the school bus? And here was girl-loving Germaine, Jesus's child no matter what, wanting her baby in the worst way. Glen said, "Shit."

"She's your mother," I said. "And she's here. That's something."

"She's right," Bud said, behind me. "Florine's right." When Dottie, Bud, and I passed by Germaine, we said hello, and went on home. If Glen hadn't stopped to talk with her, I would have clouted him one. But he did.

21

Bud introduced me to his new girlfriend one Saturday in October.
I was hanging out clothes in the fall sunshine in the side yard, sheets slapping back against me like wet sails, when I heard footsteps crunch up the gravel road. I peered around the sheets and saw Bud holding hands with a girl, walking up toward Ray's. The girl stopped and smiled at me. "Hi," she said. "You're Florine, right?"

I stepped out from behind the sheet, wearing my old jeans and a holey white T-shirt that Grand kept begging me to get rid of. But it had been Carlie's shirt, and I'd reduce it to rags before I tossed it out.

Both the girl and Bud looked down when I stepped out.

"Hi," I said.

Bud, still looking down, said, "This is Susan."

Susan's hair was long, a soft, straight brown like a mink's coat. Her eyes were the same color as her hair. She was small enough to fit into a teacup. I'd seen her in school surrounded by friends.

Grand came out with a basket of clothes and set it down next to me.

"Hi, Bud," she said. Bud looked up at her and smiled.

"Hi, Mrs. Gilham," he said.

"Mrs. Gilham?" she said, and then she giggled like a girl.

"Grand," Bud muttered.

"Who's the young lady with you?" Grand said.

"This is Susan Murray, from school," Bud said. "Susan, this is Grand."

"Nice to meet you," Susan said.

"You sew on them patches?" Grand asked her. Susan's jeans were covered with colorful squares.

"I did," Susan said. "Each of them means something to me. This one"—she pointed to a flannel patch on her thigh—"comes from one of Bud's old shirts." She bumped against Bud, who bumped her back and blushed. He looked as if he'd been hit upside the head with a honey-coated two-by-four.

"Well, aren't you clever," Grand said to Susan.

By this time, I'd figured out why Bud and Susan had looked down when I'd stepped out from behind the sheets. Carlie's shirt was thin, it was wet from the sheets, and flat as I was, my nipples still stuck out in the cold. I covered my breasts with my arms.

"Well, we're going to Ray's," Bud said.

"Nice to meet you," Susan said. They walked on, my old friend and his new girl.

"She's nice, and some cute," Grand said. "Good for Buddy."

"I got a headache," I said, and went up to my room, tore off the T-shirt and swamped myself in a thick gray sweatshirt that read BUBBA'S STEAK HOUSE.

Stella came over later in the day to see Grand and to talk about Susan. She usually didn't come alone, and I wasn't pleased to see her. She said hello to me, then sat down with Grand to have a cup of tea.

"Sweet girl," she said to Grand. "Looks good with Buddy, too."

"It's Bud," I said from my place on a stool near Grand's kitchen cupboards. I had cleaned them out and was putting new contact paper on the shelves.

"Point of fact, it's James Walter," Stella said.

"He's Bud to me," I said. I smoothed a sheet of contact paper down on the top shelf so hard my hand got hot from the friction.

"Lee says she's the prettiest girl he's seen in these parts since . . . ," Stella said.

I stepped down off the stool and I said, "Since what?"

"Carlie," Stella said.

"She doesn't come close to Carlie," I said.

"Now," Grand said. "It's apples and oranges. This girl right here is just as pretty as her mother, and as pretty as Susan."

"I'm not pretty," I shouted, and I stormed upstairs to my room, where I headed right for the mirror to stare down a pale girl with muddy green eyes. My cheekbones were so sharp you could slice cheese on them, my mouth turned down, and my chin was like Daddy's chin, strong. If I saw me, I wondered, would I think I was pretty? I shook my hair out of the rubber band that had been holding it back. It twisted and squirmed away from my head. Except for some red highlights that reminded me that I was Carlie's daughter, I hated it.

Someone clumped up the stairs and then Dottie stared at me from the doorway.

"They let me in," she said.

"They'll let anyone in," I grumbled.

"Strange car over at your dad's house."

"Who?"

"I don't know. Some woman looks like she works in an office. Your father came out of the house to meet her. They shook hands, then went back in."

That confused me. How could a strange woman get past Stella's eagle eye and why would she let Daddy be alone with her?

"I'm going to see who it is," I said. "But don't let Stella know I'm doing it. You go down the stairs, make a lot of noise, say hello or something, and I'll go out the side door, through the garden, and cross the road."

"Why don't you walk downstairs and go out the front door?"

"Where's the fun in that?" I asked. Sometimes, Dottie could be a few sandwiches shy of a picnic. Any chance to pull one over on Stella was not to be missed.

Dottie clumped downstairs and started talking loud to Stella and

Grand while I tiptoed out the door into the side yard, ducked under the sheets, and went across the road and down Daddy's driveway.

The car parked there was a new one; a town car, no doubt. I passed it and walked into the house. Daddy and the woman sat at the kitchen table. She was writing in a notebook and a tape recorder sat in the middle of the table. Daddy looked at me like I'd caught him doing something wrong. The woman looked at me and said, "Hi."

"Florine, this is Elisabeth Moss. She's a reporter. She come to talk to me about Carlie being gone."

As I thought about backing up and leaving, Elisabeth Moss got up and came toward me with her hand outstretched. "Hi," she said, and her voice was as warm as a heated, buttered muffin. "I work for the Long Reach paper, Florine. Your dad has just been telling me about you."

"Florine don't have to be here," Daddy said.

That set me off. "Why don't you want me here?" I asked him.

"I didn't want you to have to talk about something that might make you feel bad."

"How could I feel any worse?"

Daddy shrugged. "Suit yourself," he said. "She's stubborn," he said to Elisabeth.

"I've got one of those," Elisabeth said. "Thirteen going on twenty."

"Well, sit down," Daddy said, and I slipped into a chair between them.

Elisabeth said, "I know that there was a story about your mother disappearing when it happened, but I thought I'd do an update. It was a little over a year ago, right?"

"One year, two months," Daddy said.

Elisabeth nodded. I liked her face. It wasn't fussy. She looked me in the eye.

"Let me catch you up, Florine. Parker Clemmons told me that the police haven't had much to go on. So, I thought that if I wrote something about it, it might shake something loose. I called your dad here, and he agreed to talk to me. This will go into the paper, probably in a couple of weeks. I want to talk to some other folks, make it a feature."

"Will my picture be in the paper?" I asked, thinking about the whispers in school.

"Only if you want it to be," Elisabeth said.

"I was thinking of using the picture in Carlie's wallet—the one of the three of us," Daddy said. "I was going to ask you first, of course."

"So, if you don't mind, I'm going to ask you a few questions," Elisabeth said. "Do you mind if I tape you?"

I shrugged. "Okay I guess."

"All right then, I'll start with this question, Florine," Elisabeth said. In the gentlest voice possible she said, "What did you think, at first, when Carlie didn't come back?"

"A lot of things," I said. "I thought maybe she'd decided to take a trip. Then I thought she ran off. Then I thought worse things."

Elisabeth nodded, and said, "How has your life changed, Florine, without her here?"

To my surprise and embarrassment, sudden tears ran down my cheeks. Daddy fished a handkerchief from his pocket and handed it to me. As I caught his eye, I saw the fear in his face and I knew he was thinking about the part Stella had played. I could give him up now. I could tell this reporter about the slut who had marched in and kidnapped my father. I wiped my eyes and blew my nose.

"If it hurts too much, you don't have to answer," Elisabeth said. "But I think readers might like to know how it feels to lose someone and not know what happened to them. They would be sympathetic to you, I'm sure, Florine."

"It isn't that," I said. "It's just that it's none of their business."

"How do you mean?" Elisabeth asked.

"They might read the paper and feel bad, but then they go do what they do. We got to live this." I looked at Daddy. He was looking down at his big, scarred, salt-dried hands, folded on the table. The knuckles were white.

"It's changed everything," I said.

The article on Carlie came out in early November. A photographer took a picture of Daddy and me standing by the harbor, and they used the picture of the three of us. For two weeks in school, I was once again the center of attention, only this time it was pity instead of rumor that made me stand out. I didn't want people feeling sorry for me.

The police got tips from people who swore they'd seen Carlie as far away as San Francisco. Daddy got a marriage proposal in the mail, which fried Stella's ass. But nothing panned out. When Thanksgiving came, the crowd turned to turkey and I gave thanks when it quieted down.

22

It was good that Grand loved me, because in the spring of 1965 I turned fourteen, and anyone else would have dropped me off the wharf with a one-hundred-pound bag of cement chained to my legs.

I was so ugly Stella Drowns didn't dare come to Grand's house when I was around. I didn't realize how brave Daddy was at the time. Maybe years spent rolling on a bitchy ocean had set him up to weather my storms and silences.

I stayed in my room and cried. I talked back to Grand. Once. I yelled at my body in the bathroom mirror. A full crop of light fuzz had finally settled in between my legs, but I was still flat and my feet were big and my period was nowhere in sight.

"You don't even want your period, and you've got it," I grumbled at Dottie one Sunday about two weeks before my birthday. We were walking toward the ledges in the State Park.

"You're lucky," Dottie said. "It's a pain."

Dottie was almost as tall as me, now, but much bigger through her hips. She whistled a little bit as we reached the edge of the rocks and plunked herself down on Mr. Barrington's bench. "Madeline wants me to go on a diet," she said. "I hate to break the news to her, but I think I'm just big."

"Least you don't look like a fence post with straw stuck on the top."

I sat down beside her and we looked out over the water. "Remember when you found me?" I said.

"Christ, you was a goner," Dottie said. "You was blue, you was that friggin' cold."

"I felt warm," I said. "I felt good."

"You couldn't see you from where you sat," Dottie said. "You looked like hell."

"Thanks for finding me that day," I said.

"'Course. I got to get back," Dottie said. "Barb Raymond's bowling on TV this afternoon."

When I got back to Grand's house, I found four large boxes, one stacked on the other, in the hall. I undid the flaps of the top box and found it filled with Carlie's clothes.

"How'd these get here?" I asked Grand.

"Stella brought them by," Grand said.

"Why did she do that? She has no business doing that."

Grand said, "Florine, like it or not, she's been living there for a while now. She needs the room. She asked me if you might want your mother's clothes to keep here with you. She said she would never toss them out. You want some fresh apple pie?"

"Shove the damn pie," I said, and ran upstairs to my room. I studied the pictures of Carlie I'd hung on the wall opposite the bed. I said to her, "I'll bet they said, 'Well, you know Florine's going to have a fit but she'll settle down. It'll be hard for her but she'll get over it.' But I won't. I'll never get over it." No matter how much Grand insisted, I couldn't believe that Stella wouldn't throw out the rest of Carlie's things. In fact, I could see her cackling like a witch as she burned them in a pile. I had to go and rescue whatever might be left. As the dark fell down and night came on, I lay on my bed and hatched out a plan to do that.

On Monday, I dressed, ate my breakfast, and grabbed my school books about a half hour earlier than I usually did.

"Why you headed up to the stop so early?" Grand asked, handing me a bag for lunch.

"I feel like getting some fresh air," I said.

"I packed some apple pie," Grand said.

"Bye," I said, and took off for the bus stop. But I veered off and snuck into a part of the woods. There were no paths, just spiky branches, stubborn prickle bushes, dead leaves, and brambles. I clutched my books to me and fought my way through it all, scratching my arms and catching my clothes. By the time I had made my way in a hard-fought straight line to The Cheeks in back of Daddy's house, I'd ripped my skirt and run my nylons. I crouched behind a decent-sized set of pines and watched Dottie and Bud walk to the stop, heads close, gabbing about something or someone. Probably about what a joke I am, I thought. After they'd gone by, I took a seat on a rock pile in the middle of the pines, opened my lunch bag, and took out the slice of apple pie. I bit through the top and bottom of Grand's fine flaky pie crust into tender, sweet and spicy apple slices, and waited.

Daddy had long since gone out on the water for the day. I could see the dinghies, left back while the big boats roamed the ocean, take the tide against their bows.

Carlie loved our dinghy. We'd named her *Ruthie*, for no particular reason. We'd gone out in her often, hugging the shoreline up and down the harbor. We rowed like a double person, me on one oar, Carlie on the other, drinking in the salt and the sun. We had a special place we'd named Pirates Cove. We would pull ourselves into the cove, slip *Ruthie*'s line over a pointed rock, scramble onto the shore, and make our way up onto the stubby cliffs above it. Then, Carlie would shout, "One, two, three!" And we would jump off the cliffs, plunging feet first into the deep green, nipple-freezing water below.

"One, two, three," I whispered. "One, two, three." I repeated this until Stella finally came out of the house to go to work at Ray's store. She was dressed in a pair of Carlie's jeans. I could tell because a small blotch of white paint sat up near the right hip. I'd accidently done that during a buoy-painting session, and it had never faded. The jeans were big on Stella's skinny hips, and short. "Take those off, bitch," I hissed at her from my hiding place.

When she disappeared up the road, I set down my books and my lunch and slipped around to the back of the house, hoping that the door to Daddy's workshop was open. I didn't want to go around to the front, where Madeline or Ida, or even Grand, might have been able to see me. I was in luck. I pushed on the door and it opened. I paused to drink in the smell of fresh cut wood from Daddy's shop. It reminded me of another piece of who I had been not so long ago. A new wooden door had replaced the tarp that had separated the living room from the shop. I opened the door to look inside the workshop. I could see it was spotless. Stella's influence, no doubt.

I walked into the living room, closing the shop door behind me. I hadn't been inside the house since February and, during that time, Stella had changed things around. Two new chairs and a sofa, all a soft green, faced a new coffee table that I guess Daddy must have built. Women's magazines and fishermen's journals were spread just so on top of it. I was happy to see that Daddy's old chair still faced the corner where the television squatted.

The kitchen looked pretty much the same, except that I could almost see myself in the floor, it was that clean. I opened the door to my room. I'd hauled most of my things over to Grand's. What remained of my books and toys sat where they'd always been.

But Stella had claimed Carlie's bedroom, replacing the bright yellow walls with a dark-piney-green. The green bedspread and the white curtains were new. On the wall in back of the bed were pictures of Stella and Daddy in some restaurant, holding hands and grinning across the table at whoever had taken their picture. Another picture showed them in Ray's at the deli counter, with Stella puckered up, leaning over the counter to kiss Daddy. A third picture showed Stella in a black bathing suit, draped over the back of the boat, her thin white legs dangling over the words *Carlie Flo*.

The way her legs half hid our names set me off, and made me forget that I'd been on a rescue mission. Rage, in the form of blood, pounded in my ears. Not asking my brain's permission, my hand reached out and took the photograph of Stella on the boat from the wall. I threw it on the floor and stepped on the glass, breaking it. I did the same to the other two pictures. I took the bedding off the bed, opened the bedroom window, and threw it into the backyard. I went into the closet and took Stella's clothes from the hangers and threw them on the floor. I took her clothes out of Carlie's dresser and dumped them on the other clothes. Then I walked out through the back door and slammed it shut before I hurried up over The Cheeks and into the woods.

"Teach her," I said out loud to the trees.

I gathered up my books and my lunch bag and walked through the path in the woods to the State Park until I reached the bench by the rocks. I sat down and looked at the cloth-strapped Timex watch Grand had given to me for Christmas. It was nine o'clock. School let out at 2:30 P.M.

"More time to spend here," I said to myself.

"Aren't you supposed to be in school?" a stern male voice said in back of me.

I turned around and saw a thin-faced ranger wearing thick wire-rimmed glasses. His oversized brown eyes looked as if they were used to peering into thickets and up into trees. His name patch read DICKIE. He wasn't smiling. "You're supposed to be in school, if I'm not mistaken. You're dressed for school and your books are with you. You wouldn't be skipping, now would you?"

My stomach hurt and I wondered if Grand had mistakenly put some bad apples into her pie. I decided to tell the truth. "Yes," I said. "I'm supposed to be in school. I skipped because it's a nice day. I've never done it before. I'll never do it again."

Dickie squinted hard at me. "It's against the law."

"Okay," I said. "I'll go home now and turn myself in."

"You *should* be going home," Dickie said. "But I imagine you'll spend the day here, then head home when the bus is due."

"No," I lied. "I'll go home."

"Be sure you do," Dickie said. "Don't let me catch you here on a school day again."

He walked down the trail, his thick boots kissing the hard-packed ground. I headed back up the path, an occasional cramp joining the flutter of discomfort that appeared to be settling in for a long stay.

"I can't go home now," I said. I took the side path that would lead me to the summer cottages, planning to either hang around the edge of the woods, or maybe sit on the Barringtons' porch, eat lunch, and look at my books until it was time to go home.

But when I reached the Barringtons' property, Louisa was unloading linens from a wood-sided station wagon. I watched her for a while. I loved the way her skin drank up the sun like a rich dark brew, instead of tossing the light back, like my pale skin did. As she moved between the car and the back kitchen door, she sang a hymn I'd heard that I knew Grand would have known. Louisa, it appeared, was friends with Jesus, too.

I wandered back into the woods. Because it was spring, the undergrowth was sparse, and that's how I discovered a thin path leading to the left, about halfway back from the cottage. I followed it through scrubby brush until, unexpectedly, I reached a tiny clearing in the dead center of a circle of old, thick pines.

In the middle of the clearing, three large, reddish brown rocks flecked with mica provided a good sit for a picnic lunch. I eased myself down onto the sun-warmed rocks and listened to the wind and the birds sing. I looked at my watch again. It was ten thirty.

"What have you done, Florine?" a voice said. I stood up and looked around, but I only saw three small birds flitting through the clearing. A crow called from somewhere in back of me.

"I did it for Carlie," I said out loud.

"You did it for you. Carlie was an excuse," the voice said.

"I did it for us," I said. But what had seemed to make perfect sense this morning suddenly seemed wacky. My stomach cramped up again.

A baby green grass snake wove across the tip of the warm rocks, near my toes. It paused before it slithered off, becoming a slight shiver in the soft moss.

"I got to go back," I said out loud. "I got to clean up before anyone finds out what I did." I jumped up and beat it to the State Park trail. Along the way, I met Dickie again. I dodged him, shouting, "I'm going, I'm going." I bolted over The Cheeks and down to Daddy's backyard. I burst in through the back door and into the living room, then the kitchen, where I stopped cold. Stella was tossing a dustpan filled with shards of glass into the garbage can. The scar on her face stood out like a whip that I had the feeling could be pulled off and used at will. Her storm-lashed eyes could have capsized me. She walked to the kitchen door and she opened it. "Get out," she hissed through gritted teeth.

The door slammed behind me so hard that the house bounced. I mumbled something to Grand about being sick and getting a ride home from a janitor and I went up to my room for the rest of the day. That night, Daddy came by and came upstairs to say hello. He put his big hand on my forehead. "Grand says you're sick," he said.

"It's my stomach," I said. He doesn't know, I thought. She didn't tell him.

She never told him. But she wouldn't talk to me for a while. We did a clumsy dance whenever we were thrown together, but somehow we avoided each other. If I had to go to Ray's for something, and she was at the register, I set my stuff down, she rang it up, bagged it, put it on the counter, and then turned her back on me, unless there was someone behind me. Then, they got all of her attention.

Three days after I had vandalized the bedroom, my long-awaited period finally started.

I helped Grand more and more that summer. She was eighty now, and she was having trouble bending over. She couldn't stand for long periods of time. Her legs hurt her. She never complained, but watching her limp across the kitchen floor, or watching her struggle up from a chair or the sofa, I knew. It was hard to see her in pain. She was dizzy sometimes, too. One Sunday, after church, she suddenly clutched my arm as we walked up the aisle toward the front door after service. It surprised me so that I gave her a look.

"Got to get my bearings, Florine," she whispered to me as if she didn't want anyone else to know. But watchful Ida must have seen her take my arm, because suddenly she was on Grand's other side. "You okay?" she asked her, taking her other arm.

"Fine," Grand said. "I'm fine." She freed herself and walked straight as a pin up to Pastor Billy to talk to him about the sermon.

I planted her precious petunias and pansies and kept the garden free of weeds. She supervised me in the vegetable garden, in the kitchen, and everywhere else. Sometimes, I snapped at her when she hovered, but I didn't want to do that. What I wanted was for her to be able to be who she had been just a few short seasons ago. She was my white rock, my strength, and I needed her to always be there.

One afternoon, after she'd caught my struggle to be kind to her, she said to me, "I never thought that getting old would happen to me, but that was vainglorious of me, I guess. I'm as young in my head as I ever was, that's the funny thing. It's as big a surprise to me that things aren't working like they used to as it is to you."

"Sorry," I said. I looked up at her. I was holding a soil-covered spade in my hand. The spade was close enough to my nose so that I could smell the fresh dirt, and I got a whiff of life and death in one sniff.

"Well," Grand said, "I'll just trust that Jesus knows what he's doing as far as my welfare's concerned. He had it worse on the cross."

I never argued when Grand brought up Jesus. I had my own reasons for mistrusting his judgment, but I didn't want to throw that in Grand's face. I don't know if he had anything to do with it, but I did become more patient, and the garden yielded up a fine crop of tomatoes, carrots, cucumbers, and zucchini that summer and fall.

23

"**I** love Elvis," I said, getting hot under the collar. "Elvis is the King."

"I didn't say he was bad," Susan said. "I just said the Beatles were better."

"Gin," I said, and Susan, Bud, Dottie, Glen, and a girl I didn't bother to name because soon she would be a piece of Glen's dating history groaned and counted up their points.

It was New Year's Eve, 1966. We were at Bud's house. Sam and Ida had gone up to the Buttses' house and let Bud have us all down for New Year's Eve. Grand was already in bed, it being nine thirty or so.

"You can't top 'Love Me Tender,'" I said. "It's the most beautiful song ever sung. Elvis didn't have to grow his hair long to get noticed. Elvis is a natural. The Beatles are fake."

"'Yesterday' is the best song of all time," Susan argued.

I didn't want to say that I hadn't heard it, that I refused to listen to the Beatles. It was hard to find Elvis on the radio now, but I kept turning stations looking for him, or settling for Roy Orbison, Del Shannon, or Dion, Carlie's music. "The Wanderer," one of my favorite songs, was playing on Bud's record player. I appreciated that he had put the song on for me. *I'm the type of guy that likes to roam around . . . ,*" I hummed.

Bud loved Elvis and the others, too, as much as I did. He'd been getting used to the Beatles, though, for Susan's sake. And he liked

Susan, it was plain to see. Whenever I saw them at school, they were hand-in-hand, or he draped his long arm over her small shoulders. I was surprised he'd invited Glen, Dottie, and me to his house at all. I would have thought he wanted Susan all to himself.

"No way Ida's going to let him do that," Dottie overheard Madeline telling Stella at the store. "She's not leaving them alone. That's flirting with disaster, for sure."

So I took it we were chaperones for Bud and Susan, which set wrong with me. But I didn't want to sit out the New Year watching television while Grand snoozed upstairs.

Susan was wearing a red minidress with black tights and shoes. Her hair hung over her shoulders like beautifully cast tinsel, except when she brushed it back and little pieces fell back over her shoulders. She was good at gin, too; almost or as good as I was. I wasn't having much fun. She got up and took "The Wanderer" off the record player.

"Hey," Dottie said, "leave that on—that song makes me feel lucky."

"I think Florine was listening to that," Bud said to Susan, "and so was I."

"I know," she said. "But listen to the words to this song, Florine," she pleaded. She looked at me as if she would die if I didn't hear it, so I shrugged. She put a 45 onto the record player and lowered the needle. When the needle hit the vinyl, little pops and scratches marred the beginning guitar. *"Yesterday,"* one of the Beatles sang, *"all my troubles seemed so far away . . ."*

"Let's play another hand," I said. "Susan, you in?"

"Oh, Florine," she said. "I wish you'd give it a chance. I think you'd really like it."

She sat down, but then she popped up again and took the record off. She handed it to me. "Here," she said, "take this home and give it a listen. Just a listen." She walked back over to the record player and put "The Wanderer" back on.

"Gin," I said, five minutes later.

But as the night wore on, I got agitated. When Bud kissed Susan's ear, I felt his lips as surely as if he'd kissed my ear. I watched Glen run his large hand up his girl-of-the-minute's leg. I lost concentration as I imagined Bud's hand moving up my leg and reaching the place in the middle. Susan won the whole game.

It was ten o'clock when we pushed back from the table and went into Ida's spotless living room. Susan and Bud sat down on a tan couch together, while Glen and his girl took up Sam's large chair. Glen's girl cuddled into his neck. Dottie and I sat down across from them in two other chairs.

"Well, what do you want to do now?" Dottie asked.

Bud said, "I don't know. We could watch some television, I guess."

"I'm going home," I said. "I can watch television there. Coming with me, Dottie?"

Dottie shrugged. We got up, humped into our winter coats, and headed for the door.

"Don't forget to listen to 'Yesterday,' Florine. I think you'll love it," Susan called.

"Want to come in?" Dottie asked when we reached her house.

"No," I said. Stella and Daddy were inside.

"You letting me go in there with all them grown-ups?" Dottie asked me.

"You can come and stay overnight with me," I said.

"Nah. Guess not. Wish me luck with the old folks."

When I walked into Grand's house, I was surprised to find the television on. But Grand wasn't watching it. She was sitting on the porch, rocking, looking out over the dark water. I joined her in my rocker.

"Thought you'd be in bed," I said.

"Couldn't sleep," she said. Her flowered housecoat sat over a long, flannel nightgown. She had pulled on her ugly pink slippers and she rocked up, then back, showing brief flashes of her thick ankles.

Grand said, "Franklin and I used to go dancing up at the Rod and Reel Club every New Year's Eve. He was a wonderful dancer. Quiet, but he talked loud with the way he moved. All the other wives were jealous of me. He took each one of them for a spin, but he came back to me for the last dance."

"What else about him, Grand?" I asked. She didn't talk about Franklin, much.

"The flower garden on the side?" she said. "Franklin planted it for me when we was first married. He dug up all of them side gardens for me and we picked out the flowers we wanted in them. He had to haul in so much dirt. Used to have Daniel Morse, up the road, bring down a couple loads of chicken shit. We dug up seaweed and mixed it all in with the dirt and got them gardens planted. On summer nights when the moon was full he'd wake me up in the night and bring me out to the garden to dance."

I tried to picture a much younger Grand with Franklin, but I had trouble getting past the way she looked now, with her old lady hair in wisps around her head, holding on to a tall, thin old man who thought it was romantic to dance in a full-moon garden. It wasn't such a horrible picture. I liked the thought of growing old with someone, being woken up to go into a garden he'd made for me and taking a turn around the peonies and roses.

"I miss him so, Florine. I never got to grow old with him. I would have liked to grow old with him," she said, soft as the new snow outside. We rocked for another minute or two, then she said, "Well, I had him for some good times, anyway." We went upstairs and said "Happy New Year" to each other at the doors to our rooms.

I couldn't sleep. I thought about old people loving one another, summer gardens, my mother dancing on my father's shoes, and Susan cuddled next to Bud on the couch. When midnight came, I heard a muffled "Happy New Year!" from the Butts house. A car drove down the hill, and I heard Susan and Glen's girl call, "Goodbye." Glen walked up the hill by Grand's house and hummed "The Wanderer." When the sound of his footsteps faded out, I got up and walked down to the kitchen and looked out the window over the night. All of the lights in the other houses were off. I looked out for a little while, and thought about Susan and Bud.

Then I remembered Susan's record. I figured I might as well listen to it, so I could tell her how much I hated it and get her off my back. I went back to my room and popped "Yesterday" onto my old record player with its worn-out needle. I kept the sound low.

"*Yesterday,*" the song began. By the time the second verse started, I had slipped off of my bed and onto the floor to sit in a puddle of sadness. After four times through the song, the needle got stuck in one place, and I kept letting it skip.

Why she had to go . . . skip. *Why she had to go* . . . skip.

I don't know.

24

At ten o'clock on Monday, February 24, 1966, the phone at Grand's house rang. I was home on winter vacation from school. I was close to the hanging phone on the kitchen wall, so I picked it up.

"Hello," I said.

"This is Parker Clemmons, Florine," he said.

My heart stopped. "Have you found her?"

Parker said, "Florine, honey, we haven't found her. But I need to talk to Leeman. I couldn't reach him or Stella at home, so I thought I'd try Grand's house."

"You can tell me what you need to tell him," I said. "He's uptown, but I'll let him know when he comes home."

Parker paused. "Well, thank you. But I need him to call me."

I hung up. "Who was that, Florine?" Grand asked, walking into the kitchen. "Parker," I said, then I heard a truck and saw Daddy turn into his driveway. I was out the door, down the driveway, and beside him before he could turn off the truck. "Parker said for you to call him," I said. "He just called over to Grand's looking for you."

Daddy handed me a paper sack as he rushed into the house. It was heavy, filled with nails. The points pricked my palms and fingers through the bag, and I dropped it. Nails scattered along the walk.

"Damn," I said, but I left them there as I hurried into the house after Daddy.

Daddy's hands shook as he dialed Parker's number. When Parker answered, Daddy said, "Florine said you called. Yes. *(Long pause.)* What? Where'd they find it? Why there? Well, should I go up there or what? Okay. Okay, I'll wait for a call. Okay. Thanks. Thanks." Daddy hung up the phone, looking confused.

"What'd he say?" I said.

"They found Carlie's purse. That pink one? The one with the shiny gold buckle?"

Like it was yesterday, I remembered her getting into Patty's car that summer day so long ago with it slung over her shoulder.

"In Crow's Nest Harbor?" I asked. "The police up there found it?"

Daddy shook his head. "No," he said. "Blueberry Harbor. In some woods off an old road. A guy walking a dog. Dog dug it up through the snow. Guy turned it in. Had everything in it, Florine. Her license, her wallet. Money. Everything." As he said the words, I saw his face change as he realized what that meant. Carlie's money. Carlie's identification. If she was alive, she had nothing. It hit me, too.

Blueberry Harbor was almost an hour south of Crow's Nest Harbor, back our way.

"When you go, I want to go with you," I said, blood pounding in my ears.

"I don't know as that would be such a good idea," Daddy said.

"I'm going with you," I said. I wouldn't take no for an answer, and Daddy didn't try too hard to talk me out of it. I went outside to pick up the scattered nails and wrap my mind around the fact that my beloved Carlie, my sweet, sassy mother, had walked through the horizon and was now on the other side of it and more than likely would never return. I clenched a fistful of nails to feel that pain of their points before I put them into the bag with the others. Then I took them inside and we waited for Parker to show up.

Parker drove us up to Blueberry Harbor later that afternoon. We walked into the tiny police station and were shown into a Detective Pratt's office. Detective Pratt appeared to be about Daddy's age. The skin around his mouth was loose. He had large pores in his nose and black hairs peeked out of his nostrils. Time and trouble had plowed a deep line on his forehead between his watery brown eyes.

He shook Parker's and Daddy's hands and nodded to me. "Young lady," he said, and we all sat down at a small round table. He reached behind him and brought back a clear bag that contained Carlie's pocketbook. The "contents," as Detective Pratt called them, were in another bag. He opened the bag and put the pocketbook on the table in front of us. Then he put "the contents" beside it. Carlie's red wallet and a red change purse. Her small, light-blue hairbrush. Clove gum and a small white handkerchief with a yellow *C* stitched into one corner of it. A dark compact with a mirror inside of it. A book of matches that read LOBSTER SHACK on the lid. A bright pink lipstick.

I reached for her wallet. "Florine," Daddy said.

I looked at Detective Pratt. He nodded and I took Carlie's wallet and opened it. On the left side, a compartment for change that Carlie never used because it was too small. On the right side, a clear plastic window showed a picture of three people. The photograph was water stained, but I could still see us. Madeline Butts had taken our picture down by the wharf the summer I'd been ten. Daddy knelt on one knee and Carlie sat on his thigh. She held me in front of her, her arms around me. Daddy had his arms around both of us. Daddy said, "That's my wife."

We followed Detective Pratt's car to where the purse had been found. He led the way down a tramped-down slushy path into a patch of woods above a snow-covered pond.

"This is where the dog dug it up," he said. Clumps of dirt from the dog's claws had sprayed backwards, outside a small circle surrounded by yellow tape. That dirt and the empty shallow hole where the purse had lain among some crushed leaves were not half as interesting to me as the frozen pond, and one by one, everyone turned to look at it.

"She's not down there," I said, but my voice wobbled.

Daddy shouted, "Jesus!" and clutched his head. He walked over to a birch tree and kicked it, hard. "Why the hell does my daughter have to worry about that?" he yelled into the woods. He gathered himself together and turned back to us. I looked at the birch tree and saw the bare wood where his foot had connected with it.

"It's all right, Daddy," I said, not knowing what else to say.

"No, by Christ, it's not," he said, shaking his head. "It's all wrong."

"Tomorrow we'll conduct a search," Detective Pratt said.

The wind that came up from the pond was soft for a February day. A blue jay flew to a branch overhead. It cocked its head and looked us over with its black sharp eyes. "THIEF!" it cried, then flew off, its bright feathers dipping over the ice on the pond.

Going home in Parker's car, Daddy asked him, "What now?"

"Now, we work on why the hell the pocketbook was where it was and how it may have gotten there," Parker said. "And we wait for them to search the pond."

"She's not there," I said again. I don't know how I knew, but I did. It was just one of the places where Carlie wasn't, and never would be, again, at least in this world.

I was right. They found nothing in the pond. But the odd clue riled Daddy and me up in new ways. What had happened? Why was it there? If Carlie was not among the living, where was she? My grief took a right turn as I imagined where she might be, and how alone she was through whatever had happened. I tried to bat away the worst-case scenarios, but there were so many of them that I found it easier to let one come, ride it out, then wait for the next one. After a while, my imagination ran out of options, and I spun reruns of what might have happened until I was spun out.

25

Maybe it was the full moon on that early March night, or maybe we all read each other's minds at the same time, but Bud, Dottie, Glen, and I ended up going for a moonlit walk. The night before, a wind storm with some snow, but mostly noise, had blown in from the ocean and up the harbor, making the houses on The Point shiver and shake. I don't know how everyone else felt, but I curled up like a periwinkle, worried that Grand and I would be picked up, house and all, and hurled into the harbor without so much as an apology. So maybe the relief we felt when the next night gave us a moon bright enough to see the pimples on each other's faces made us want to band together and just take a hike. I guess I might have started it, or maybe Bud. I was sitting on the porch at about nine o'clock that night, rocking away and soaking in the moon rays, when I saw him come out of his house and start to walk up the hill. It seemed a perfect time to join him, so I threw on my coat, told Grand that I was taking a walk with Bud, went outside, and waited until he walked up to me.

"Mind if I come along?" I said.

"Company would be good. Ain't the moon something?"

We heard a door slam and looked over to see Dottie coming up from her house to us. "What's going on?" she asked.

"We're taking a walk," Bud said.

"Where we going?" Dottie asked.

"Let's see if Glen's around," Bud said, so we trudged up to Ray's and convinced Glen to leave the television behind him. Then the four of us, bundled up and moon mad, stood in the middle of the road, huffing our breath out into the cold air.

"Well, you got me out here," Glen said. "What now?"

"Let's go into the State Park," I said. "Not too much snow. I'll bet it's pretty in the moonlight."

We walked through Daddy's yard to The Cheeks, which were only a little icy, scrambled up over them, and headed into the woods, single file. I thought about that summer night only a few short years before when we'd gone on a mission.

"Remember?" Glen said, and we did. We laughed about it as we walked along, although I got quiet thinking about Carlie, for not realizing back then that she wouldn't be around much longer after that adventure. Would missing her ever go away? I didn't see how. It was different now, like a deep splinter grown over by skin. I could see it but I couldn't get to it, yet if I pressed it, my heart broke every time.

Dottie led the way that night. She plowed along, snow boots and thick legs making short work of what snow there was. I followed her, then Bud, then Glen behind him. A couple of times, I could have sworn that Bud touched my shoulder, then my back, but this was a night that anything was bound to happen. We all felt it.

We walked to the cliffs and looked out over the grumbling, tired ocean, so recently tossed and thrown by the wind. "I wonder if we'll always come back to this spot," I said.

Bud cleared his throat. "Don't know if I will," he said. "But if you do, be sure and wear your coat." Dottie and Glen laughed, and I punched him, and we started back up the path.

"Home?" Dottie asked when we got to the crossroads in the woods. The path leading to Barrington's was to the right.

"Let's go that way," Bud said, and pointed into the woods. So we walked to the summer houses, the path lit this time by the light of the full moon instead of a small flashlight. As we came out of the woods, the eye of the moon stared us down, causing us to blink, then take it in full on.

I wondered at the big dark house, left behind by summer to stand against the loneliness of the winter. "Hard to believe summer's ever going to come," I said.

Glen pointed past the house, to the lawn. "Look," he said. A big pine had snapped, probably in last night's storm, and it now covered half the lawn. We headed that way, drawn to its downed splendor. Glen and Bud climbed up onto its trunk and began to walk along, grabbing and weaving around branches. I breathed in the scent of freshly fallen pine, took some of the needles, and crushed them in my hand.

I turned to let Dottie take a whiff, but there she stood, hypnotized by the moon. The moon sapped the color from her face, leaving her all eyes, nostrils, and mouth. Her eyes held the moon, or the moon held her eyes. It was hard to tell. "Can't remember when I've seen anything like this," she said. "Looks like heaven's bowling ball."

Bud jumped from the tree and headed down the lawn to the private beach and we followed him. When we reached the edge of the lawn, we all gasped at the same time, because the edge of the lawn was what was left of the beach. The ocean had taken a bite out of the earth and chewed up and swallowed the beach, whole. Wave and wind had won this round. In its place, the ocean had hurled snarls of lobster traps and gear onto slick rocks.

"Think we should call someone?" I said. "Maybe they don't know."

"They'll know when they show up here," Glen said.

"They'll have to rebuild the beach," said Bud. His eyes glittered and threw back the moon at itself. "Well, the bastards can afford it." He turned away and walked up the hill, past the fallen pine. His hand touched the needles. I did, after him. "Sorry," I whispered to the tree.

We walked into the woods, away from the mess, back toward home. As we passed my secret path, the place where I went to talk to Carlie, I stopped suddenly, and Bud put his hands on both sides of my waist to keep himself from falling. "What?" he said. Glen stopped, and then Dottie. I couldn't say anything for a few seconds, because Bud's hands on my waist, even over my thick coat, felt like fire.

"Want to see something?" I asked them. I led the way down the narrow path, to my clearing in the woods. Under the moon, the circle was an ivory carpet, surrounded by black-walled trees.

"What's this place?" Dottie said.

"I came here one day," I said. I didn't add, ". . . after I trashed Stella's bedroom." I thought it might be a good idea to leave that alone.

"Good place to come," Bud said. And then a bloodcurdling scream split the night into a million pieces and we stood frozen in time and space, the moon looking down on our smallness and terror with a smirk on its face. Glen grabbed Dottie and she grabbed him back. "Jesus Christ," she shouted, her voice muffled by Glen's winter coat. Bud and I had turned toward the sound and I had my back to him. Suddenly his arms were around me and he breathed into my ear, "What the hell . . ." I put my hands onto his arms as we all withstood another godless shriek, and then Bud began to laugh and he let me go.

"What is that?" I said, missing his touch even as I wanted to know about the noise.

"Listen," he said, and the scream came again. "It's a screech owl," he said. "Gotta be. What else could it be?" And he hurled his own shriek toward the woods. Glen let go of Dottie, who let go of him first.

The woods gave nothing back for a few seconds, and then the screech came again, and we all screamed and shouted back at the sound. Then, on quiet wings, a disgusted white-feathered ghost flew out of the darkness of the trees, crossed over our heads, and headed for where it wouldn't have to listen to bad imitations of its nature-given voice.

The owl, the moon, Bud's closeness, and the night had shaken me

up, and I wobbled a little bit as we trekked down the path and found
ourselves at the crossroads of The Point again. "See ya," Glen said. We
stopped at Grand's house. "Night," Dottie said, and started down the
road. Bud followed her, but before he got too far, he turned to see me
watching him. He stopped, gave me a half wave and a smile, then trotted after Dottie.

26

By the time I turned fifteen in May, my fingers had grown into the beautiful emerald ring that Carlie and Daddy had gotten me for my thirteenth birthday. I took it off the gold chain and slipped it onto my right ring finger. During boring classes, I shone it so that a shaft of green fell on my classroom desks, warming their scarred metal tops. My fingers grew perfect half-moon nails, and I painted them pink or red. The colors reminded me of that day at Mulgully Beach, when Carlie's and Patty's pearly nails had glistened against their summer hands.

One day after school at Grand's house, Susan said to me, "You have the most beautiful hands." These days, she often rode down on the bus with us to spend the afternoon with Bud. Sometimes, she joined Dottie and me at Grand's house first for a cup of cocoa and snacks. We'd sit around the kitchen table and shoot the breeze until she wandered down to Bud's house. I liked her in spite of myself. Not liking her would have been like hating Bambi.

Susan held her own hands up against mine. I could have bent the first joints of my fingers over the tops of hers, they were so small.

"I'll never be a model." Susan sighed. "Too short."

Dottie, who had been picking the chocolate chips out of one of Grand's homemade cookies and putting them in a pile to eat last, said,

"Why would someone want to look like a bony-ass broomstick? Can you imagine not being able to eat cookies?"

"You could be a model, Florine," Susan said. "You're tall. I can see you on some runway somewhere."

"Maybe I'll run off to Portland and give it a shot," I said.

"Why think small? Try New York or California," Susan said.

"Shoot!" Dottie said, slapping her hand on the table. Susan and I both jumped.

"What?" I said. I took a cookie, watching the way my slender fingers—the fingers of a future model—clutched it as I brought it toward my mouth.

Dottie said, "I need two people tomorrow for bowling. You up for it?"

The last thing I wanted to do was stick my beautiful fingers into the hard, cold, dirty holes of a bowling ball. "What if I break a nail?" I said.

"What, now you're some friggin' pinkie girl?" Dottie said.

"No," I said. "But it takes awhile to grow these things just right."

Dottie shook her head. "I never thought I'd see the day," she said.

Dottie's bowling team, the Gladibowlas, was in first place in their league. Susan, who substituted sometimes, said it was because of Dottie's high scores.

"Come on, it'd be fun," Dottie said. "We could kick some butt."

"I don't know," I said. The thought of taking the bus to the bowling lanes along with thirty-two other girls gave me the hives.

"Don't be a poop, Florine," Susan said. "Come on. Live a little."

"I suppose you won't leave me alone until I go," I said.

"Probably not," Dottie said. She reached for another cookie.

"That's four," Susan said.

Dottie arched a perfect brown eyebrow. "Stop counting my food," she said. "I got to keep up my strength. I'm a growing girl."

On the bus ride to Bowla Rolla, the three of us sat in the very back seat of the bus. Dottie was as excited as I'd ever seen her.

"I'm going to knock 'em all down," Dottie said. "I'm going to get a perfect score."

"I'm going to be right behind you," Susan said.

"You're going to wipe the floor with me," I said.

"Stop thinking that way. You got to think you can beat everyone," Dottie said. "That way, you start thinking up here"—she raised her hand and touched the roof of the bus—"instead of settling for something down here." She touched the floor of the bus. She sat back and birthed a huge, pink bubble full of veins from the three pieces of bubble gum she had crammed into her mouth. The bubble stretched until the light outside the bus windows shone through it.

"Oh my god," Susan squeaked. Dottie's eyes went wide and I held my breath. When it finally popped, it covered Dottie from her hairline to the top half of her blouse. When we reached Bowla Rolla, we were still picking pieces of it out of her hair. In spite of her gum handicap, Dottie was the first one off the bus.

By the time Susan and I caught up, she was at the counter, trying on her used shoes.

"We have to wear other people's shoes?" I asked.

"You going to take this serious?" Dottie said. "I don't want to look like an asshole."

"That happened before you got up this morning," I said. She ignored me and I gave my shoe size to the person behind the counter. She passed them over to me as if handling stinky used shoes was second nature to her. I didn't know whether to admire her or feel sorry for her. Susan and I walked down to our lane behind Dottie and Holly, her other teammate. We put the shoes on in our little seating area. I double-knotted mine, like Carlie had taught me. "Two knots is stronger than one," she'd said.

Holly and Dottie sat together a little apart from Susan and me, talking over their plan for the game. They looked over at us from time to time, then went back to talking.

"What do you suppose they're saying?" Susan whispered.

"Holly's asking Dottie how she got stuck with the loser with the bushy hair. She's wondering if it wouldn't be just as good to tell me to go back to the bus now."

"They need four to a team," Susan said. "I can do this. You can do this, too."

I watched a girl walk up to a line and throw the bowling ball down the lane. Some pins fell. "Doesn't look so hard," I said.

"Let's get our balls," Dottie said.

When we reached the rack, I picked out a pretty red marbled ball. It was much heavier than I thought, and I dropped it about six inches from Holly's foot.

"Watch it, for chrissake," Holly said.

"Here," Dottie said to me, handing me a scarred black ball. "This is a ten-pounder. You can handle this."

I cradled it to my chest to see how it felt, stuck my fingers in the holes, and hefted it. "I can do this," I said.

"Atta way," Dottie said.

It went downhill after that. My first ball went crooked and headed for the gutter like it was the shortest way home. I couldn't look Dottie in the eye. After one throw, I said to Susan, "I think my ball is afraid to hit the pins."

"Maybe if you broke a couple of nails, you'd do better," she suggested. She got a strike the first game, although she was all over the place as far as what she knocked down. Sometimes three pins fell, then eight the next time, then one. Holly kept a steady score, with eights, nines, and an occasional spare.

Dottie was on fire.

Whenever her turn came up, she stood back to us, her thick legs—the calves shaped almost like bowling pins themselves—ready to go. She went still for a few seconds, like she was praying to some bowling god. She quick-stepped from foot to foot, glided forward, bent down on one knee, and let her ball fly. Straight it went, right to the heart of the lane. Pins scattered. She stayed in her crouch until she knew the verdict, then she stood up, turned around, and walked back to us, grinning like a sassy gull. She sat down, wet her score pencil with the tip of her tongue, and colored in her score boxes. In spite of my pathetic efforts, or because of her high scores, Dottie's team still remained on top. Afterward, we went to the snack bar and bought French fries.

The big guy at the snack bar, Dottie called him Gus, said to her, "You're good, Dottie. You're gonna be a champ."

Dottie sucked ketchup off a fry, bit little pieces off it, and swallowed it down before she said, "Thanks."

On the ride home, we missed grabbing the back seat of the bus. I sat next to Susan, while Dottie and Holly sat across from us. I looked out the window at the dark flying by, fingering my broken nails and wishing I could have bowled better. Carlie, I was sure, would have done a fabulous job. Her little form would have sashayed up to the line, said a few words to the ball, and let it go home to strike heaven.

"You're good at other things," Susan said, beside me, like I had spoken out loud.

"Like what?" I asked.

"You can knit great scarves. You make good bread. Bud and I think you're pretty."

I was glad the bus was dark because my face went bright red. "I'm not," I mumbled.

"Well, if Bud says it, it's true," Susan said.

I knew that, well enough. I didn't need Susan to tell me that.

"Sometimes," she said, changing the subject, "I wish he talked a little more."

"He's just quiet," I said. I pictured his dark eyes and his sudden, sweet smiles. My memory caught hold of the candy heart he'd left for me in Petunia once, and the thought of our game made me smile out the window at the dark.

"Why are you smiling?" Susan asked.

"No reason," I said. Maybe I couldn't bowl like Dottie, and maybe Susan had Bud for a boyfriend. But I had a heart that said SOME GIRL hidden in the bottom of my underwear drawer. I had a feeling that somewhere deep in Bud's heart, he remembered setting it on Petunia's seat for me.

27

All through that school year, and as winter turned the corner from 1966 into 1967, I found myself itching for freedom in a whole new way. I pictured myself behind Petunia's steering wheel, heading out for that far horizon. My determination to keep my lips sealed and not bug Daddy lasted until early spring. And when I couldn't take it any longer, I broke down and asked Daddy if I could get my license when I turned sixteen. Bud already had his license and was close to buying the car he'd been saving for since he was thirteen years old. Glen had failed on his first attempt because he went through a stop sign to beep at a friend on the opposite side of the intersection. Dottie had permission to get her license. I had my permit, but Daddy and I hadn't practiced much because he was so busy. Still, I wanted my license. But Daddy said that I should wait until I was seventeen to go for it.

"Why?" I asked him as we walked up the hill from the harbor.

"I just think it would be a good idea to wait," Daddy said.

"Why would it be a good idea? What's good about it?"

"I don't see the reason for it, really. I can get you where you want to go. The truth is, I would feel better if you was a little older."

"You think I'm going to take Petunia and drive off into the sunset? Never come back?"

He looked at me and nodded as he stopped to catch his breath at the crossroads. "Maybe that's it," he said and sighed. "Maybe that's it."

"Daddy, I didn't mean that," I said. "I'm not going anywhere, but it would be nice to be able to go places. Take Grand places. I'm too old for the bus. I feel stupid."

"Another year isn't that far off," Daddy said. "Grand gets where she wants to go."

"I'm already a freak. Now I'll be a freak without a license."

"Can't be helped," Daddy said. "That's the way I feel, Florine. You think of something else you might want for your birthday and we'll see what we can do."

We parted ways and I went into Grand's house. She sat at the table surrounded by some of her ruby glass. I frowned. It wasn't time for ruby glass cleaning.

"How come you have the glass out?" I asked.

"Don't know," Grand said. "I went by the cabinet and I just got a bug to take it out and shine it up. I like looking at the color, I guess."

"You're weird, Grand," I said.

"You live with me," she said. "What does that say about you?"

She had a point. I picked up a teacup made of red glass and ran my finger along its cold inside. "I'm sorry I threw your heart away," I said.

"Well," she said, "you was awful upset that day." She heaved herself out of the kitchen chair, carrying a vase toward the cabinet. I saw how she hitched herself at the hips with each step she took. It occurred to me that I would look like that someday; that it would pain me to walk, and that I might become forgetful.

"Daddy told me that I have to wait a year before I get my license," I said.

Grand walked back to the table and picked up one of the teacups. I handed her the other one and she walked them to the cabinet.

"Everyone else on The Point is getting their license," I said.

She walked back to the table and picked up a pile of dessert plates.

"He's probably just afraid I'll drive off into the sunset and never come back."

"He might be a tad protective that way," Grand said. "I guess he's earned it. Might be a little hard on you, but you'll bear up, I guess."

My mind flashed to Carlie and Patty driving off. And suddenly, I knew what I wanted for my sixteenth birthday. "I'm going to ask Daddy to take me up to Crow's Nest Harbor," I said. "He asked me to think of something else I wanted. That's what I want. I want to see where Carlie stayed and where she might have gone."

Grand lowered herself into the chair across from me and squinted. She said, "I don't know as it's such a good idea, but I can see why you want to do it."

"Why isn't it a good idea?"

"I know you want to figure out what happened," Grand said. "But it might be just as good for you to tuck your mother close to your heart and claim something of your own. Carlie would be the first one to tell you that."

"I know," I said. "I know she's not coming back, Grand. I just want to see the last place she was."

"Maybe it's best to leave it alone," Grand said. "I'm not so sure Leeman wants to relive it. You might want to think about something else for your day. I'd be happy to have a party for you. Invite some friends down. Don't know as you've ever done that. I bet they'd like it down here. See where you live."

I didn't want to tell her that I hadn't made any friends. I suddenly felt like a double freak, a friendless, license-less freak. "I'll think about it," I said to Grand.

"No you won't, but the invitation is always there," Grand said. She patted my hand and I took in how tired she looked. I stood up and kissed the pink scalp where it shone under her fine white hair.

I asked Daddy the next day. He said no. "I can't do it right now," he told me. He was sanding down the hull of the *Carlie Flo*, preparing her for her launch in a couple of weeks, which happened to be on my birthday. Usually, she was taking him out into the bay by late March, but he was running late this year. "You can see that, right?"

"No," I said.

He picked up a bucket of white paint, a mixing stick, and a brush and handed them to me. "If this is going to be a long conversation, Florine, do something useful while we talk. The inside of the cabin needs a good whitewash."

He looked tired. Everyone, it seemed, looked tired. It had been a long, harsh winter and spring had been slow in coming. I climbed up the ladder into the boat and took the paint into the cabin.

"So, why can't you take me?" I asked, mixing the paint with the stick. Thin rivers of amber-colored oil disappeared into the white.

"I know it's going to make you mad no matter how I put it, so let me just say that I don't want to travel up there, Florine. It don't set well with me. Won't do me any good, and it won't do you any good."

"How do you know what will do me good?" He'd already cleared the cabin of everything. He'd taped newspapers over the windows and spread them over the floor, so all I had to do was slap paint on the walls and ceiling.

"I knew you was going to say that," he said. "I don't know, for sure, what will do you any good. I just know it will make me think about the whole thing all over again, and I don't need to go through it again." I ran the paintbrush slow along the edges of the wall leading out to the deck. I stared into the white, until, when I blinked, reds and oranges and yellows faded into blues and greens.

"Daddy, I know she's probably dead," I said. Dead. It was the first time I'd said the word out loud. The sound of it went through my body and down through the bottoms of my feet and slunk into the deep, cold earth. Daddy stopped sanding and we looked at each other, then he gave a slight nod and went back to sanding.

"Thing is," I said, "you know what the last place she was looks like. When I picture it, it's different every time. I don't know the streets. I don't know what the motel looks like. It all changes in my head, every time. I keep thinking of it, different. If I knew what it looked like, then I could stop making it all up."

"Florine," he said. "I can understand that, I guess, but honey, I just can't go through it again. Maybe when you've had your license for a little while and you've got some experience under your belt, you and Dottie can go up, or Grand might like a day's ride."

"I can't get my license for another year, though, right?" I said.

"We been through this. No," Daddy said.

"You won't do this for me?"

"Not when I don't think it would be good for either of us."

I ducked back into the cabin. No wonder Carlie got so agitated with you, I thought. Jesus, it's like talking to a friggin' rock stuck into cement. I painted the cabin out as fast as I could go, then I climbed down the ladder and walked away from the boat.

"Florine," Daddy said.

I didn't turn around, just said, "I don't want to talk to you," and kept walking away. He went back to sanding before I was out of earshot.

When I was almost to the end of the driveway, I heard the low chug-chug of a motor up by Ray's store. A shiny black car with a red top turned down The Point road and headed toward me, beeping the horn. It took me a minute to make out the driver, but then I saw that it was Bud. He stopped the car next to me and rolled down the window.

"Want a ride?" he asked.

I ran around to the passenger side and jumped in. The whole inside was red and warm, like being inside someone's mouth. I stroked the leather seat and looked around. I grinned at Bud.

"When did you get it?" I asked.

"Just picked her up now. Runs like the tide's chasing her into shore."

"What kind of car is this?" I asked.

"1961 Ford Fairlane," Bud said. "Dad knows the guy was selling her. Got me a good price." He pointed out all the knobs and buttons to me, and I listened, although mostly I was aware of his thin, strong fingers playing over the instruments and his coffee-flavored breath. And I knew how I would get to Crow's Nest Harbor.

Starting that Monday, Bud took Dottie, Glen, and me to school. No more bus for us.

"You drive safe, now," Grand said to Bud when he stopped for me that first morning.

I rolled my eyes as I climbed in beside him. He said, "Don't worry, Grand, I'll be careful." Dottie ran across from her house and climbed in the back. "You making me sit back here with Glen?" she asked me. "You get back here with me. I don't feel like fighting him off first thing in the morning." When we got to Ray's, I hopped in back and Glen rode shotgun. We drove to Long Reach that day, feeling like we were on top of the world. We walked into school with a new lift to our steps.

"Isn't it great?" Susan said to me as we walked the halls between classes. "I can't wait to go parking." She glanced up at me from underneath her minky eyelashes.

I pictured her small body straddling Bud's thin thighs in some dim place under a grove of pine trees. "I have to go," I said to her, and turned into my English classroom.

I sat at my desk looking up at the mild blue sky, trying to think of a way to get Bud to drive me up north. But it turned out to be easy. With some surprise help from Dottie and Glen, he fell into my idea like a melted marshmallow into a campfire. We'd been driving uptown together for about two weeks. It was Friday, May 17, the day before my sixteenth birthday.

"What you want for your birthday?" Dottie asked me on the way to Long Reach that morning.

"I already know what I'm not getting," I said.

"What's that?" Bud asked.

"I wanted Daddy to drive me up to Crow's Nest Harbor so I could see where Carlie stayed and put that to rest, but he won't do it."

We were driving up over Pine Pitch Hill. I looked into the woods where all those kids, except for Stella, had lost their lives. Why, out of all of them, had she lived?

Glen said, "Let's skip school and go, today. We can get there by noon and walk around a little bit, then drive back. Get back by six or so. We can say we stayed uptown for a while. Or we had to wait for Bud to stop balling Susan."

"Jesus, Glen," Bud said, "shut the hell up."

"Trying to think of excuses for us," Glen said. "You come up with something."

"I'm not coming up with anything," Bud said.

"Oh, come on," Glen said. "Where's your sense of adventure?"

"I have some money," I said. "Grand gives me five dollars a week and I've saved up fifteen. I've got enough for gas, and a little for food."

Bud looked at me in the rearview mirror. "You're as crazy as Glen is," he said.

"That's not news," I said, and we locked eyes until he had to look back at the road.

Dottie sealed the deal. In a rare burst of sappiness, she said, "Soon, we won't be together. Seems we could do one last thing before we get booted in different directions."

"What do you say?" Glen asked Bud.

"I say, 'Firecrackers,'" Bud said, and caught my eyes in the mirror again. I gave him such a big, sloppy smile that his eyes danced before he looked away.

"Florine should get her birthday wish," Glen said.

"One more time," Dottie said.

Bud shook his head, but when we reached the high school, he drove past it. He looked back at me in the mirror. "Be careful what you wish for," he said.

We drove through Long Reach and crossed the high bridge that straddled the river. Immediately over that bridge to the right was the road to Mulgully Beach. I looked down that road and pictured Petunia driving toward the beach, carrying a red-haired, fire-crotched woman and her daughter. Inside her plush interior, the two of them listened to summer songs on the radio, wanting to reach the beach so they could soak up some sun.

28

We stopped for gas in Wiscasset, bought a map, paper cups, orange juice, and chocolate donuts. After I promised Dottie that she could have half of my birthday cake, Glen and I switched seats so I could ride shotgun.

White and brick houses dotted the towns winding along the dips and bends of Route 1 and always, to the right, peek-a-boos of the ocean. Woods and fields greening into the spring set between the towns, and Bud rolled his window down and invited the May air inside to tickle our nostrils. He drove the speed limit, just in case we passed cops. He cranked the radio. *"It's a beautiful morning,"* the Rascals sang, just like a flock of butterflies rising to catch the sun on their wings.

I imagined Patty and Carlie looking at the views we were seeing now. What things would have caught their eyes? What scenes were special to them, year after year, as they'd traveled the same road we were on? Wiscasset, Thomaston, Rockland. Camden. A town built to slide along the coastline's curves. Hooded mountains to the left of us, cat-backed islands soaking their toes in the wide and bright blue ocean to our right. Little shops lined the crooked street. Had Carlie and Patty stopped here, every year? Had this been part of their weekend away? Which shops would they have lingered in?

"Let's stop," I said, but Bud said, "I want to get there, Florine. We're probably not even halfway yet. Look at the map, would you?"

I wanted to give him a good argument but he was taking a big chance by skipping school, driving his new car all this distance, and not telling his girlfriend about any of it.

I thought about Susan moving down the corridors, looking for Bud, expecting to see him, brown eyes worried even as she hurried to class, her little butt swaying from side to side underneath one of the short skirts she liked to wear. Susan had such a happy little ass, perky and twitchy, like a mischievous cat's tail. "Won't Susan miss you today?" I asked Bud. "What if she calls down to The Point to ask where you are?"

"She's not in school today," Bud said. "She and her family went to Connecticut. Some relative getting married tomorrow. They asked if I wanted to go. I didn't."

"Jesus, look at that place," Glen said, pointing out his window at a forest-green mansion behind a stone wall. The house loomed over a scilla-showered lawn. Needle-sharp turrets stabbed at the sky to shoo it away from the gabled, rambling roof. Thick iron bars crisscrossed the glass windows.

"It's like that show, *Dark Shadows*," Dottie said. "Wonder if they got any vampires?"

"Wonder how much money is in there?" Bud asked.

"Probably more than all of us got put together," Glen said.

"Couple three million," Dottie said.

"I wouldn't want to live there," I said. "How would people ever find each other?"

"I wouldn't mind it for a change," Bud said. "Christ, seems as if we're all on top of each other at our house."

"I love the way your mother has it fixed up so nice, though," I said.

"You can only love it so much when Sam's pissed off and steam's coming out of his ears," Bud said. "Kind of hard to know where to go when that happens."

"Bert don't steam. He just yells," Dottie said. "We don't listen. Evie gives him the big-eyed doll look and I just walk off. Madeline's the one to watch out for."

"I can sit on Ray now," Glen said. "Not much yelling from him anymore. Germaine talks soft. When I get the 'Now, Glen,' with the eye-to-eye, I know I'm in trouble."

"Carlie never yelled at me," I said. We'd slipped past the castle and were riding beside long, lean rows of trees. The soft green buds on the limbs made me sleepy. "Daddy yelled, when I lived with him. I wouldn't dare to get Grand mad."

"No, neither would I," Bud said. "Her being so close to Jesus and all."

"Only one person can call me Dorothea without me smacking her," Dottie said.

"She's my ideal woman," Glen said. "If we was the same age, I'd go for it."

We moved on up the road toward Belfast, passed it and kept moving.

The trees thinned out and soon we were tucked between boulders in dead-grass fields that lined both sides of the road. I remembered from fifth grade learning about the glacier that scraped across Maine and left behind this mess of rocks and scarred land. It came to me that while these boulders sat for a few more centuries, everything I felt, thought, or did would be swept up and tossed out like the gravel I tracked into Grand's kitchen. It wouldn't matter that Carlie had disappeared or who Daddy slept with. Cold shuddered through me like a Popsicle burn.

"You okay?" Bud asked. "Want me to roll up the window?"

"No," I said. "This place is bringing me down, though."

"Me too," Dottie said. "How much more?"

"Not much," Bud said. "Look at the map, Florine."

"About three-fourths of an inch," I said.

"Long damn drive," Dottie said.

I had to agree. What did Patty and Carlie talk about all this time? They saw each other almost every day. What could they say that hadn't already been said? Did Carlie talk about how stubborn Daddy was?

Did Patty bring up the latest boyfriend? Did they talk about me, ever? If they did, what did they say?

"We're just ahead of the tourists," Bud said. "Come Memorial Day, we'd be stuck in traffic somewhere."

The just-before-town signs and rows of motels began to crop up. Tourist traps, seafood restaurants, and views of the ocean that made Camden's bay seem puny. We drove down a little street into Crow's Nest Harbor, passing a small town square with a bandstand in the middle of it. Shops surrounded the square. Carlie had crisscrossed this square into these shops buying things for me, or her, or for Daddy.

We came up to a stop sign. In front of us was the building that housed *The Crow's Nest Harbor Howler*, the local paper that had run Carlie's photo and a story about us and how we were waiting at home for her return.

"None of it did any good," I said out loud.

"What didn't do any good?" Bud asked. "Where did Patty and Carlie stay?"

"The Crow's Nest Harbor Motel. Down by the water."

Bud steered us down a street, close to the ocean, toward a big blue sign with a smiling crow wearing a sailor's cap sitting in a messy nest.

"That's got to be it," Glen said.

Bud parked on a side street near the motel. "Let's go," he said.

The motel formed an L of white units on one level, with a fenced-off swimming pool sitting in white concrete in the middle of the units. The pool was empty, but it wasn't hard to imagine Patty waving goodbye to Carlie, then diving into the warm silky water, not knowing she would never see Carlie again.

"What do you want to do?" Dottie asked. They were all looking at me.

I started to shrug, and then I saw a maid go into one of the units. "I wonder if she'll let us look inside," I said. "I want to know what the rooms look like."

"Glen and I are going to take a walk down to the slips," Bud said. "Probably scare her if we all shuffled over there and asked to go in. Come get us when you're done." He gave me a half smile and he and Glen walked off. Dottie and I walked toward the open door and Dottie poked her head into the darkness. "'Scuse me," she said. "Would you mind if we looked at the room? My bowling league is thinking of taking a trip up this way and we're trying to decide where to stay."

The maid, a short, dark woman with a body as plump as a well-fed partridge, pulled a white bedspread up over one of the twin beds. She smoothed down the spread as she moved around the bed. "I don't care," she said. "Just don't touch anything."

She hustled into the bathroom, and Dottie and I stepped in. White spreads covered twin beds set against a light-blue wall overlaid with a dark-green fern pattern. Two tiny blue-shaded lamps, the base of each clear and filled with shells, sat on a honey-colored wooden table between the beds. A television sat on a dresser against the opposite wall. A heavy blue drape hid a big window at the other end of the room. A small table and two chairs with light-blue cloth backing sat underneath the window. I walked over and pulled open the drapes. The white light of the bay plunged into the room and landed on Dottie's already-tanned face. Her shiny brown eyes took in the view. "Nice," she said.

The maid flushed the toilet in the bathroom. She hummed a few notes of something, then stopped. She whizzed back the shower curtain and turned on a faucet.

"I wonder which bed was Carlie's," I said. She'd slept on the left side of the bed at home. Daddy had slept closest to the door, as he was first to get up.

"I don't know," Dottie said. The maid turned off the bathroom faucet and walked into the bedroom carrying a small trash can with her. "You girls want to see the bathroom, go ahead. But be quick. I got to get done in here."

We peeked in. Tiny. Straight ahead, a toilet, with racks above it to hold clean towels. To the right, a tub and shower with a white curtain. A sink and white countertop with a mirror in the middle of the wall over it.

"Barely room to move," Dottie said.

"Excuse me," said the maid from behind us. We both jumped. She cradled an armful of folded, fluffy towels. "If you don't mind my asking, why would your bowling league be coming up here? We don't have a bowling alley."

"Did I say we was bowling?" Dottie said. "We're just looking to relax, is all."

"How old are you?" the maid asked her. "You look like you should be in school."

"Day off," Dottie said.

"Let's go," I said. I turned and walked out of the room, Dottie close behind me.

We looked back toward town. Carlie had walked that way one morning, never knowing that she would not be coming back.

The maid came out of her room to her cleaning cart. I gathered up some grit and said, "Can I ask you something?"

She shifted her weight to one hip, ready to listen for as long as it took to get rid of us.

"My mother used to stay here," I said. "She used to come every summer with a friend of hers."

"Lot of people do," the maid said.

"She disappeared from here about four years ago. No one ever found her."

The maid's hazel eyes opened wide and she straightened up. "Carlie Gilham," she said. She looked at me, closer. "You're her daughter. I knew Carlie. She was a hoot. She and Patty Higgins, right? Used to come into town when they was here and join us in Frenchman's Folly for a drink sometimes. I felt bad about what happened. Everyone talked about it. My Lord, you're her daughter, here. For heaven's sake."

My eyes welled up. She'd known Carlie. She'd liked her. People had cared. The town had cared. They'd come up empty, but they'd cared.

"My name is Jorie Rich," the maid said. "Used to be Marjorie, but I sliced off the Mar when I was a teenager. What's your name? Carlie told me, but it's been years."

I told her and I introduced Dottie.

"You look like your daddy," Jorie said to me. "He's a handsome man. Stood out when he was up here looking around. Big man. Felt so bad for him. Came back two years in a row after that around this time. Always looked me up for coffee. We'd drink it down and he'd walk into town, trying to figure it out, he said. Same thing you're doing. How is he? I haven't seen nor heard of him for a while."

"He's fine," I said. My brain twirled to learn that Daddy had come here, alone, looking for her. And did Stella know? Jesus, did anyone talk to anyone anymore?

"I came up with my friends," I said. "I just wanted to see where she was last."

"Of course you did," Jorie said. "Well, let me think. Nothing much has changed. That's the way to town. Carlie liked to look around in the bookstore at the end of the street straight ahead. She liked to read them thrillers. She liked Grundy's Dress Shop, too. About halfway down that street. And the Lard Bucket—don't ask, been there so long I can't remember why they called it that. It's got some tourist-trap things in it, fun to poke around. Mostly, though, she liked to sit around the pool, go into town for dinner and a couple of drinks. Patty and her splurged and took a couple of sunset cruises on the sloop *Cordelia* a couple times. That was about it."

My mind danced through space and time, picturing her here, walking there, shopping there, gabbing with the girls over beers. All this was overlaid with seeing Daddy taking that long drive up here, alone, on the off chance he might find out something new.

"She had some pictures of you," Jorie was saying. "She had baby pictures, and on up through. She was some proud of you."

"Oh," I said, and choked. Jorie walked over to me, stood on tiptoe, and gave me a hug that bent me like a bamboo fishing rod in her direction. "I'm all right," I said, moving back gently. "Thank you for the nice things you said," and I turned and walked toward town, following on the heels of my mother's ghost. Dottie trotted along in back of me like a faithful dog. We walked toward the boat slips, where the boys had headed. They were admiring a small yacht at the end of the wharf. We hollered to them and they joined us. We all went into the bookstore.

The bookstore clerk looked at us as if we were high school students skipping school. The thing that confused him, I guess, was the fact that he didn't recognize us as locals. I moved up and down the aisles, looking up at the book titles. "Where's your thriller section?" I asked the clerk. He tore himself away from eyeing Glen and Bud, both of whom were looking at magazines.

The clerk pointed to a wall right behind me. "Have they always been here?" I asked.

"Bud," Glen whispered so that we all heard him, "get a load of these."

The clerk frowned, trying to figure out, I guess, why I had asked that question, and whether or not Glen was looking at what he seemed to be looking at.

"Yes," he said. "I've owned this shop for years, and the thrillers haven't moved. Are you thinking of buying those magazines?" he said to Bud and Glen.

Bud moved away from Glen and walked to the register with his car magazine. He pulled out his wallet. The clerk watched Glen put his magazine back, underneath the latest edition of *Good Housekeeping*.

"Doesn't go there," he growled at Glen. Glen slunk outside.

I stood in front of the thrillers with my eyes closed, willing my mother to walk in and take control of me, give me some information, even let me know which books she'd bought to read by the pool. I stood there until Bud whispered, "Let's go," into my ear.

I followed him out the door. We joined Dottie and Glen on the bench seats inside the bandstand in the little park.

"Clerk was an asshole," Glen said.

"Cop," Bud said. We followed his eyes to a blue-clad figure walking along the sidewalk opposite us. He went down a side street and soon was out of sight.

"We're not doing anything wrong," Glen said.

"We skipped school," Bud pointed out. "You got the shortest memory there is."

"Where is Grundy's Dress Shop?" I asked. I stood on the floor in the middle of the bandstand and turned a quarter to my left. Didn't see it. Turned another quarter, and another, until I began to spin around. The absence of my mother and the surprise that was my father blended and blurred as I whirled around and tried to make some sense of it. Dottie stopped me mid-spin and hissed, "Stop that. The cop is walking this way."

"Ah shit," Bud muttered.

The cop walked up to the bandstand and put one shiny-shoed foot on the lowest step. He was thin and handsome in a Bing Crosby kind of way, with clear, far-seeing eyes that told us he spent a lot of time on the water.

"Afternoon," he said. "You kids supposed to be in school?"

Dottie said, "Yes," just as Glen said, "No."

Bud said, "Yes, we are."

The cop nodded. "Why aren't you in school?"

Bud started to say something, but I said, "My mother disappeared from here about four years ago. I wanted to come up and see the place for myself. Her name is Carlie Gilham, and I'm her daughter, Florine. I got my friends to drive me here. It isn't their fault. I wanted to see."

The cop studied me. "I remember her," he said. I reached into my dress pocket and pulled out her photograph. He nodded. "Yes," he said. "Of course."

He said, "That was four years ago this summer."

"I was twelve. I'm turning sixteen tomorrow."

"Happy birthday," he said, and he gave me a sad smile. "Florine, I'm sorry we weren't able to find your mother. We followed every clue we could. Your father still calls, once a year or so around the time it happened."

Daddy, again, still following up.

"We talk with the State Police; talk with Parker Clemmons, down your way. Talk with Detective Pratt in Blueberry Harbor. We never quit, Florine. Believe that."

"Everyone says that," I said, low.

The cop nodded. "You'd best be getting on home," he said. "You have a long ride."

"That Jorie woman was nice to tell you all that stuff," Dottie said. I was huddled into the backseat with her. Glen was in front with Bud.

"I know," I said.

Dottie said, "Well, at least you went up there. Now you know what it's like."

"I thought if I showed up, something would come to me," I said. "Something would change. I might know what had happened. It was a stupid idea."

"No it wasn't," Dottie said. "You did something about it, anyways."

We rode some more, for a long time. Sadness circled my side of the backseat, but I didn't cry. I just watched the scenery fly by, thinking more about Daddy's quiet, lonely search than I did about Carlie.

About two hours into the drive, I said, "Thank you," to Bud.

"No need to thank me," he said, looking at me in the mirror. He looked back at the road and I studied the back of his head. Thick hair, a little too long for me, small ears tucked in tight. His neck looked sweet where the hair dipped into it. I wanted to stroke that spot, but I left it to my imagination.

We reached home at about five o'clock. As we drove down the hill, I noticed the *Carlie Flo* sitting beside the *Maddie Dee* out on their buoys.

"Daddy finally got the boat out," I said.

Bud dropped me off. "I hope it helped a little bit," he said. He gave my hand a warm squeeze, then drove down the hill toward his house.

I woke up on my sixteenth birthday to the smell of angel food cake baking. Grand had the radio in the kitchen set on the oldies station. Big band music drifted up the stairs. I turned and looked at my Mickey alarm clock. His hands told me it was eleven.

I heard Daddy come into the house, go into the kitchen, and talk in low tones to Grand. My daddy, who I didn't know. His secret trips up north. His choice of Stella to keep his bed warm. For a set-in-his-ways man, he was filled with surprises.

Turned out he had one for me.

"Happy birthday," he called up to me. "Come down a minute."

I tugged on bell-bottom jeans and threw on the last of Carlie's sweaters that fit me. The short sleeves were frayed, and the waistband rode my belly button, but I didn't care.

I met Daddy in the kitchen, sipping coffee at the table. "Come with me," he said.

"Where we going?" I said.

"It's a surprise," he said. I followed him down to the wharf.

My soul leapt as I watched the *Carlie Flo* bob in the harbor.

"She looks good," I said.

"Give a look aft," Daddy said. Just as if she knew that he'd asked, the wind moved her so that I could check out her rump board, and I saw that Daddy had changed her name to the *Florine*. No *Carlie* and, surprising to me, no *Stella*. The letters of my name were bright white against the dark green.

"Now, I know you probably wonder why I took your mother's name off," Daddy said. "I got to tell you the truth. I don't think any less of your mother. I never could. But you take a boat out to sea with her name and, well, it makes me nervous. I need a steady name for her. We've been through it all, thick and thin. We don't see eye to eye sometimes, but I know we see things clear heart to heart. I know I can count on you."

I reached around him to give him a big hug. The last time I'd done that, my nose had pressed against that place where the center of his rib cage met muscle. Now, my nose pressed into the lower part of his shoulder. "Happy birthday, Florine," he said.

29

I went to my clearing often during the fall of 1967. I loved the colors: the reds and browns that some of the bushes took on, the paling of the moss and lichens, the occasional yellow, orange, or pink leaf from an oak or maple that twirled its way down through the pines and spruce that surrounded the little clearing. Crows cawed in their scraggly rooks, warning each other about owls and hawks. Geese, fretful about a possible early winter, honked to one another as they passed overhead. My sorrow for Carlie had seasoned, and she appeared in my mind wrapped in October's colors and moods, set for a long winter before spring.

Except for my three best friends, I kept this place secret. I made a game out of getting there. Turning off the State Park trail and making sure no one was following me, I looked both ways before I ducked down the side path near Barrington's house. Once I reached the clearing, I opened an old knapsack of Daddy's I'd found in Grand's crawl space, took out and spread onto the rocks a small, crocheted blanket I'd made that reminded me of Carlie—spring green for her eyes, red for her hair, and white for her skin—on the three flat rocks. I sat on the blanket, knees up by my chin, arms wrapped around my legs, and I talked to my mother. I no longer pleaded for her to come home. That was out of my hands. Instead, I told her about what was going on in my life. "Grand's been better lately. Not so tired. She's still taking afternoon naps. I'm

baking most of the bread, but I don't mind. It's selling good. I'm knitting more, too," I'd tell the clearing.

If anyone heard me talking out loud to the rocks and the trees and
any animals that might be listening, they probably thought I was nuts,
but I didn't care. They also might have thought it crazy that I buried
small things Carlie had owned in the clearing. Scraps of cloth, used
lipstick, a pack of gum I'd found in a pair of her shorts.

One late October day, when the air nipped my nose with the scent
of the sweet-sour juice of a cold apple, I came back from Carlie's Clearing and went over The Cheeks through Daddy's backyard to find him
loading up the truck. Stella was going through another binge of redec-
orating. The house needed a new roof, and she'd managed to get Daddy
to agree to insulate it so that the upstairs rooms could be opened up and
heated. While he was doing that, she planned to clear them of the junk.

Grand had told me all this beforehand so there wouldn't be any
surprises. "Now, she's not touching your room at all, Florine, and the
things she's throwing out are no good. She wants to make a sewing
room out of one of the rooms. The other one will be storage. You can
check to see if there is anything you want, she told me."

I didn't bother. I'd been up there a few times in my life before. Two
broken bureaus stuffed with old, mouse-turded-and-pissed-on clothes.
A hanging rack filled with Hattie Butts's old lady dresses. Boxes of old
records, some magazines, more mouse turds. Stella could have it.

Daddy said good morning to me as I came out of the woods. The
truck bed was heaped with the upstairs trash. "You got it all," I said.

"Most of it," he said.

"Going to plant some bulbs," I said. A little while later I was in the
side yard, sticking in tulip and daffodil bulbs. I did this every year, in
different places. Grand liked to be surprised at where they came up in
the spring. That morning, as I finished poking about two dozen bulbs
into six-inch holes, I heard the storm door at Daddy's house slam and I
glanced up to see Stella sit down hard on the front steps. She stared out

over the harbor for a minute, then got up and wove her way up the driveway like a drunk on a three-day bender. Her face was white as sifted
flour except for the scar. When she saw me watching her, she covered her
face and stood, her shoulders shaking. I hollered, "Grand. Something's
wrong with Stella."

Grand came out to the side yard. "For heaven's sake, what's happened now?" she said, and walked toward her. When she reached her,
she put an arm around her shoulders and Stella caved into her chest.
Grand turned her around and walked her back to Daddy's house and
they went inside. I waited to see what would happen next, but she didn't
come out, so I made myself some lunch. Grand came back an hour later
while I was rocking on the porch and looking out over the harbor.

She sat down hard in her own rocker. "Floor gets lower every year,"
she said.

"Stella okay?" I asked.

"Well, no," Grand said.

"What's wrong? Daddy give her the heave-ho?"

"Now, I'm going to tell you and you're going to feel bad for saying
something so mean," Grand said. "She had a miscarriage."

We rocked back and forth a few times. Then I said, "How far
along?"

"Not more than a month."

"I didn't know women could get pregnant at forty-five."

"Ain't common, but it happens," Grand said. "I was thirty-five when
I had Leeman. That was ancient in those days."

"I'm sorry I was mean."

"Don't forget to tell it to Jesus, too," Grand said. "I invited Stella and
Leeman to supper. I might as well invite the rest of 'em over, too. We'll
throw together something simple. Winter's almost here and we haven't
had time to get together. Pretty soon, all you kids will be flung to the
four winds and we'll have missed the chance."

Grand and I made up a Saturday night supper of beans and biscuits and hot dogs. Madeline brought brown bread and Ida supplied an apple crisp. Everyone on The Point joined us, except for Bud, who was out with Susan.

I hadn't really seen Bud since our trip to Crow's Nest Harbor, after he and Susan had gotten into a fight about it. She came at me in the school hall on the Monday after our trip.

"Who the hell do you think you are, getting Bud to drive you up north?" she yelled.

"He chose to do it," I said, as people slowed to take us in. "He wanted to."

"Well, it was stupid and selfish. It better not happen again." And she stomped off.

Bud was in a foul mood for days. He picked me up, but we barely spoke.

"You going to talk to me, or do you want me to take the bus?" I finally asked him.

"Maybe you should take the bus for the rest of the year," he said. But lucky for me, Dottie got her license about then, and she drove me to school for a while, until he simmered down and began to give me rides again, now and then.

At the supper at Grand's house, Dottie, Glen, Evie, Maureen, and I sat in the living room eating off TV trays.

Stella clung to Daddy. Every once and a while, when we were in the same room, I'd catch her looking at me and when I did, she'd look away quick. I wondered if she was thinking that the child she'd lost might have looked sort of like me, only with a scar on its face, had it been born.

30

Winter brought the flu and a couple of bad colds to Grand. She fought being sick like the trouper she was, with cold medicine, both store-bought and one she concocted herself made out of honey, ginger ale, and melted Canada Mints. She drank strong tea until it steamed out of her ears, and even dipped into the whiskey for medicinal purposes.

I made soups and stews and made sure she was comfortable before I went to school. Most of the time she was up and around when I left, but it was obvious that something nasty was dogging her every step. By the time I got home, she was usually lying on the couch, watching television or napping.

Susan decided to talk to me again, although she wasn't nearly as friendly as she had been. "I'm sorry I yelled at you," she said. "I guess I was jealous for not getting to go. You're like a sister to Bud, he told me. He made that pretty clear."

I didn't tell her that I didn't think of Bud as a brother. In fact, these days, I had a hard time thinking in a sisterly fashion about any male that caught my eye or brushed my arm, or breathed in my general direction. My body was hot to trot.

Martin Luther King was assassinated in April 1968 and Robert Kennedy was killed in June. Even our tiny place in the world mourned the losses. I turned seventeen in May. Grand called me Mooney Mulrooney, because my attention sputtered and my moods wavered, dipped, and then straightened like a guttering candle. Days, I worked in the gardens, or baked bread, or sat on the porch and waved in the boats. Nights, I rode twisted wads of blankets jammed up between my legs. I was turned inside out with touching and wanting, wishing someone would touch me back. That wishing felt more real than the rest of my life did.

Spring bumped into summer, excused itself, and moved on. Dottie got a job at the State Park for the summer, leading nature walks during the days. It was interesting, she said, when it wasn't driving her crazy. She had great stories. "So the other day," she said, "I says to some numb nuts guy, I says, 'That's poison ivy, sir, best not touch,' but didn't he do it anyway. He says, 'That's not poison ivy,' and I says, 'Yes, it is,' and kept walking down the trail. Well, don't you know he comes back a week later and he walks up to me and a group of kids from the YMCA camp and he turns around back-to, hauls down his shorts, pulls up his shirt and he says, 'See what you caused to happen?' Jesus, he was scabbed to the gills. I says, 'I warned you not to touch it, sir. See why?' I says to the campers—they was standing with their mouths open like they was catching midges—'This is why we don't touch poison ivy.' That man asked for the manager, I pointed to him, and off he went."

"Sounds like an asshole," I said.

"Probably itched there, too," Dottie said.

We sat at the end of the wharf, swinging our legs. I looked up into the sky and saw the moon shining through the bright blue daytime sky. "Huh," I said. I pointed it out to Dottie.

"That's pretty clever, I think," she said. "You don't see the sun in the middle of the night, but here the moon is hogging part of the sky."

"I wonder if Carlie is up there," I said.

"Good a place as any," Dottie said. We studied the moon for a little while, and then Dottie said, "I add her to my prayers every night, still."

"You do?" I said, touched to think that she would. "I didn't even know you prayed."

"How do you think I get all of them strikes?" she said.

One Saturday night about nine o'clock in the middle of August, Grand and I were watching television. I was just thinking about going upstairs when someone knocked at the door.

"You expecting company?" I asked Grand.

"Jimmy Stewart said he'd drop by," Grand said. "Might be him."

Jimmy Stewart was Grand's favorite movie star. "He seems like he'd be good company," she'd say. "Just a nice fella."

"I'll get it," I said. I opened the door to find Susan standing there.

"Can you come outside for a minute?" she whispered as if she held a secret that only I should know.

"Who's out there?" Grand shouted.

"It's Susan," I yelled back.

"Hello Susan," Grand shouted. "Come on in. Bring Bud, too. Tell him I got some of those molasses cookies he likes."

I rolled my eyes. "I'll be right back," I said. I caught Grand halfway up off the sofa, ready to go fix us snacks.

"Don't do that," I said, sharper than I meant to say it. I took a deep breath and said, softer, "Susan wants to talk to me outside. You okay with that?"

"Well, I guess," she said. "She's welcome to come in, though."

"She knows," I said, and almost ran from the room.

Susan was looking down toward the wharf.

"What's going on?" I asked her.

She stuck her little hands into her patched pockets and sighed. "Well, I hope you're cool with this. I got you a date."

"What do you mean, you got me a date?"

"Oh man, don't get all weird, okay?"

"Who said I needed a date?" I said.

"No one, but if you want a date, you can have one. I hope you do because he's here."

"Who's here?"

"Kevin Jewell."

"Who is that?" I asked, although I knew. He was part hippie, part football player. He was part good-looking, too, and he had a nice smile.

"We met up with him in Long Reach when Bud was getting beer and he rode down just to see you," Susan said. "Kevin thinks you're groovy, but he told me he was too shy to talk to you in school."

I snorted. "Sure he is," I said.

Susan's eyebrows knit a cross-stitch and she said, "He's a good guy. You should give him a chance. If you don't want to do it, I'll make something up. It's up to you."

She turned and started to walk toward the wharf, while I pondered on it. Inside was Grand and some bad TV, upstairs was a pile of abused blankets and another night French-kissing my pillow. My feet moved to follow Susan to the wharf. I squinted to see if I could see Bud and Kevin, but all the shapes threw shadows.

The tip of a cigarette burned a hole in the dark. I hated that Bud smoked now, but who was I to tell him not to if his girlfriend didn't mind. When we got closer, he said, "Hey." He took a drag off his cigarette and his eyes glowed orange above it. The glow also revealed a tall boy with hair to his shoulders. Another drag from Bud and the boy smiled and bobbed his head.

"Hey," I said.

"Hi," Kevin said.

"Well, now that's out of the way, let's have a beer," Susan said. Bud reached in back of him and a paper bag rustled. He pulled out a pint can of 'Gansett and handed it to me. I stood against the railing and popped the top. I'd never had a whole can of beer before. But I'd seen them guzzled down, sucked down, belched loud, and pissed out into the snow. I had all of those things in me to do, so I figured that what might happen to me wouldn't be much different.

Kevin came and stood beside me. He smelled of smoke and cloves.

The hairs on his arm touched mine and I rubbed my arm. We all took a swallow of beer.

Kevin said to me, "Want to show me around?"

"Take him down by the rocks and the little beach," Susan said.

"Be careful. Tricky getting down there," Bud said. "Might fall and get hurt."

"I know that way just as good as you," I said to him.

"I know," Bud said. "And I'd worry about getting stoved up on the rocks."

"She's a big girl, Buddy," Susan said. "She can take care of herself."

"Take my lighter," Bud said, and handed it to Kevin.

In the small light cast by Bud's lighter, the path looked like a white snake winding its way down toward the beach. Then the path disappeared behind a wall of boulders.

"You got to go round this boulder," I said. Kevin put his hand on my shoulder and held the lighter up higher. "And then you go this way. Step down," I said, and I did, and fell, and I twisted my ankle, and then I was on the beach on my butt, hissing pain in and blowing it out through my teeth. The beer in my can blooped as it spilled out onto the sand. Kevin righted it as he knelt beside me.

"You okay?" he said. He held the lighter between us and I saw the beginnings of a mustache above his upper lip. His eyes were light green.

"'S fine," I hissed. "Just fine."

"No it's not," Kevin said. "Hold on to me." He helped me hobble to a boulder and lowered me against the back of it. He pointed the flickering lighter toward my sneaker.

"Great," I said. These were my faded blue house sneakers and they were too small. My growing feet had whittled holes over the big toes and the smallest toes. They looked so awful that I put my hands over my eyes and groaned.

But Kevin didn't say anything about the holes, and his hands were gentle. He cupped one palm under the heel of my sneaker and undid the laces. "Double knots, huh?" he said, and smiled. "Me, too." He worked the sneaker off, then cradled my bare foot in his hand. He held the lighter close to my ankle, warming it up as he peered at it.

"See if you can move your foot," he said.

I winced, but I did it.

"Wiggle your toes," he said. I did.

"I think it's okay," he said. He handed me my beer. "Take a swig," he said. It tasted like cold metal, but a couple of good swallows took the bite out of the pain.

Kevin sat down beside me.

"You okay?" he asked. I nodded and he moved my hair back behind my ears. "You got the grooviest hair," he said. "All wild, like some kind of river in the spring." He nudged me, put his mouth against my ear, and whispered, "I think you're beautiful."

I giggled, and when I did, I moved my ankle. A bullet of pain shot through it.

"You sure you're okay?" Kevin asked when I jumped.

"Yes," I said.

"Good," Kevin said. He took one of my hands and kissed it. "Because all we have is now. What if the world was going to end in thirty minutes, and this was all the time you had? Wouldn't you rather be with someone than be alone?"

Before I could laugh my ass off at this bunk, his tongue was in my mouth, and my tongue touched his tongue back and then we were on the sand and he was half on top of me and we were kissing to beat the band. Kevin reached between my legs and squeezed. This was much better than my bedding. I moaned and he did it again.

"Like that?" he asked.

He moved my legs apart, dragging my ankle, which he'd been so careful with only a minute before, through the pebbles and sand. As I cried out from the hurt, he said, "Sorry," and unzipped his pants.

And then, a frail warble hailed my ears, from where, I couldn't tell, but it sounded weak and frantic to find me.

"Florine," it whined. "Florine." I pushed against Kevin and he tumbled backward. I struggled up, hopped around on one foot, and looked out at the water, heart thumping hard against my chest. Kevin followed me.

"Who's calling you?" he asked. He put a hand on my back to steady me.

Then, the voice again. "Floorrriinnneeee."

At the sound of footsteps, Kevin walked away from me, trying to zip up his jeans. I wobbled, trying not to put too much weight on my ankle. Bud said from somewhere above the rocks, "Grand's calling you, Florine."

"Florine," the voice came again, and then I recognized it, and could even tell where she was standing—in the road outside the house.

"It's my grandmother," I said to Kevin.

"Oh man," he said. "Can't she wait?"

"Florine?" Grand called.

"You want me to tell her you're down here?" Bud asked.

"No, I'll go up," I said.

"Well," Kevin whispered into my ear. "Later then. We have a date with destiny."

With Susan following us, Kevin and Bud helped me up the path to where Grand stood in front of her house.

"I was just about to go get your father," she said. "You hurt?"

"Just twisted my ankle," I said.

"Well, thank you boys for bringing her home," Grand said. She looked at Kevin. "Hello," she said and stuck out her hand. "I'm Florine's grandmother, Mrs. Gilham."

"Kevin Jewell, ma'am," Kevin said, and took her hand. Grand invited them all in, but Kevin said no, he'd best get uptown, and Bud and he and Susan drove past the house as I was limping upstairs to bed. Bud beeped the horn as he drove by, and Grand said, "He seemed like a nice boy."

I choked down my aggravation as Grand wrapped my ankle in an old Ace bandage. She stood behind me as I made my painful way up each riser. I used one of my pillows to cradle my ankle, and I finally settled down long after Bud drove back home. I wondered if and when Kevin would be back. Something told me never. It turned out that Something was right.

31

During the last week I would ever spend in high school, I ran afoul of a pack of idiot girls led by a dumpling of a bitch named Angela Hill. Everyone knew these girls and steered clear of them. Angela's girls stuck close to her, like sucker fish to a shark. I don't know what made Angela so mean, but even those of us that tried to be invisible could be a target at any time. Even Dottie had been zoomed in on because she was such a good bowler. Dottie told me that Angela was on another team that the Gladibowlas always beat, so maybe that pissed her off. When word got around to Dottie that Angela was making fun of her weight, Dottie handled it like she handled everything, straight on. She walked up to Angela and told her that if she didn't shut up, she would sit on her until she begged for mercy.

My time came in the high school gym locker room in November of 1968. We shared a gym class that fall, which was hell for me during the best of times. I hated being naked in the locker room. I wasn't built like many of the girls; they were small and curvy, and I was the opposite. During the gym classes I managed not to stick out too much, save for one horrible moment during my sophomore year when the gym teacher asked me why I didn't go out for basketball, I was so tall and the team could use me. I mumbled something about not having time to practice and fled from her as fast as I could.

Gym classes were awkward, but the shower was a nightmare. We all had to take showers. I turned around once in freezing cold water, wrapped a towel around myself, and faced the tomalley green walls of the locker room as I fumbled my tiny bra on and dressed as quickly as I could. But on the last Tuesday of my last week of high school, as I hurried to dress and get out of the locker room, I heard a voice behind me. Angela whined like a buzz saw. "Florine Chlorine," she said. "I'm talking to you."

I turned around to find her about three feet away from me, flanked by two of her cronies. I didn't say anything.

Angela sniffed the air. "Chlorine, like bleach. Smells like bleach. Ewww." One of her friends, a dirty-blond girl, brushed her hair and smiled. The other, a dull brunette, just looked at me with her dead eyes. "No, wait, not bleach," Angela went on, "more like hot tuna." Both of her friends laughed.

I said nothing.

"Do you know what hot tuna is?" Angela asked me. "Can't talk? Well, ask someone then. It's all over school what you smell like." She and her friends left me alone, and I finished dressing in peace, wondering what the hell she was talking about.

"Why did she call me that?" I asked Bud and Glen later, in Bud's car. A silence a little too long to be comfortable filled the air and I said, again, "Why?"

"Don't tell her," Bud said to Glen. "Just don't tell her."

"I got a right to know," I said.

"Shit, Bud, we should tell her," Glen said.

"No," Bud said. "Don't do it."

"WHY DID SHE CALL ME THAT?" I shouted into poor Glen's ear.

"The hot part means a good lay," Glen said, shrinking down into his seat. "The tuna part means you smell like fish down there. Don't hit me."

"Who the hell says that?" I asked him.

"Kevin Jewell started it," Glen said.

I sat back in my seat, my burning face outdoing the car heater. "Why would he do that?" I said. "We didn't do anything."

"He's an asshole," Bud said.

On my last day of school, a Thursday, Angela struck again. This time she didn't bother to come around the lockers. She started in on me from the other side. "Hot tuna," Angela said to her giggling friends, "is only good on the first day. After that, it goes stale and it smells bad."

I had just come from the shower, and I stood swamped in my towel. I shook my head, wishing Dottie, with her negotiating skills, was here. Then, the shit hit the fan for me.

"Florine Chlorine Hot Tuna, is it true that your mother ran away?" Angela asked.

The locker room went quiet, except for the hiss of the showers.

My hands shook as I grabbed my hairbrush from the locker.

"Chlorine, did you hear me?" she said.

I heard her. I dropped my towel and walked around to the other side of the lockers, still holding on to my hairbrush. Angela was looking up over the lockers, no doubt waiting to spew some more garbage at me. When she saw me standing there, she almost looked startled. She opened her mouth, but I chose that moment to find my voice.

"It's none of your goddamned business," I said to her and her friends. They moved closer to one another and gasped as if they were one thing.

"I don't blame her for leaving you and your drunk daddy," Angela said. "Can't imagine her putting up with you."

"You'd better stop, now," I said. I stepped toward her, naked and ready to kill her.

I looked at all of the girls and I said, "I'll tell you what I know about my mother. She disappeared when I was twelve. We never found her. She's probably dead. I haven't stopped missing her. Any other stupid questions? No? Then you leave me the hell alone." I looked at Angela. "And by the way, I never screwed Kevin Jewell."

I stomped back to my side of the locker, breathing hard. Very little talk took up the air as I dressed, took my books out of the old locker, slammed the door, and left.

Right outside the locker room, I bumped smack into a tall man.

"Hey, watch where you're going, there," the man said. I glanced up at him.

"Sorry," I said. Then I gave him a good look. His hair wasn't greased back anymore, and the black was mostly gray. But his eyes were still blue and he was smiling, and a snaggletooth showed at the side of his mouth. *"I just need to know the rules,"* I had heard him say to Carlie that day at the beach.

"It's you," I said.

"Who?" he asked, and he laughed a little.

"Snaggletooth Mike," I said. He stopped smiling. "You were on the beach with Patty and my mother. You knew my mother. You acted like you really knew her."

"What are you talking about? Who are you? Who was your mother?"

"Carlie Gilham," I said.

Mike crossed his arms over his chest and squinted hard at me. "Oh, you're her daughter," he said. "Lorraine? Is that your name?"

"It's Florine," I said.

"Florine," he said, and he nodded. "I remember you now. I remember the cops asking me a lot of questions. Got my wife all worked up for no reason."

"Seems like you weren't too worried about that on the beach," I said.

"Whoa, whoa," Mike said. He stepped back further and held out his arms as if I was going to rush him. "Look, Florine, I'm sorry about your mother. She was a nice lady. We flirted, that's all. At the restaurant. I had a job delivering milk for Maplehurst Dairies that summer. I'd stop at the Shack, get funny with Patty and Carlie. We had some laughs. Patty told me to come along to the beach one day on a day off. I would never have done anything to your mother," he said.

I stared at him, turning to stone inside.

"Listen, Florine, I'm substituting for the men's gym teacher today, and I need to go. Are we okay? I promise you, I wouldn't ever hurt Carlie. She was a good girl. A fun girl. And she loved your father. Everyone knew that. Are we cool?"

I turned away and walked down the hall, late for class. I sat in a fog through the rest of the day, thinking about Carlie, the beach, Mike, that awful, awful time. I was still thinking about these things when I got into Bud's car. He was alone.

Bud said, "I heard you gave 'em hell in the locker room."

"I did," I said.

"Good for you," he said.

We didn't talk until we reached Grand's house.

"You know," Bud said, "you're better than any of them, don't you?"

"I wish none of this had ever happened. I wonder what my life would have been like if it hadn't happened."

"Different, for sure," Bud said. "But I think you've done good, anyway. Don't know as I could have done it without going crazy. You're some girl." He patted my hand, and then he squeezed it before he took his hand back.

"Thanks for the ride," I said.

"See you tomorrow," he said. I watched him drive down the hill, and then I went into the house to have a cup of tea with Grand.

She wasn't in the kitchen. But the teakettle was fussing so I turned off the burner. When I picked it up, I found that most of the water had boiled away. "Oh Grand," I said. I picked up the kettle to tease her and went into the living room. She was lying on her side between the coffee table and the sofa. She groaned, and I went to her.

32

I covered Grand with one of her crocheted afghans, shut off the television and then called the ambulance. She mumbled and moaned, and I listened hard to catch anything that might make sense. The lights in her eyes showed through the slits in her eyelids and I hoped those lights wouldn't go out.

As we waited, the November dusk put the brakes on the day. My heart knocked against my head and I breathed deep, trying to keep calm. I hummed the tune to "Amazing Grace" over and over. "Help is coming, Grand, hold on," I said between humming.

After endless minutes, I heard the siren, and red lights flashed as Bert Butts and his brother, Wayne, wiped their shoes on the welcome mat in the hall, as Grand had trained everyone to do.

"Where's the light?" Wayne hollered.

"Switch to the left," I called, and lights went on there, then in the kitchen, then in the living room, then they were tending Grand and I watched them with my hands tucked beneath my armpits to keep from shaking apart.

More shoes scraped the mat, and Bud and Glen walked in. They stood in the doorway to the living room, their breath visible in the light.

"Go get the gurney," Bert said to them.

The four of them eased Grand onto her back, counted to three, and hoisted her onto the gurney. They counted again at the back of the ambulance and loaded her up. I climbed in back with Bert and Grand. Wayne turned on the siren and we bucked up the rocky hill. The lights at Ray's showed people standing outside, wondering who was passing. Then the dark gobbled up all but the lights inside the ambulance.

We sped toward Long Reach. Cars hugged the sides of the road as we flashed by—all but an old Chevy with a bumper sticker that read How'd you like me up your ass, Chummy? It wouldn't move over and we couldn't pass on the twisted road.

Wayne beeped the horn. Nothing. "Jesus," he said.

"Must have the radio cranked," Bert said.

"I'll mess with his crank if he don't pull over," Wayne said.

Grand groaned. I took her cold, dry hands in mine. "She worse?" I asked Bert.

He placed his fingers against the pulse in her neck. "Gun it," he said to Wayne.

But the Chevy blocking us moved as slow as a dreamer who can't outrun a nightmare.

Bert yelled at Wayne, "Either pass the bastard or run right over him."

"I'm on it," Wayne said. Then he hit the gas and we zoomed past the Chevy, whipping around the curve at Pine Pitch Hill. I waited to take flight, or waited for the jolt that meant we'd hit a car coming toward us, but it didn't happen. I looked out the back window and saw the Chevy still moving as if nothing else mattered.

Bert muttered, "Shit," and moved a stethoscope from atop Grand's sheet-covered chest.

"What?" I cried, my own insides ticking down to a stop.

"Wayne," Bert said, "floor the bastard. Florine, you got to move." I scrambled to get out of the way while he placed his hands on Grand's chest and began to push and count.

It took Wayne about five more minutes to make the emergency room. They whisked Grand out and wheeled her inside, where they moved her into a curtained room. I tried to go in, but a woman in blue put her hand up and said, "Wait outside, please. The family room is right over there."

I backed up toward it. One old man sat on a brown sofa watching the TV mounted on the wall. He didn't look up at me, and I didn't want to go in, so I turned and looked down the hall. A man about Daddy's age swished his mop over the floor. I wanted to be him. He had nothing to worry about except his floor, even as people were going through some of the worst moments of their lives. It might come around to him, but not right now. Now, he was just washing the floor.

"Come in and sit down, young lady," the old man called to me, and I turned around. His eyes were still on the TV, but he signaled me with his thin hand to join him, so I took the blue chair beside the sofa. As soon as I did, Bert came into the room and we went back into the hall. He looked at me, straight on.

"Florine, they're trying," he said. "She's not doing good though, honey. She's tough, but she's had a bad stroke and they think she's still having 'em."

A chill raked its nails down my back.

Bert put his hand on my shoulder, left it there.

"Will Grand die?" I asked.

When Bert took his hand away from my shoulder I knew the answer. But he said, "Not if they have anything to say about it. Your father's on his way up."

He walked off and I went back to the waiting room and sat with the old man. We watched a newscaster deliver the news. The sound was off so we couldn't tell if the news was good or bad. Her expression stayed the same, no smile, no frown, just her mouth moving at us. A bomb could right now be ending the world and she'd let us know without so much as a blink.

"I got you some cocoa," someone said and I looked up. Glen held out a big red cup, and Bud stood beside him.

"I'm not that thirsty," I said. "Grand's really bad."

"Got whipped cream," Glen said.

"Jesus, Glen," Bud said. "Think she cares if she gets goddamned whipped cream?"

"It'll make her feel better," Glen said. "Good for what ails you."

I took the offered cup and took a swig. It was dark and sweet and half whiskey. Fire and sweetness tickled their way down my pipes and jolted my pale soul.

"One of them Irish coffees without the coffee," Glen said.

"My wife died," the old man said.

We all turned and looked at him.

"When?" Bud asked.

"About an hour ago."

"Why you still here?" Glen asked. "You by yourself?"

"Yes," he said. "Tried to call my boy. No answer. He's probably at work."

Bud pulled a whiskey flask from a pocket inside his flannel jacket, and he passed it to the old man, who lifted it to his mouth and drank deep. His Adam's apple roamed up, then down, then settled in the middle of his throat. He passed the flask back to Bud and rubbed his mouth with his sleeve.

"Thanks," he said. "Now can you tell me what the hell I'm supposed to do?"

Just before Grand died, Daddy and I were allowed into the emergency unit. We watched her take her last breath. It rose in a high swell before she settled forever on a calm sea. Daddy and I stayed with her for some time, then Daddy said, "We got to be strong when we go out there," and so we were.

The morning Grand was buried, no one on The Point went to work or school, and all the boats stayed in the harbor. The store and the gas station closed. The gravediggers dug past the first frost and made a deep, clean hole for her to rest in. The whole Point and people from the surrounding areas filled the little church at her funeral. People we didn't know showed up—old ladies Grand's age who had gone to The Point school with her, and craft fair and shop people who sold the sweaters she'd made. A few summer people showed, too, those who had bought her bread and sweaters. A couple of older gentlemen with gloom tracing the road maps of their wrinkled faces sat toward the back of the church. I wondered if they'd been in love with Grand at one time or another. Any man would've been happy with her, if she hadn't only loved one man for her entire life.

After the service, people bustled into and out of her house with the casseroles and stews. Stella looked as though she might want to comfort me, if I would give her the chance. But the only person who might have comforted me was more than likely having a high old time with her good friend, Jesus.

The Point women worked like a machine; they ran the wake and the after-funeral gathering, made the men drink and smoke outside and pick up their empties and butts, and cleaned up afterward. Then they were gone.

Daddy, Stella, Dottie, and I were the only ones left. We slumped at the table, tired and sad. Dottie still managed to chow down on chunks of this and bites of that from the leftover casseroles, while Daddy and Stella drank coffee. I wasn't hungry or thirsty.

"You eat anything today?" Stella asked me.

"No," I said. Sorrow was beginning to work its way up inside me like unchecked bittersweet settling in for a lengthy growing season.

"You got to eat," Daddy said.

"You want to come home with us?" Stella asked.

"I'm home," I said. I'd seen the will. Grand had left the house to me when I turned eighteen next spring. She'd left me a little money, too, enough to tide me over for a year or two. And her bills were paid ahead, as she'd always done.

"I know, Florine, but I thought you might be lonely."

Dottie said, "I can stay with you, if you want."

"That'd be good," Daddy said.

"Okay," I said to Dottie.

Daddy hugged me close before he left and I hugged him back. This we understood about each other; that we were veteran soldiers on the battlefield of grief. Then he and Stella left and it was just Dottie and me at the kitchen table. The only sound for a few seconds was Dottie's top and bottom teeth clicking together as she ate.

"You okay?" she asked.

"Kind of numb."

"It's weird here without Grand."

"Yeah."

Dottie stood up. "I'd better clean up or she'll come back and have my ass." As she washed her plate at the sink, she said, "I wonder what was up with Stella. Usually her dishes come out so decent they get you to groaning, but that macaroni and cheese was gummy as pitch and half again as good. How could she screw up something that easy to make? Madeline's always making it because she can throw it together."

"Makes you wonder," I said.

"Glen flushed his plateful down the toilet. Caught him in the bathroom, using the plunger to get it all the way down. Before I saw what he was doing, I thought he was jerking off, but then I saw the mac and cheese in the bowl."

I smiled.

"Hope it doesn't muck up the septic system," Dottie said. "Can't you just see some Roto Rooter guy saying, 'Best to toss this out into the bay, or bury it so's it won't kill the fish. I don't want to see it in this tank again. I find it, you get a big-ass bill and a fine for cooking this crap up in the first place.'"

I had to laugh, but when she put a cup of tea in front of me, something she'd never done before, I cried.

She didn't follow when I ran upstairs to Grand's room. I spread myself over the bed to fill myself with her presence and sobbed. I fell asleep clutching her pillow.

Much later, I woke when the door creaked. I sat up and cried out, "Grand!"

The hall light backlit Dottie's stocky form.

"It's me," she said, quiet. "I was just checking on you."

I stared at her, stupid with sleep and grief.

"Can I get you something? Water?"

"No," I said.

"You want me to sleep in here with you?"

It would have been nice to have her warmth, but nothing would comfort me tonight, and she needed to sleep, so I said no. She shuffled in and kissed the top of my head, then she left the room, closing the door so that it never made a sound.

Too tired to squeeze out any more emotion, I stumbled toward the ragged edge of sleep. Then I thought of something.

I got up and went to the window that looked across the road to Daddy's house. I remembered the night I had stood out at the end of the driveway by the big white rock, feeling alone and unwanted. I recalled the way Grand had come for me, saying, *"Oh for heaven's sake, that's not true. Now, I was sound asleep and I heard you crying and I woke right up. Guess that's love, don't you think?"* Moonlight kissed the white rock with a pearly glow, then the clouds took back the moon, and it turned dark.

33

After the funeral, Dottie stayed once and awhile, but she was busy with school and bowling and I didn't want to make her feel like she had to take care of me, so I didn't push it. She'd been through so much with me, being there for me when Carlie disappeared. Enough was enough. As Grand had said, "Well, she's a restless soul."

I didn't return to school. It made me tired just thinking of trying to get through every day at home, let alone trying to fake it in a place that had never set right with me in the first place. I didn't have the energy to face any of them. Mostly, I just wanted to sleep.

I was abed one morning when a horn beeped outside and someone knocked at the door. "No," I said into my pillows, both to getting up and to answering the door. The horn beeped again, and I knew it was Bud, and I knew they were waiting for me.

Dottie hollered up the stairs. "You ever coming back to school?"

"I don't know," I said. I heard Dottie stomp upstairs and then she stood in the doorway.

"Been three weeks," she said.

"I know," I said.

The horn beeped again. "You'd better go. You'll be late," I said.

"Yeah," she said, and clomped downstairs and out the door. The

Fairlane chugged up the hill as I stared at the thin morning light on the ceiling. "Get up," I said. Grand wouldn't have brooked my slacking.

So I got up, I cleaned downstairs, then went upstairs and made up Grand's bed. I hadn't the heart to change her sheets. Her musty lavender smell was fading, but if I breathed deep, I could catch a whiff. Days, I wore her dresses, though they hung off me like popped balloons. It was a comfort to me.

After I picked up the house, I turned on the television, cranked up the volume, and settled back. I sat through soaps, talk, crafts, and cooking shows. During commercials I made tea and grabbed snacks. Naptime was three thirty. After my nap, I rocked on the porch. I hummed "What a Friend We Have in Jesus," much as Grand might have done, and when the winter sun set, I washed my face and hands and maybe took a bath.

If Dottie came over, I'd make some kind of dinner, mostly from the frozen stores in Grand's freezer, along with the canned goods we'd put up. The stash was beginning to go down and I knew that sooner or later I was going to have to buy more food. But I didn't want to leave the cocoon of the house just yet.

After a month, the school called. I only answered the phone because I thought it might be Dottie or Daddy.

"This is Vice Principal Brown calling from Montgomery High School. May I speak to Florine Gilham, please?"

"She's not here."

"Do you know when she'll return?"

"No, I don't."

"Would you take a message down?"

"Sure." I clunked the phone down and mumbled, "Now where's that pen?" loud enough for Mrs. Brown to hear. Finally, I picked up the receiver and said, "All right."

"Tell Florine that she needs to come back to school, or she's in danger of flunking out. She hasn't been in class for over a month, and the school is concerned about her. We know that she lost her grandmother, and we're sympathetic to that. But she has her future to think about, and she's a good student and we would hate for her to not finish high school. It would be a shame."

"Okay, I'll tell her. Thanks for calling."

"Did you get all that? It was quite a lot."

"Oh yes."

"Be sure she gets the message."

"I will."

"Goodbye, Florine. Come back soon."

I slammed down the phone. I thought about calling her and asking her to describe me. If she could do that, maybe I'd consider coming back. But chances are she wouldn't recognize me. Hell, I didn't recognize myself.

December's dark mornings tamped down my efforts to get up in the morning. Why bother? I wondered. I felt tied down with invisible ropes, like the story I'd read once about a man named Gulliver, who had been staked to the ground by the tiny Lilliputians. I didn't want to jar my heart awake. That would bring tears and upset, and it just seemed easier to shut it all out.

I began sleeping until 9:00, then 10:00 A.M. Then past noon. Clocks danced away the minutes as I drowsed. Cars and trucks went up the hill and growled as they came back down to the harbor. Seagulls yonked and Ray Clemmons's beagle, Hoppy, barked the day away while I burrowed under the covers, safe. I thought about shutting the bedroom door and leaving a sign on the outside that read Do Not Disturb Till Spring. I'd all but decided to do that when a couple of things happened that got me cranked up.

34

I always made sure I was up when Daddy stopped by on afternoons on his way home from carpentry jobs. He'd bring me milk, sugar, and tea to keep me stocked up.

"You okay?" he asked me every day. "You need anything?"

"I'm fine," I'd answer. We'd talk a little in the kitchen, then he'd say, "Well, I got to go across the road. You're welcome to supper. Stella would love to have you over."

I doubted that, but I let it lie. "I have leftovers, Daddy, but thanks," I said.

The school had called him, too. "Might help you take your mind off Grand. Keeping busy helps. She'd be the first one to tell you that," he said.

"I'll go back soon," I lied.

One Wednesday night in December, I was watching the news when someone kicked at the door with what sounded like a big boot. I jumped before a voice yelled, "It's Bud."

I opened the door and he walked through it, carrying a large cooking pot.

"Ma steamed up some mussels at home," he said. "Too many. She doesn't want them going to waste, so she told me to bring them over, see if you wanted some. Lots of butter and garlic and some wine she threw in on a notion. Ain't half bad."

I was so far from hungry that I almost didn't know what it felt like anymore. "That's nice of her," I said. He thrust the pan at me and I took it.

"Want to stay a minute?" I asked.

"Okay. But I got to pick up Susan. She wants to see some movie."

"How's she doing?"

"Good."

I put the pot on the kitchen counter.

"Sit down," I said.

He started to do it, and then stood up. "I forgot," he said. He reached into the back pocket of his flannel pants.

"You like lemon?" he asked, holding it out to me. In the callused darkness of his palm, the lemon shone like a piece of summer sun.

I took it from him, my fingers brushing his smooth skin. The lemon was warm from being in his pocket, and I cupped it between my hands.

"You better eat them mussels up," Bud said.

"I will. Tell Ida thanks."

He headed for the door, but then he turned around and said, "I forgot to tell you about that old guy. Remember his wife died and he didn't know what to do? Bert saw to it that he got some help. So he got taken care of."

"That's good."

"Ma said not to worry about washing the pot." And he was gone.

I tossed the brightness that was the lemon from one hand to the other for a while, remembering how Carlie had loved yellow. I bit into the skin and the zest tingled in my nostrils. I cut it in half and squeezed it over the mussels. I ate every one. I dreamed of gold that night, of lemons. Of people walking away into the sun. Of Bud's hands.

I got a rude awakening the next morning at about eleven o'clock, in the middle of a good drowse.

"Florine?"

Stella's voice grated through the four layers of blankets over me and I raised them up to see her standing in the bedroom doorway. The white apron she wore at the store had grease spots on the front. She looked mad.

"How'd you get in?" I asked. She didn't answer.

"I'm going downstairs, and I want you to join me," she said.

I tucked myself under the covers again and hoped she would just go away.

"Florine," she called from the bottom of the stairs. "I'm not leaving until you come down here. I mean it. The sooner you get down here, the sooner you get rid of me."

That gave me a reason to get up. I hauled my butt out of bed and pulled on Carlie's old Popham Beach sweatshirt and a pair of dirty jeans, went to the bathroom and peed. I ran my fingers through my tangled hair, then caught it up in a rubber band. I considered brushing my teeth, but figured that tea would just undo that chore so I went downstairs to the shrill of the kettle on full boil.

"What's wrong?" I asked.

"Set down," she said. "I want to talk to you."

"Is Daddy okay?" I asked as I stayed on my feet.

"What do you think?"

"He looked fine last night when he stopped by."

"Of course he did," Stella said. She set the mugs on the table and sat down. I needed milk, so I went to the refrigerator and brought a quart back to the table.

"Want some?" I asked.

"No. Set down, Florine," Stella said, and her voice shook. I took my time lowering my ass into the chair seat. The tea bag dangling in my mug had a tear in it, and some of the leaves floated on the top of the water. I poked at them to make them go down, and then I bobbed the tea bag up and down, releasing even more leaves.

"I took your father to the hospital this morning," Stella said. "He had chest pains."

I stopped the tea bag in mid-bob.

"He's okay," she went on, "but the doctor said he needs to slow down, stop drinking, and not get so worked up."

"Don't get him so worked up, then," I said.

"Jesus, you make me tired. You're the reason your father is in the shape he's in."

"Well, that's bullshit."

"He's worried himself sick about you. He's on the verge of a heart attack, because you're sleeping all hours and you've quit school. How the hell can he not be worried?"

"Tell him not to worry. I'm fine. It's a waste of his time."

Stella got up and pushed in her chair. "No. You do that. You say that to his face. And by the way, hating me only hurts your father more. I don't give a damn if you think I'm scum, but I won't have your father sick over it. He thinks he's lost you, too."

"He can come and see me anytime. I'm right here," I said.

"Oh, you're here, all right. Even when you're not in front of him, you're here. I'm sick of you playing on the fact that you've lost your mother. He thinks you think he's to blame. He's taken it all on, you stupid girl. And, by the way, you're not the only one who has lost someone. I know a little about that, too." Her hand moved toward the scar on her face.

"Talk about playing on the fact," I said.

She took her tea mug to the sink, ran water inside of it, put it down with a clunk, turned back to me, and said, "I love your father. I wouldn't have had him go through what he's gone through, but he did, and I was blessed to have a chance with him. I hope you get to be with the love of your life someday. And I hope you don't have to put up with some brat who hates your guts just because you're not who she wishes you were."

"I wish you'd died," I said. "That's what I wish."

She sucked in a deep breath. "I have to get back to work," she said. "I came by to tell you about your father. Grand would be ashamed of the way you've talked to me. If you keep up with this nonsense, and Leeman gets to feeling worse, I will be on you every day until one of us kills the other one. Do you want me in your face every day?"

I clenched my hands into fists deep within my pockets.

Then her gray eyes filled with tears and she said, "It wasn't my fault, Florine."

She went back to work and I tossed what was left of my tea into the sink. The tea leaves scattered over the bottom. I knew there was a fortune there but I didn't know how to read it so I turned on the faucet and flushed it all down the drain.

Daddy came by at about five o'clock. "What's cooking?" he asked.

"Mac and cheese," I said. "Grand's recipe."

"Good," he said. "Is Dottie coming by?"

"Isn't for Dottie."

"Oh," he said.

"You going to tell me you went to the doctor?" I asked.

"I told Stella not to tell you," he said. "Nothing to worry about." I looked into his face. Really gave it a look. The shadows around his eyes broke my heart. He shuffled his feet and said, "I'd better get home."

I picked up the casserole and said, "I'm coming with you."

He paused. Then he said, "Let's go, then."

We found Stella at the stove. She turned to greet Daddy with a look that made her look about seventeen. But when she saw me, she stopped and stared.

"I thought you could use a lesson on how to make good mac and cheese," I said. "Yours is terrible."

35

The next morning I went to the loose brick behind the stove where Grand kept her pin money. I fished a twenty out of the wad and put the brick back. Then I stepped outside for the first time in a month and took a walk up to Ray's.

The cold air pinched my nostrils together and I wrapped my jacket around me as I bustled up the road. Ray was reading the morning paper by the register. He looked up over his reading glasses and said, like I'd been there yesterday, "Cold enough for you?"

"Few more degrees and we can call it winter," I said.

"What you need?" Ray asked.

"Bunch of stuff," I said.

"You know where it is," he said and went back to the paper.

I moved down the little aisle trying to think about what I needed. I hadn't made a list but it didn't matter. I was thinking about buying chocolate squares for brownies when Ray said, "You selling wreaths this year?"

"Oh my God," I said. I had completely forgotten about the annual wreath making. I must have looked like a fish gasping for air, because Ray said, "We can skip a year."

"No. We can't," I said. Grand wouldn't stand for it.

"We got five orders from Connecticut," Ray said. "And two come from Mass."

"Okay," I said. My mind slid like slippers on a waxed floor as I tried to gather my thoughts. How could I make this happen? I didn't know if I was up to it.

"Might talk to Madeline," Ray said, reading my mind. "She can probably help."

I bought the milk and a Heath bar and walked back to Grand's house, thinking how she'd left me everything except instructions on how to understand what she'd really meant to everyone. I sat in my rocker on the porch and ate the Heath bar for breakfast. I was working the butter toffee off my teeth with my finger when the phone rang.

I tripped over Grand's knitting basket, scattering balls of yarn.

"We just got another two orders," Ray said, when I answered. "Wreaths for Mrs. Caldwell. And she wanted to know if Grand had her sweater made. Grand told her she'd make one for her granddaughter."

"Damned if I know, Ray. She didn't leave me a list."

"Well, you find a sweater looks like it would fit a kid, bring it up and I'll ship it out."

I hung up and rubbed away a fingerprint that was smudged on the phone box. "What else have you got me into?" I said to Grand.

I gathered the yarn up and put it back into the knitting basket. Beside the basket was a little bag. I peeked inside and saw a half-made child's sweater. I held its tough little stitches to my nose and inhaled the lanolin in the wool and I almost keeled over from memories of Grand knitting and humming while I read a book, her bulky form beside me, her hair mussed up, and her silver-framed glasses catching light. I hugged the little half-made sweater to me until I could stand without crumbling. Then I went to find Madeline to have a talk about Christmas wreaths.

She said, "I've got it covered. Has to be soon—how about this Sunday? I can get Bert out there and I know Stella will boss your father out. I've talked to Ida and Stella about it and they'd be happy to come to our house this year. You don't mind, do you?"

"No," I said, relieved beyond belief. "I don't mind at all." Madeline would make it her own event, but it probably would have happened, anyway. The wreath making had passed on.

Or passed out. At the wreath making, Madeline filled a punch bowl with wine and god knows what else and she, Stella, and Ida got lit and made their version of a holiday wreath with toilet paper rolls and unused tampons. They took off their bras and hooked them onto the wreath and laughed so hard it's a wonder they didn't wet themselves.

"Let's swipe some wine and get out of here," Dottie said. We took a half fifth of Gallo Rosé into her bedroom and took a couple of swigs from it.

I said, "Carlie liked little wreaths. 'Not everyone has a big door,' she'd say."

"I remember 'em," Dottie said. "They was sweet. Remember that one she made out of lobster claws she saved up from the Shack?" I did. I had it hanging in my room.

In the living room, Ida and Madeline laughed at something Stella said. It was hard for me to imagine Stella being funny. I took a gulp of wine. "Grand would have a cow if she saw them now," I said.

"They're being assholes," Dottie said.

The rosé warmed my face. "I think I'm getting drunk," I said.

"Kinda lightweight, aren't you?"

"Don't you feel anything?"

"I been drinking for a while now," Dottie said. "I down a six-pack no problem."

"Where you drinking?"

"Bud's car. Glen's truck. Parties. You should come out with us."

But I couldn't imagine chugging beer and going to a party. I could never go back.

The women in the living room exploded into laughter. "That's it," Madeline screamed, "that's all he does. That means I'm supposed to roll over and open up wide and say, 'Come on in honey, the water's fine.'"

"Oh, Jesus," Dottie said. "I don't friggin' need to know this crap. Let's get them back to business and finish up."

It took us till ten or so that night, but in spite of our wooziness, or because of it, we ended up with thirty beautiful wreaths that would have made Grand proud. Madeline handed the most beautiful one to me as I went out the door.

"Don't mind us," she said, swaying a little as her brown eyes filled up. "We miss Grand, too, honey. I would have given up all this silliness just to hear her laugh. You need anything, you holler. You're one of our own." She gave me a sloppy kiss and a hug that squeezed the breath out of me. "Night," she said. "Careful out there, it's slippery."

I walked toward Grand's house, still floating in a pink glow from the wine. When I slipped and fell on my ass on the road, I picked myself up and turned to see if anyone had seen me, but all seemed clear, except for the two ghosts who now followed me; one small and slender, carrying a red claw wreath that clinked as she walked, and one big-boned and older, holding a fragrant, soft-needled wreath with brilliant scarlet berries and prayers woven throughout it.

The day after the wreath party, I picked up the child's sweater and studied it. It was a fairly simple pattern, one that Grand had taught me years before, and I decided to try and finish it up. I hadn't clicked two needles together since she'd died, but after a few starts and stops it started to make sense again. I hustled the ivory-colored stitches back and forth along the rows, and the creamy ball of yarn shrank as the sweater grew. I pictured Someone's mother pulling it over a small head, popping it past a little nubbin of a nose and down over a stubborn chin, then smoothing electrified hair while Someone stood, impatient to travel on to bigger things. This sweater would become part of Someone's life. If I knit it well, it would be passed down to Someone Else.

By two o'clock, it was done. I held it up and looked it over. Although I could see where Grand's work stopped and mine began, I was pretty sure that no one else would be able to tell. I had a few sad seconds thinking that, from now on, all the sweaters I made would be my own work.

But I shook it off because I needed to wash and block the sweater and get it up to Ray so he could ship it out.

I was rolling it in a towel to squeeze the water out of it when Bud drove by on his way home. I looked out the kitchen window and he caught my eye and we smiled at each other. To my surprise, my nipples went hard, and I realized I was so horny that I would have welcomed the hands of a clock on me.

When someone rapped on the door that night at about ten, I was watching television and casting stitches on for another sweater. Dottie stood there. "Just got back from bowling. We played a team in Brunswick. We won," she said. "Saw the TV light and decided to come over and say hi." I let her in and she pulled off her boots. She was wearing nylons and her toes looked mashed. She pulled them off.

"Want some socks?" I asked.

"Good idea," she said.

I put on the kettle. "You get out the cocoa and I'll go get socks. You staying here?"

"Not tonight, I guess. Just a visit."

When I came downstairs with the socks, she was sitting in front of the television with a sleeve of saltines in front of her. The kettle shrieked as I handed her the socks. I went into the kitchen and found the box of cocoa by the sink. I spooned it into two mugs, mixed in sugar and milk, and stirred until it all melted. I took the mugs and some milk into the living room and set them on coasters on the coffee table.

"You got any peanut butter?" she asked, and I fetched it and a knife to spread it.

"See the sweater I made?" I asked her. I held it up to her.

"Ain't that cunnin'," she said. She touched a little sleeve and ran her hand over the front of the sweater. "Soft," she said.

She layered peanut butter on a cracker. "Want one?" she asked.

"No."

She munched, I knit, we sipped, and we watched *Hawaii Five-O* for about ten minutes. Then Dottie set down her cocoa cup, walked over to the TV and turned the volume down. She looked at me as serious as I'd ever seen her.

"I come to a decision," she said. "I'm going to be a pro bowler."

"Can you make money doing that?" I asked.

"Sure can. They got pro leagues. Barb Raymond does it, why can't I? The guy manages Bowla Rolla, Gus—he said I should go pro, and he would know. He sees hundreds of people bowl every day. Says my style is a lot like Barb Raymond's."

"What makes her so special?" I asked.

Dottie crouched and looked through the living room wallpaper to a V of pins at the end of an imaginary bowling lane. "Moves like a cat down to the line. Lets her ball go and WHAM! Strike. WHAM! Strike." Dottie straightened up. "Know how it hits you that you were meant to do a thing? Well, God spoke unto me and said, 'Dottie, thou shalt bowl.'"

"Madeline know?"

"Not yet."

We went back to looking at Jack Lord. A lock of black hair fell over his forehead. It killed me when that happened, and it also reminded me of Bud. I smiled.

"Book 'em, Danno," Dottie said.

A commercial came on and Dottie went on about the plan she had to get a job at Bowla Rolla, so she could get in some free practice when the lanes were shut down.

Then she said, "What you going to do?"

I shrugged. "Don't know. Maybe get married. Have kids."

"You got a guy in mind?"

"Maybe Bud," I said.

"How's that going to happen?" Dottie said. "I thought we talked about him and Glen being like our brothers. Besides, he's hot and heavy with Susan."

"Look," I said, "you got your dreams, I got mine." My face got hot. "I tell you something I got in my heart, and you make fun of it."

"Don't get so riled up."

"Might seem stupid to you, but it isn't to me."

"Don't take it so hard," Dottie said. "I didn't mean nothing by it. Calm down." She got up and stretched, and then she knelt down and pretended to throw a ball down a lane. Then she shouted, "Strike!"

"No," I said. "You missed a pin to the right. Definitely a spare."

She shrugged and started for the door. I followed her. She pulled off the socks, pulled on her boots, and put her coat on. She stuffed the nylons into her coat pocket. The wind tagged us both when she opened the door.

"I'll be seeing you," Dottie said, and she shut the door. She hadn't gotten two steps when I opened it again and hollered, "I was wrong! The pin just fell over. Strike!"

She smiled. "I knew that. Dottie Butts don't spare nothing."

I closed the door. "You got your dreams," I said again to her back. "And I got mine." But a part of me knew she might be right. I needed to get out more. Maybe I could take a chance and walk over the mountain, so to speak, without worrying about someone keeling over or driving off to God knows where.

36

Next morning I put the sweater into a little box and hugged it to my chest as I walked it up the hill to Ray's. Stella was dusting shelves when I showed up, but she came right over when she saw I had business with Ray.

"Mind if I take a peek?" Stella asked.

I opened the box and she ran her hand over the wool. She said, "You got the touch."

"Put some more together," Ray said. "Grand's sweaters always sold."

"How much did Grand get?" Stella asked.

"Not a lot," Ray said. "She said she just liked making them."

"Florine's got to make some money," Stella said.

"I'll pay her, Stella. Don't you worry. It'll be between her and me."

" 'Course, but she needs a job. She's got to do something."

"I'm right here," I said. "I can hear just fine."

They looked at me as if I had just showed up.

"This is what I'm planning," I said. "There's the bread. And making sweaters will bring in some extra. I'm hoping Daddy will take me on next spring to help on the boat. Maybe I can housekeep at the cottages when the summer people come in. There's plenty of stuff to do around here." I didn't mention working at the Lobster Shack. I would never be able to waitress there without thinking of Carlie.

Ray nodded. "Maybe you can help out here this summer. We'll see."

"That'd be good," Stella said. "We can have her do what I'm doing so I can get going on the sandwiches, or she can sell ice creams."

"She's going to help me, Stella, not you," Ray said.

"I know," Stella said, "but I could use the help, too."

Since they didn't seem to need me there to carry on about what I should be doing with my life and for whom, I left the store. Ray would pay me for the sweater later.

Once outside, I sucked in a season's worth of winter air: cold, clean, filled with snow. The gray swells in the harbor huddled close, as if to keep warm. I thought about what I had just told Ray and Stella. Most of it was talk. I didn't know if Daddy would take me on, wondered how many sweaters I would have to make, how many loaves of bread.

My head filled with half-risen plans, I headed toward the path that led to the State Park. About an inch of snow covered the ground. I meant to take the path to my little clearing that day, but my feet changed my mind and took me through to the Barrington place. I stood on the edge of the woods. I thought back to how Mr. Barrington had kissed my hand and called me lovely, like my mother. I thought about the fire. The old man pissing on Bud and me. Seeing my first Negro. Getting talked down to by Mr. Barrington. The way Carlie had squeezed my shoulders when he had done that. "My little criminal," she had whispered into my ear. The wind in the pines picked up the word "criminal" and spread it amongst themselves. I thought about the walk the four of us had taken last winter. The downed pine was gone, cut up, no doubt, last summer. I walked down to the edge of the lawn to see if they had put a new beach in. A pile of rocks edged the soil ledge carved by the ocean, and a strip of new, imported sand faced the sea. "Foolish," I said. "Just going to happen again, sooner or later." I turned and walked back toward the cottage. It was beautiful in the winter sunshine. Each weathered gray shingle stood stern and stark, and the lupine-blue trim of the windows and porch shone bright. I walked up onto the porch and peeked through a large window. Furniture slept in lumps and curves under white sheets, except for one big, rose-colored sofa sitting in front of a pink quartz fireplace the size of Daddy's boat. Charred logs filled the hearth.

"Huh," I said. "That's kind of strange." The caretaker for the cottages lived a couple of miles away from The Point. I'd seen him come into Ray's on this and that errand for the summer people. Always wore thigh-high rubber boots, even on the hottest days. Always walked fast, as if he had long distances to cover in those boots.

I wondered why he hadn't cleaned the fireplace. Maybe he had something going with someone's wife and they used this place to get away together. Or maybe he liked to come here and drink. Whatever he did or thought was beyond me, though, so I stepped off the porch and looked out over the ocean. I wondered how far Carlie's horizon would be by boat. Ten miles? Twenty miles? "If you'd stayed in school," I said out loud, "they might have told you."

"Probably not. They're ignorant bastards," a man's voice said behind me.

I whipped around. The man was so close that I hopped backwards.

Then, given distance and the fact that he was smiling, I studied the speaker. Brown freckled skin where his red beard didn't grow. Light brown hair, dark brown eyes. Dressed in an old pea jacket, jeans, green flannel shirt, and beat-up Bean boots.

"How you doing, Florine?" he asked.

"I'm okay," I said, looking deep into his face to figure out how I knew him.

"I saw you looking into the house. I figured it'd be a matter of time before you saw my truck. I thought I'd save you the trouble of trying to guess who was here."

"Who *is* here?"

"I'm crushed," he said. "Andy Barrington. I helped you set off firecrackers." He took off his right glove and held out his hand for me to shake. His was warm. Mine was cold.

The whole summer rushed back and passed through me like a high-speed train and I stepped back again to get out of its way.

"You okay?" Andy asked.

"A lot happened after we saw you," I said.

"Well, if it makes you feel better," Andy said, "I got busted for spiking Aunt Camilla's Virgin Mary. They didn't appreciate it, seeing as how she'd been on the wagon for a while. They sent me back to Connecticut after that."

"Why are you here now?"

"Christmas break at school. Early time for good grades. I was sitting in English class one day thinking about this place and something told me that I had to come. Mother is going to the Bahamas and Dad is spending the time with a bottle somewhere in the Berkshires. So, I drove up from Boston a couple of weeks ago."

"Your folks divorced?"

"Yeah. About a year ago. Edward started drinking like the world was running out of booze and he went from a part-time asshole to a full-time one. Wouldn't quit drinking and Mother left him. I see him maybe twice a year. Always a good time when we get together—he picks me apart and I count the hours till I can leave. Jesus, sorry. Probably more than you wanted to know."

I shrugged. I wasn't surprised, somehow. "How are you keeping warm?" I said.

"Fireplace throws off a lot of heat," Andy said. "I sleep pretty close to it. Might move my sleeping bag up to the master bedroom. Room's smaller but there's a fireplace there, too. How's your family?"

I blinked. It was weird that someone didn't know everything and then some about my family. I decided on the short version. "My mother disappeared. Grand died almost two months ago. Daddy's living with Stella, the deli woman from Ray's store. I quit school and I live at Grand's house. Otherwise, same old thing," I said.

Andy went right past Carlie to Grand. "Your grandmother died?"

he said, and his voice went sad. "No. She made me sweaters for years. I got one every year at Christmas. Mother ordered them. I'm sorry for your loss."

I nodded.

"And you lost your mom?" he said.

"Yes, she disappeared the summer I last saw you."

"Like, poof?"

"Yes," I said. No one had ever put it that way before. Poof.

"I'm sorry," Andy said. We just looked at each other for a few seconds. I studied the way his face changed second by second. His expressions were never still.

"So, everyone else around?" he asked. "The big girl, the big guy. That skinny guy that jumped in and rescued my father's money from a briny death?"

"We don't go far."

"What do you do all day with no school?"

"Knit sweaters. Bake bread. Clean house. I keep busy."

"Whatever it is you're doing is good," Andy said. "You're lovely."

Lovely. Shades of his father. I could see Mr. Barrington telling Andy, "Son, call 'em lovely. Gets them every time." Truth is, it did. It was a—well—lovely word. "I mean it. You're a good-looking woman," Andy said. "Do you have a boyfriend?"

"No," I said.

"Well, I know the place isn't heated, but would you consider joining me for dinner tonight?" Andy asked. "It's quiet here and I'd love to have some company."

When I balked for a second, drinking in the fact that this was the first time someone had asked me for a date, he added, "You can bring the others, if you want."

That confused me. Did he want them to come? Or did he want just me to come? I said, "They're probably busy."

His smile went wide and he said, "Good. Five thirty work?"

People came home from school and work at about that time. They would see me walking up the road and through the woods and wonder where I was going. I wanted this for myself. I didn't want them to know. "Later," I said. "Six thirty or so?"

"Okay," he said. He held out his hand again and I took it. His eyes winked like stars as he lifted my hand to his lips and brushed it with a kiss. His lips, I noticed, were like his father's lips. He grinned and his breath appeared in clouds of white that floated up into the blue sky.

Walking home through the woods, I noticed that red berries dangled from bushes ranging in color from brown to maroon. Dark green moss poked through the thin layer of snow. Blue-green pine needles brushed against my face. The belly of a blue heaven stretched above me. I felt so light that I turned around to check my tracks to see if they showed. They did. Barely.

The rooms in Grand's house were quiet. The clock ticked, a faucet dripped, the furnace grumbled on and the heat whooshed up through the floor register in the living room. I stood over it and let the warmth seep into my bones. I took off my coat and gloves and looked at the clock. It was noon. What the hell would I do until six thirty?

To take up some of the time, I got naked and checked myself out in the full-length mirror on Grand's closet door. From the side, my ribs showed and my back curved in a little. My tummy had a little pouch. The things that stuck out furthest were my feet, which were long and flat, like wharf ramps. Front-to, my mouse-sized boobs, with nipples the color of new pencil erasers, perched high on my chest. Nice calves like Carlie's. Square hips. Red brown triangle of pubic hair. Belly button with a small brown birthmark to the north. Long neck. Freckles starting at my chest and walking up my face to my hairline. Long arms, like a monkey. I smiled. Ivory teeth. Not as white as Andy's, but Grand had made me brush twice a day and floss. When she died, she had most of her teeth, and I guessed she had intended that I keep mine.

I turned back-to and studied my butt. Dimples above it. Carlie once told me that they were special dents the angels made when they touched you to see if you were done. I bunched one, then the other butt cheek. They reminded me of loaves of bread, and that gave me the idea to make some to take to supper. *"You never go calling without a small gift,"* Grand always said.

While the dough rose, I took a bath. I kept heating the water, using my big toe to turn the faucet on and off. I was dozing in the tub when I heard Bud's Fairlane slow down as it passed Grand's house, chugging almost to a stop before moving on. I wondered if Susan sat beside him. I wondered that it had mattered as late as this morning. Dottie had been right about getting out more.

I climbed out of the tub, dried myself, and dabbed on some Lily of the Valley perfume. Just a whiff which, according to a magazine article I'd read some time back, would keep Andy searching for the source until it drove him wild.

At about five o'clock, while I was looking for something to wear, someone knocked on the front door. "Damn," I said. I didn't want to answer it but if it was Daddy, he might worry. I threw on jeans and a sweatshirt and went down.

It was Bud.

"Hi," he said.

"Hi," I said.

He frowned.

"Do you want to come in?" I asked.

"Okay."

He stood in the kitchen and looked everywhere but at me.

"What?" I said. I took the moist dishtowel off the loaf of raised bread dough, put it into the warm oven. A whoosh of hot air blasted my face. I stood and looked at Bud. His face was as sad as I'd ever seen him.

"Bud," I said, scared now. "Did someone die?"

"Nothing like that," he said. He turned for the door. "I shouldn't have stopped by."

I walked him to the door.

"What's going on?" I said. "You're acting funny."

He turned and looked at me. "I got a girlfriend, Florine," he said.

"I know," I said. "Susan. Unless you got a new one."

"No. It's still Susan."

"Good," I said. "Everything all right?"

"You tell me," Bud said.

"Bud, what the hell are you talking about?"

"I talked to Dottie today."

"You talk to her every day."

"Yeah, I do. But she was saying something about . . . ," Bud said. "I just wanted to tell you that if I didn't have Susan, you and I . . ."

Shit on Dottie, I thought—so much for best-friend secrets. I'd deal with her later. But right now, all I wanted to do was finish baking the bread, get dressed, and hightail it up to Andy's place. I said, "It's okay, Bud. I know you got Susan. I'm glad."

"Good," Bud said. "That's all I wanted to say. It ain't that I wouldn't consider it, but I'm taken. I wouldn't hurt your feelings for nothing."

"I'm okay," I said. "Thanks for being honest. We're friends, right?"

"I guess the hell. You're a hot shit, Florine. Don't ever let them tell you different."

37

For my dinner date, I chose a purple peasant dress with paisley designs on it that Dottie had given to me because, as she'd said, "It's too jeezly small and I hate it." I wore black tights under it. I pulled on my winter boots, shrugged myself into my coat, hugged the warm bread to me and left the house, with the television and the overhead kitchen light on so people would think I was home. I started through the woods, shining the flashlight I'd brought with me along the well-known path.

Andy met me on the snowy lawn. He kissed me on the lips. "To get that out of the way," he said. Then we walked hand-in-hand around the porch, our feet thudding over the wide wooden boards. He let me in before him and shut the door against the night.

A small kerosene lantern sat on a table in the hall, its light flickering over the dark shiny wood on the walls. A set of stairs led up to a square landing, then turned and followed themselves up and out of sight to the second floor. A dusty crystal chandelier dangled overhead like a spider. The sharp smell of mothballs made me sneeze and I let out a cloud of white mist.

"Bless you," Andy said.

"I know you said you were keeping warm," I said, "but how again?"

"Oh, I'm Mr. Outdoor Guy," Andy said. "I've been to Outward

Bound four times. I'm getting by." He put his hand on my back and guided me toward the soft glow of lights in what turned out to be the kitchen. Six more kerosene lamps were placed around the kitchen to throw off as much light as possible. Something in a large pan bubbled on top of a gigantic woodstove.

When I handed the loaf of bread to Andy, he put his nose to it and breathed in the yeast. "This is too much," he said. "May I cut into it right now?"

"Go to town," I said.

I lifted the lid on the pot. Chunks of beef and carrots and potatoes rose to the top, than sank in the simmer.

"I went to Long Reach and bought groceries," Andy said. "Kind of a mix."

"Smells good," I said. While Andy sliced the bread, I looked around. The same dark wood in the hall covered the kitchen walls. With the lamps throwing soft shadows everywhere, it felt as if we were in a cave.

Andy put the bread on a small butcher's block between us. "I'm going to eat it raw," he whispered. He ripped off a small piece, popped a chunk into his mouth, and laughed out the smell of yeast.

"Glad it's a hit," I said. "It's just bread, though. It's simple."

Andy said, "Sometimes just bread is pretty close to heaven. Take it into the living room and set it on the table in front of the fire," he said. "I found some red wine in the cupboard this morning. Pour us a couple of glasses and I'll be right in."

The size of the hearth in the living room and the number of logs lit up almost the whole room. Pillows were scattered over a deep red rug with blue designs set in front of the fireplace. I poured the wine into glass goblets and held it up to the fire. Ruby as dark as the glasses in Grand's cabinet shimmered in the flames. I toasted myself and took a mouthful of the pretty wine, and found it so sour that Grand could have pickled beets in it overnight. I spit it back into the glass and swished spit around in my mouth to try to smooth down the puckers.

When Andy carried in a tray with two blue crocks of steaming stew, I kept quiet about the wine because I wasn't so sure the taste was off. I decided to wait until Andy tried it, then take another stab if it seemed like it was supposed to be good.

I tucked my arms over my knees and admired him as he set the tray on the table. He'd gotten hot in the kitchen, I guessed, because he'd taken off his old sweaters. He'd tucked the red T-shirt underneath it inside his jeans, showing off a sweet butt and flat stomach. He sat down beside me on a faded yellow pillow, picked up his wineglass, and said, "Cheers. To getting reacquainted." He took a big gulp, gave me a funny look, then held up his glass and spit the wine back into it.

"That's what I did," I said.

"Jesus, I'm sorry," he said.

"Don't tell Jesus," I said. "Put it back in the cupboard."

"Humor dry as dust," Andy said so soft that I had to lean into him to hear it.

He had me on my back before I knew what to say. He slid his body over mine and kissed me until my lips swelled to the size of juiced-up slugs. I was good to go further, except that Andy sat up.

"Man," he said. "Man."

"What?"

He studied me with his dark and shiny eyes. "You. Wow."

The sleek way he fit his body back over mine again made me spread my legs and hold his hips between my thighs. We took stock of each other's faces for a few seconds and just breathed, listening to our hearts, the silence around us, and the popping of the embers in the fireplace. He put his finger on my lips.

"I want you," he said. "But first, let's do something that'll blow your mind." He jumped up and headed for the kitchen.

While he was gone, the lumpy ghosts of the sheet-covered living room furniture claimed my attention. Here, a big overstuffed chair. There, what appeared to be a tall rocking chair. A low table sat between the two. I pictured Louisa coming back in the spring to clean, then moved on to imagine the room filled with people during a summer evening, drinks in hand, playing games or laughing. Could I ever be one of those people? Would I want to be? Would they want me to be?

Andy hummed an off-tune song in the kitchen. I sat up and smoothed my hair and moved my dress back down over my hips. I threw a couple of dry logs into the greedy fire. It gobbled the splinters before it started eating into the heart of the wood. Andy returned, holding a big, fat, home-rolled cigarette. He grinned. "Ever fucked stoned?"

I almost said, "Never fucked," but didn't. I did say, "Never stoned."

His mouth dropped open and he backed away as if I had some awful disease. "What the hell? Everyone's been stoned."

I shook my head. "Not me. But I'm willing to give it a try. Hit me."

He lit it up and a sickish-sweet smell hit my nostrils. "Whoa," I said.

"You'll get used to it," he said. "Suck it down into your lungs like you would a regular cigarette and hold your breath until you can't anymore, then let it out."

I didn't dare tell him I'd never smoked.

"Okay, I'll give her a try," I said. Andy took a hit and held his breath. His face was red and his eyes watered and a whimper slid from between his lips. He handed the joint to me and I sucked it down. And then I rolled in agony on the pillows, my lungs bucking and heaving as they tried to remember what they were supposed to do. I dropped the joint and clutched my scorched throat, coughing up smoke.

"Jesus, don't waste it," Andy said, and dove for the joint.

"What the hell is that?" I rasped.

"It's gold. The best," Andy said, holding the joint as if it was a precious jewel.

"The best what? Way to kill someone?" I sipped on the red wine vinegar to soothe my throat while Andy inspected the joint for damage. It was out, but ready to party.

"You all right?" Andy asked.

"Just dandy," I said.

He said, slow and soft, "You don't have to suck in the whole thing at once." He lit it up again. "Watch." He took a little toot. "Little breath," he said. "Then hold it."

We made our way through half of it before it hit me that he had the shiniest, most beautiful hair that I had ever seen on any human being. "Oh my God, your hair," I said, and I pawed at it like a kitten.

He pawed back and we started to laugh. And laughed. And laughed. It could have been for hours, or for five minutes. It didn't seem to matter and we couldn't stop. We rolled and tumbled on the dusty hardwood floor through paths between the ghost furniture. The giggles rolled from his body to mine and back again.

"I feel so connected to you," he said. It sounded so corny I hooted some more.

Then time disappeared into a fog bank. I'm not sure which one of us began to undress the other. Button by button, snap by snap, gentle tugs and fumblings, until he was naked on top of me and I was kissing his chest, breathing in the scent of his skin.

"This isn't quite how I imagined it," I said.

"Imagined what?" Andy said. Then he said, "You're a virgin?"

"I am," I said. "You?"

"No," Andy said. "Far out."

We made short work of my virginity. In what seemed like seconds later, I cried out and Andy groaned as he moved inside of me. It hurt like hell, but I didn't want him to stop. I watched his face, the way his eyes were closed and his mouth open, forehead creased. I wanted to take that crease away, so I put my hand on his face. He opened his eyes and smiled. His eyes were filled with stars and I could see that he was traveling somewhere else.

"You're all right?" he whispered.

I nodded, and he kissed me and pulled himself up onto his hands from an elbow position, then he drew himself out of me. I throbbed for him to enter me again, but he sat back on his haunches, lit up the end of the joint, took a toke, and said, "I was deflowered by a—uh—woman of experience, in New York City. Taught me to touch her where it mattered most. Places like this." His fingers parted me and moved to the little bump that made me crazy. He ran his thumb over it, soft, then hard, soft, soft, hard, changing the game so that I didn't know how much pressure was coming down on me.

And I came before he could make it back inside. I arched my back and screamed into the dark ceiling overhead. "Wait," Andy cried. He entered me mid-arch and then he pulsed out a warm, thick wetness. Then he pulled himself out of me again and lay beside me on the pillows. I ran my fingers down his goose-bumped back.

"Well?" he said.

"Well, what?" I asked.

He smiled. He was beautiful, with his face flushed and his hair mussed. "I would like to know how you liked it."

"Best ever," I said. He laughed and tucked two thick sleeping bags over us. Not soon after that I fell asleep in his arms.

I woke up in the pitch black of the backside of the moon. It was cold and I wondered if Grand's furnace had broken down. I cupped my nose to breathe warm air on it. I couldn't see my hand in front of my face, save for a dim glow somewhere off to my right side, which wasn't where leftover light spilled into Grand's room.

I turned my head and saw the dying embers of a fire and it came back to me on an inhale that I was with Andy Barrington in the cottage we'd almost burned down, and on the exhale that I'd been deflowered, and that my crotch hurt and I had a splitting headache. My thighs ached and my face burned from his kisses.

I was thirsty and hungry, but the thought of drinking that wine and eating cold, greasy stew turned my stomach. I wanted a big glass of water and a nice bowl of oatmeal with honey. No matter that it was the darkest time of night. The urge to clean up, eat, and wake up in my own bed was stronger than the butt end of a romantic night.

When I stood up, warmth trickled down my thighs. I fumbled under the sleeping bag for my underpants and I pulled them on fast in the cold air. I found my dress, which was spread out by the top of my head. I found my tights nearby and hauled them up. I fed the fire the last two logs in the carrier and gave it twigs and dried moss to chew on. I estimated that it was about two thirty in the morning. If the fire burned until three thirty, Andy, who never broke with his steady sleep breathing, would begin to feel the cold at about four thirty or five, if he slept that long. He would be fine. He seemed to know what he was doing in more ways than one.

The renewed fire showed me my coat and boots on the other side of the room near the big front hall. I knelt down, kissed Andy's hair, and tiptoed away. I slipped into the heart of the night, showing the flashlight in front of me on the snowy path through the woods. I huddled into my coat and scurried over the footprints I'd made coming here as a virgin. The little trip to heaven I'd experienced only a few hours before was fading fast. Besides the pain in my crotch and my thighs, Andy had also bitten my neck and it smarted. My throat was coated with ashes and pitch. Words like water, aspirin, tub, hot food, and bed kept my brain busy, until I reached the path that led to my special clearing.

And suddenly Carlie's presence filled my being and left me rooted to the ground.

The sense of her was so strong that I whispered, "Carlie?" into the night. I moved the flashlight around, as if she would walk up to me. No sound but the wind answered me, but I decided to talk to her, anyway. "I miss you," I whispered. "I'm not your little criminal anymore, but I don't miss you any less." Then, like a sigh let loose after a held breath, the feeling eased enough so that I could move. I walked on, shaking all over, wanting only to sleep.

All the houses in The Point were dark when I reached home, but I knew that someone somewhere was watching and that it would be all over town the next day that Florine Gilham had come in some time between late night and early morning. I turned off the television, drank two full glasses of water, made up some oatmeal, spooned half the honey jar over it, and took four aspirin. I stood over the heating grate in the living room, blessing the warmth that whooshed up my dress.

The rest of the night whirled in a confusion of tastes and smells as I ran a bath. I faded in and out of a half sleep until I heard a car start and realized it was time for all good children to go to school. I staggered out of the bathroom and went to bed, leaving Andy, Carlie, Grand, and anyone and anything else cluttering up my mind hanging on the bedpost.

38

I woke to so much blood on the sheets that I wondered if Andy had stuck me through, but then I figured I was having my period. It was always a surprise. It didn't come on a monthly basis, it came when it damn well pleased, and I was never ready for it. I hauled myself out of bed and pulled on some clothes to make the trek to Ray's for supplies.

It was bitter cold and I hoped that Andy hadn't died in the night. When I slipped into Ray's, I heard Stella cackle as she told Ida about a movie she and Daddy had gone to see the night before. I managed to get to Ray's register with my pads before she decided to walk over and include me in on her conversation.

"We stopped at Grand's to see if you wanted to come to the movies with us," she said to me. "The TV was running, but you weren't home."

"I stepped out," I said, setting down my pads on the counter.

"Oh," Stella said. "Where?"

"Two dollars seventy-nine cents," Ray said. He stuffed the pads into a bag.

"Where did you go last night?" Stella asked.

"Crazy," I said. "How about you?"

"Guess it's your business," Stella said.

"Yep," I said.

She went back to Ida at the deli counter and left me with Ray.

I handed Ray three dollars for the pads.

"You got home late," Ray said. " I saw you come down the road from the woods."

"It was a pretty night. I felt like walking. You felt like looking out your window. I'd a waved if I'd known you were looking at me."

"Don't get your panties in a twist," Ray said. "Just saying what I know."

"Not much to know," I said.

"Tell you something else I know," Ray said. "I know the Barrington boy is staying at the cottage."

"Wonder how he's keeping warm?" I said.

"Bring me some bread tomorrow," Ray said. "I can sell five loaves uptown."

I groaned as I walked down the hill. The last thing my aching body needed was to stir, mix up, and punch down lumps of dough. But I needed the money.

At home, I trussed myself up and took myself back to bed until about four o'clock, when Dottie came into the bedroom and took a seat on the bedspread.

"Ray says you went over The Cheeks," she said. "Is that right?"

I sat up. My arms ached. What had we done with my arms?

"Ray said what?"

"Says that Andy Barrington is staying in the cottage."

"Oh for pity's sake," I said. "Is it on the front page of the paper now?"

"No," Dottie said. "But you being my best friend and all, I thought I'd ask."

"Speaking of being best friends, how come you told Bud I liked him?"

"Just come up," Dottie said. "Happens sometimes."

"How am I supposed to trust you?"

Dottie shrugged. "I see your point. Won't happen again. I promise."

"Okay. I got laid," I said. "You want to take that back to the store and announce it?"

"Jesus to Jesus, that's some news!" she whooped. "You got laid?"

I nodded.

"Was it Andy Barrington? The firecrackers guy?"

"The same one."

"Thought you was going to save yourself for Bud."

"As you pointed out, there's no chance of that happening."

"True. You going to tell me about it?"

I did, from the stew to the sex.

"How'd it feel?"

"Good," I said. "I can't remember much."

"Did you come?"

"A thousand times," I said.

"I should try it. Gus told someone on my team he'd ask me out in a minute."

"Go for it."

She shrugged. "Not my type. Can't picture him going at it and me yelling, 'Gus, Gus' underneath him." She left a little while later.

I was changing my pad upstairs in the bathroom when someone else knocked on the front door. I wondered if it was a reporter come to get the juicy details.

"It's open," I yelled. When I went downstairs, I found Bud in the hall.

"Seen you more in the last couple days than I have in a month," I said.

"I got to say it," he said. "He's no good for you."

"Who's no good for me?"

"Andy."

"Did Dottie tell you?"

"Heard up at Ray's."

"What do you care?" I said. "What's it to you?"

"I heard some things."

"Everyone is hearing things today," I said. "Maybe the whole damn Point should get their ears checked."

"I don't want to make you mad," Bud said. "Just thought you should know about it."

"Thanks," I said. "Straightened me right out."

"I shouldn't have said nothing," he said.

"Seems to be what you're best at," I snapped.

He went out the door, closing it with a quiet click behind him.

The way he closed that door, so polite, so calm, like he was leaving a crazy person, set me off. "You never say nothing!" I screamed at the door. "Could have been you."

I clenched and unclenched my hands, wanting something to fill them with. Then I remembered I had to make bread for the store. I went into the kitchen and mixed the dough for the first two loaves, then pummeled the shit out of it, muttering at Bud, Stella, Ray, Dottie, even Andy. I had the period blues, for sure.

But mostly, I was mad at Bud. For someone who didn't talk much, he'd managed to open my eyes to the fact that I'd given myself to someone I hardly knew. I'd snuffed out any chance of ever being with him by screwing some summer boy in a freezing house where I wouldn't have been welcome as a guest during a cocktail hour.

"God damn you, Bud Warner," I hollered, and I threw a wad of dough at the kitchen wall, then another one, until all the dough in the bowl was stuck or sliding slowly down the wall to the floor.

I was too down to be jumped when Daddy said from the kitchen doorway, "You okay, Florine?"

"No," I said. I walked over to where he was standing by the doorway and put my arms around him. "I feel like crap," I said.

He patted my back and said, "Shhhh," for a few seconds, until I got myself back together. Then I walked over and started peeling dough off the wall.

"Stella told me you went somewhere last night," Daddy said.

"I did," I said. "Over The Cheeks. You must know that. Everyone else does."

"Small place," Daddy said.

I threw the dough out, wet a dishcloth, and went back to the wall. I scrubbed at the oily stains but they had set in, leaving me a nice reminder of my temper.

"Florine, I ain't real happy about you seeing this boy."

"Well, I wasn't real happy about you seeing Stella. Didn't stop you, did it?"

"We're talking about you and this boy."

"His name is Andy."

"I'd appreciate it if you'd listen for a minute."

I crossed my arms over my chest and waited for him to talk.

"Don't you think it's odd he's up here without no heat or nothing?"

"You asking me or telling me?"

"I'm asking you to think about this. How come he ain't in school?"

"He got out early for Christmas break for good grades and he decided to come up here. He's had all this outdoor experience and he thought it would be fun to camp out. What's wrong with that?"

"Nothing, on the surface. You get a chance, you bring him to meet us. Do that for me, please?"

"Got it," I said.

"You want to come over and have supper with us?"

"No," I said. "I'm tired."

"Be careful," Daddy said, and left.

I baked bread for Ray and between loaves I knit on a baby sweater that was part of a set. I spun what everyone had said around in my head until I had it all dried, folded, and sorted, but I wasn't able to put it away. Every time I thought of Andy as evil, I pictured his eyes, sparking and full of me. At about eleven o'clock, I turned off the lights and pulled myself up over the stairs to bed.

Tomorrow, I thought, The Point will move on to something else. I sank into the sheets, ready to let my dreams do the driving. But I didn't get too far down the road before I heard a soft knock at the door in the side yard. I knew it had to be Andy because no one ever knocked on the side door. I bounded out of bed and ran downstairs. I opened the door and he lunged over the door stoop and pinned me against the stair banister. Everything inside me took off like a twitchy flock of birds as we kissed and clenched with the door wide open. December whooshed in, scraping its boots on the doormat and bellowing out, "Where's the party?" If my feet hadn't gotten cold, we would have been there forever. I finally managed to shut the door.

39

We were out in the open after that. Some may have thought I was throwing it into their faces but that wasn't the reason I trotted Andy around. I liked him. Partly I liked him because he thought different, he'd seen different things, and he told me stories about the things he'd seen and done. Partly I liked him for the sex. And he was a person who had come back from the past. He was living proof that it was possible that lost things could show up again. He listened to me talk about Carlie. Telling someone new about her was such a relief to me. It shifted the heaviness in my heart, moved her loss around a little bit so that there was more room to breathe.

"I remember her," he said. "She was so pretty. I only saw her that day on the lawn when she came over with you, but I remember she had the reddest hair and a happy face. I hated that my father was such an asshole that day. He hit me. Did I tell you that?"

"He hit you?" I said. I must have been staring at him as if he had two heads, because he said, "What? You think because we have money that this shit doesn't happen?"

"What about your mother?" I asked. "We've talked about Carlie, but you never talk about your mother."

He was quiet for a minute, looking at the fire. We were dressed, for once, and had just eaten fish chowder I'd thrown together for us.

Somehow, he'd managed to get a bottle of red wine that sat on my tongue like velvet and made me sleepy.

"Mothers can disappear in more ways than one," he said. "My mother—she sleeps a lot. Sometimes, she'll sleep the whole day away. That's when I'm home. Probably, she sleeps more than that when I'm gone. Her sister, my Aunt Meggie, took her to the Bahamas to get her away for a while."

"When Grand died, I was so sad that all I wanted to do was sleep," I said. "I might still be there if people had left me alone."

"Sometimes, I feel like I'm an orphan," Andy said. "I mean, I got two parents, but where the hell are they? And when I'm with them, it's just a pain in the ass."

By that time we'd been together every day, except for Christmas. I spent that time with Daddy and Stella. I had invited Andy, but he had wanted to be alone.

"No one wants to be alone for Christmas," I argued. "My father wants to meet you."

"Some other time, Sweetness, okay?" Andy said. "This year, I want to write some, think some, sleep some, take a walk. Besides, I'm not alone. You're not that far away."

Christmas night found us curled around one another like greedy vines. We toasted in 1969 wrapped in a thick sleeping bag on the porch with a bottle of champagne that made me giggle and feel ticklish. We snuggled and picked out stars for ourselves and named them. We got stoned, too, although I wasn't as sold on it as Andy was—I didn't like the smoke and heat hitting my lungs or the dull depression afterward.

It went on like that into January. Him and me, prone, heating one another against the freezing weather and the storms that raged outside. We stayed in his cottage, mostly, for the adventure Andy liked, and for the privacy I craved. We managed by keeping the fire going and wearing layers of clothes. When we needed showers or warmth, we headed for Grand's house. We did our business in chamber pots, then flung out the slops into the ocean at the end of the lawn. Emptied pot in hand,

I would turn to look back at the house, picturing our children rolling down perfectly mowed summertime grass.

Andy didn't seem to be in a hurry to get back to school. That seemed odd to me, but I'd quit, so who was I to ask anyone about their own plans? Still, he was supposed to graduate in June, and it was coming up on the second week in January. Finally, I asked, "When you going back to school?"

We were face-to-face, naked in bed. He smiled and gave me the tender eyes. "Independent study," he said.

"You're not going back to school, are you?" I said.

"Would it bother you if I stayed?" Then he did something that made me forget I'd asked the question.

A couple days after that conversation, we both got a hankering to clean up. We walked hand-in-hand through the quiet of the midmorning and met Bud driving up the road from his house. He passed by without looking at us, his mouth set taut like nylon rope.

"He's late for school, I guess," I said.

"He's cool," Andy said. "That look in his eyes. He could be a dangerous character in some movie, someone you least expect to do what he's doing. A spy or something."

I snorted. "Bud? Nah."

I knew someone had been in Grand's house the minute I opened the door. I listened for the echo of what had gone on while Andy headed upstairs to check things out. Then, in the kitchen, I found a piece of paper on the table, held down by Grand's bluebird pepper shaker. At first I didn't recognize the writing, but then I saw that it was in Daddy's hand. He seldom wrote more than a list. His cursive was big and loopy and the words sloped down on the paper.

> *Florine, dear,*
>   *I got to tell you how I feel. You ain't here much, so I can't do*
> *it. But I need to say I'm worried about you and I want you to*
> *come home to Grand's house. I know we don't talk much at all,*

but I'm still you're father and you got to know I love you, even
if I don't say it much. If you don't want to come by youreself,
bring that young fella along and we can work things out. I told
you to bring him to supper and I ment it. Please come and talk
to me.

You're loving Daddy.

"Oh Daddy," I said, feeling tender about the wrong spellings and the way he'd borne down on the pencil so hard it had ripped the paper in a couple of spots. To write me a note, Daddy had to have been bothered. Maybe Stella had put him up to it but it didn't matter. I had been a bad daughter. I hadn't been thinking about him, or Grand's, or bread, or knitting, or anything or anyone else downwind of Andy's cottage.

When Andy got out of the bathroom, I said to him, "Do you want to meet my father?"

He looked at me out of the sides of his eyes. "Is he here?" he asked.

"No," I said. "He wants us to come to supper. It'll be okay," I said when he looked like he wanted to bolt. "Stella will cook something good and there will be lots of it. Daddy won't say much but Stella will do all the talking. We won't be there long, couple hours, maybe. He just wants to meet you, look you over."

"I don't know," Andy said. "He's a big guy. I wonder what he thinks of me poking his daughter."

"I don't see that coming up," I said.

"I don't have too much luck with fathers," Andy said.

"So you don't want to go to supper?"

When he caught the low growl in my voice, he said, "I'll do it for you. What time?"

"Let's go ask Stella if tonight is okay," I said. "Get it over with."

We walked toward Ray's to ask her there, but before we got there Andy said, "I'm going back to the cottage. You come for me when it's time for dinner. We're almost out of wood and I should bring some in. It might snow."

The sky was as blue as Daddy's eyes.

"Well, it feels like it's going to snow," Andy said.

"What is wrong with you?" I asked.

"Nothing," he said. "I just have this feeling that if I don't bring in wood, it'll snow. Why wait when I can do it now and prevent that from happening? Your father would approve of me taking care of you by making sure you're warm and dry, right?"

I knew he was stalling. But I let it go.

"See you later," I said.

He gave me a lip-smacking kiss in front of Ray's, then walked toward the path.

I went inside. "Got Daddy's note," I said to Stella. "How about we come over tonight?"

She lit right up. "Oh, that would be wonderful," she said. She leaned over the deli counter and said, "I saw you kissing Andy."

"What time do you want us?" I asked.

"About five," she said.

I went back to Grand's for a little while. It was well past the New Year and the ruby glass hadn't had its January cleaning. I took each piece out, cleaned the cabinet, washed and dried the pieces and put them back. I touched the spot where the red ruby heart had lain, wondering if anyone would ever find it; maybe in the belly of a fish or swept up in a net. What would they think if they did find it?

I went up to the cottage around four. It was dusk but I could see smoke rising from the tall chimney over the central fireplace. When I went inside, the place reeked of pot. Andy had taken the fire screen off and was feeding the fire little twigs, rocking back and forth and humming.

"I see you got the wood," I said.

"Hey," he said. He turned to me. The whites of his eyes were cherry red.

"You can't come to supper like this," I said.

"What?" he asked. Then he giggled and said, "You're pretty."

"What's my name?" I asked. "Do you even know my name?"

He laughed and slapped his thighs. "What's your name?" he asked me. "I know your name. It's my darling Florine of The Point. She's the girl for me."

"Damn," I said. "Andy, I'm going to have to go on to supper. If I don't, they'll be worried."

"Oh," Andy said, face suddenly serious. "Well, help me up and we'll go."

"You're too stoned," I said.

He laughed and when he did I turned around and walked out into the dark. He caught me by the edge of the woods. He tackled me and I fell into the icy snow, scraping the palms of my hands. Andy fumbled under the fresh, ironed skirt I'd put on for supper.

My eyes stung as I shoved his hands away. "Don't," I said. "I have to go. Go back to the house, you'll get cold."

He stroked the side of my face with the backs of his fingers and gave me a look that held so much love that it hurt me to see it. I struggled to get out from under him.

"I'll talk to you later, okay?" I said.

He rolled off me and helped me up. He smiled and said, "I love you."

"I know," I said. My hands and knees hurt like hell. "I love you, too." I did at that moment. How could I not, when he needed me so much?

He kissed me so hard that one of my teeth pinched my lip and I tasted blood.

A little ways down the path, I looked back to see him watching me go. In the faint light, he seemed to be floating on white. I got to Daddy's house at five thirty.

I told them that Andy had gotten a cold that had come on fast. But Stella's eyes shone like high-beam headlights and I knew she was dying for morning to come so she could spread the word. Andy's not showing up would make him stand out like a sore thumb and turn the spotlight on him and on me in ways we had never, ever wanted.

40

I stayed in my own bed that night. I waited for Andy to show and worried when he didn't. Somewhere around dawn I fell asleep.

The phone rang at around ten o'clock Saturday morning. It was Dottie, wanting to know if I was home. Dottie hardly ever called—usually she dropped by—and her call brought it home to me that I hadn't been around enough to be dropped in on. I suddenly couldn't wait to see her. I made cocoa and a stack of cinnamon toast and we sat at the kitchen table and wolfed it down while Dottie unloaded some news.

"I almost bowled a three hundred," she told me. "Well, more like two seventy, but that's closer than two hundred."

"It would take me about forty games to get that," I said.

"Most likely, but you got other talents. How's things with Andy?"

"Okay," I said. "No. Not okay."

"Okay. Not okay. Which is it?"

I told her about the supper and about Andy being stoned, and how he'd been dragging his feet as far as meeting Daddy went. "He told me that Mr. Barrington hit him a lot and that he's a drinker," I said to Dottie. "Every time he talks about him, it's like a black cloud sets down over his head."

"Well, he *was* like some general on that day we had to tell him we was sorry," Dottie said. "He passed down the line of us like we was fresh recruits. I was waiting for him to bring out a whip and beat us all foolish."

Thinking of Mr. Barrington trying to beat Daddy, Sam, and Bert made me smile.

Dottie said, "Madeline's made me apply to a couple of colleges. She thinks I need a Plan B in case bowling doesn't work out."

"Why does she care if you go to college?" I said, thinking about how that would take Dottie far away from me. "She didn't go and she's fine."

"I know," Dottie said. "But she pulled a funny one at the supper table a while back. She suckered us up with a homemade Boston cream pie and while we was eating it, she went on about how no one on either side of the Butts family ever went past high school. And then she got to crying about it and Bert said, 'There, there,' and Evie and I just looked at each other. I says, 'Well, maybe I'd give it a shot if I wasn't so damn dumb.' She says maybe I can get some kind of scholarship and why don't I just give it a try? Bert says, 'Your mother never asks for much, for chrissake, Dottie. You've had an easy road. Do something for her, for a change.' So I got some applications and she's writing them for me. So, yours truly might be heading off to school in the fall."

"Wow" was all I could think of to say.

"But I made sure that wherever I go has a bowling alley in town, or close by."

"Good thinking."

"I might as well do it to shut her up."

"I guess so. What are you going to study?"

"Gym teacher, I think. They don't look like they need to know too much. I'd get to wear shorts all day and yell at people to move here and go there. I could do that."

"You'd be good at it."

"When's Andy going back to school?" Dottie asked.

I decided to keep his secret. I said to Dottie, "Tell the truth, I don't know. We aren't much past the staying in bed part of things. He's just told me he loved me."

"You tell him back?"

"Yesterday," I said. "Now I'm wondering if it was the right thing to do."

"Why?"

"I don't know. He was stoned. I was mixed up. I didn't know what else to do."

"Some guy told Evie he loved her," Dottie said. "Well, he paid for that because she chased him all over school. He finally got another girl-friend just to fend her off. Evie was all upset. Madeline told her to let them come for her. I say the hell with the whole thing. Someone shows up for me, he's gotta have money to support my bowling career."

We drained our cocoa and felt like having more, so I got up to heat some water for it.

Dottie said, "Bud doesn't like Andy."

"Bud can just stick it where the sun don't shine."

"I'll tell him you said that."

"You do that. I've never said anything bad about Susan."

"Bud says Andy gets his dope from Kevin. You remember Kevin Jew-ell? Dope dealer. Pusher man. Bud says Andy's Kevin's best customer."

"How's Bud know all this stuff?"

"Gets it from Susan, I guess. She gets around more."

"Well, good for Susan."

When Andy said a soft "Hello" behind us, we both jumped out of our rocking chairs.

He looked better today, eyes clear, hair combed, and beard trimmed. I wondered if he'd heard a lot of what we'd said but before I could ask, Dottie stood up, stuck out her hand, and said, "I'm Dottie Butts. Not sure you remember me."

Andy shook her hand. "Of course I remember you. You'd be hard to forget."

"I'll take that as a compliment," Dottie said.

"I meant it as a compliment," Andy said. "I've heard so much about you from Florine. I was hoping I'd get to see the famous Dottie again."

Andy let go of her hand and they took each other in for about five seconds. Then Dottie did something I'd never seen her do or would ever see her do again. She blushed. Then she said, "Well, I got stuff to do. Nice to see you." And off she went.

Andy and I looked at each other, then Andy said, "I let you down. I'm sorry."

"Told them you had a cold. We pretended it was true."

"I made a mistake and I'm sorry."

"You did," I said.

"What can I do to make it up to you?" I was surprised to see tears on his cheeks.

"I mess up a lot, Florine," he said. "I don't know why, but I do."

Then he ran shaking hands down the sides of my face. He said, "Please don't leave me. Please, please give me another chance."

Because I knew what it felt like to be left, I said. "I'll give you another chance."

He nodded and we held each other for a minute.

"Are they home right now?" he asked, wiping tears from his cheeks.

When I nodded, he said, "Let's go over."

We walked across the road, hand-in-hand, and he knocked on the door.

"I'm Andy Barrington," he told Daddy when he answered the door and let us in. "I'm sorry I missed supper."

"You don't sound like you got a cold," Stella said.

"I heard I missed a fabulous feast," he said with a smile.

Stella put on a pot of coffee and we sat around the table. Like I'd told him, Daddy didn't do much talking, but Stella made up for it, asking him about his folks, where he'd grown up, and his school. We finished our coffee and stood to go. Andy shook Daddy's hand and looked him in the eye. He thanked Stella for the coffee, and we walked toward Grand's house.

"Was it as bad as you thought?" I asked.

"No, Angel," Andy said, and squeezed my hand.

Ray's truck was parked in front of Grand's house. Hoppy the Beagle sat in the truck bed, tongue lolling, eyes half closed in the winter sun. Ray came around to the driver's side and spied us. "I was just knocking for you," he said to me. "Need some bread. Special—four loaves for a dinner. You got time to make it up by five? Hi," he said to Andy. Andy nodded and scratched Hoppy behind an ear.

I said "Yes" to Ray and he reversed the truck up the hill and disappeared out of sight.

"I'll go clean the cottage," Andy said. "Fix dinner. Make us a loaf and bring it up."

"Thanks for coming down," I said.

"You're my baby," he murmured, cupping my chin. "I got to take care of my baby."

I felt as warm and flexible as the dough I kneaded and shaped that day. The smell filled my head and heart and I understood what it was Andy found so special about it. Once, when he'd been only a little stoned, he'd cut off the end of a loaf of fresh-made bread. He'd held it up and breathed in, deep. "I could live in there," he said. "It's warm, and soft, and I could just crawl inside of it. It smells like home should feel."

I'd laughed but as I sat at the kitchen table, watching the dough rise beneath the damp dishtowels I'd put over the tops of the bread pans, I had to agree. I lazed around the house while the bread baked. At about four thirty, I bagged it up and headed for Ray's.

A strange car with Massachusetts license plates was parked in front of the store. It shone white in the late January twilight and I wondered if these were the people who had ordered the bread. It was a Mercedes or a BMW. I could never remember which symbol stood for which car. I peeked inside at butter-colored leather seats. I wanted to climb inside and sit down just to see if I would melt into them.

Inside the store, Stella was talking to a man who stood with his back to me. I put the bread down for Ray, and Stella caught my eye, stood up straight and looked afraid. Then the man turned around.

"You're lovely," I heard him say inside my head, clear as day. Then I heard Dottie's voice just as clear. *"I was waiting for him to take out a whip and beat us all foolish."* And Andy's voice. *"He hit me, you know."*

When Mr. Barrington spotted me his eyes went snake black, flat. But his smile was beautiful, just like his son's smile. I didn't know whether to run or stay. I scowled at Stella to give me somewhere else to look.

Stella's face was red as she said, a little too brightly, "Mr. Barrington's come up to bring Andy back to school. He's got to get back this weekend."

"Hello, Florine," Mr. Barrington said, softly. "Stella has been telling me all about you two."

I shrugged. "Not much to tell."

"My boy has good taste," he said, and smiled.

I turned away, my heart hammering hard, my head saying run. I wanted to get to Andy before he did, to warn him he was coming. But I tried to be calm as I waited for Ray to pay me. He looked hard at me as he gave me my fifteen dollars. I said, "Thank you," and left the store. The minute the door shut behind me I ran as fast as I could through the woods, toward the cottage and Andy.

I burst into the lantern-lit kitchen to the smells of roasting chicken and pot. Andy was setting wine goblets down on the rug in front of the fireplace. He looked at me with a smile as raw as a child's. It was the last smile I ever saw him give me, because when I said, "Your father is here. He's come to get you," it was replaced by a look much as a wild thing might wear when caught in a trap.

"Shit," he said. "Shit. I'm so dead."

A chuckle came from the hallway. "Don't be so dramatic, Andrew," Mr. Barrington said. He leaned against the living room doorway and said to me, "You're a fast runner."

When I didn't say anything, he said, "It's a compliment. Please don't look at me as if I'm the big bad wolf. I'm here to take Andy home, that's all." He looked at Andy. "How are you doing, son?" Andy shrugged, eyes unfocused, darting, cornered, confused.

Mr. Barrington sniffed the air. "Hmmm. Is that chicken I smell?"

When Andy didn't answer, I said, "Yes."

"I thought so," Mr. Barrington said. "I'm starved."

I looked at Andy. His arms hung by his sides, and the fingers on the hand that wasn't holding the wine bottle twitched. What on earth was wrong with him, I wondered? Although I didn't trust him, Mr. Barrington wasn't being unpleasant, and he didn't seem drunk. Maybe we could get through this over supper. Maybe we could figure out a plan.

"Would you like to have some supper with us?" I asked him. Andy looked at me, eyes wide, as if he couldn't believe what he'd just heard.

Mr. Barrington said, "I would love to. And I see you have some wine."

Andy looked down at the bottle as if he wondered how it had gotten into his hand.

"What can I do to help?" Mr. Barrington asked me.

"Andy, what can he do to help?" I asked Andy.

"Nothing," Andy said in a dead voice. "It's all ready."

"Great," Mr. Barrington said. "Now, the rug is a fine thing," he said, "but how about we take the sheets off the coffee table and move it in front of the fire. Give me a hand?"

Andy walked over to the table and put the bottle of wine down on the floor. The two moved the heavy oak table so that it covered the same rug I'd been deflowered on and where we'd eaten, talked, slept, and made love many times.

"There," Mr. Barrington said. "Now, shall I help bring in the food? Florine, why don't you sit on the divan and Andy and I will wait on you."

"It's okay," I said, "I'll help, too."

Andy had cooked up carrots, potatoes, and the chicken. He served them up as I sliced up the bread. Mr. Barrington hovered between us, talking about the drive up. Half a joint sat in an ashtray on the top of the stove. Mr. Barrington must have seen it, but he made no comment, even when Andy slipped it out of sight behind the dirty potato pan.

We sat down in front of the fire at the table, Andy and me on the divan, Mr. Barrington in a creaky rocking chair beside me. He picked up the bottle of white wine and looked at the label. He said, "Not bad," and said, "Give me the corkscrew, son, and I'll open it."

Andy looked around for it. He finally spotted it on top of the hearth and fetched it, brushed it off, and gave it to his father.

"So," Mr. Barrington said. "Where did you get this wine?"

"Long Reach," Andy said.

"How did you get this wine?" Mr. Barrington said.

"I bought it."

"How?"

"They sold it to me."

"Who is they?"

"Market in Long Reach."

"They didn't ask for identification?"

"No."

"Oh. Well, give me your glass," Mr. Barrington said. "You won't be driving home, anyway. And you, Florine?"

"No, thanks," I said.

"Oh, come on. It's very French to have a glass of wine with dinner." He poured me some and waited until I took a sip.

"I'm taking the truck home," Andy said.

"You are?" Mr. Barrington said.

"I was planning to stay another week or two, anyway," Andy said. He took a big gulp of wine. "Then head back."

"Oh?" Mr. Barrington said. "Head back to what?"

"Not sure yet," Andy said.

"Not to school, I guess," Mr. Barrington said.

"No," Andy said.

Mr. Barrington leaned over to me and said as if he and I shared a secret, "Andrew was tossed out in November. Did he tell you that he's been kicked out of four schools?"

"Stop messing with her," Andy said. He didn't look at his father, but studied his chicken as he moved it from one side of his plate to the other. He herded orange carrot coins into a small corral he'd made out of his mashed potatoes.

Mr. Barrington said, "I'm not messing with her. I wondered if you'd told her."

"It doesn't matter to me," I said.

"Oh. Then that makes it all okay, doesn't it?" Mr. Barrington said. "Yes, that makes it fine." He sniffed the air. "I smell something else in the air. What is it? It's not chicken. It's not potatoes or carrots. No, it's sweetish. Dessert, perhaps?"

"You know what it is," Andy said.

Mr. Barrington winked at me. "Just teasing you, Andrew. Of course I know what it is." He leaned toward me again and whispered, "Andrew's pot smoking has cost me thousands of dollars—what with changing schools and fines and bail and such."

"I don't care," I said again.

"Well, of course you don't, Florine. Then again, you weren't saddled with the fines," Mr. Barrington said. "Would you like a ride home when we leave for Boston?"

"I'm not going anywhere with you," Andy said.

"Yes, you will," Mr. Barrington said in a cheery tone. "I've called the sheriff to come by, in case you needed persuasion. He knows you're living high—excuse the pun—on the hog up here. I gave him permission to search the cottage, if it comes to that. You can be his guest for a while, if you like. Or, we can finish our meal, clean up, and go home. The truck will be all right here."

"How'd you find me, anyway?" Andy said.

"Stella—is that her name, Florine?—gave me a call. Told me you were up here and said she was worried about you being in this cold house. I said to her—Stella, Della?" He looked at me.

"Stella," I said.

"Thank you. I said to Stella, you must be mistaken. He's being tutored in New York and he's living with his mother. But then I called your mother and it turns out that she is in the Bahamas. So I called her there and she told me she thought you needed a break. You told her you wanted to come up here and she gave her permission as well as some of the money I pay her each month for your sorry keep." Mr. Barrington stood up and walked over to the fireplace, glass of wine in his hand. He looked into the flames. "You lay a nice fire, son," he said, his voice almost a whisper. "Logs stacked just so. Fine job. Fine job." Andy sat very still. He looked at me and his face went white.

"What's wrong?" I mouthed, but he shook his head.

Mr. Barrington said, his voice low, "Andrew, I don't give you permission to be here," and he threw his glass of wine against the side of the fireplace. The glass shattered and he aimed a kick at the heart of the flames. Logs and sparks snapped and hissed and I jumped and spilled my glass of wine into my lap. Andy didn't move, just shut his eyes.

Mr. Barrington turned to us and said, through gritted teeth, "You have cost me too much money and embarrassment for you to be able to just waltz up here, buy dope and booze, and screw the fisherman's daughter. Now finish up your meal and let's go."

Except for Mr. Barrington's breathing, the cottage went silent. I heard a drip outside as an icicle melted, or maybe it grew thicker, even as things cracked and broke inside.

Andy said, "D . . . D . . . Don't insult Florine like that. I love her."

"Oh Andrew," Mr. Barrington shouted and threw his hands into the air. "Andrew, my son, you wouldn't know what love was if it came up and bit you on the ass." He looked at me sitting on the divan, a puddle of white wine warming my thighs. "She's lovely right now," he said, and he moved his hand as if to make me disappear. "But many, many women are, and it doesn't last. It isn't important in the long run. Please use your head—the one on your shoulders. I beg of you. Go back to school— whatever school will have you. Then go to college. Do it. FINISH this one thing."

Andy stood up and came around the table. He held out his shaking hand and I took it and stood up. Wine trickled down my legs. Andy turned around and faced his father.

"I'm not going with you," he said. "I have everything I need here. Florine has a house on The Point and we can live there. I don't need you."

I tried to think back to when I'd asked him to live with me and I couldn't think of when, but now wasn't a good time to bring it up. He was facing down his father, and I could see what it was costing him to do it. Right now, he was my man. My scared but brave man, and I had to stand by him.

"You are eighteen years old," Mr. Barrington said. "She is seventeen years old. There might be some law against you two fornicating, I'm not sure. At any rate, Andrew, I meant it when I said the sheriff was coming. I told him to give me thirty minutes. Now, I'm sorry I did that, but I had a feeling you might get stubborn."

"Well, I'm leaving right now then," Andy said. "We're going to Florine's house. You have no right to come after me there." And he pulled me and we went out into the hall, where he grabbed our coats.

"Andrew," Mr. Barrington said. "You will be under arrest the minute you step out of her house. I swear you will. And it will be for your own good."

"Come on," Andy whispered to me and we slipped out the kitchen door. I looked across the driveway and pictured a younger Bud, Dottie, and Glen hiding in the bushes on that summer night so long ago. They looked at me sadly as Andy and I walked down the stairs and started for the truck. Mr. Barrington wasn't far behind. "Andrew," he called. I turned around just in time to see him step down, slip on a patch of ice, and fall backward onto the steps, hard. He went still, out cold, or maybe dead. "Shit," Andy said, and we hurried back to Mr. Barrington. His face was waxy in the night, his body limp. A dark liquid gleamed on the step in back of him. I crouched down and lifted his head as gently as I could. Warm, sticky blood covered my fingers.

I said, "Andy, we have to call a doctor," and Andy said, "Okay." I lowered Mr. Barrington onto the step again. Andy reached into his father's pocket, snatched the car keys, grabbed my hand, and said, "His car is faster than my truck. Let's go."

He led me to the passenger side of the Mercedes BMW, opened the door, and sat me down on the soft, butter-colored leather seat. But instead of melting, I froze as he slid into the driver's seat, turned the key, backed the car up, and threw it into gear. We bucketed down the dirt road. I thought we would turn toward The Point, but we kept on going straight toward Long Reach.

"Where are you going?" I asked. "What are we doing? We need to find a phone. We can't leave him there."

"Get help," he said.

"The Point is closer, Andy. Let's go back."

"I can't go back," he said.

Parker passed us in his sheriff's car and I turned around in time to see him disappear around a curve.

Andy and I drew ragged breaths against the strains of some classical symphony on a station Mr. Barrington must have been listening to on the way up. I looked at the almost dried blood on my hand.

"Andy, we got to call a doctor," I said again.

"Sheriff will find him."

"You're mixed up. Let's go back to The Point and let them help."

"No," Andy said. "No. I'll take care of it."

He pressed down on the gas pedal and the Mercedes BMW roared into another gear. "Andy, you need to slow down," I said.

"I need to slow down," he repeated. He took his foot off the gas pedal and braked just as we crested Pine Pitch Hill. But it was too little, too late. We sailed up and into the very trees that had spit back Stella Drowns from the dead. In the headlights of the car, those trees gleamed bright and toothpick-thin. This will be okay, I thought. The trees will break in half and we'll set down nice and easy in the bushes.

41

The first thing I saw when I woke up was Daddy, who was sitting in a chair beside me, looking like he'd drunk poison and it was slowly killing him.

"What's wrong?" I said. "Did they find Carlie?"

Daddy said, "No. You were in an accident." I looked around then, at least, as far around as I could look with a neck brace. "Where am I?" I asked.

"We're in Portland," Daddy said. "You been out for a couple of days. You're in intensive care at Maine Medical Center. You got in a car accident with Andy Barrington. They took him to Boston. Broke both legs and a hip. He's going to make it, though. Parker found Mr. Barrington—they stitched up his head. You're all lucky."

Lucky, lucky me, I thought, as I went under.

I wound up with a twisted, badly sprained back and neck, a broken right leg, a mangled right arm and shoulder, cuts and abrasions, and a bad concussion. I drifted in and out for about a week, mostly out.

They kept me in intensive care until the concussion went away, and then they wheeled me into a semiprivate room with an old lady named Hazel who had pneumonia. She hacked up phlegm while I floated down rivers of medication. We were quite a pair.

Hazel was so small that only the tips of her feet and her hands folded on her stomach showed under the blankets. Her face was yellow against the white pillowcase, and her white hair was in bad need of a trim. When she could talk without coughing up her lungs, and I could speak without jarring some nerve, bone, or muscle, she told me she lived alone with her twelve cats. She told me the story of each one. Hazel couldn't wait to get home to her cats. "A neighbor's watching them, but it's never the same," she said.

Jane, a student nurse only a few years older than me, told me one day when Hazel was sleeping that she wasn't going home. A couple of nieces had found a nursing home for her. Hazel's house had been sold to pay for Hazel's spot in the home. The poor cats had been sick and about half of them had been put down. The other half had been taken to the local shelter.

I went along with Hazel and her cat stories for as long as she was there. The day the nurses wheeled her out with her nieces on either side of her chair, Jane and I had a good cry thinking about what must have happened when she realized that she wasn't going home, and that her cats were gone.

Without Hazel to distract me, each injured body part took a turn putting on a show-and-tell of pain. It was hell not to remember what had happened. For a long time, the last thing I could remember was Andy saying, "I got to take care of my baby," in front of Grand's house. Then it began to drift back to me: Stella talking to Mr. Barrington, Mr. Barrington smashing the wineglass into the fireplace.

I wanted to talk to Andy in the worst way, to get his take on things. But like most of my life, during those early days after the accident, he seemed like a dream to me, as if we had never happened. It was almost as if he and what we had meant to each other had been jarred out of my head. To bring him back, I did something I'd done when Carlie had started to fade in my memory. I went through each sense; how Andy looked, smelled, tasted, felt, and sounded.

When Dottie wasn't bowling, she showed up after school and stayed until closing time if she could. She sat with me, along with Daddy,

Madeline, Bert, Ray, and once and a while Glen, Bud, and Susan. Ida and Sam Warner visited once, but Sam was nervous and Ida explained that he hated hospitals. I told him not to come back if he was going to be spleeny. He kissed my forehead, thanked me, and left.

I wouldn't let Stella near me, no matter how Daddy tried to smooth things over. "She was afraid you would get into trouble. She was protecting you," were some of the reasons Daddy thought were enough for Stella to have ratted out Andy.

"She did a bang-up job of it all," I said to Daddy.

"She feels terrible, Florine."

"Good."

"Well, honey, you got to forgive her, because you have to come home with us to our house when you leave here," Daddy said. "You got to have a first-floor bathroom."

"Cold day in hell," I said.

"You don't have a choice," he said.

"What will happen to Andy when he leaves the hospital?" I asked.

"He can take a flying fuck through a rolling donut hole as far as I'm concerned," Daddy said.

Dottie wasn't quite so plainspoken. "Parker said Mr. Barrington is sending Andy to some kind of military school. He'll get taught at home for the rest of the year and go there all next year."

It broke my heart to think about the military whipping him into something wooden. It would be like hauling a seagull out of the sky and turning it into a chicken. I ached for the free spirit in him. I got Jane to help me as I tried to call him one night. I told her the number, and she did the rest. She dialed a friend in Boston who worked in the hospital where Andy was a patient, but when she spoke to her, she found out that Andy wasn't allowed a phone.

When I was higher than a star in the sky, I thought of us under layers of blankets on the freezing floor in front of the cottage fireplace. I talked to Jane about him in the middle of the night, when she was on shift. I told her about Carlie, too, and she said she remembered reading about that and wondering what had happened. I told her I wondered every day.

Parker came to see me in the hospital to get my version of the Mr. Barrington and Andy show and I gave it to him, trying to make Parker see that Andy had been scared and that he hadn't meant for us to get into an accident. Before Parker left he promised, once more, to look for Carlie for as long as it took. "Don't you think I won't," he said, and I pretended I believed him.

42

It took me almost a month to heal enough so I could move without swearing or crying. When I could use my crutches to get to the bathroom, wipe myself, and flush, it was time to go home, Jane said.

She wheeled me out of my room, Daddy and Dottie beside me, on February 24, exactly a month after the accident. Daddy had brought Madeline's car instead of his truck, and he, Jane, and Dottie loaded me into the back so my leg stuck out on the seat. They put a pillow under the truss tied around my back and the collar that held my neck in place and settled my leg on the seat. I made Jane promise to come and see me at The Point.

"Lobster for free," I said. "And so is the view."

She said she would, but I knew she wouldn't. Angels come and go.

Stella met us in the driveway but I wouldn't look at her. Glen and Bud helped Daddy get me into the house where they carried me into my old room. A hospital bed waited for me, along with a little radio and a small television and a tray for food, books, or whatever I needed or wanted. A bud vase with a pink rose sat on the tray, with a Welcome Home card that everyone on The Point had signed.

Then Bud and Glen left and it was just Daddy, Stella, and me.

"Are you hungry?" Stella asked.

"Why did you rat on Andy and me?" I asked.

Daddy said, "Can't this wait for at least fifteen minutes?"

Stella said, "That's all right, Leeman. She's got a right to ask."

"Damn straight," I said.

She took a deep breath, and her scar went scarlet. She said, "I know you're upset. And if I'd known what would happen, I wouldn't have done it. But Florine, the boy was living in a freezing cottage. He was dealing dope and he could've gotten you pregnant. Or you could have gotten busted."

"Or we could have gotten in a near-fatal car accident, for chrissake," I said. "And I didn't get pregnant, and we were plenty warm in that cottage. You didn't have any right to interfere with my business."

"I told you I wouldn't have done it if I'd known what was going to happen," she said, tears filling her eyes. "But your father was upset. Jesus, Florine, you just don't know how he worries about you."

"Stella," Daddy said. "Now, Florine, both of you just stop, now."

"Well, if I'd been dead, that would've really bummed him out, don't you think? Or maybe you wanted to get me out of the way?" I hollered at Stella.

"Don't be so goddamn dramatic," she yelled back. "I don't want you dead. I wanted you safe, and I wanted your father to stop his worrying. Now know I didn't mean any harm to come to you. And we got to put up with each other, whether we like it or not." She walked out of my bedroom and into their bedroom and slammed the door.

"I have to pee," I said to Daddy.

"Okay." Daddy sighed. He got me into the bathroom and onto the portable toilet and we made it back to my bed.

"I'm sorry to be such a nuisance, Daddy," I said. "I hate it."

"I don't mind helping you," he said. "I'm just so goddamn glad you're all right and you're safe. I don't know what I would've done if I'd lost you. But Florine, you got to make some sort of peace with Stella. You two got to get along. She's here to help you, and I'm not going to be here all day, every day. I got to work. I got house customers and I got to get the boat ready. Do you think you can work it out with her? 'Cause if you can't, I don't know what we're going to do. You ain't well enough to be alone just yet."

"I guess I'll have to," I said.

"I guess you will," he said.

He left for a carpentry job two days later, leaving Stella and me alone for the first time.

"Do you need anything?" Stella asked about twenty times.

"No," I answered, and I made sure I didn't, unless I needed the bathroom, or I had to do my three times daily walk from my bedroom, through the kitchen, around the living room, and back. She walked beside me, saying, "You're doing so much better today," like she was Nurse Nancy. "Don't you feel better? You look better."

"Better, better, better," I mimicked in the same cheerful tone, until she stopped saying anything, just walked nearby in case I took a tumble, which I never did, as luck had it.

She had taken two weeks off from Ray's, but I guess the daily cocktail I made her swallow—two parts silence, one part nastiness, shaken not stirred—got to her and off she went after a week, up the muddy road, deli apron tucked around her waist. She came back every two hours or so to check on me.

It was quiet after she left the house. It was haunted with memories of Carlie, and of the first days without Carlie. Even though Stella had painted the kitchen a cheerful apple-green and new, green-flecked linoleum shone on the floor, I was zipped back to being twelve years old, waiting for word and hoping as hard as I could. When the phone rang, it drove me crazy. I couldn't get to it, and I had to wonder if this was the call we'd been waiting for. I remembered being tied to that phone, not daring to go anywhere. The loneliness of that memory made me almost glad to hear Stella walk back down the driveway.

One day in March, Daddy and I had a talk that had been a long time in the making. He was home that day, between carpenter jobs. Stella was working. He cranked my bed to a sitting position and turned it so that I faced the window. He opened the window so I could get a sniff. Spring was creeping back to The Point like a whipped cur. It was raining, and I could hear each splat of water chonk away at the dirty winter snow. Daddy sat beside me in a rocker he'd made a few years back. It creaked every time he rocked back.

"Have to fix that," he said. "Always something." The light from the window reflected on Daddy's face. Once, that face had lit up like spring, but time and weather had darkened it to the leathery colors of late autumn.

I said, "Being here reminds me of Carlie. It brings it all back."

"I know," he said.

"What do you think happened, Daddy?"

He rocked some. "Well," he said, "I honestly don't know."

"Do you think she was happy here? I used to hear you argue about taking trips."

"We had talks about that all the time," he said. "Don't you think I don't regret not taking a trip with her? It was like to tear me apart after she left—all the things I didn't or wouldn't do, or told her to wait on."

"She didn't like to sit still, that's for sure," I said.

"She didn't have nowhere to sit," he said.

I had no idea what he meant. We'd had chairs when she'd lived with us. She'd used the sofa plenty of times. I must have looked confused because Daddy said, "Not chair-sitting. That's not what I mean. I mean, she couldn't relax any. You know how you had Grand to live with when I was being such a crazy bastard after she left?" he said. "You had somewheres to go that you knew you were welcome. You felt at home."

"Yes," I agreed.

"Well, Carlie didn't have that. Carlie didn't have nowheres to be where she could just set and feel safe. Feel that no matter what she did, it was okay. Growing up the way she did, she was always jumpy. Do you remember when we visited her house? You wasn't very old, so you probably forgot about it."

"I remember it," I said. "I wanted Robin for a sister."

"You remember that man in the chair?"

"The one watching the boxing match?"

Daddy looked at me, amazed. "Christ, you got some memory on you!" he said, then continued, "Well, he was a mean son of a bitch. Used to pick fights with Carlie when she was growing up. Get drunk, smack her around, call her ugly names. Mother wasn't much help. Nice woman, I guess, but afraid of him. Carlie got out every time she could. She told me she used to climb out her bedroom window to the back porch roof and jump down. She used to go into town, get herself into all sorts of trouble, then sneak home."

"I guess I take after her, that way," I said.

"Well, she got herself in real trouble," Daddy said. "When she was sixteen, some boy in town got her pregnant." He looked down as he said this, maybe watching the way his feet stayed still on the floor even as his body rocked back and forth. I thought, I have a brother or a sister somewhere in the world. I did the math in my head. I was seventeen, so that meant my sister or brother was twenty or so. "Where's the baby?" I said.

"Lost it," he said. My heart fell. "Went into early labor at about six months and delivered a dead baby."

"How come that happened?"

Daddy rocked and looked out of the window. "When she got pregnant, her father called her all kinds of names. Told her she was no good, a lowlife piece of shit, whore—things like that. She had to quit school when she was pregnant. Stayed at home, hiding. No one was supposed to know. No one in the house was talking to her much—she stayed out of her father's way, stayed in her room. Now, you know how your mother loved people. How that must have driven her crazy. One night she couldn't stand it anymore and she went out onto the roof, figuring to go to town. Get out for a while. This was in the middle of winter and she slipped and fell. Went into labor. Didn't dare call for help. She had the baby in the yard before they found her. The baby was stillborn.

"After that, she just waited, worked, saved money to get out. Bought Petunia with all the money she'd saved and she packed up and left. She ended up here. You know the rest. Father told her not to come back and, believe me, she didn't have any intention to go back. That's why we only went to visit once. I thought it might be good for you to know her family, but it was all I could do not to choke the living shit out of him when I saw him in that chair. You didn't know it, but she cried a lot about it. She wasn't always the sunshine and light she showed you. She got some sad, sometimes. Some nights she just cried herself to sleep."

I wondered how I could have missed this part of my mother. I thought I'd heard everything from my room. How could this have slipped by my eagle-sharp ears?

As if he'd heard me, Daddy said, "She would have talked to you about things when you got older. She didn't like to think about it but it was part of who she was."

I thought back to the beach, to Carlie's story of meeting Daddy. I heard her, word for word, talking in her voice. *"When I was little, I used to go to bed and before I'd go to sleep, I'd put myself to flying. I'd go to all these places and touch down, look around, see if I recognized anybody. Then I grew up, drove up here, and recognized your father. He's a good man, Florine. One of the best men I've ever met."*

"She loved you," I said to Daddy. "She told me all the time."

"I'm happy she told you," Daddy said. "I talk to her on the water sometimes. I go over everything we ever said to each other. Mostly, it's a comfort to me."

We were quiet for a minute, then Daddy said, "I wish we could find out what happened. I wish we could put her to rest. Bring her home."

"I do, too, Daddy," I said. Someone dear to me whispered into my ear just then and I said, "Grand would say we need to give her soul a place to settle. "We need to have some kind of ceremony. Put her to rest where she can feel welcome forever."

Daddy's eyes got shiny and he wiped at them. He said, "Next summer it will be six years. We'll do it then, Florine. What do you think about that? Can you wait?"

I could. We'd waited all this time. What were a few more months?

43

Around the middle of April, I wanted to jump out of my skin, to fly out of the window. I wondered how people trapped in their bodies year after year could stand it.

"I'm freaking out," I told Dottie. "Think of how you would feel if you couldn't bowl."

"It would just about kill me. By and by, though, you'll be up. Might as well wait for good weather," she said. "Wait for May." But it seemed such a long way away. Time inched its way along.

I hadn't seen Bud or Glen since they'd helped me into the house after I'd gotten home from the hospital. Dottie told me Bud was working at Freddie's garage when he wasn't in school or with Susan. Glen was thinking about joining the Army, going to fight in Vietnam. The thought of big stupid Glen carrying a gun in a jungle didn't comfort me.

Then the nightmares began, and I remembered one big reason I'd left this house for Grand's house. They crawled up through the cracks in the deepest part of my brain like daddy longlegs spiders. *Trees. Screaming. Andy calling my name over and over again, then not calling my name at all. Lights. Wind. Mr. Barrington smashing the windows in the car with a fire poker, trying to get at Andy and me even as we lay dying. Carlie walking through the trees and past the hood of the car with a little smile on her face, ignoring me as I writhed in pain and cried to her to help me.*

Sometimes, after one of these horror shows, I woke up to find Daddy wiping the sweat and tears from my face. But it was Stella who understood what was going on. One night she was there as I struggled to escape a night terror. She was dabbing at my forehead with a damp washcloth when I opened my eyes. When my ragged breath settled down, she said, "I went through that."

"Was it this awful?" I asked, too frightened to remember that I hated her.

"Oh, ugly, horrid stuff."

"How did you get through it?"

"I tried not to sleep, but of course I did, so off I'd go, down the chute to hell. Metal on trees. Blood in my eyes. Jimmy's dead body pressing me down into the seat. All of them pissed at me because they died and I didn't."

She smoothed some hair from my forehead. "The dreams will pass," she said. "You're strong. One of the toughest people I've ever met. Tough like me."

I wasn't sure I liked that, but she said, "Tell you what it did do for me, though. It taught me to go after what I want out of life. It's too short not to do that."

"You went after Daddy."

"You never saw me do that when Carlie was here, did you? I never would have done it if she hadn't disappeared. I saw what her being gone was doing to your father, Florine. I couldn't have him go through that. I loved him too much."

"What if she'd come back?" I said.

Stella got up from the bed. "I would've gone back to what I'd been before. Maybe moved away again. Think I don't know he still loves her? I don't care."

As she started out of the room, I said, "I'm sorry about your baby."

She turned and looked at me. I could see she had no idea what I was talking about. "What did you say?" she said.

"Your baby. Grand said you miscarried awhile back."

Stella's face went white and wobbly. "Oh," she said. "The baby. Yes. The baby."

As she left the room, her wake turned black, then grays and whites filled in the space.

In early May, they cut the cast off my arm and gave me a sling. I thought that meant that my leg would be set free, but the doctors said, "Another month. Be patient." They put a bar on the end of the cast so I could put weight on it. I ended up back in my bed, itchy and miserable.

The nightmares didn't end. One night, after a nasty one about Andy walking toward me with no head, I woke up and thought, "If I get out of here, this will stop." Back in Grand's house, these dreams would go away and my leg would heal. But I knew that Daddy and Stella would let hell freeze over before they'd let me go. So I sat on the nest of a breakout plan, waiting to hatch it out. I practiced walking around the house with one crutch underneath my left armpit because my right arm was still tender, bearing as much weight on the bar of my cast as I dared.

One rainy Friday about a week before my birthday, after Daddy went to Long Reach to work and Stella left for Ray's, I got myself up, tucked my crutch under my arm, and made it to the coatrack by the kitchen door. I shrugged my slicker on, took the spare key Daddy kept for Grand's house and put it into the slicker pocket, lowered myself into a kitchen chair, and dragged Daddy's left-footed boot to me with my crutch. I rested as I savored the next step.

It wasn't a long way from Daddy's house to Grand's house. I could hop, skip, and jump it in no time. Then, I would unlock Grand's door and get myself inside. Grand's radio was upstairs and the bathroom was just across the hall. I would move up and down the stairs on my butt, coming downstairs only to eat. It made perfect sense. Going home would give Stella and Daddy a break, I would be free, and the night-mares would stay across the road in my childhood bedroom.

I pulled the boot onto my good leg, wrestled the door open, hop-walked down the four front steps, and gimped up the driveway. Blessed May rain fell on the hood of my slicker and hit my face. The smells, the birdsongs, the feel of that rain, made me feel alive in a way I hadn't felt in months. I smiled as I moved toward the shuttered arms of Grand's house. Step, swing, step, swing. This was easy. My heart soared.

But the soft Maine mud and the tip of my crutch were determined to mate. When the crutch sank into the mud, I tugged hard to get it out, but as I did that, I lurched hard to the right, almost falling to avoid put-ting too much weight on my right leg. "Not happening," I said. I eased my crutch out of the mud and took another few steps. The crutch became mired again.

"Shit on a brick," I muttered. I pulled. The crutch slipped and sank back. My leg throbbed in its cast. The sky opened up and the rain hit my exposed skin and dribbled down my neck into my shirt.

The sound of a car coming down the hill told me I was about to be seen and maybe helped back into bed. "No," I said. I hopped a few steps forward before my left foot slipped out from under me and I fell back-ward and landed on my butt in the driveway.

The car's purr sounded familiar. I said, "Oh no," as Bud's Fairlane came into view. He looked my way, looked away, looked back. He jammed on the brakes and started to laugh. And laugh. He used up so much air laughing at me that the driver's window fogged up and I couldn't see him anymore. I struggled to get up, but it was no use. He opened the car door and got out and laughed some more. Then he shook his head and walked my way.

"Florine, Florine," he said.

"Help me up," I snapped and he bent down and reached behind me to pull me up until I was standing.

"Put your good arm across my shoulders," he said. He began to turn me around, back toward Daddy's house.

"Toward Grand's house," I said.

"Leeman know you're making a break for it?"

"No, Leeman doesn't know. But he'll be fine."

"I don't know," Bud said. "Doesn't seem like you can get around real well. Looks like you need more help than you might think."

"I would have been okay without the mud," I said.

"That's true," Bud said. "But the bathroom's upstairs. How you going to get around, on your butt? That's a picture."

"No one has to see it," I said. "Please take me over there. I'm going nutty. I need to get out of there." I looked at my bedroom window, and I swore I could see the nightmares peeking out from behind the curtains. "Please, Bud."

The rain poured down on both our heads and he looked at me. His dark eyes still laughed, but he turned me around in the direction I wanted to go. "We'll figure it out," he said, and he became my crutch for the rest of the way. He unlocked the door for me and we went inside. I breathed in lemon furniture polish.

"Someone's been here," I said.

"Ma's been over a few times," Bud said. "Stella asked her if she'd mind. Let's get this off," he said, helping me shed the slicker. He took in my pajamas and giggled. "Which way we headed?" he asked and I said, "The living room." We hobbled that way. At my orders, he went upstairs and brought down a towel, which he set on the sofa. I sat my muddy butt down on the towel and breathed as deep as I'd ever breathed, tired, but happy as a clam at high tide. I grinned like a fool at Bud, who shook his head and gave me his crooked smile.

"I got to move the car," he said. "I got to get your other crutch, too. I'll be right back. For chrissake, stay put, will you?"

I was still sitting and smiling when he returned. "You want anything?" he asked.

"Cup of tea," I said.

He headed for the kitchen. The faucet went on, the water splashed into the hollow bottom of the old metal kettle. The match scratched against the stove as Bud lit it, the burner whooshed on, and the water on the outside of the kettle hissed as the flame hit it. I heard all this from the living room, music to my ears.

Bud shuffled back and leaned against the doorway.

"Why you here?" I asked. "You're supposed to be in school."

"Yeah," Bud said. "But I didn't feel like it. Don't give me any shit about it, either. You can't really say nothing about it."

"Not going to," I said.

"I'm sick of it all," Bud said.

The water hummed.

"You going to be in trouble?" Bud said. "Will they be pissed?"

"Probably," I said. "But I'm going to stay here."

"Well, you got your mind made up. I know no one can change it."

"I needed to be here."

The kettle whistled and Bud went back to the kitchen. He brought me Grand's favorite mug, a white ceramic thing so old that the cracks on the inside were stained brown. I sipped at the strong, milky, sweet tea. It was just the way I liked it.

"How's Susan?" I asked.

"Good. Thinking about colleges. Wants to be a teacher."

"She's smart," I said.

"Yeah. You're almost out of sugar. What else do you need?"

We made a list of basics and I told him about the brick in back of the stove. He took some cash and started out.

"Wait," I said. "What if Stella gets her radar up?"

"Told Ida I'd pick up some stuff for her on my way home." Off he went. As the sound of the engine in the Fairlane died away, the telephone on the hall table rang. Did Daddy know already? Had someone else seen us? Should I just let it ring?

Then I knew.

I pulled myself up using the arm of the sofa, and I lurched to the hall and picked up the receiver.

"Hello?" I said.

Just the smallest of pauses, then Andy said, "Florine?"

I lowered myself by inches into the telephone chair by the desk. "Andy," I said, and we both started to cry. For about a minute, that's all we did, listen to each other sob, sniffle, and take in and let out broken breaths. Then he said, "You're alive."

I laughed. "Yes," I said. "And so are you."

"I've been having horrible dreams," Andy said.

"Me, too," I said.

"I'm sorry," he said. "I'm so sorry."

"It's okay, Andy. We're going to be okay."

"I was crazy. I almost killed you. I'm so sorry. I can't even think of the words . . ."

"It's all right," I said. "I'm just glad to hear your voice."

"I've been calling for about two weeks now, every day. I didn't dare call your dad's house, but I was hoping that you were going to be at Grand's some day. I kept trying. I sent you a card. Did you get it?"

"No," I said. "But I'm not surprised. Don't worry about it, Andy."

"I'm going to have to go to an army school, Florine. I don't know if I can stand it. I'll go out of my mind. How will I get through it?"

"You're Outward Bound boy," I said. "You can get through anything. You're strong. Tougher than you know."

"Florine?"

"What?"

"I meant it when I said I loved you."

"I know."

I heard a door open on his end. "Did you love me?" he whispered.

"I did, Andy."

"I have to go," Andy said. "I love you. I'll try to call later. Goodbye." And then he was gone.

Bud found me crying by the phone. He put the groceries down and helped me back to the sofa. He went upstairs to the bathroom, grabbed a box of Kleenex, and then came back down.

"I know you don't like him," I said. "But there's good that people don't see."

"He must be a good guy, somehow. You ain't a stupid girl."

I threw the balled-up Kleenex across the room. "I am a stupid girl," I cried. "Look at me! I'm sitting on my dead grandmother's sofa with a broken leg, a twisted back, and an arm that's about as well knit together as a cracked branch. I quit school. I got no mother. I got no Grand. I got no future. I'm just going to bake bread for Ray and the rest of you are going to move away, and I'm going to turn strange."

"You ain't going to turn strange," Bud said.

"Oh," I said. "But the rest of it is true?"

"Hell no," he said. "Well, you quit school and Carlie's gone. Grand died. You couldn't help those last two things. You didn't have nothing to do with them. Lighten up on yourself. You ain't so bad. You got us."

"I don't," I said. "Dottie's going to school. You're going to fix cars and marry Susan. Glen's going to Vietnam."

"We'll see about marrying Susan. And Glen won't be in Vietnam forever," Bud said. "Maybe you can get together with him."

I shot him such a look that he got up off the sofa. "I got to put the groceries away," he said. "Then I think we better help you upstairs. I'm going to get Ma to help you get cleaned up. She can fix you supper, get you settled in for the night. I'll come by in the morning, see if Stella and Leeman have killed you."

"Thanks," I said. "Thank you so much, Bud."

He shrugged and went to put the groceries away. He helped me upstairs and waited outside the bathroom while I had a good, long pee. Then he helped me across the hall to Grand's room. He sat me in the rocker. "I'll go tell Ma you're here," he said. "She'll be glad to help."

The thought of a visit from gentle Ida cheered me up. I nodded and said thanks again.

Bud's heavy steps creaked down the stairs. I heard him open the front door, then shut it again. He clomped back upstairs and came into Grand's bedroom. He knelt down in front of me and said, "I'm glad you didn't die, Florine. I was scared you might, and I would have missed you all my life." He kissed my forehead and pounded down the stairs and out the door.

"I appreciate everything you've done," I said to Daddy and Stella when they came hustling over to see if I'd killed myself. "But I feel better already and you can relax."

"Well, since you say so, and since we trust your judgment, Florine, we'll just relax," Stella said. "Thank you. My mind is at ease. What about your mind, Leeman?"

"You don't have to be sarcastic," I said.

"What if there's a fire?" Daddy asked.

"Won't be one," I said.

"You never know," he said.

"No," I said. "But the chances of it are slim to none, don't you think?"

"The chances of you getting into a car accident with a summer kid were slim to none," Stella pointed out, "but it happened."

"I'm not going back," I said. "If a fire takes me, it'll take me here."

Stella looked at me as if to say, That would solve everything, as far as I'm concerned.

"How are you going to get downstairs?" Daddy asked.

"Oh," I said, "that's easy. Watch." I slid my crutches down the stairs, then bumped down each riser on my butt.

"Great," Stella said. "Just great."

"Daddy, I'm happy here," I said. "It's home to me."

"If I hog-tie you and carry you across the way you'll just come back here," he said. "How the hell did you get so stubborn? Never mind. Your mother."

I didn't like him talking about Carlie in front of Stella. I gave him a look, and he said, "Come summer, I'll rewire the place. Hasn't been done since Dad was alive."

I woke up sometime later that night, not because of a nightmare, but because I wondered how Bud had known that I liked my tea with milk and sugar.

44

The accident and the long time I'd had to lay in bed and think changed me. Stella's words about going after what you wanted seemed like the truth to me, too. Some kind of determination had taken hold in my brain and made things clearer. One of the things I was pretty clear about was that Andy and I were over.

Andy called me once more during the day when I was downstairs and could answer the phone. By then, I'd come to the conclusion that without him in front of me, it was as though he didn't exist. Everything we had been to each other had been so loaded with touch and feel. And his voice on the phone was thin, with a trace of whine in it.

He told me that he was staying with his mother. "I'm going to come up and see you when my legs are better," he said. "We'll work this all out. We'll make a plan." When I didn't say anything, he asked me if I loved him. Again I said that I had, but it didn't sound real to me and I realized I was saying it to make him feel better.

"You do love me, now," he said. "Right?"

Tears slipped down my cheeks, and I said, "I don't know anything anymore, Andy."

"Hang on," he said. "Hang on to what we had. I'll be coming up as soon as I can."

We hung up shortly after that. He called a few times at night, but I was upstairs and couldn't get down to the phone in the hall without risking life and limb. When the calls stopped, I was almost relieved. I knew he would not be up, at least not for a long time, and probably never, for me, anyway. I stopped trying to recall him in my head, and concentrated on getting well.

Rain took up my eighteenth birthday. Stella made me a passable angel food cake, but I missed Grand and Dottie, who was too busy to get together with me. But we spent time together at the movies a few days later. Madeline tagged along after talking us into seeing a movie called *Midnight Cowboy*. She cried at the end and thought it was "brilliant." I thought Joe Buck was sexy, but I didn't get much of what the plot was about. Dottie slept through most of it.

On June 5 the temperature went up to sixty-five and the sun shone almost every day. I bumped downstairs every morning and hobbled into the kitchen to make myself breakfast. I sat on the porch and rocked and watched the water turn from murky green to the bright blue that meant summer was coming. Stella came by every morning to find me up, fed, and ready to roll. Daddy came by in the afternoon to find me busy with a knitting project or making myself some dinner. They began to relax, just as I'd told them to do.

I settled into a routine of cleaning as best I could, calling up to Ray's for supplies, and knitting sweater sets. I would be ready for the season, for the fairs and for the new craft show that had opened in Long Reach for the Fourth of July celebration.

At about one o'clock every day, my heart picked up the pace and my ears strained past seagulls and wind, boats and rattletrap trucks for a low chug-chug, and here Bud would come, stopping outside to drop off groceries. He'd put them away and we'd sit on the porch and watch the water and talk.

One day he talked about why he didn't want to be a lobsterman. "It's too hard. Jesus, have you had a good look at our old men? I'm going to be a mechanic," he said.

"How does Susan feel about that?" I asked.

"She's fine with it," he said. We watched two seagulls catch drafts over the water. One rose, then the other, back and forth.

I said, "Why do you like her?"

He frowned. "What do you mean, why do I like her? Why wouldn't I like her?"

I backed up, slow. "She's pretty, she's sweet, and funny. I just wondered what makes people like each other."

"I don't know. You think weird things, sometimes, you know that?"

I laughed. "I'm crazy," I said. "*You* know that."

The seagulls were side-by-side now, balanced on the wind.

Then Bud said, "I don't know why she picked me. She could have gone out with anyone. She makes me feel smarter than I really am. She makes me think I can be something. She thinks I'm special."

One seagull rose above the other one, turned, and flew down the harbor toward the bay. The other stayed with the wind for a few seconds, then flapped off the other way.

"I know you're special," I said, soft. "I don't just think you're special."

Bud smiled. "You're my friend," he said. "We've known each other a long time." We sat quiet for a minute, and then he said, "I got no right to say this to you, and I know it, Florine. You deserve someone special."

"What do you mean?" I asked.

"Florine, he almost killed you."

"You're talking about Andy, I guess?"

"You know I am. And I got no right. But don't even think about ever going back to him. He almost killed you and he left his father—now I ain't saying he's much better than his son—to die in the cold, maybe from freezing or from hitting his head. Doesn't matter. You got to find someone who will take care of you and himself. Someone who has his head on straight."

"I know that," I said. "I do." I did.

"You ain't mad at me for saying all that," Bud said.

"No."

"Good," he said. "I had to say it." He got up, patted my shoulder and left. I smiled.

Dottie told me that she was going to the college at Farmington, no doubt due to Madeline's determination to get her there. "And they got a bowling alley down the hill from the dorms," Dottie said. "You can bet I'll be there any chance I get."

Glen had made up his mind to go to Vietnam. The thought made me sad, but his decision sat on his brow, solid and true to him. I hoped that he might keep himself out of trouble, by thinking about coming home to Evie Butts. Evie was all curves and giggles and Glen was a fool for her.

"Madeline's fit to be tied," Dottie said. "Glen swears to her that he won't touch Evie until she grows up. Says by the time he gets back, she'll be the right age for him."

"Will he wait?" I ask.

"If he wants to keep his balls. Oh Christ! He could be my brother-in-law."

"You always said he and Bud were like our brothers," I said.

"I did, didn't I? Never miss an opportunity to keep your mouth shut," she said. "That should be my motto."

In the middle of June, I went to graduation with Bert and Madeline and watched my friends get their diplomas. As I sat through the ceremony in the hot June sun with the rest of the crowd, I pictured myself up there, and in my mind, I saw my proud parents watch me walk across the stage to shake hands with the principal, take my diploma, move the tassel on my cap to the other side, wave and smile. That vision disappeared as I realized that my arms were turning too pink. Carlie would have taken me home at that point, but I made it through the long ceremony and put ointment on when I got home. Someday soon, I vowed, I would try to find a way to get my diploma.

All this planning for the future made it clear to me that, before I got my diploma, what I wanted was across the road and down the hill. I was going to marry Bud. Susan was gone. She just didn't know it yet.

But she might have picked up on some kind of radar that I was sending out, because one afternoon when Bud came through the door with the groceries, she was with him.

I hadn't seen her since my stay in the hospital. She was thinner and prettier than I'd remembered her being, all smiles and shiny hair. Bud put the groceries on the table and Susan put her arm around his waist and they looked at me sitting in my chair at the table.

"How you doing?" Susan asked.

"I'm fine," I said. "Just fine."

"You look fine," Susan said. Her eyes narrowed, like a cat's eyes will when it might pounce. And I knew that she knew. "Cast coming off soon?" she asked.

"Soon," I said.

"Must be good, knowing you'll be able to take care of yourself."

"I get along," I said. Then I narrowed my eyes. And she knew that I knew that she knew. And she knew I didn't care.

On weekends, Bud worked on the Fairlane in his driveway. I loved to sit in the kitchen, look out the window, and watch my future husband bend over the engine. I would watch him for as long as he was out there. To my mind, there was no finer thing to do.

In late June, I got my cast off and set myself to learning to walk normally again. My leg was weak, but my will was strong, and although I limped, I kept on going. I gave the house a thorough cleaning and started gardening outside, when I wasn't watching Bud and Susan.

She spent the last part of June in a lawn chair reading a book near Bud as he worked on the Fairlane. She wore shorts and cinched her shirt up and tied it into a knot that showed off her belly, back, and her curvy sides. While Bud tinkered with the car, she would do things like run her hand up the back of Bud's thigh and bring it to rest on his butt. Sometimes after she'd done that, he'd pull himself up from under the hood and give her a kiss. But it didn't bother me. It had nothing to do with my future. I knew she knew I was watching her—why else would she put on such a show?—and one Sunday afternoon she put the book she was reading down beside her lawn chair, got up, and walked toward Grand's house. She let herself in, came directly to the kitchen and stood in front of my chair, her long hair framing both sides of her pretty face. "What is going on?" she asked.

"What do you mean?" I said.

"Why are you watching us?"

"I like the view," I said, and I smiled. She moved her hair back with her hands.

"Okay," she said. "I knew that, I guess. So, I'll be honest, and I hope I don't hurt your feelings. Bud's been really nice to you, but that's all. It's one reason I love him. But I hope you're not mistaking him being nice for him falling for you."

"No, no mistake," I said.

"Good," Susan said, "because we are definitely together."

"Then you shouldn't mind me admiring your happiness."

"You're giving me the creeps."

"Why? I'm not looking at you."

"You're looking at Bud?"

"I am," I said. "Don't you think he's worth looking at?"

"Of course I do," she said. "He's my boyfriend."

"For now," I said.

"What does that mean? I thought you were my friend."

"I am, but he won't be your boyfriend in a few months."

"Why do you think that? We're together now more than ever."

"If you say so."

"I do. Look, I don't want to be mean, but you need to start asking other people to help you out. He's tired of it. He told me."

"I don't think he's tired at all," I said. "I think he's just warming up."

"No," Susan said. "No. He told me he feels sorry for you."

"I feel sorry for you."

"Why?"

"Because he's going to marry me."

Susan turned pale. "You're crazy," she said.

"No, I'm not," I said. "You need to get going now."

She stomped back to Bud and tapped him on the back. He stood up as she waved her hands and pointed at the house. He looked over and saw me looking out the window. I smiled and waved. He waved, but he didn't smile. He slammed the car hood down and Susan climbed into the passenger side of the Fairlane. He got in on the driver's side and they drove away. He didn't beep as they passed.

But I knew he'd be back.

Late that night, when he knocked at the door, I was snuggled down in bed with a book. He let himself in and mounted the steps two at a time. He stood in the doorway, a scowl in his eyes, hands gripping either side of the doorframe.

"Did you have a nice date?" I asked.

"Susan is my girlfriend. Stop staring at us. It's weird."

"No law against looking at the scenery, is there? We live in a beautiful place, Bud."

"Florine, we talked. I thought you understood everything."

"It was fine, then. Things have changed."

"Not with me. If I got to choose, I got to stop seeing you."

I swung myself off the bed and stood in front of Grand's lamp. The warm yellow light backlit my thin nightie and showed each curve and angle, the soft darkness on my mound, and my nipples. I knew how it looked, because I'd checked it out in the mirror.

"I don't think you can," I said.

His eyes moved to my breasts, down my belly. "Jesus," he said.

I yawned. "I'm sleepy, Bud," I said, and I tousled my hair. His eyes went down everywhere, and he moved back from the doorway, toward the stairs. "Good night," I called. "Thanks for your help."

He stomped down the stairs and went out the front door. The Fairlane roared to life and he rumbled down to his house.

45

O n that high-summer morning in late July, the sky sucked me into its blue soup like a willing and thirsty fly. "You okay?" Daddy yelled from the *Florine*'s stern. I sat in a tall deck chair with a pillow against the back in the wheelhouse, taking her down the channel while Daddy baited traps and tossed them overboard. I was helping because Sam was too sick to come aboard. He had what would be diagnosed as liver cancer, but none of us knew that yet.

I hollered to Daddy, "I'm okay," over the flock of gulls that spoke in loud tongues for Daddy to toss them bait. The *Florine*'s engine growled as if she was hung over and paying for it.

"Take your pills?" Daddy yelled.

"Yes," I lied. I was trying to get by without them because they made me sleepy. I wore pain like an itchy wool sweater. Besides, the doctor had told me I might have back and leg troubles all my life, and I didn't want to be tired, to boot.

Daddy tossed a trap into the greedy harbor's mouth. In my head, I followed it down to the bottom, to where some scavenging lobster would get wind of it and follow its claws into the funnel. If it was too small, it would eat and leave. If not, it would have to cancel its appointments and hope that its relatives would divvy up its belongings.

A larger boat, the *Molly B*, passed us on the left. We waved, they waved, and I waited for the wake to rock us sideways over the hill of the swell, then down into the gullies. I slowed the engine and eased back in my chair.

Daddy came into the wheelhouse when we reached the end of his line. I took the engine to a crawl. She coughed, but guttered along.

"Good day," Daddy said. He took off his black rubber gloves, opened his thermos, and poured coffee into the little red cup that topped it.

"How long have you had that thermos?" I asked him.

"Since before you was born," he said. "Grand got me this lunchbox when I was in high school. Same thermos as then," he said. "That's hard to do without breaking it."

"Guess it is," I said. "I broke about three in grade school."

"I remember," Daddy said. He took a sip of coffee and puckered up. I gave him a sympathetic look and he winked at me. "I'm used to it," he said. "Stella can cook some good, but her coffee's always been too strong. Eh, what the hell."

"Can't you teach her how to make a decent cup?"

"I could," he said. "But why bother?" He shrugged. "Got to get along," he said. "Stella's been good to me."

I surprised myself when I said, "She has been good. She's taken care of you."

He smiled at me as if I'd given him a present he'd asked for but didn't expect. He nodded and said, "You find someone like that, you take care of each other. Best thing you can do for you and for them."

Daddy looked out the front window of the wheelhouse. One big, freckled finger curled itself around the thin red handle of the little cup. A bubble of tenderness floated from my toes to my head. I thought, I will knit this picture into my brain forever. I'll put it alongside the time Bud and I dove down to the bottom of the mooring, all the times Grand and I waved in the boats, and the time Carlie pointed out the horizon to me.

Then the *Florine*'s engine sputtered and quit.

"Damn it," Daddy said. "She's been running rough. Let me give her a try," he said. I climbed down from the chair, being careful not to wrench my back or my leg, and stepped to the other side of the wheelhouse. Daddy turned the key in the ignition. Nothing. Not even a clunk.

"Well, hell," he said. "Guess I got to tinker with the bitch."

"Let's eat lunch first," I said. "Sit in the sun." The fickle gulls now hovered around the *Molly B*, way over by the edge of the horizon.

I went out onto the deck and opened the cooler we'd brought along. The sun massaged the back of my neck with warm fingers and it felt so good, I groaned. I breathed in salty air, drunk with summer. I unfolded a lawn chair and lowered myself into it, sprawling my legs out in front of me.

Daddy dropped anchor, then sat across from me on an overturned bait pail. "Good idea," he said. "Give her a rest. Maybe that's what she needs."

"Maybe you need a rest, too," I said.

"Nah," he said. "I'm tough." He squinted into the sun and I saw where one of his top teeth was a funny color, almost blue.

"You got a bad tooth?" I asked.

"Yeah. Stella wants me to see to it, but it don't bother me yet. Looks kind of funny, but then, so do I."

I bit into my peanut butter and jam sandwich and slugged down cold milk. We didn't talk, just ate. Being quiet, with the motor off, is probably the reason we saw the whale. It breached about ten feet from the boat, made a bow out of its long, shiny back, swam on the surface for a minute, then sank.

"Minke," Daddy said.

We waited, and the minke swam back alongside the boat. We could see it as clear as if it were above the waves, the way its body moved smooth and silent. Then it rose, exhaled from its blowhole, and arched toward the *Molly B.*

"Kick dive," Daddy said.

The giant tail fin slapped the water, blessing Daddy and me with salty spray.

We let it dry on our skins as we finished lunch. I raised my face to the sun and Daddy got up, walked to the middle of the boat, and opened the trapdoor to the engine crawl space.

"We'll fix her up, then haul on the way home," he said. He lowered himself down and I put his toolbox next to him.

I fell asleep in the chair soon after he started working on the engine. The sun and general well-being lulled me away and I sank down, down, down with the whale, swimming with the whole ocean ahead of me and the rest of it behind.

When I woke, the sun had moved from the top of the sky to somewhere around two o'clock. My back hurt and my face burned. I didn't hear the engine. Damn, I thought, we'll have to radio in for some help.

"Hey, Daddy," I called. I struggled up out of the chair and limped over to the trapdoor by the engine. "Haven't you got that bitch fixed yet?"

He was looking up at the sky, braced against the back of the hatch, his hand open on the deck, a wrench across his palm.

"What are you doing?" I said.

He kept looking at the sky, so steady that I looked up. I saw nothing. "What are you looking at?" I asked. He didn't answer.

And then I knew.

My heart throbbed in deep, painful jerks.

"Daddy?" I touched his face. It was clammy and wet with sweat that he would never wipe with a hankie again. I jerked my hand away and began to wail in wide loops like a little girl, sending seagulls over to study me before winging away again.

I don't know how long I dropped tears down onto my dead father's face. But after a while, I stopped and studied the expression on it because he looked both happy and surprised, as if someone he hadn't seen in a long time had come by. I followed his eyes up again, and got caught in the layers of blue that separated us from space.

"She found you, didn't she, Daddy," I said. "She came for you." I swiped tears off my face with a fist. "It's about time," I said to Carlie. "It's about goddamned time." Then I thought about Daddy and Carlie dancing in the kitchen, her small feet on his big ones as he lifted her around in a clumsy waltz. I let them dance all the way through "Love Me Tender" before I thought about calling for help.

I looked at my watch. It was about three o'clock. Daddy had died between about one o'clock and two thirty or so. "I should have been there," I said. Then I heard Daddy's voice, clear as the sky above, say, "Nothing you could have done, Florine. It's all right. Right as rain." And Carlie said, "You'll be all right, my little criminal."

The horizon was clear of boats except for a tanker inching its tiny way along the line between sea and sky. I went to the radio. I should have called the Coast Guard, I suppose, but the time for emergencies had passed. I called into Ray's store and Glen answered.

"This is Florine," I said. "I'm out on the boat with Daddy. Glen, he's died. Heart attack, I think. I need you to send someone out to get us. The engine quit."

"Holy shit," Glen said.

"I know," I said.

"Holy shit," Glen said again, and then he said, "Oh, no." I heard the sadness in his voice, and that's when it hit me that he wasn't just mine, that he belonged to The Point and everyone in it. Stella. Oh God, Stella.

"Glen," I said, my voice shaking, "he was trying to fix the engine. I took a nap and when I woke up, he was gone. Please send someone out. Please be gentle with Stella."

I sat with Daddy for almost another hour. We'd gone pretty far out, as far as his line extended. Some boats motored past me, but I didn't call out to them. I stroked the top of Daddy's head with the tips of my fingers, letting sorrow wash over me, riding it up and over and down. Up and over and down. Down and over and up.

Finally, Bert, Glen, and Bud pulled up next to us in the *Maddie Dee*. Bud clambered over the side and I went to him like a baby. He held me and let me go on, rubbing my back, kissing my hair, saying, "It's okay," as if I had fallen down on a gravel road and skinned my knee.

Finally he whispered, "I got to help out," and he walked back to the trapdoor, where Bert and Glen stood. Bert said in a voice that was none too steady, "We got to move him and try and start up the boat. Pretty sure I know what ails her. Florine, honey, you and Glen go back in the *Maddie Dee*. Bud and I will bring your father home."

"I don't want to leave him," I said.

"He's gone, darling," Bert said. "You ain't leaving him."

Bud said, "Why don't Glen stay? I'll take Florine back."

Bert looked surprised and then he didn't, and he nodded.

Bud steered the *Maddie Dee* back to home with me in between him and the wheel. I leaned back into him and he held me and the boat steady as we neared The Point. The wharf was crowded with people come to greet Daddy.

"I can't do this," I said.

"You don't have to do it alone," Bud said. "You got us to help you."

Then I remembered the whale.

"What kind?" Bud asked.

"Minke."

"Supposed to be good luck," he said. "Or maybe not."

46

Stella went out of her mind. She was there on the wharf when Bud and I docked, and she threw herself on me and shrieked, "It can't be true. Say it's not true. Oh my god, Florine, we've lost him." Despite her skinniness, when she launched herself at me I cried out, not just from the loss, but because she hurt my back. Dottie was on the dock with tears running down her own cheeks, but she took the time to unwind Stella from me.

Later, when Bert and Glen had brought Daddy into port and burial arrangements had been set in motion, Stella, when she could talk, said she wanted Daddy to be buried in their plot on the hill by the church near to Grand. They'd planned this a while back, she said, which surprised me, but then, I hadn't been paying attention.

"There's room for you," she told me the day after they brought Daddy in and took him up to the funeral parlor. "You can be buried between Grand and Leeman, if you want."

"Don't know where I'll be buried," I said. "Hope that time is a long way off."

"Well, that's where we'll be, if you don't have anywhere else to go," she said. "You'll always be welcome."

I hoped the hell there would be more to my life than ending up like that. But I had something else on my mind. I took a deep breath, and

said, "Now, don't go all weird on me, but what would you think of giving Daddy a burial at sea?"

"What?" she cried.

"Daddy loved the ocean better than anything," I said. "I'm wondering how you would feel if we took him out on the boat and gave him a
water burial."

"Over my dead body," Stella said. She started to shake. "I will *not*
have him out there all alone. If I can't be with him now, then I'll settle
for eternity with him in our graves. On the hill. Forever. I know that
you're next of kin, but I'm next to nothing without him. You've got to
understand that if you know nothing else." And she started to sob, so I
handed her a Kleenex and that was the end of that.

We went with Madeline and Dottie to choose the coffin. "He has to
have the best," Stella said, although Madeline talked her down from a
mahogany number that probably cost more than the house. "Florine,
what do you think?" Madeline asked me from time to time.

"Well, maybe . . . ," I'd start, then Stella's cries would drown me out.
During the height of one of her squalls, I pointed to a simple, dark coffin, and Madeline nodded. Stella, thank heaven, agreed with us.

The night before the funeral, Dottie, Bud, Glen, and I sat on Grand's
porch. Dottie cracked open a bottle of rosé and I held up my red ruby
wineglass and studied the richness of the color in the porch light. Glen
and Bud sucked down beers and leaned back in the rocking chairs.

"Don't do that," I said. "The legs will break." They rocked down.

"How come no one knows what to say when something like this
happens?" Dottie asked. "No one ever knows what to say."

"The way Stella's carrying on, it's hard to say anything," Glen said.

"She loved him," I said. "He's all she ever wanted."

"She keeps saying that," Dottie said.

"It's true," I said.

"Maybe she can get a dog," Glen said.

Bud burst out laughing, followed by Dottie. I even giggled.

"You think a dog's gonna replace Leeman?" Dottie asked.

"Well, maybe then she wouldn't be so lonely," Glen said. "Dogs are good company."

I thought of Daddy, who looked so uncomfortable in his blue suit with his big freckled hands folded over a Bible, being stuck for eternity in a box. Two things hit me at once. I would never see him again, and I would know that he was trapped in the earth in an uncomfortable suit forever. It was too much to bear. "No," I said. I dropped the red ruby wineglass, which miraculously didn't break as it hit the floor. I held my hands over my face, trying to rid myself of the vision of crawly things chewing through poor Daddy.

Pictures of him flashed through my mind. Him waving at Grand and me from the boat, walking up from the wharf, down the hill to the harbor, tossing traps, drinking coffee from his little red cup, watching the whale, holding his hand, holding him close. Us fighting. Me hurting him. Us making up. Us loving each other, no matter what. Us getting on with it during the hardest time in our lives. I started to cry.

"Get her a Kleenex," Dottie said. "She's finally exploded."

Bud was ready with a clean white handkerchief in his pocket and I blew my nose loud into it. I balled it up, wiped my tears, and hiccupped.

"I can't stand to think of him in the ground," I said. "Being eaten by worms. Sucked dry. He'd hate it."

"Well," Dottie said. "It's the way things go."

"I know," I said. "But he'd rather be out in the water."

"Sleeping with the fishes," Glen said.

The day of the funeral was like the day he died. We filed into the church under a warm blue sky. The pews were filled, as they had been for Grand's funeral. Stella hunkered next to me, one arm hooked through mine. She sobbed throughout the teary service, while I sniffled and tried to listen to Pastor Billy, who stopped a couple of times to blow his nose. Glen told me that Billy had wanted to talk about how they'd all lost a good poker player, but that he'd decided against it, thinking that people might misunderstand. He did talk about men going down to the sea in boats, about Daddy's love of the water, his love for his family and friends, and for his beloved Point.

After the service, we shuffled out of the church and walked Daddy to his burial plot. I got the vision of him being underground again and I shivered and the tears slipped down. Stella put her arm around me and said, "I know. What are we going to do without him?" She threw her arms around Madeline. "What am I going to do?" she sobbed.

The sun hit the back of my neck, much as it had only four days before, only this time it dug its nails in, too hot, too sharp. Sweat trickled down my chest and fell into my belly button before it spilled over and wet the front of my slip and underpants. I looked up at the sky and the day faded to white and I woke up on the ground by the grave with the pallbearers bending over me, Bud touching my face.

"You all right?" he asked.

"Oh, poor Florine," Stella cried from somewhere. Bud and Glen raised me from the ground and I wobbled between them. They helped me back to the car and I never saw them lower Daddy into the ground, which might have killed me.

At the get-together at Stella's house afterward, I sat in a lawn chair in the shade of a maple tree that held the remains of the swing Daddy had built for me when I was about five. The wood seat was rotted out but I ran my hands up and down one of the thick ropes that held it up, feeling little splinters catch in my palms and in the pads of my fingers.

The men all stood outside the house, smoking, drinking, talking and not talking. Sadness set like shiny stones in their eyes. They'd grown up together, fished together, loved women together, raised kids together, and now the first one of them was gone. To a man, they looked smaller, as if they could be struck down at any moment, too.

People kept checking on me, which got to me after a while, and when Dottie came around, I said, "Give me a hand. I'm tired of feeling so damn precious." She hauled me to my feet, and I mingled until four o'clock or so, when I decided to go to Grand's house to nap. "I'll be back later," I said to Madeline, who was running the show.

"You sure?" she asked. "You look peaked."

"I feel okay," I said. "Tired mostly."

I went home and crawled upstairs to bed. My body sank into the mattress, but my mind played Daddy's life like a movie. I cried until I got to the end, and then it was dark, and Dottie was shaking me.

"Get up," she said.

"Why?" I snapped.

"Just come on," she said. "And be quiet."

"What time is it?"

"About one o'clock."

"In the morning? Jesus, Dottie."

I hauled myself out of bed and pulled on shorts and a sweatshirt lying on the floor beside the bed. I forced my feet into my sneakers.

Dottie pulled me out the door, down the hill, and toward the wharf. We took a right toward the beach, where I saw a dark figure standing by a dinghy. Bud.

"Get in," he whispered, and he rowed us out toward where the *Florine* sat moored. We passed her, though, and I said, "What are we doing?" Bud didn't answer, just kept rowing toward the *Maddie Dee*, which sat farther out in the harbor. Onboard her I saw the faint outlines of several figures. Lit cigarettes punched orange holes into the night and I realized that Daddy wasn't going to rot in the ground. He was going home to sea and we were taking him there. The men hauled me and Dottie up over the gunwale while Bud tied off the dinghy next to two others and climbed aboard. Sam, Bert, Ray, Bud, Glen, and Pastor Billy paddled the *Maddie Dee* out toward the mouth of the harbor. Dottie and I stood over the remains of my father, now bound in a white sheet that glowed as if a chip of the moon had fallen from the sky and landed on deck.

When we got far enough out, Bert fired up the *Maddie Dee*'s engine

and we puttered out into the silent bay toward the ocean, past the lobster pots, past the place where we'd seen the minke whale, and where
Daddy had died.

Finally, Bert stopped the boat and shut off the engine. The water
lopped against the sides, and we formed a circle around Daddy.

"Well," Sam said, "we come to bring you home, old man."

"Should we say a prayer or something?" Glen asked.

"Enough prayers got said this morning," Ray said. "Sorry Pastor."

"I agree," Billy said. "We don't need words."

"Well, let's do it," Sam said.

"Wait," Bud said. "Maybe Florine's got something she wants to say?"

I looked at the men standing around Daddy and moved closer to
Dottie. "Thank you," I said. "Daddy will be all right now. Thank you
for this."

"Don't tell Stella," Glen said, and we laughed.

Then the men hoisted up Daddy like he weighed no more than a
chunk of Styrofoam and they put him on a wide board, tilted it up, and
Sam said, "God rest you, Lee." Daddy slid off and smacked the water
like a seal going home. Phosphorus sparked off the sheet as he floated
down to the fishes and the lobsters, who knew him better than the
worms, and would make quicker work of him.

Then everyone stepped away and left me alone to stare down into
the empty water. A light breeze lifted my hair and tickled the back of
my neck with a soft touch. I smiled through my tears. "This is so you
won't be alone," I said to Daddy. I pulled off the emerald birthstone ring
Daddy had given me so long ago, the ring he and Carlie had picked out
for my thirteenth birthday. I tossed it into the spot where Daddy had
gone down. In my heart, I put the spirit of my mother alongside him
and brought her home to him.

"Take care of each other," I whispered to my parents. "Don't worry
about me. I'll be getting on with it."

47

Despite our stubborn streaks and our disagreements about Stella, I missed Daddy something awful. I had never realized how much his being just across the road had kept me moving in some kind of direction. My insides spun in circles, searching for north. Still I got on with it, as I'm sure Daddy would have told me to do. About one hundred times a day I doubled over with grief, but I rode it until I could move again.

One early Sunday morning in August, shortly after Daddy's burial at sea and just after the sixth anniversary of Carlie's disappearance, I sat on the porch in my rocker, looking at the water and thinking about how it wouldn't be too long before all of us were gone to dust or became cookie crumbs for bottom-feeders. "That's a happy thought, Florine," I said. "You keep that up." I turned to look at the boats to clear my head.

The *Florine* moped at her mooring, where she'd been since Daddy's death. The *Maddie Dee* rocked close beside her. Suddenly the *Florine* lurched as if she was being goosed from underneath. The wake moved over to rock the *Maddie Dee*. Then, from around the *Florine*'s bow, came Daddy's dinghy. The rower sat back to me, but I could tell it was a woman with a black cloud of hair. Stella. She was having trouble rowing in a straight line. She jerked hard one way, then the other, as she made her way to the wharf. When she finally reached it, she hauled herself up onto the dock as if she was wearing cement shoes.

"She's drunker than a skunk," I said out loud. Securing the dinghy's line to the tie-off took her another good part of forever, but finally she zigzagged up the ramp. As she staggered up the road, I began to think about helping her, but before I could move she bent over and puked up a bucket full of brown liquid right outside Bud's house.

Evidently, Ida had been watching her, too. She came out of the house with a washrag and handed it to Stella so that she could mop her face with it. Then she put her arm around Stella and helped her up the hill to Daddy's house. She came out about ten minutes later and hurried down to her own house to get ready for church.

Later that afternoon, a strange blue car pulled into Daddy's driveway. A stout woman got out and walked right into the house like she meant it. She didn't come out, and after a while I went about my day. I was weeding the flowers in the side garden when the screen door across the road slammed. I looked up to see Stella come out of the house. The stout woman beside her carried two suitcases in her hands. She opened the trunk of her car, tossed them inside, and slammed it shut. Stella caught me looking at her and they both walked up the driveway until they stood in front of me. I saw that they had the same gray eyes.

"This is my sister, Grace," Stella said to me. "This is Florine," she said to Grace.

Grace and I didn't exchange any pleased-to-meet-yous. The way she scowled at me made the skin on my face shrivel. I could just imagine what Stella had told her about me. Grace said, "I came to take Stella with me. Think you can watch the house until she comes back?"

"Probably," I said.

"Just a few plants to water," Stella said. "I left Grace's number on the kitchen table. I'll be in touch." She gave me a clumsy hug and I put my arms around her to hold her up. She clutched at me and whispered in my ear, "I don't blame you, you know." Then she let go. Grace glared at me again and she and Stella went back to the car, got in, and left.

Dottie stopped by later that day. "Did you know that Stella has a sister?" I asked her. "Her name is Grace. Looks like Stella except there's more of her."

"No," Dottie said. "But Stella probably has a whole family we never even heard of."

"Well, you'd think I'd know," I said.

Dottie shrugged. "You been busy."

"Stella said she didn't blame me."

"For what?"

"Daddy dying. She was right. I was hard on him." Sadness washed over me.

"You didn't do nothing that wasn't normal for what was going on at the time," Dottie said. "Nobody's perfect. Not you. Not Leeman. Not Stella. Not even me, though I come close."

I had to agree with her there. Dottie didn't have to bowl 300s to prove it to me.

Stella called a couple of days after she'd left, wanting to know about her plants. I lied and told her I'd taken care of them. I didn't tell her that I had yet to work up the gumption to do it, but I didn't want to let the plants wither away, either.

I hadn't set foot inside Daddy's house since his funeral. The screen door whined as I walked into a kitchen that reeked of spilled booze and loneliness. I opened the door to his workshop, breathed him in and cried him out. I gave Stella's plants a drink and left as fast as I could go.

The house may have been Stella's, but Daddy had willed the *Florine* to me. I knew that, come fall, I would have her hauled out, but right now her bobbing in the water with nothing to do was bugging me, as was the thought of the traps probably filled with lobsters sitting on the bottom of the bay. Then, as if they'd read my mind, Glen and Bud stopped by.

"We come to see if you wanted us to take the *Florine* out early mornings for a couple of weeks," Bud said. He sat across from me at the kitchen table cradling a cup of coffee. Glen sat beside him, making fast work of a piece of blueberry cake I'd made that morning.

"Don't you guys have other jobs?" I said.

"We'll go as soon as we can in the mornings," Bud said. "Fred will let me come in at noon."

"Ray don't care," Glen said. "Anyways, I'm leaving in a month."

"I'd be glad of the help," I said. "I'll go, too."

"You don't have to do that," Bud said.

"I know," I said. "My boat, though."

"Wait till your leg gets normal," Bud said.

"Make sure we got something for breakfast in the morning," Glen said, sucking cake from his fingers with a smack.

So I filled thermoses with coffee and made muffins and cinnamon bread and coffee cakes. Glen stopped by every morning at about four thirty to pick up the goodies, and out they went. They came back before noon. Although I told them to keep half of the money, they gave me all that Stinnie paid them. I stuffed most of it behind the brick in back of the stove.

Madeline held a going-to-college cookout for Dottie in the middle of August. She was due to leave on Saturday, the 23rd of August, for freshman "orientation." She was pleased to go early, because, as she told me, "I can get the hang of the bowling alley."

"Things will be hectic then," Madeline said to me at Ray's a couple of days before the party. "You know Dottie. We'll be packing her up while she's driving up the road." I baked chocolate chip cookies—Dottie's favorite—and took them to the Buttses' house on a beautiful Saturday afternoon. Bud and Glen were there, along with Ray, Ida and Sam, Evie and Maureen, and Susan.

I hadn't seen Susan since before Daddy's death, and I hadn't noticed her around The Point, either. It appeared that she had forgotten or put our talk behind her, though, because when I put the cookies down on the table, she walked up to me and hugged me. Her long hair whispered over my shoulders as she said, "I'm so sorry about your dad."

"Thanks," I said.

"How are you doing?"

"Okay," I said. Dottie came over then, snatched the plate of cookies off the table and ran for the house with them tucked under her arm, which made everyone laugh. I followed her into the house and helped Madeline and Ida with the food.

After we ate, Susan, Dottie, and I found ourselves sitting close together, chairs facing the harbor. The summer sun sank its needle claws deep into the pores of my face. *"You have my skin,"* Carlie had said. *"You burn easy."* I opened my eyelids to slits, watching the glitter on the water, half listening to Dottie and Susan talk about school. I was happy to just be sitting there, but Susan drew me into the talk. "What are you going to do, Florine?" she asked.

"About what?" I said.

"Your life," Susan said. "I mean, will you stay here or what?"

"I don't know," I said. "Who knows?"

Susan plowed on. "You can get your GED," she said. "Go to night school."

"I plan to do that," I said.

"Bud is coming up to Orono. He can work up there and he might go to school. We'd be close, that way," Susan said.

My heart thwacked against the front of my thin summer shirt.

"It'd be great," she continued. "In a couple of years, he can get a business degree and run his own garage, if he wants to, or do something else with it."

The contents in my stomach churned into a squall as she kept on about Bud and herself setting up housekeeping. Finally, I got up and headed for Madeline's kitchen. She said, "You okay, honey? You're awful flushed."

"Sunburn," I said. "Tired, I guess. I'll be heading home." I thanked her, we hugged, and I crossed the yard. But before I got too far, Bud called my name. I turned to face him, going to stone so I wouldn't cry. "Madeline said to give you this," he said, holding out the cookie dish.

"Thanks," I said. It amazed me that I had been so sure of us such a short time ago. Daddy's death had set me to reeling, and I now knew that nothing was certain. I could plan all I wanted, but things went the way they went, and I would have to weather the changes. Still, Bud's ignorance over how he must have known I felt was getting on my nerves. He could have his stupid girlfriend. I would be fine. That, I knew.

"You okay?" he asked.

"Why does everybody ask me that?" I snapped. I took the dish from him. I started to walk away, but then I turned around and said into his startled face, "You know, I would have gone anywhere with you, you dumb ass," then I crossed the road to Grand's house. I went right to bed and sank into sleep to shut down my head and calm my heart. Tomorrow I would begin my life, again, but for now, sleep was what I craved to keep both the dead and live people at bay.

It was dark when I woke to the sound of someone driving a car very fast up the road toward Ray's. The tires spit pebbles that hit the side of Grand's house as the car flew past. "Hey, I'm sleeping here," I said out loud, and rolled over to do just that for the rest of the night.

Summer twitched its tanned hips and sauntered deeper into August. Stella called to tell me that she was doing better, but that she would probably be staying with her sister at least until fall. I went over to Daddy's house twice a week and began moving the things I had left over there to Grand's house to sort through. Every item brought a memory as piercing as a mosquito bite. When the memories got to be too much, I got into my bathing suit and headed for the beach. The cool water and the sunshine cleared my head.

Dottie came over to my house the night before she left for school lugging some rosé she'd snuck from Madeline's liquor cabinet. I poured some into two red ruby glasses and we sat on the porch and pondered the wind herding the water this and that way.

We clinked our glasses together. "Knock 'em dead," I said. "The world needs a dose of Dottie Butts."

"Could use a dose of you, too."

"Don't know about that."

"You can do all them things Grand taught you," Dottie said. "No reason you can't do anything else you want to do, too."

"You sound like Susan."

"I come to this by myself."

We took big gulps of wine at the same time and rocked back and forth for a bit.

"Truth is," I said, "I'm scared something might go wrong. Someone might die."

"Can't live your life thinking that," she said. "If I die, it won't be your fault, most likely. Probably be something stupid I do to myself. Can't worry about that."

"I suppose not," I said. We got drunk that night, but she managed to rumble up the road in her overpacked car the next morning as her family and I waved goodbye to her. *No reason you can't do anything you want to do,* she'd said to me.

I was picking tomatoes in the side garden on the Monday of the last week in August when Bud and Glen came by to tell me that Tuesday would be the last day that they would take the *Florine* out into the bay.

"I got to leave on Friday," Glen said. "Army ain't going to wait."

"I guess not," I said. "Anyway, thank you both."

"You want us to have her hauled out?" Bud asked.

"No. I'll take care of it. You both have other things to do."

Bud shrugged. "Not really." My nails dug into the skin of the ripe tomato I was holding and my fingers plunged into the warm, wet center of it. I sucked the juice off my fingertips.

Glen said, "We got to get going."

"I know," I said, and they left, walking up toward Ray's store. As I watched them go, I sent a silent prayer to Glen's back, wishing him a safe journey and return. I sent the lump in my throat Bud's way.

I couldn't sleep that night. What was left of the August moon cast a dim glow on Grand's bedroom wall. My head spun, trying to untangle itself from the past, from my near-death experience with Andy, from my wasted love for Bud, and from my own fear. I needed to clear a path to a possible future. "I don't want to be left behind," I said to the wall. Dottie, Glen, and Bud were leaving The Point. If their luck held, they would come back, but they would live their lives outside of it, most likely. Did I want to stay here without them? Did I want to live across from Stella and fade away? Did I want to ping-pong between Ray's store, the harbor, and the woods? Did I want to grow old alone?

Was this it?

My body wriggled on the bed, seeking relief from the churned-up thoughts swamping my brain. "You would think," I said to the wall, "that all the dead people in my life might put in a good word for me with someone." Then I felt bad. Maybe they had other things to do. "I'm sorry," I said to them all. "I don't know how to get going. I don't know what to do. If you get a minute, drop a hint, okay?" That said to whoever might be listening, my mind settled. The warm night held the promise of a good morning. Things would be clearer then.

I was well on my way to drifting off when I noticed the faint light on the wall brightening to the gold of a sun-kissed summer sea. The wall melted away to reveal the summer sea yielding up diamonds too dazzling to ignore, all the way to Carlie's horizon. I lifted up from the bed and floated down until I was walking along the path to the cliffs in the State Park in my bare feet and my nightgown.

As I reached the water, I saw that the diamonds were on fire. But I wasn't afraid. I sat down on the sitting bench and waited. I didn't wait long. A boat that may have been the *Florine*'s twin glided into view on the molten water, Daddy at her helm. My daddy as he had been when he was living life full tilt, when everything he knew made sense. He smiled at me and I saw the man that Carlie must have seen when she'd first come to The Point.

And she was with him. She sat starboard, her freckled arm over the side of the boat. She skimmed her fingers over water that gave off sparks where she touched it. She gave me a look filled with so much love that it turned me inside out.

"Oh" was all I could say, but it contained everything I had ever felt and could ever feel about both of them. With that, Daddy turned the *Florine* and they sailed into the horizon and disappeared. Then someone next to me said, "You got company." I looked up to see my Grand with flour on her apron, her white hair falling from its pins, her blue eyes bright and light as a cup of sky with cream. Someone stood beside her. He was dressed like I'd seen him in pictures and I didn't need an introduction, but Grand said to him, "This is my granddaughter."

I said, "Pleased to meet you, Jesus," because Grand liked manners.

Grand patted me on the shoulder. "You need to tend to your company," she said, and then she and Jesus walked out of the bedroom and I came back to myself.

"What company?" I wondered, now awake. I got up from the bed, feeling light as the down on a baby duck. I wandered downstairs, through the darkened living room, into the kitchen, and out to the porch. I had a mind to sit in the rocker and ponder what had just happened under the silent night stars, but found myself too restless to do that. I walked back into the kitchen and looked out of the big windows over the harbor toward the bay.

A dark form moved up the hill from the wharf. My heart hopped into my throat. "Who . . . ?" I whispered. As it grew closer, I saw that it was Bud, on one of his night prowls. I watched him until he reached the front of the house. To my surprise, he stopped and looked through the window at me and then I moved, because although nothing was for sure, what I wanted right now stood about ten feet away from me. Stella would have shoved me out the door, but I didn't need that push. I walked myself outside into a summer night so perfect that it felt like part of my skin.

"Hey," I said.

"Hey," Bud said.

"Couldn't sleep."

"Me neither. Funny, isn't it?" Bud said, and he smiled.

"When are you leaving?" I asked.

"Leaving for where?"

"Word has it you're moving north."

"No," Bud said. "Someone got their story wrong. I'm not." He smiled into my eyes and I stopped breathing for an instant. He said, "I come out to go for a walk. You want to come along?"

"I don't feel like walking," I said.

His mouth twitched. "I thought you said you'd go anywhere with me. Dumb ass."

I laughed, but I couldn't see him through the blur in my eyes nor answer him. It appeared that, for once, I had nothing to say. But for once, he did.

"Well, maybe I've walked far enough," he said.

I reached for his hand and he took it and we went inside. We turned right and went through the living room and into the hall. The risers creaked as we walked up the stairs.

We fell into Grand's bed like one body, coiled around each other like eels. He was part of me before I knew it. His hands touched me in ways that didn't hurt, as if he knew where all of my scars were. My legs wrapped him tight and we dove deep, past the seaweed, past the bottom of the ocean, until I surfaced, crying out his name even as I tried to breathe him in.

Dawn found us lying on our sides looking at each other. I traced the map around his eyes, his nose, his mouth. He moved a strand of hair from my face and nested his fingers in my hair.

"I ain't leaving you, Florine," he said.

"I know that," I said. And I did.

"I ain't sure what's going to happen, but I'd like you along for the ride," he said.

"Front seat, passenger side?"

"Shotgun all the way. You bet," he said. We reached for each other at the same time.

The warm night yielded up a good morning, with promise of many more to come. Where we would wake up in the future and what would happen to us were questions we had yet to answer, but we would wake up together. But one thing was for sure. We would always come back to The Point to keep an eye on the change of seasons, walk the rocky, pine-scented paths with our children, if the powers that be saw fit to give us any, and play with them on the beach that led to the bay, the ocean, and to the horizon, beyond it.

Here, where endings and beginnings met in the middle of the dirt road leading to the harbor, we would stoke up the fire we had set for each other since the beginning of our time in this tiny place in the world. We would live our lives as best we could, guided by the sweet memories of those tender souls, missing and missed, who had blessed us with their love as they had best understood it.

It hadn't been so very long ago that I had thrown the red ruby heart into the cold blue sea and begged for my mother's return. Although I would most likely never see her as she had been here on earth and in my life, she had never left my heart, and she never would. In its own way and in its own time, the red ruby heart had come back to me, and I would hold tight to it, forever.

Acknowledgments

"Praise the bridge that carried you over."—George Colman

I'm so grateful for the love, faith, honesty, and friendship of so many people in so many walks of life for their assistance in writing this book that I hardly know where to begin.

First, I want to thank those directly responsible for bringing Florine and The Point to life. My gratitude goes out to my agent, Gail Hochman, for her quirky genius, and for her warmth and persistence. This also extends to Marianne Merola, who has taken me to Germany and Spain. My humble appreciation extends to the Viking Penguin group, and to my editor, Laura Tisdel, for her energy, her kindness, and her determination. My thanks also go out to Ann Hood, a remarkable woman and author.

A honey-drenched dose of gratitude to those who have had to take me in whether they wanted to or not. Fran, Smudge, Mary, Mickey, Leo, Cindi, and my five beloved babies, I love you all more than you're comfortable hearing about, being Mainers. Also, love to my aunts, uncles, and cousins, particularly to Janie. To my Quaker Point family, the Bennetts. Without you all, there would be no story.

Charlotte Eckel Brown, Barbara Lee Gaul, Lee Kennett Paige, and Tootie Van Reenen, you are my rocks. Edith Gaul, thank you for keeping the candy jars filled and the kitchen table available. Karen Gaul

Bessey, your belief in the unseen has kept my imagination fired since we were in third grade. Thank you to Elisabeth Wilkins and Peggy Moss, my precious pearls, and to fellow New Englander and friend Brenda Edmands, who picked me to go to a Bruce Springsteen concert.

My everlasting appreciation extends to friends and teachers at the University of Southern Maine's Stonecoast MFA in Creative Writing program, particularly to Baron Wormser. Your encouragement meant so much to me. Thank you to Lee Hope. And thank you to extraordinary teachers and writers, including Suzanne Strempek Shea, Elizabeth Searle, Michael Kimball, Clint McCown, Richard Hoffman, Joan Connor, Michael C. White, and Jack Driscoll. To Barbara Kelly, who keeps the books alive. I am also thankful for the friendship of Bruce Pratt and Hank Garfield, my brothers in writing, and my colleagues in the program, who are all amazing and all a bit mad.

Go raibh maith agaibh to my Irish family, Claire Foley, Michael Connolly, and Rebecca Hitchcock. Big hugs go out to my Flatbread women for the pizza, sundaes, and friendship. Mary Beth Gray, thanks for the awesome quilt. It is an honor to have Frank and Jean Woodard in my life. Thank you for believing in my voice. To Central Station, Portland Fire Department, all shifts, I'm grateful for the brunches, lunches, and for quiet time on weekends in the office. Rua and Jessie, thanks for your patience and devotion.

To Maine, and to its tough and tender characters. I keep coming back. Guess that's love, isn't it? And to western South Dakota. You just have to love somewhere that Rand McNally altered on a map.

Finally, my love to Robert. The adventure continues.